Kissing Madeline

USA TODAY BESTSELLING AUTHOR

LEX MARTIN

Copy editing by RJ Locksley

Cover design by Najla Qamber Designs

Model photograph by Lindee Robinson Photography

Cover Models: AC Parker & Shannon Lorraine

August 2022 Edition

ISBN 978-0-9915534-5-7

ABOUT THE NOVEL:

What's the worst thing about wanting a sexy NFL football player? Everyone else wants him, too.

After catching my boyfriend getting deep-throated by a cage girl, I've learned my lesson – never date a professional athlete. Never. Besides, I have more important things to worry about, like not blowing my shot to make it as a broadcast reporter. I won't let anything get in my way, not even the new "it boy" of the NFL and my hot-as-hell neighbor.

What's the worst thing about getting death glares from his new neighbor? It doesn't make him want her any less.

I've worked my ass off to make it to the pros. The last thing I need is the complication of a relationship, especially since my last one was a total train wreck. But I can't stop thinking about the feisty girl next door with the smart mouth. And I'd love nothing more than to show her what to do with that mouth.

Friends with benefits might be the best idea he's ever had. Or the worst.

KISSING MADELINE, the third book in The Dearest Series, can be read a standalone novel. This new adult romance is recommended for readers 18+ due to mature content.

To Matt & my little bears

"Our greatest glory is not in never falling, but in rising every time we fall."

- Confucius

PROLOGUE

DAREN

(Early May)

SOME PEOPLE THINK I have it made. I say looks can be deceiving.

The white lights blare down on me, and I smile. That's my answer for everything. I've broken bones, sprained ligaments, twisted joints, and I always smile. It's how I get through the pain until the numbness settles in and I can breathe again.

The cameras crowd closer to the conference table, and the answers roll off my tongue. "I'm the new guy. I'm just looking to be a part of this team, to do my part and fill in the gap." I glance at Coach Reynolds and Shawn Brentwood, the veteran quarterback. "That is, if there is a gap."

Everyone chuckles, but underneath Brentwood's grin, I know what he's thinking. Because I'd be thinking the same thing. That I'm the asshole here to take his job. He's right. Because what the hell kind of QB would I be if I were content to sit my ass on the bench all day? I'm here to win. It's what I'm good at.

The coach fields a few questions, and my eyes travel to the back of the room where I spot wives and girlfriends of fellow players. Hell, even my father took time off from corporate domi-

1

nation to come, and he and I aren't even talking. He's standing in the back next to my mother, who looks like she might pass out from the euphoria of clutching my NFL jersey.

I should be just as elated. After thousands of hours of practice and games, I have arrived. Achieved my dream. But as I search the room, that numbness swells.

She didn't come.

My jaw tightens. I shouldn't be surprised. But I am. Because I'm the dumb asshole who thought that after all this time she'd be different. That she'd actually mean those promises. That she'd change.

She's probably off buying some Armani luggage or a new Gucci watch or some shit that's only going to crowd her overflowing walk-in closet.

I never ask her for anything, but I asked her to do one thing for me. One. To be here today, the biggest day of my career.

My temple throbs, and I rub it with my palm.

Deep down, I know I deserve this. What do they say? Payback is a bitch. Yeah, they got that right.

"Daren! As the Heisman winner, do you feel extra pressure to perform?"

Of course.

I shake my head. "Titles mean nothing. Only wins. While I'm honored to have received the Heisman, that award represents my college career. My NFL career starts now. As any athlete will tell you, the only thing you can control is the here and now. So I don't let titles or previous wins or awards dictate how I think about the game. I play to win. That's it."

He nods, ignoring the fact that I didn't answer his question. They always do because they only see my stats, my completed throws, my touchdowns.

It's easy to see why people think I have it made. When I look in the mirror, sometimes I think the same thing. That the victories are too easy, that there has to be the other side of the coin, the dark side, the part no one sees. Because no one can walk between the raindrops like I can. I'm a fucking master.

But the tightrope comes with a price. Pride. Hubris. Vanity. Call it what you will. It's the head game I play to make myself think I'm better. So when the ball snaps, when I can feel the leather stitching between my fingers and my heart pounding in my ears, the training takes over and I actually feel the swell of invincibility. Sure, I put in the time. I sweat. I train. I fight. But at the end of the day, the winners think they can do it, and the losers know they can't.

Does that sound like total bullshit? Yeah, it is. But if I chant that crap long enough, I believe it. And when I believe it, I win.

So what happens when I don't believe it? When I know I'm just full of shit?

I fuck up. Big.

My phone buzzes in my pocket, and anger surges through me. When the press move on to interview the new wide receiver, I pull out my cell.

Her message is typical. *I got held up. I'm coming.*

I can't type my response fast enough. *Don't bother.*

Thanks for missing the NFL Draft, bitch.

CHAPTER 1

MADDIE

(Late May)

AFTER A YEAR-LONG INTERNSHIP WITH NBC, I finally did it. I got a coveted position as an on-air reporter. It's meant long hours at the studio, missing meals, and having no social life, but I nailed it two weeks after I graduated from college.

I wish I could say NBC offered me the job, but my boss told me right off the bat he didn't have any positions for newbs. So I got the next best thing—a gig with New England News Network, which boasts a reputation for hard-hitting stories. It also means that unlike most of my peers who are trekking off to report the news in bumble, I get to stay in my hometown.

And there's only one person I want to celebrate with tonight.

Jacob is going to die when I tell him I nailed it.

Walking in to his apartment, I set my bag down in the entryway and kick off my heels. Jacob is probably napping. He always takes a snooze after practice. He's a mixed martial artist and a gym rat. I've never dated a professional athlete before. Usually, I've gone for the quiet econ or history major, but I couldn't resist Jacob's allure. I was shooting footage for a friend who had to cover a local match last summer when we first met. After Jacob pummeled his opponent, he strutted up to me and asked me out.

Two weeks ago, he asked me to move in, but he's training for a big fight, so we're waiting until after his trip to Vegas next week to make it official.

Glancing at my watch, I know I'm a few hours early, but I can't wait to tell him.

On the bar, next to a dozen roses, a bottle of wine chills in a cooler. Did he find out my secret? My tummy jumps with excitement.

I tiptoe down the hall, ready to strip out of my clothes to give him a proper wakeup call, when I hear the laughter. A woman's laughter.

I jerk to a stop, my heart suddenly pounding.

"You like that, huh?" His voice cuts through the silence and sends goosebumps up my arms. "Suck it harder. That's right. Show me how much you love my cock in your mouth."

Oh my God.

Trembling, I don't want to go any closer. I don't want to see for myself, but my legs move of their own accord until I don't have a choice but to witness this with my own eyes.

I see him through the crack in the door, sitting on the edge of the bed with his fingers threaded through her dark hair. Their faces are in shadow, but his head motions yes as she bobs up and down in his lap.

She pauses to look up at him. "Can we do it like we did yesterday?"

He moans. "Yeah, baby, just like yesterday."

The bitch crawls up the bed, and he follows, straddling her chest. She reaches up and grabs the metal headboard as Jacob directs himself into her mouth.

Nausea twists in my stomach.

Yesterday, my boyfriend and this girl had sex in his bed. Just before I had sex with him in his bed.

I cover my mouth, fighting hard not to vomit because, yesterday, we had unprotected sex. When I thought he was monogamous and the man I would marry, I let him put his dirty dick in me.

All at once, my life doesn't make sense. Tonight should be about my future and planning a life with someone I thought loved me. I'm such a fool. Ignoring the rumors he was promiscuous, I let my guard down with him, let myself believe his lies about being with lots of girls simply because he hadn't found the right one. And he let me believe I was it. His forever.

As I watch this woman deep-throat Jacob, the hurt and pain dissipate, and all I feel is rage. Blinding, white-hot, I-might-kill-someone rage. My hands move like I'm on autopilot, my training kicking in. I'm barely aware of my phone shaking in front of me as my finger slides across the screen to activate the camera.

I push the red button. A few seconds is all I get, but it's exactly what I need to remind myself of my stupidity. Because I know he'll lie. He'll twist this around until I can't see straight, and he'll somehow get me to think this is my fault.

No, this is on him, and I want to remember every ounce of humiliation so I never repeat this mistake again.

The cocksucker pauses to ask where they'll hook up once I move in, and he tells her they'll do it in the locker room at the gym. Classy.

I turned down date after date so this jerkoff could cheat on me.

Tucking my phone back into my jacket, I stomp past them and dump the shit out of his gym bag before I yank open drawers and toss my clothes in.

"Shit. Shit. It's Maddie," he mumbles. "Baby, what are you doing?"

"Fuck you, asshole." I storm into the bathroom and grab my

makeup. When I emerge, Jacob is pushing the girl away, and I see her face for the first time.

"Oh my God. This just gets better." Staring at Kimmy the cage girl, I can't believe I got this whole thing so wrong.

"Baby, this isn't what it looks like," he stammers.

My knuckles turn white as I grip my bag. "Really? So your dick magically landed in her mouth? What an interesting phenomenon."

I take the keychain he gave me with a miniature boxing glove and chuck it at his head.

"Kimmy, now you don't have to blow him at the gym. He's all yours."

CHAPTER 2

MADDIE

WHEN THE DOOR OPENS, Sheri laughs. "Maddie, you have a key. You don't need to knock."

I shrug, and my messenger bag slides down my arm, dragging my blouse with it. Tugging up my shirt so I'm not flashing her, I blow my bangs out of my face. "It felt like the right thing to do. I'm your guest. Your very grateful guest."

"No, you're my roommate. None of this guest shit."

Smiling weakly, I acquiesce, but only so she'll stop arguing because we both know she's not charging me anything close to half the rent. She lives in a luxury brownstone in Boston's Back Bay, something I could never afford in my wildest dreams. But my friend caught wind that I needed a place to stay since I had already given my notice for my old apartment, and she all but demanded I move in.

I've been here before, but I'm still a little awed by her condo. Dark, polished hardwood floors draw my eyes to an enormous brick fireplace, which is flanked by sleek modern furniture. It's sophisticated and elegant, and about a million times better than my futon fold-out bed and cinderblock book shelves.

There's only one thing missing from the view.

"You moved my boxes." Because, holy crap, that was a lot to move.

"I had a little help. My neighbor stopped by, and he lent a hand. Speaking of that hot man—"

"You went through too much trouble. I could have done it." When I brought over my moving boxes last weekend, I was afraid I'd get a ticket for double-parking the small van I'd rented out front, so I just left everything in the corner of her living room.

She waves me off. "It gave me an excuse to skip the gym. Besides, I had fun analyzing how you labeled your stuff."

"What do you mean?"

"Bathroom makeup and moisturizers. Winter bedding and thermal layers. News-writing textbooks and notes. Everything color-coded. Did you use a label maker?" She doesn't wait for my response. "By the way, what was in the 'bedroom nightstand' box that started vibrating when I accidentally dropped it?" My mouth drops open, and her chuckle grows into full-blown laughter. "Hmm, let me guess. Jacob's replacement."

Clearing my throat, I shake my head, and with it, my embarrassment. "Jacob wishes he was as hung as the Power-Boy 3000 or that he gave me nearly as many orgasms."

Her eyebrow raises. "The Power-Boy 3000? Where can I find one?"

"I bought it at my friend's sex toy party."

"We are *so* going to have one of those! Maybe when we wrap up this film." Sheri works for her dad, who's this big movie producer, so she travels a ton. It's one of the reasons she wants a roommate. To keep an eye on her place when she's gone. It would be so much easier for her to move to New York or LA, but she's a Boston girl through and through and gets a little crazy at the mere mention of relocating.

After I change out of my work clothes and into a pair of jeans and a fitted v-neck t-shirt, Sheri suggests we check out a new bar that opened up down the street and grab a few drinks.

Twenty minutes later, we settle into a corner table in the dimly lit bar, and by the time we get our second round, the effects of the alcohol have me on the verge of crying into my beer. I never drink for a reason. I get too emotional. And right now, my heart feels heavy. "Sheri-berry, I really appreciate you taking me in."

Her eyebrows raise. "You're the first friend I ever made at BU. Of course I'd take you in."

Sheri and I were roommates freshman year in the dorms at Boston University. We didn't get along at first. I think she found me too uptight, and I found her to be too rich. I know that sounds terrible, but she's a Park Avenue transplant, and growing up, I was a second-hand clothes kind of girl—not because I thought that was cool or because I watched too many old John Hughes films, but because we couldn't afford more. But I eventually began to look beyond Sheri's designer labels and French manicures to see a girl with a heart too big for her pixie-sized body.

Together, Sheri and I make for odd-looking friends. If she's the size of a walnut, then I'm an oak tree. She's petite and tan with cropped blonde hair and big blue eyes. I'm a little over five-eight with long black hair, pale skin and blue eyes. She looks like she waltzed off a movie set, and I look like a character from *Wicked*. But I love her, even if her whole body could fit into one leg of my jeans.

"Mads, I would totally sucker-punch Jacob's gonads for you if I could. Is that douchebag still calling you?"

"Just once or twice a week now. I let them go to voicemail."

She watches me, her frown growing. "How are you doing with everything?"

I take a quick sip of my beer to buy me a moment. "I'll be honest. It's been a rough few weeks." Especially once I realized I had lost my apartment. Since I'd been planning to move in with Jacob, my old roommate had already found another living situation, and the landlord had found a new tenant, so I was doubly screwed. My fingers play with the corner of the wrapper on my beer. "Make that a rough month and four days."

As much as I wish I could forget the date of our breakup, it coincided with getting my new job, making it that much tougher to block out.

But I have to look on the bright side. At least my tests came back negative. Because the first thing I did after our breakup was bolt to the clinic to make sure the asshole didn't give me something nasty.

Sheri scoots her chair closer and reaches over for a side hug. I drop my head onto her shoulder and sigh. I'm an only child, but if I had a sister, this is how I imagine she'd be. It's times like this that I ache with more than the pain of losing Jacob. I miss my dad so much right now, my chest feels hollow.

"I realize you're mending a broken heart, but I want you to know how psyched I am to have you as a roommate. I'm still pissed at you for ditching me sophomore year."

I gasp. "I did not ditch you! As I recall, you wanted to live in West Campus, and I needed to be next to the Com School on East Campus for six a.m. call times."

"Oh, yeah." She chuckles and glances down, a serious expression crossing her face again. "I'm so sorry that dick hurt you, Mads. Are you okay? Really?"

"Mmm." My eyes well with tears. "Aside from the fact that Jacob ruined my five-year plan?" I let myself think about the video on my phone, and the anger surfaces. This is what I have to hold on to because hatred is a more valuable emotion than grief.

Sheri's mouth twists. But before she can say anything, I go on a rant. "I get that he was tempted to sleep with other women. They threw themselves at him wherever we went. And maybe I was a fool to think I had somehow tamed him. But what's really been bothering me is how he…" I close my eyes and the scene flashes before me in graphic detail. Lowering my voice, I say, "How he talked to her."

Show me how much you love my cock in your mouth.

I can't say the words, but they ricochet in my head like a gunshot going off in a canyon.

Tilting my head so my hair falls forward to hide my face, I clear my throat. "He was never that way with me."

"What do you mean he was never that way with you?"

How do I say this? God, this is humiliating. "He, uh, he was... careful with me. More... proper."

"So he didn't talk dirty."

"It's more than that. He treated me like he was afraid he'd offend me somehow. Here was this intimidating fighter, but he was surprisingly gentle and maybe... too respectful? Uh, that sounds terrible. Am I crazy that I wanted him to be rougher?"

She snorts. "Fuck, no. Rough is good. Rough rocks my world."

"I guess I wonder if I was too anal for him."

"Anal works for me too."

I smack her in the shoulder. "You know what I mean. Like you said, I can be particular, and I can't tell you how much I loathe sleeping on the wet spot. He hated how I'd bolt from bed the moment we were done, but I can't have *that* dripping down my leg at two in the morning."

Sheri giggles. "It's totally his loss for not sexing you up properly. And so what if you like to clean up? To each her own." She takes a sip of her beer and gives me a once-over. "Look, I know you had boyfriends before Jacob, but you definitely have this good-girl vibe. I wonder if he couldn't get past that. You know, that whole Madonna-whore complex."

"So I was the virgin and that woman in his bed was the whore?" Sheri nods reluctantly. "I guess that would explain why he had her deep-throating him like he was trying to reach her bellybutton through her esophagus."

"Jacob might have been sleeping around, but he wanted to marry you, so maybe some part of him had to keep you pure."

At this I laugh half-heartedly. "Pure. Right." Had I not purchased a half-dozen see-through nighties for this man? What part of him thought I wanted to be pure? Did he need me to spell it out for him? I mean, he didn't have to go all Christian Grey on me, but it's like he never lost control when we were together. And isn't that what every girl wants? To make her guy so crazy in lust he can't control himself?

Damn, Jacob. Wasn't the sex good enough? I thought he seemed satisfied. And I might not have always had an orgasm, but what girl who works sixty-five hours a week achieves the mighty O every time?

I'm so tempted to think this was my fault. That I drove him to be unfaithful. Because I worked too much or seemed preoccupied with my job. But he's the one who strayed, and I'm not some broken-down girl who lives for her man's approval.

Screw that. I tip my drink back to my lips. No, I dodged a bullet.

I recently read that over seventy percent of married men would have an affair if they knew their spouse would never find out. No, Jacob isn't an anomaly, and I am not the problem. Men are.

After my internal pep talk, I'm feeling a little more resolved. I'm going to be okay as long as I keep reminding myself that men are the enemy. Especially good-looking men.

Sheri elbows me. "Don't look now, but my favorite neighbor just strolled in." Her eyes widen as she stares at someone behind me.

I twist in my seat, and my eyes bug out as I take in the small entourage at the other end of the restaurant. "*That's* your neighbor? Daren Sloan?"

"I see you're already familiar with this nearly mythical creature."

I turn back to her as I put two fingers against my jugular. "Hmm. Let's see." I wait a few seconds for dramatic effect. "I have a pulse. Because that's all one requires to take notice of your 'favorite neighbor.'"

Inwardly, I growl. Even from here, his expression grates on me. Daren Sloan has this irritatingly smug look on his face, like he knows women everywhere are envisioning him ripping off their underwear with his teeth.

Of course Sheri and Daren are neighbors. Because her dad is a movie mogul, she knows everybody. When she says she loves Brad and Angelina, she actually means she loves them because they all vacationed together last Christmas.

"Let's call Daren over." Sheri starts to wave, but I yank her arm down before anyone sees her.

"Let's not."

"Why?" She gives me a look that tells me I might be insane.

"Because no."

"Maddie, I need more than that. You're going to love Daren. God, he's such a great guy. Thank Jesus and the little lamb he finally broke up with that slore Veronica." She clinks her beer against the bottle in my hand. *Slore?* "You should see him after a workout. All hot and sweaty and hard." After a quick swig, Sheri gasps so loudly I'm half afraid she's choking on her beverage, but before I can pat her on the back, she drops the bomb. "You should totally go out with him!"

Huh?

She wiggles in her seat, a giddy expression on her face like I just told her Charlie Hunnam wants to hump her. "He went through a manwhore-rebound phase this summer, but I think he's getting over it. I haven't heard his bed frame banging against the wall lately."

"Wait. What?"

A devilish grin spreads on her face. "His bedroom shares a wall with your bedroom. I *might* have listened in. And if I'm right, he's a beast in the sack. We're talking Godzilla. And holy crap, you guys would make the cutest couple!"

A little snort escapes me. I'm still laughing when I realize she's serious. She actually wants me to go out with Daren.

"Um, no, Sher-bear. That will never happen. Ne-ver. Never ever."

"Never say never." She tugs on my arm. "Don't be a fool. He's Boston's most eligible bachelor. The Heisman winner. The number one draft pick. A god among men." Sheri turns my face toward his table. "Look at that chin dimple. I mean, that alone gets girls to drop their panties. Never mind those eyes. I'm telling you, Maddie, if I were into jocks at all, I would scale Mount Everest over there so fast, I'd break the sound barrier."

"Mount Everest?" My eyebrow tilts up.

"Yeah. Earth's highest mountain. The Big Kahuna. The Big Enchilada. The—"

"I get the idea." I'm trying to be patient because I know Sheri just wants to be helpful. "I'm not into athletes. Not anymore. There's too much temptation for them, and I'm not good at being a doormat. It would never work. I'm going back to dating econ majors. Those guys might not be able to throw me over their shoulder or bench-press my body weight, but at least they're not going to rear-naked-chokehold my heart." I rack my brain to think of something to get her off my case. "Hey, Brad, the tech guy at work, asked me out."

She looks at me suspiciously. "And did you say yes?"

"I don't date coworkers, but we still had a nice chat. He's a decent-looking guy. And I didn't think about Jacob once."

"I'm sure the poor schmuck will find that comforting when he's jerking it with his left hand instead of boning the hot reporter."

"Ew." I do not want to think about Brad and his left hand.

My eyes trail back over to the table where Daren sits with a couple of friends. Thoughts of my coworker fade as I take in this elite athlete. To call him beautiful is an understatement. He's a five-alarm fire of a man, and that's with his clothes on.

I roll my eyes at myself.

That's the old Maddie talking. The new Maddie realizes Daren is just a pretty boy who thinks he's God's gift to women. Been there, done that. Having grown up in the area, I'm probably better acquainted with Daren Sloan's reputation than I care to be.

Daren runs a hand through his thick, dark hair that's cropped short on the sides but long enough on top to flop onto his forehead. I don't need to get closer to see the effect those hazel eyes have on girls as three women saunter over to his table.

Sheri flicks me in the shoulder. "At least let me introduce you two before some slussy gets her hooks into him."

A cynical smile plays on my lips, one that I hope says I'm a no-fly zone for players. Because Daren's a player just like Jacob, and players only do one thing. They cheat.

I shake my head. "No need. We've met."

* * *

Go out with Daren. That's the worst idea ever. I want to punch myself in the face for the two-point-two seconds my brain found the suggestion appealing.

I finish tying my shoelaces before I trudge down the stairs and out into the humid morning. Well, night for most people.

Reaching behind me, I grab my ankle and stretch my quad. At quiet times like this, I always think about Jacob. Not that we ever worked out together. He never got out of bed at this hour. Maybe the fact that he didn't says something about us.

I can't stop doing this, replaying our relationship to try to pinpoint what went wrong. It's been torture to not take his calls —I miss him like crazy—but I'll never forgive him for what he did. Because it wasn't a one-time thing. It wasn't some crazy drunken accident. It was deliberate. Calculated. Habitual.

My hand twitches on my phone.

When I get desperate, when I get tempted to contact him, I watch the video on my cell. That's a different kind of torture. Watching the man you thought loved you screw another woman feels like a slow death of a thousand lies. *I love you. I want to marry you. I want you to have my children.* All lies.

But rather than distance myself from these thoughts, I force myself to think about those excruciating details to harden my resolve. *His dick. Her mouth. Their moans.* Yeah, fuck him.

When I'm done stretching, I jog slowly and let the ache from last night's drinking spread through my limbs. I've never run in Sheri's neighborhood before, but I know the main streets well enough from attending school nearby, and I'm on the familiar ground of the Esplanade before I know it. The path meanders around the Charles River, which laps against the banks this morning with the steady breeze.

By the second mile, Jacob's betrayal feels duller, less like a knife to my heart and more like a bruise to my ego. But I'm tired of feeling sorry for myself. For questioning my self-worth. Moving in with Sheri and getting my new job means I get to start over, and I intend to take full advantage of these opportunities.

Perhaps that's why Daren sounded briefly alluring. A gorgeous face to distract me. God, I could use a distraction. That's why I love work. It keeps me so busy, I barely have time to breathe.

By the time I loop around and reach Sheri's building, the sun is starting to warm the horizon. Guns 'n Roses blasts from my iPhone as I push into my final sprint. My blood is thrumming through my veins, and I'm drenched with sweat, but it feels good. I'd never admit this to a sane person, but I like having to get up this early. It forces me to stay on top of my life.

Internally, I'm ticking off today's call schedule. I have a meeting in an hour, an on-air interview at eight a.m., three stories I'm researching for the week, the web report to update, and at least a dozen follow-up calls to make.

When I turn the corner, I never see it coming. But when my body slams into the brick wall, all the air escapes my lungs as I fall backwards and onto the pavement.

CHAPTER 3

DAREN

IT'S STILL EARLY as fuck, but if I don't hit the road soon I'll be stuck in rush-hour traffic, and I don't want to be late. Plus, I need to check how long the drive takes at this hour since training starts at seven a.m. Although camp doesn't begin for a few weeks, I'm meeting with one of the trainers to take a tour of the locker room and gym. The coach knows this is as much of a head game as it is about physical ability, so he agreed to let me work out there a few days a week and get a feel for the team's facilities until preseason starts.

My key turns in the lock as I ask myself again why I've kept this condo. The parking is terrible, my commute sucks, and the building is old. I purchased it for Veronica and me to live in after we graduated because I knew she wanted to stay in the city, but since we broke up the night of the draft, she never even knew about it. I've been thinking about scoping out some condos closer to the stadium.

Thoughts of that failed relationship automatically put me in a foul mood. Four fucking years wasted. Even the eight months we spent apart sophomore year were plagued with her drama and lies.

I'm good at a lot of things, like football and school, but even the word "relationship" feels like a live wire waiting to electrocute me.

The problem with Veronica, aside from how she and I got together in the first place, was football, the one thing that gave her the attention she wanted. Ironic.

That's just it. I can't have a woman jealous over what I do for a living. I've busted my balls since I was a kid to get here. People can say I'm rich already, that it doesn't matter how my football career pans out, but that shit makes me want to bust my ass more. Besides, that money isn't mine, and I need to make my own way.

If I do this, if I make our demise about her shallowness instead of her betrayal, my chest doesn't feel like it might explode. Like I might put my fist through a concrete slab. Because that confession...

My stomach twists when I think of what she told me that night. Even though she begged me to forgive her, there are some sins that can't be washed away with words.

Swallowing the lump in my throat, I realize the sun is rising and I need to haul ass. I toss the gym bag over my shoulder and head toward my SUV in the back lot. As I round the corner, I pull my phone out of my back pocket to see if the realtor returned my call.

Deep down, I think I dodged a bullet. Because at least Veronica never moved in with me. That would have been a nightmare.

Suddenly, I hear an "oomf" and my cell goes flying.

It takes me a second to realize what just happened, and that's when my heart starts to race. Holy shit. A woman is on the pavement.

I drop my bag and lean down to her. "Ma'am, are you okay?"

She turns her face toward me with a groan.

Wait a sec. *I know that face. I could never forget that face.*

"Maddie?" What's she doing outside of my building at five thirty in the morning? She's wearing yoga pants and a tank top. Her iPhone is on the ground a few feet away. "Maddie, shit. I'm so sorry. I wasn't looking where I was going."

She blinks a few times. Finally, she groans. "Jesus Christ, Daren. Are you trying to kill me?"

Did I hurt her? Fuck.

I brush her hair out of her face until those piercing blue eyes peer back at me. Without thinking, my hand trails through her hair and cradles the back of her neck.

We stare at each other, and she sucks in a breath.

Why am I holding her like this? The same question registers in her expression, and I back away and clear my throat, trying not to notice the way her tank top reveals all kinds of creamy cleavage.

Why is she still sprawled on the ground? *Oh, yeah, asshole. You knocked her down. Help the girl up without trying to grope her this time.*

"Here, let's get you off the sidewalk." I extend my hand, which she ignores as she pulls herself up.

She shoots me a dirty look as she dusts off her ass, which I'm wildly curious about seeing how she's wearing snug-fitting workout clothes.

Wow. Maddie McDermott. Her thick, black hair sits in a messy ponytail, made even messier by our collision. She's tall for a girl. Slender but curvy in all the right places. The last time I saw her in person, she was wearing a slate-colored business suit and was interviewing the mayor. And Maddie in a business suit is a sight to behold.

But shit. She's even hotter when she doesn't have any makeup on.

She leans over to grab her iPhone, and I avert my eyes from her rear because I don't want to be the skeeve who checks out girls' asses.

When she turns back to me, she's frowning. "Someone should put you in charge of the welcoming committee. Is that how you greet all of your new neighbors? Don't you think you should save the tackles for the field?"

Despite the non-staring pact I've made with myself, I can't help but take in her pouty lips and the way her nose wrinkles in the cutest way when she frowns.

Wait. What is she talking about?

"I'm sorry. I was on my way to Dunkin' Donuts for some coffee, so my brain isn't fully functional yet. Did you say we're neighbors?" She nods. My eyes widen. "You're Sheri's Maddie?"

Her eyebrow raises. "I don't label myself as such *per se*, but yes, I'm Sheri's Maddie."

My mind instantly flashes to the box her roommate joked was likely full of sex toys.

Fucking hell. Maddie and sex toys.

Down, boy. I need to go before my dick gets any more excited to see her.

"Sorry, Maddie. I'm running late. Tell Sheri hi. If you're around this weekend, I'm having a Fourth of July party on the river. You guys should join me."

She shakes her head before I finish talking, her eyes darting down to the ground. "Sheri is heading out of town, and I have to work. But thanks." She's frowning like I've just asked her to grout my tub.

Okay. That was a fuck-off vibe if I've ever seen one.

Nodding, I grab my gym bag. "Well, have a great Fourth, then. Sorry about knocking you on your ass." I don't wait for her answer before I take off for my SUV.

* * *

FORTY-FIVE MINUTES LATER, I'm almost at the stadium, but I'm thinking about Maddie. I don't know why it's still bugging me, but she couldn't have turned me down any faster. Which is so different from the first time we met last fall. Okay, she might have been on the fast track to getting drunk with one of my best friends, Clementine, but Maddie was chatty and sweet and, fucking hell, gorgeous.

I'm wondering if I've offended her somehow. This is probably a dickish thing to think, but I'm not turned down often.

Rubbing my neck, I'm tempted to feel paranoid right now. I wonder if she knows the truth behind Clementine's book. That's how Maddie and I met, after she interviewed Clem, when Clem's identity as a bestselling author was revealed.

I shake my head. It's probably for the best that Maddie's not interested. For a million reasons.

Preseason means I don't fuck around, so my summertime activities have to stop anyway. With a new team, about a hundred new plays to learn, and the stress of the NFL, the last thing I need are head games. And women definitely mean head games. Because I am great at a lot of things, but dealing with female drama is not one of them.

I've spent the last two months since my breakup embracing the fuck-till-you-forget lifestyle until the wasteland that was my former relationship is a distant blur. If anything, this summer made me realize my ex and I were over months ago, maybe as far back as Christmas.

Jax, my best friend and Clementine's twin, likes to tell me it's about fucking time Veronica and I parted ways. I think he's right.

Now it's time to get serious. To focus on football. To play like my life depends on it.

So the last thing I should be thinking is how I'd love to get Maddie McDermott horizontal on my sheets, maybe in my tub, and definitely on the living room floor, preferably near the fireplace.

My cock might be cheering yes right now, but I know better.

But when my phone rings with a call from my realtor, suddenly moving doesn't seem as pressing as it did this morning.

Maybe living in the city won't be a hassle. Because living in the Back Bay has at least one perk.

CHAPTER 4

DAREN

SWEAT DRIPS down my face as I survey the defensive line. I may have been the shit in college, but the NFL is a whole new stratosphere of intense. Training camp is about three things: getting in elite-level shape, bringing the new players into the fold, and cutting guys who can't handle it. I'm already in shape. I worked my ass off all spring and summer, but even so, I'm still going to be sore as hell tomorrow. But that's not my biggest concern.

We've run this drill five times, but something's off with LaDuke, my wide receiver. So much of this game is chemistry, and he and I aren't clicking. I spot Brentwood, the veteran QB, laughing by the water table, but as we line up again, he stills to watch.

The ball snaps, and as soon as my fingers grip the leather, I drop back into the pocket and eye the field. Bodies shuffle, and I check my options. Finally, LaDuke breaks from his defender, and I reach back for the pass.

The ball leaves my hand in a perfect arc. But at the last minute, the asshole slows down, and my pass sails wide.

LaDuke jogs back and shrugs. "Did that one slip out?" he asks, knowing full well that's not the case.

Gritting my teeth, I wait to get reamed out by the coach. I make eye contact with the rookie receiver on the sidelines as he paces back and forth. Quentin Alvarez is hungry. He wants the ball.

I jog over to Coach Reynolds so he doesn't need to raise his voice to chew my ass off. He blows out a breath and frowns. But instead of yelling, he drops his hand on my shoulder and turns me to face the empty field behind us.

"Daren, I like the way you keep a level head. It takes time for the veterans to accept the rookies. Don't take this personally."

Taking a deep breath, I nod. He's right. "No problem, Coach." That's usually my answer out on the field. I should keep my mouth shut, but I decide to take a chance. "Do you think we could try Quentin for a few plays?"

Reynolds works his jaw back and forth. "He'll have his turn. Besides, it's more likely than not you'll play with the old guard, and that's who you need to win over."

"I hear ya. But I also think Quentin really wants it."

Coach nods, his tan brow furrowing. "We'll see. Go grab some water."

Ten minutes later, we're back in formation when Coach blows the whistle. "You know what? Let's try Quentin." He shouts for LaDuke, and points his chin at the sideline.

It's hard to fight my smile, so I clench my jaw until I'm focused again. Quentin stalks by, and when our eyes connect, he nods.

This time, when my wide receiver breaks from the defense, he's on fire. Everyone on the sideline pauses to watch my pass, which lands in Quentin's hands about two steps before he blazes into the end zone.

That's how it's done, motherfuckers.

I'm still grinning when I head into the locker room a half hour later. Until Brentwood sidles up to me like we're old friends. Then he leans close with a smile on his face.

"What the fuck was that?" he whispers even though the stereo is blasting Eminem.

This is getting old. A week and a half into camp, and I've lost count of how many times Brentwood has bitched me out. "Sorry? What the fuck was what?"

"Why did you suggest that Quentin play?"

"I'm not sure I know what you're talking about." I'm not in the habit of declining credit where credit is due, but I'm also not looking to piss off Brentwood any more than whatever crawled up his ass today.

"Daren!"

Jeanine Cartwright, Vice President of Marketing and PR, saunters in, totally unbothered by the fact that half of the men are in jock straps or naked. She motions toward me while she talks on the phone, and Brentwood gives her a wink and heads toward his locker on the opposite wall.

She nods, continuing her conversation. "That's a great idea. Yes, I have him right here." She looks up at me and smiles a half second before she holds up her hand, telling me to wait. Jeanine is the first female executive and the youngest. She's an attractive woman, but her ice-cold eyes have a predatory gleam. NFL players are not the politest group of guys, but no one bothers her. Probably because they don't want their balls removed from their bodies. She smooths back her red hair, which is cropped in a short bob. "I'm sure he'll be on board. Rookies never have a problem doing interviews."

I get the message, Jeanine. No need to rub my face in the fact that I'm the low guy on the totem pole.

She hangs up while her eyes make a slow perusal down my bare chest and linger around my waist, a flash of disappointment registering in her eyes that I'm still wearing gym shorts. Finally, her attention lifts back up to my face. "I'm going to need you to be available tomorrow morning after your weightlifting session.

In fact, you might need to cut it short. I'll let everyone know you might be late to your second session. Oh, and be sure to shower before you meet me on the practice field. You need it."

Well, no shit I need a shower. I just spent two hours in ninety-five degree Massachusetts weather in the middle of July.

Jeanine taps her phone and enters the appointment on her calendar. "You and Quentin have an interview with one of the local news stations doing a series of sports segments for women. We're calling it *Football 101*, and we'll likely feature different players each time. But since you're the hot draw right now, I wanted to capitalize on it."

"I'll be there." I force a smile, and I know she thinks it's sincere because she grins back, taking the time to check me out once more before she stalks over to Quentin.

One of the guys waits until Jeanine leaves before he whips out his phone. "Come check out the pussy I snagged last night. She fit my cock like a glove." Several players huddle up to check out the footage.

If he were my Boston College teammate, I'd tell him he's being a dumbass. It only takes one viral video to make your life a living hell, especially if it's twisted up with gossip someone made up to get those fifteen minutes of fame.

But this isn't college. And I'm not at the helm of this outfit. My eyes travel over to Brentwood, who doesn't chime in on the video. He's too busy watching me. God, he's a weird asshole.

I keep my expression blank as I grab a towel and head for the showers. I still have another practice session later this afternoon, and I need to clear my head. I'm used to drama, but there's enough in this stadium to choke a man.

When the hot water is pelting my skin, I close my eyes and try to shut out the noise. Finally, a moment of peace.

And that's when I think of her face. Those plump pink lips the hue of sweet berries. That pale skin that looks silky soft. Those kohl-rimmed eyes that remind me of the waters off Santorini, Greece. Blue like ice melted from the sky.

It's been two weeks since I knocked her on her ass, and I haven't seen Maddie once. And I've been looking.

Despite my better judgment, I want to look harder.

CHAPTER 5

MADDIE

I'M SCRIBBLING down the last of the fire chief's comments from our phone interview when my boss Roger sticks his head into the cubicle.

"Madeline. Nicole. My office. Now."

My cubicle-mate Nicole blows out a breath. I close my spiral notebook and glance at her.

"Off to see what little man wants," she mumbles to herself as she grabs her notebook. "At least this interruption got you to stop gnawing your pen cap." When she faces me, I can tell from her expression she's about to unleash her not-so-inner bitch. "Can I just mention that it would be awesome if you had someone oil the swivel in your chair? Because you jiggle your leg like you're having some kind of seizure, and that noise is about to make me batshit crazy."

For some reason, Nicole's not my biggest fan. Even though we were both hired at the same time and should be helping each other in this cut-throat industry, she looks at me like I might give her an STD. I'd say I'm usually a confident person—you don't make it in broadcasting if you're a wallflower—but there's something unnerving about this girl.

Normally, I ignore her comments, but I've been averaging less than five hours of sleep a night since I landed this job, and my nerves are shot.

"Nicole, how about we try to pretend we're on the same team here? Enough with the eat-shit-and-die attitude, okay?"

Her eyebrow pops up. "I've never heard you curse before. If I piss you off more, will you do it again?"

That's her response? No, I don't curse. Not really. Because all it takes is one slip-up on live television to end up on the back roads of Montana doing segments on the mating patterns of bison.

I don't even know why Nicole and I sit in the same cubicle aside from the fact that we're both new. She should be hanging out with the sports department on the other side of the hall, but that office is already packed. I think she's pissed she got stuck with a news reporter and can't listen to ESPN all day.

She ignores me, as usual, and curls a long strand of her blonde hair around a French-manicured finger. Nicole looks like she was bred by some cheerleading team in Southern California. There's even a perky little bounce to her step.

Smoothing down my gray pencil skirt, I watch her indecently short dress flounce as she practically skips down the hall.

When we enter Roger's office, Nicole turns on the bubbly personality. "Hey, boss, can you believe the footage from training camp today? Man, Daren Sloan has one hell of an arm."

The moment I hear his name, my heart starts racing. *Jesus, Madeline. Chill out.*

I don't know what my problem is, but ever since I plowed into him, whenever I hear his name, little bolts of electricity shoot through me. I blame those hazel eyes... the way he stared down at me... the way he cradled my neck. And, yeah, the way he remembered my name. *Damn him.*

Nicole flips her hair over her shoulder, and internally, I roll my eyes. The dazzling smile on her face is one I only see directed at other people, typically men. She would never waste that much energy on me.

Roger doesn't seem enchanted like every other guy who gets sucked into Nicole's vortex of charm. Maybe it's because he's older, maybe early sixties. With a worn expression, he rubs his stubbled jaw.

"That's what I want to talk to you about, girls." He sits back in his squeaky chair and frowns. "I'm going to need you both to head over to the Rebels' stadium tomorrow morning to do a new football segment targeting women. If it's a success, we'll do it every week. Nicole, I don't need to tell you this could be huge for your career."

I'm so confused right now. "Sir, why do you need me?" She's the sports reporter.

He smiles. It's tired, but it warms his eyes. "I loved your suggestion to investigate how expanding the team's parking would affect the neighboring wildlife in the adjacent park reserve. This is your chance to interview the Rebels' public relations rep to get a few answers and some footage. With the vote coming up on Friday, you'll have everything you need to do a full report."

I can barely contain my glee. So far, I've mostly written for the anchors or done small, live spots about human interest stories. But this could be significant. Solving real problems is what attracted me to journalism in the first place. I could care less about being on TV or getting recognition. I love fighting for the little guy and helping the community.

He waves between us. "You two should go prep. Spencer will brief you on the logistics of tomorrow."

At that, my face falls. Spencer is the new producer corporate hired to increase ratings. And he's a total asshole.

As though sensing my trepidation, Roger nods. "You'll do great, girls. I have faith in you."

God, I want to kick ass for him. He's been under so much

pressure about our ratings lately. Corporate wants him to do more about viral videos and feature celebrity bullshit. He's been holding out, but I know if he doesn't turn things around, he's losing his job.

Here's the crazy part. I heard through the grapevine that Roger wasn't excited about hiring Nicole or me. He wanted more seasoned veterans but gave in because he didn't have a choice. According to the gossip, corporate made him hire young, attractive girls. I don't know why that endears him more to me. Maybe it's because I know he really cares about the news and getting it done right.

I plan to make him proud.

* * *

SPENCER'S EYES are alight with enthusiasm as he goes over his notes with Nicole. I might as well be a piece of lint.

"The Rebels hope to increase their viewership among women, and they want to use this weekly segment to tap into a whole new viewership. I think you're just the girl to do it," he says to Nicole, not hiding his interest in her artificially high breasts.

Spencer is not a bad-looking guy. He's in his early thirties and has an impressive resume that boasts consulting gigs with major news networks across the country. At least, I'd be impressed if he didn't creep me out.

Nicole doesn't seem to care that our boss is leering at her tits. She's too busy jotting down ideas in her notebook. "I can't believe I get to interview Daren Sloan. Fuck, yeah."

I cringe at the expletive, thinking back to my professor who would ream us out if we cursed around him for fear we'd drop an f-bomb on live television, but Douchebag Spencer doesn't bat an eye.

Nicole looks over tomorrow's schedule with a frown. "We don't have a lot of time for the interview."

This is where I *could* tell her Daren is my neighbor, that we have mutual friends, that I could probably get her more than the ten minutes the team promised us. But then I'm reminded of the many times Nicole's handed me a big, fat serving of snark during the last month, and my usual pay-it-forward philosophy disappears faster than Kanye's false sense of humility at an awards show.

Nicole taps her pen at the edge of her notebook. "Spence, what approach should I take? Would you prefer that I ask the totally clueless questions like the idiots out there who don't know jack about football?"

Spence? I'm vomiting on the inside.

"No, just do your thang, girl. Get Daren talking about the game. Use your charm." He clicks his tongue. "Give the ladies watching a show."

I resist making a gagging sound. But only barely.

He starts to walk away, and I call out, "Did you have any special direction for me?"

Spencer doesn't look up from his call sheet. "Touch base with news. See what they need." And then he shuffles out of the office.

His commitment to journalism is heartwarming.

Nicole talks through her questions like I'm not in the room. *How did you feel when you won the Heisman? What can we expect from you this season? How much time do you think you'll play? Are you dating anyone?*

Somehow, I don't think those are the questions the team is hoping she'll ask. Finally, I can't take it anymore. "Nicole, have you considered just asking basic football questions for girls who want to learn the game but don't know where to begin?"

She makes a "pft" sound and shakes her head at me like I'm an idiot.

Okey-doke. I'm done. Nicole trots off to talk to the sports department, and I return to my notes.

At least I can finally do the segment about the wildlife

preserve. The Rebels don't seem concerned that expanding their parking will endanger the golden-winged warbler, which is on the brink of extinction.

I'm trying to pull up some research when my laptop freezes, and I get the pinwheel of death. "Goddaaaa... Motherfuuuu... Shhhhh... Gah." I slam my fist on my desk.

"What's the trouble, Madeline?"

The voice behind me makes me jump.

Brad, the tech guy, is leaning into my cubicle as though he heard my cries from afar. He pushes up his black-rimmed glasses on his nose and smiles, his green eyes crinkling at the corners. Brad is a nice guy. Why can't I like nice guys? He brought me an iced mocha last week when he ducked out for a coffee run. I know several of the secretaries have little crushes on him. It's that laid-back demeanor and sandy blond hair that do them in. Even though I never date coworkers, I wish I felt an inkling of attraction for him. He's so much more my speed.

I smile in relief. "Thank God you're here. This wonderful technological invention that should make my life easier is driving me insane. It keeps freezing. I know you said it was that last system update, but Nicole's laptop doesn't have the same problem. Can you take a look?"

He smiles and folds his hands in front of him. "I'm here to serve."

CHAPTER 6

DAREN

THE MORNING COMMUTE is a bitch due to an eighteen-wheeler that overturned, effectively shutting down the Mass Pike. I barely make it on time, and guys stream in late all morning.

After an hour and a half of weightlifting, I head for the showers. Coach rolls his eyes when I remind him about the interview, but he waves me off to meet with the news crew.

Jeanine directs me toward the practice field, but the sight of Maddie McDermott in the vestibule of the stadium having a heated conversation with some guy stops me in my tracks. Their voices, although low, echo in the glass enclosure.

"Spencer, I haven't prepped for this. I'm here to cover the wildlife preserve. Let's just wait for Nicole to arrive."

He stares her down. "She's at least an hour away because of the accident. The team gets dozens of requests to do shit like this, and I'm not taking the chance they won't reschedule. So get your ass in there and change." He points to the bathroom across the enclosure and shoves a gym bag in her hand.

I can't handle the tone he's using with her and before I realize it, I'm beside her. "Is there a problem, Maddie?"

She presses her palm to her chest. "God, Daren. Stop sneaking up on me."

Spencer looks from her to me and grins. "You two know each other?"

Before I can tell him we're neighbors, Maddie interrupts. "We've met once or twice."

I don't miss the warning in her eyes to keep my mouth shut.

He tilts his head as though he's trying to reconcile why I'm glaring at him since I apparently barely know Maddie, but then he shrugs. "Great. Whatever. Look, Madeline, we're going to table the Save the Earth tearfest for another day, and you're going to tape the sports segment."

She squeezes her eyes shut and pinches the bridge of her nose. "I'm not a sports reporter, Spencer. I do news. Thus, the suit."

She's decked out in a form-fitting burgundy suit that instantly reminds me of all the reasons I'd love to get her between my sheets. I force my eyes up and try to stop thinking with my dick.

Maddie sighs and hands the gym bag back to the guy I'm assuming is her boss. "I'm not going to prance around on a foot-ball field in yoga pants and a tank top during an interview." She blows out a breath. "I don't even *like* football."

I laugh, and they both look at me.

That's something most people never admit to my face. She's got balls, this one. I don't know why, but her comment makes me want to mess with her a little. "Aww, come on, Maddie. Do the segment with me. I promise I'll be gentle." And then I give her a wink.

Her mouth falls open and her boss's sleazy smile widens. He motions between us. "Perfect. See, this is going to be great."

* * *

SPENCER IS GETTING IMPATIENT. I glance at my watch. If Maddie doesn't hurry up, we might need to reschedule after all. I'm about to knock on the bathroom door when it opens.

When she steps out, her jaw is clenched, and she's gripping a binder to her chest like it's a life vest. After a second, she lowers it, a resigned expression in her eyes.

She's tied her long, black hair up into a high ponytail, and she's wearing a tight gray Rebels tank top and running pants. And fuck me if she doesn't look edible.

That Spencer guy is on the phone, and when he sees her, his eyes take an indecently slow perusal down her body before he gives her a thumbs up.

She sighs and shakes her head, looking a little defeated.

"Hey, you look great," I tell her, trying to cheer her up, and she growls.

"I hate you," she says under her breath.

"It'll pass. Then you'll love me. I promise."

She turns and glares. "You shouldn't make promises you can't keep."

I grin and motion toward her. "You need to be careful. I always keep my promises."

Maddie mumbles something I can't quite make out as Jeanine stalks out of her office. "Spencer! We need to get this going. Daren has a whole day of training ahead of him."

Five minutes later, we're out on the field. A burly guy named Joe hands Maddie a mic before he trains the lens on us and does a quick countdown.

And even though Maddie looks pissed as hell, the minute the camera rolls, she pushes her shoulders back and smiles.

"Hi, this is Madeline McDermott with the newest member of the Rebels team, all-star quarterback and Heisman winner Daren Sloan."

"Stop!" Spencer waves from off camera. "You know, Daren called you Maddie. I like that better. Let's use it. 'Maddie' is much more approachable than 'Madeline.' Okay, Joe, let's roll."

"I'm sorry," she says, lowering the mic. "Yes, my friends call me Maddie, but professionally I go by Madeline. I mean, it's my name, and I would appreciate it if—"

Spencer's face tightens. "This is non-negotiable, *Maddie*."

She stills and drops her head.

Shit. I did this. I'm the one who called her Maddie. I open my mouth to apologize when she says, "Fine, Spencer. You're the boss."

She motions for Joe and starts her intro again.

"Hi, I'm Maddie McDermott…"

I tune out and watch as her whole disposition in front of the camera changes. Her eyes are sparkly and smiling. Her demeanor is confident and poised. Her voice even has a musical quality to it.

Fuck, Sloan. A musical quality? Really?

"Daren, I don't watch a lot of football, so I guess I'm the perfect candidate for this segment." She turns to look me in the eye. "Now, you promised to be gentle with me, and I'm going to hold you to your promise." She laughs and I laugh with her. Damn, she's charming. "What's the first thing someone like me needs to know about the sport? Let's assume I understand the big picture—the football needs to get to the end zone. And I think we all know you're the quarterback and control the ball. Where do we go from there?"

"Well, we start at the line of scrimmage, and I have four possessions to get to the first down, which is ten yards, and I can either pass or run, but once I run, I can only throw the ball laterally, to my side or behind me."

"That sounds easy enough. And I think everybody in New England knows you like going deep"—I raise an eyebrow, dying to crack a joke at the double entendre I'm sure she didn't intend —"that you like long passes, and you're good at making them. Which brings me to my next question. What do you think makes a good quarterback?"

"Being able to see the plays before the route clears. Having a sense for your guys and being so connected with them that you know where they're headed before they do."

Her expression is flirty. Big, luminous eyes peer up at me through thick lashes. "Sounds like a good bromance."

Laughing, I agree. "And I have all the moves."

She gives me a cheeky grin. "I bet you do." After a few more questions, she turns to the camera. "We hope to see more of Daren's moves in two weeks at the first preseason game against New York. I'm Maddie McDermott for WNEN. Back to you in the studio."

I'm not entirely sure what I expect her reaction to be when we're done, but it's not this. Her smile instantly fades, her shoulders tense, and that breezy demeanor vanishes beneath a furrowed brow.

"Thanks, Daren." She holds out her hand to shake mine.

Seriously? She wants to shake my hand? What happened to the Maddie who just flirted her ass off with me? Slowly, I extend my arm and grip her slender hand in mine.

But despite her less than friendly vibe, it's hard to miss the fire behind her eyes. It's a look I recognize every day before I get on the field. Fuck, she wears it well.

Before I can say anything, she takes off for the parking lot, at which point I can't help but stare at her ass, which is just as glorious as I imagined. *One I'd love to spank.*

CHAPTER 7

THIS IS how I know the importance of a segment. On a typical story, I shuffle out the station with a camera bag slung across my shoulders, lamenting the fact that I have to trek around Boston in heels to shoot my own footage. When a story is important, reporters get paired with a cameraman. And if the assignment is really hot, they get paired with a producer *and* a cameraman.

Apparently, Daren Sloan is hot. A hot story, that is.

Wiping my forehead, I sink into the bench seat of the van. I'm still on edge, still feeling unsettled, and I'm not sure if it's because Spencer nearly crawled up my butt when I was shooting or if it had something to do with my infuriating neighbor.

The drive back to the station is surprisingly quiet. I expect Spencer to say something, as he's never short on opinions, but he stares straight ahead as Joe directs the van through the congested streets.

Internally, I give myself a pat on the back. Aside from the whole "you like to go deep" comment, I didn't say anything too stupid during the interview despite my lack of preparation. That in and of itself is a lesson.

Maybe I should have prepped for this story even though it was Nicole's. Because if I want to make it in broadcasting, I have to be better prepared than everyone else.

Daren was his usual charming self. *You'll love me. I promise.* I roll my eyes.

Good lord, he's full of himself.

But darn it, he looked good today. And what's worse, he smelled great. Like he had just stepped out of the shower. Not that I was trying to sniff him or anything.

That's it, though. Daren Sloan probably assumes he can just smile in a girl's direction, and she'll spread her legs. Asshole.

I am so tired of men.

At least I'm done with the assignment.

Glancing at Spencer's rigid posture in the front seat, I can't help but wonder why he's so quiet.

"So… Spencer. Was that okay? The interview?"

Jeez, Maddie. Way to sound confident.

He turns and glares at me. "Which part? The part where you threw ultimatums in my face about how we were going to cover the story or the part where you insulted the number one draft pick and had the audacity to say you didn't like football? What the fuck is wrong with you?"

I suck in a breath: "I… I…"

He turns back. "Don't fucking talk right now. I don't want to hear it."

My eyes sting. I try to swallow the lump in my throat, but my mouth is dry.

God.

Spencer might be a prick, but he's right. I don't know what got into me. The moment I heard I was interviewing Daren, I threw him in the "obnoxious neighbor" category. We have mutual friends, and Sheri wants to set us up on a date, and I can't stand the way my mind drifts to think about those hazel eyes.

This is why I never mix business with pleasure. Because I can't keep my emotions in check. But it's what makes me good at what I do. I care. I invest myself in my stories, and I always dig to get to the heart of the issue.

My cheeks burn as I think back to what my old professor was always telling me. That I needed more distance. That I needed to be less involved. I never got it. I always thought he was being some out-of-touch academic. But maybe I'm not as good at this as I thought.

And now I've pissed off the Douchebag.

Swallowing my pride, I bite the bullet. "You're right. I am so sorry."

Spencer shakes his head as he pulls out his laptop. "I'm not the one you should be apologizing to."

* * *

MY HANDS SMOOTH down my A-line skirt. I reach up to knock on the door and pull away.

Glancing at my watch, I wonder if ten p.m. on a Saturday is too late to do this. But I just got home twenty minutes ago. This is the first opportunity since the interview two days ago to make amends.

I turn back and look at my door, five feet away across the hall.

Maddie, you're being a wuss. Come on. You do know Daren. Smooth this over so you can sleep tonight.

Ever since our interview, I've barely been able to sleep. The idea that I've been unprofessional makes me ill, and I need to make this right.

I knock three times, and in the silence that follows, my anxiousness grows.

Just as I'm about to leave, footsteps behind me make me whirl around to find Daren and a tiny brunette with big brown eyes.

"Maddie." Daren looks surprised to see me.

The woman places her hand on his arm and steps closer to him.

Shit. This is a date.

I open my mouth and shut it, not sure if I can apologize in front of this girl. But the sound of male voices and a small stampede cut me off. Two seconds later, I'm surrounded by several NFL players.

"McDermott! Girl, whatcha doing here?" one asks. But I'm too discombobulated to pinpoint who just spoke to me.

Daren has a curious expression on his face before he breaks out into a smile. I blink. And blink again.

And then I go on full-out autopilot.

"I'm baking brownies, and I'm out of sugar. Do you have any?" What the ever-loving hell am I talking about?

He tilts his head back and laughs. "Do I have any sugar?" His dimples peek out. "Why, yes, Ms. McDermott, I think I have some sugar for you."

The guys chuckle behind him, and I feel my face heat. Jesus Christ. *Abort, Maddie!*

Two cups of granulated sugar later, I am back in the safe confines of Sheri's condo. Leaning against the front door, I drop my head back and close my eyes.

What just happened?

I've interviewed senators and congressmen and celebrities on live television, and I never get flustered.

Letting one dumb jock with a pretty face and oversized muscles turn me into a bumbling fool is so ridiculous I want to slap myself.

I just need to look on the bright side. At least I don't have to interview him again.

* * *

45

THE WEIGHT of the deadline presses against my chest. I glance at the clock on my desk and take a quick breath. Ten minutes. I have ten minutes until this needs to be uploaded for the Monday midday broadcast.

Despite my nerves, my voice is steady as I finish recording the audio.

This is my happy place. The buzz of the chase. The adrenaline spike of getting the story done right.

I grab the phone off the cradle. When Judith, one of the producers, answers, I give her the only answer that's acceptable. "We're locked and loaded."

"One sec." She types with such heavy fingers that I can hear the keyboard through the receiver. Judith mumbles to herself for a minute and then there's silence. "Perfect. I love that last line about the food pantry's motto. Nice touch."

I grin to myself. Not that I'm the type of person who goes looking for a pat on the back, but I'd be lying if I didn't admit that my mojo has taken a hit since Spencer forced me to do that story. I watched it air from my couch yesterday morning and forced myself to sit on my hands so I didn't bite my nails.

I'm almost loath to admit that the banter between Daren and me went off smoothly. Sheri walked in mid-way through the segment and squealed something about how adorable we looked. That I could have done without.

But with the sports segment behind me, I'm feeling back in the groove as I cross off item after item on my to-do list.

When I come around the corner, I catch sight of Roger and Spencer squaring off in the hallway. Roger's brows are set low in a frown.

I glance down as I pass, not wanting to get caught in those crosshairs. Spencer points at me. "Maddie, just the person I needed to see." His faux friendliness sets my nerves on edge.

I force a smile. "What's up?"

"Congratulations. Your segment with Daren has gotten more buzz than any other sports story this summer. We've been flooded with emails and tweets."

"Great. I'm glad to hear it. I'm sure Nicole will be excited to take the reins." My cubicle partner has not been shy about the fact that she'd like to strangle me in my sleep.

Roger is still frowning, which can't be a good sign.

Spencer shakes his head. "That's just it. We don't want to mess with a good thing, so you'll be doing the series."

"But this is Nicole's story. And you know sports is not my thing. I just don't want to—"

"I could give a flying fuck about Nicole losing this. You're doing this story, and you're going to give it every ounce of your attention and enthusiasm, or you can find another news station in Boston that will take your whiny ass."

My mouth drops open. I'm not whiny... am I?

Once again, I'm speechless. I blink back the burn in my eyes because I will not freaking cry.

I look to Roger, whose grim expression confirms the worst, that he has no say in this.

Mentally slapping myself out of silence, I stick my shoulders back. "Of course I'll do the story." My words come out a whisper. I clear my throat. "Thank you for this opportunity."

Spencer rolls his eyes and takes off down the hall. Jeez, could he make me feel like a bigger idiot?

"Madeline," Roger says with a sigh, "this *is* an opportunity. Perhaps not the one you want, but if it gets the traction we think it could have, it could catapult you like no other human interest story will. Because, as you know, it'll still be a while before you get a shot at headlining news."

I nod quickly.

"But I'm sorry about Spencer." Roger leans in and whispers, "If his father wasn't on our board, I'd tell him to go fuck himself."

A laugh escapes me, along with a few tears that I quickly wipe away.

Roger averts his eyes, maybe embarrassed that I'm crying. Damn it. I've never cried on the job. He pats my shoulder. "The best revenge is success, kiddo. Go kick ass."

CHAPTER 8

DAREN

ONCE AGAIN, at the next interview, Maddie looks less than thrilled to see me. When she came over to my place last weekend to ask for sugar, I was almost tempted to look behind her to make sure no one was holding her at gunpoint.

I chuckle, a little amused by her lack of enthusiasm for covering football. "Aww. C'mon, McDermott. I can't be that bad to work with."

A lightning-fast smile replaces her frown. But it's too late. I know she doesn't want to be here. Especially wearing those workout shorts and that tank top. Speaking of those workout shorts, damn, those legs are long. And toned. They're the kind of legs I'd like to wrap around my—

"Up here, Sloan." She tilts her head until my eyes reach her face. I grin, unable to hide my obvious appreciation for her lengthy limbs. She gets right to business. "So I was thinking we could talk a little more about your offense today, maybe some of your favorite plays. I'd love to know how you decide what calls to make."

She might not be excited to be doing this, but I gotta admit I enjoy explaining the game to her. "Sure, Maddie. Whatever you want."

She flips through her notes, which have little color-coded Post-Its sticking out the side at perfect right angles.

"Actually, change of plans," some girl in a skin-tight top says as she strolls up to us with a wide grin. She holds out her hand to me. "Hi, Daren. I'm Nicole." I shake her hand, waiting for her to explain. She turns to Maddie and the chick's grin widens. "Thanks for warming him up for me. Spencer says you can go back to that bird story you wanted to do." When Nicole turns to me, she rolls her eyes.

Maddie's brow furrows. "I don't understand." She turns her back to me and lowers her voice. "Spencer made such a big deal about this when I tried to talk him into letting me back on the parking lot story."

"Well, maybe I made him a better offer. One he couldn't refuse." Nicole bats her eyelashes and plasters a fake smile on her face.

Maddie sucks in a breath, and her coworker's smile widens. A silence stretches between them a moment before Maddie pushes her shoulders back. "Right." She turns to me, her lips a tight line. "Sorry for the confusion, Daren. You're in good hands, though. Nicole is a great sports reporter." Despite what just went down between these two girls, Maddie sounds sincere in her praise of Nicole.

Maddie starts to walk away but stops when I call out her name. I take a step toward her. "It's Quentin's birthday, so I'm throwing a party tomorrow night. Why don't you come?"

Her brow tightens again. "I probably have to work late, so I don't know if—"

"We'd love to come," Nicole chirps as she hooks her arm through Maddie's. "Thanks for the invite." She turns to Maddie, who looks down at their linked arms. "Don't you usually get off at seven? That's not so late." She doesn't wait for Maddie to respond. "We should get Daren's phone number and address."

Nicole pulls out her cell and the look of exasperation on Maddie's face is priceless, so I chime in. "Maddie knows where I live, and I'm pretty sure she knows how to get in touch with me." Because no way am I giving out my number to this other girl.

Maddie nods slowly, a resigned expression in her eyes. "Sure. See you this weekend." Then she turns and walks away.

CHAPTER 9

MADDIE

IT'S BEEN A LONG DAY. I can't believe I agreed to go to Daren's party tonight.

Stretching, I glance over to Nicole, who is reviewing footage a few feet away in one of the editing booths. The face that stares back on her screen immediately sets my teeth on edge. Jacob. In all of his glory.

Beaming in the ring after his victory last weekend against another local contender, he's surrounded by his coach and several girls. After he wraps up his interview, the camera keeps rolling as he steps back and tongues up two buxom blondes, one right after the other.

Something akin to rage shoots through my veins. That jerkoff calls me every week and leaves messages asking me to give our relationship another chance while he's obviously banging two girls at a time.

I stare long and hard, wondering why I've been an unholy wreck this summer when my ex is obviously having the time of his life. My jaw clenches. I've sworn off men, hoping this approach would help me piece my life back together.

But right now, I feel stupid. Because those girls might just be one-night stands, but I swear there's more passion in those kisses than he and I ever had. And maybe that was the problem all along.

"He's so hot." Nicole purrs to herself as she splices out the full-on makeout session. I guess tongue is too hot for mid-day news.

"If you like the all brawn, no brains type."

She whirls around, a smirk on her lips. Shrugging, she motions toward my ex, whom she obviously doesn't know I dated. "I like the pretty face, big dick types."

I don't have the heart to tell her he'd disappoint her.

"We still on for tonight?" she asks as though I have a choice in the matter.

Jacob smiles on the screen behind her, taunting me. "Can't wait."

* * *

EXHAUSTION SINKS me deeper into my bed as I listen to the sound of the bass through the walls. The party next door has been in full swing since I got home half an hour ago.

A sudden slap to my ass jerks me out of my near-comatose state. "What the hell, Sheri?"

"I'm heading out to my dirty book club, and I don't want to see you when I get back." Her eyebrow pops up.

I shake my head. "I think I'll send Nicole over there by herself. I don't think she'll mind flying solo." Now that my Jacob-rage has subsided, I'm too tired to function. "Besides, I need to do some laundry and get to bed by eleven. I'm not sure how much fun I can pack in between now and then."

I let out a sigh that's been building in my chest. It's Friday night, and the old chicks on *The Golden Girls* sound more exciting than I do right now.

God, am I always this boring?

Sheri must agree with my internal assessment because she makes a little grunt of displeasure. "Seriously, get your ass up. I don't want you obsessing over seeing Jacob tonight. Go out, have a few drinks, make out with someone hot. I'm sure there are a ton of sexy men next door who would love nothing more than to service you."

"Sheri, I'm not going to have anyone *service* me, you little hussy."

She laughs and bends over to apply lipstick in my mirror. "What is wrong with getting it on tonight?" She turns back to me, hands on her hips. "How long did you wait to have sex with Jacob?"

Not long enough. "Three months. Why?"

"You waited a very respectable amount of time to sleep with someone who turned out to be a giant dick. If you were holding out because you were hoping doing so would help you see if he was serious or not, it obviously didn't work."

I stare back, feeling more depressed by her little pep talk. "Okay. Your point?"

"My point is that the amount of time some guy waits to have sex with you is not an indicator of doucheyness. Jacob waited, and yet he's the poster boy of douchebaggery." She waves her lipstick container at me. "So stop waiting around for some boring guy in a sweater vest to make you feel like it's safe to come out of your hidey hole. Be adventurous and get out there."

I'd laugh at her "hidey hole" comment except it hits too close to home.

Her eyes pass over me, and she gets a little crinkle between her eyes. "Maddie, I've watched you work non-stop for weeks now. You're gonna crash and burn at this rate. Take a break. Be social. Act your age, for Christ's sakes. You don't have to sleep with anyone, but at least go flirt with a sexy man. Flirting is like chicken soup. Good for the soul."

Laughter spills out of me. "For a second there, I was afraid you were going to tell me that flirting is like chicken. Finger-lickin' good."

She snorts. "Girl, if anything is getting licked, you're doing more than flirting. But that's not a bad thing." She winks and sashays out of my room.

Ugh. Maybe she's right. I guess I can go have one drink.

Her words are still on my mind when I step into my closet and eye all of my business suits. My job doesn't pay that much, but most of my salary goes toward my clothes, which I hate. Kids are starving in Third World countries, and I have to spend every penny on designer outfits so I can look like a responsible, respectable reporter. Ironic.

I blow out a breath. *Act my age.* I guess that rules out most of my clothes.

When Nicole saunters into our condo twenty minutes later all primped and primed for a Friday night out, the look of disgust on her face makes me wonder if I took Sheri's advice too seriously.

"You are *not* going to Daren's house dressed in a Guns 'n Roses t-shirt and jeans," she snarks.

"Well, judging by your apparel, you thought the theme of the night was street-walker chic, so I guess we both got our wires crossed."

Nicole stares at me for a moment and then breaks out into a laugh. "Hmm. The uptight bitch isn't so uptight after all. Good to know." Her hands smooth down her short dress. "I do look hot, don't I?" She doesn't give me a chance to respond. "Come on, Mad Dog. Let's get you an outfit. Where's your closet?"

And now I'd say the theme of the evening is freaky Friday. Because my snarky coworker is dragging me into my room to play dress-up. Maybe I could use that drink after all. Or four.

* * *

NICOLE WASTES no time making herself at home once we get to Daren's. Of course, first she socks me in the arm for not telling her he's my neighbor.

His condo is the reverse of ours, and his decor is surprisingly minimalist. A few leather couches, a flatscreen TV, stainless-steel fixtures and a few lamps. Simple. For a guy who's not only one of the most in-demand athlete-celebrities but also the heir to a multi-million dollar fortune, I'd say he's practically slumming it. But seeing that he's not into obnoxious displays of wealth makes me like him a teeny bit more.

Nicole flirts with at least three linebackers before she makes it back to me in the living room where I chat with a girl who's dating the kicker.

Daren works the crowd, shaking hands and doing the bro hug thing when he talks to friends. That effortless smile plays on his lips, and it's easy to see why he's known for his leadership. Girls make goo-goo eyes at him when he talks to them, and when they put their hands on his arm and pull him close, I have a sudden urge to strangle them with their product-enhanced shiny, long hair. Which is idiotic since I barely know the man.

But he does look sexy tonight. Who am I kidding? He always looks sexy.

He's wearing dark jeans and a snug white polo that shows off all of his muscles. Although he's dressed casually, he has a regal vibe about him. *It's probably because his parents own half of New England.*

"Are you two fucking?" Nicole asks in my ear.

My mouth drops open. "What?"

She makes a face like I'm a dumbass and motions toward Daren.

"No. God, no. Why would you think that?"

She studies me, her lips twisted. "Because you've been standing in this corner watching him like a sad little puppy."

"I have *not* been watching him." She hands me another beer, and I toss it back so I don't have to talk.

"Uh-huh."

Seeing Jacob tonight made me realize I need to live a little, and if that means appreciating Daren's obvious good looks, so be it. But that doesn't mean I want anyone to know it. Besides, as any girl can tell you, looking and touching are two totally different things. And I have no intention of touching. Ever.

Because one thing is certain—I'll never date another cheater again.

Fine. I don't know *for sure* that Daren cheated on his ex, Clementine, but when I interviewed her last fall about her book, most of her novel seemed to be autobiographical despite her denials. And that book very clearly detailed how her quarterback boyfriend broke her heart by sleeping with her best friend. *So you can take your charm and your cute little chin dimple, Daren Sloan, and kiss my ass.*

Realizing Nicole is waiting for me to respond, I clear my throat. "We're neighbors, but we hardly talk. I spoke to him more on the day I interviewed him than the month I've been living next door. I never see him. I mean, not that I'm looking." *Shut it, Maddie.*

Nicole's blank expression tells me she's not convinced. "I figured you two had to be fucking because you were so flirty when you interviewed him. It's one of the reasons your segment was so good, and it's why I think Spencer doesn't like my interview as much despite the fact that I promised him a blow job if he gave me the story."

"You promised Spencer a blow job?" At least a handful of people hear me shout. My cheeks start to burn.

She laughs. "No, but you should see your face."

God, this girl makes me insane.

Her manicured finger grabs a long strand of blonde hair as she sighs. "I might have mentioned that my father's best friend is the vice president of CBS. It took Spencer all of two seconds to reconsider and give me the segment. He'll be disappointed when he finds out my dad works for the Los Angeles Department of Social Services."

I laugh. "You're playing with fire." I shake my head. Even though I'd rather lose a limb than manipulate someone into giving me an assignment, a part of me admires her tenacity. "Good for you. You should go after what you want. It's a sports segment." I point my beer at her. "You do sports."

"Thank you, Captain Obvious."

"Anytime." I nod, downing my second beer.

"But you should know that Daren never looks at me the way he looks at you."

"What do you mean?"

She rolls her eyes. "Like he'd like to eat you for breakfast."

My stupid heart pitter-patters faster. "He's just playing it up for the camera."

Nicole smirks. "Yeah, okay. If that's what you want to tell yourself."

CHAPTER 10

DAREN

QUENTIN SHAKES his ass at me, and I laugh. "You have moves."

"Tell me about it," he says, thrusting his hips in rhythm to the music.

I haven't known Quentin long, but practicing together day in and day out has a way of bonding people. He and I clicked from the beginning, which could bode well for our season. While the game takes place on the field, those men watch my ass and make sure I don't get killed. So to me, they're family.

Although the party scene is not my idea of a good time, I'd rather hang out with the guys at my place than at a bar. I rarely drink in the off season, much less once football kicks in, so I'll keep it to one or two beers tonight.

Being a homebody is one of the things about me that drove Veronica crazy. That and putting football first. I see why that would bother her, but she knew that about me when we first got together. And she knew football was non-negotiable.

Surveying the crowd in the kitchen, it's hard to ignore the guys cozying up with the groupies. At least a handful of them are married. I wish I didn't know that shit. I may not have a sterling record myself, but we're all adults now, and you can't chalk up sleeping around to being young and dumb.

Ignoring that brewing drama, I reach into the fridge for a beer.

A few of the guys stand around the island and stuff their faces. "Yeah, I'd chop that up. Those big titties. That fine face. Man, I bet she be a tight fit." They're staring at someone across the living room, and when I realize who they're talking about, I want to shove my foot up their asses.

"Gentlemen," I say, squaring my shoulders to the huge defensemen. "No one is *chopping* Maddie, who happens to be a friend of mine. So I'm going to pretend I didn't hear that."

"You calling dibs, D?" one asks.

"No, I'm calling off limits." The last thing Maddie needs is one of these horny fucks after her.

"She's hot, though, right?"

"Fellas, you'd have to be deaf, dumb, and blind to not appreciate that girl. Which you should stop doing. Get your eyes off her body, and go find some other unsuspecting soul to eye-fuck."

They reluctantly meander away, and I return my attention to Maddie. Her thick black hair cascades down her back, and it's wavy and a little wild, which has me itching to run my fingers through it.

Maddie's like a grown-up version of Snow White. Those wide blue eyes and pale skin kind of do it for me. I'm surrounded day in and day out by life-sized Barbies who would stampede over their mommas for a chance to party here tonight, and there's something so refreshing about the girl across the room who looks like she could care less that she's surrounded by a team that almost won the Super Bowl last year.

And tonight, she's stunning. A silky wraparound black dress hugs her curves and reveals more than her usual outfits. But it's those black heels that make me wonder how they would look slung over my shoulders.

Her coworker, that reporter Nicole, spots me staring and nudges Maddie, who looks up and gives me a reluctant smile. And damn, it's like seeing the sun rise.

I take that as my cue and cross the room. "Ladies."

"Hey, handsome," Nicole says, pulling me into a tight hug. Then she whispers in my ear, "You don't know it yet, but I'm helping you." Then she kisses my cheek, taking her time.

Her hands linger on my waist when she pulls away. I'm not sure what to make of this aside from the fact that it's Friday night, and maybe Nicole wants to cut loose. But when I see the look on Maddie's face, I think I get what Nicole was trying to do. Because Maddie does not look happy.

Interesting.

Because up until tonight, I was almost sure Maddie hated me. Almost.

But her expression makes me rethink last weekend when she came over for sugar. I had a carload of friends with me, so it wasn't exactly the best time for her and me to hang out. What would she have said to me had I been alone? Now that I think about it, she did not look excited to see Quentin's cousin on my arm that night. It was Monica's birthday, so Q asked me to treat her special. Autograph her Rebels gear. Pay her attention before she hopped a flight the next day. So I talked to her all night and made sure she had fun. I'd do that for any of the players' friends or family.

"How are my two favorite reporters?" I ask as I reach over and pull Maddie into a hug. Just to make sure Maddie gets the hint that she's the one I'd like to investigate, I lift her off her feet until she squeaks.

I laugh at her little sound, and then she finally relents with a chuckle and wraps her arms around my neck so that she's totally pressed against me. She melds to my body from tits to hips. Yeah, I could get used to this. And she smells fucking amazing. Intoxicating. Like sweet flowers and honey.

I place her on her feet, but I have to steady her because she seems a little wobbly.

Nicole gives me a wink and trots off to get another drink.

Maddie turns to me, her face flushed, her eyes wide, and I don't think I've ever wanted to kiss a woman more. Clearing my throat, I thank her for coming.

She blinks a few times. "No prob. It was a rough commute down the hall, but I managed." She sounds out of breath, but her eyes sparkle back, and I swear to God, the air sparks with electricity.

Leaning forward until I know she is the only one privy to what I'm about to say, I whisper, "I missed you yesterday. That interview wasn't the same."

I tilt my head to see her expression, and her eyes widen a fraction more.

Maddie wasn't excited to be covering football, but her questions felt right and our vibe worked. Something was off with Nicole. Not for a lack of effort on her part. She did a full-court press, spouting facts and figures I barely know myself. But we had zero chemistry.

Maddie shrugs, ignoring my obvious attempt to flirt with her. "I'm sure your segment went well. Nicole is a great sports reporter."

My eyes pass over her. "You look beautiful, by the way."

She looks down at the beer she's clutching. "Nicole made me change. Apparently, she took issue with my Guns n' Roses t-shirt."

"This dress is wicked hot."

She laughs nervously. "Wicked, huh?"

"I am a Boston boy through and through."

She nods. "I guess I figured all that fine living up in Lexington might have stripped you of your New England idioms."

Hmm. She knows I grew up in Lexington. I shouldn't be too

flattered. She is a reporter after all. But yeah, my ego likes the idea that she's been thinking about me.

I nod at her. "Where did you grow up?"

"Nowhere exciting. Southie."

"Really? Where's your accent?"

She frowns, and I'm briefly worried I've offended her, but then her shoulders tilt back, and I'm struck by the glint in her eyes. "You mean the accent I'm gonna use to teahr your ass apaaahrt?"

I bark out a laugh. "Yeah. That one."

She grins, and my stomach does this weird little backflip. Because her smiles do something crazy to my chest. Like they're drawing out air I haven't breathed yet.

Maddie takes a long pull of her beer, averting her eyes. I love that she drinks beer. Most of the girls here tonight are downing fruity concoctions or wine, but Maddie has a dark lager in hand. I watch her mouth, mesmerized by those full lips. "I've worked hard to get rid of that accent. It wasn't easy. It still slips out once in a while, if I'm really ticked off, but I know I'll never get a national anchor spot sounding like someone off the set of *Good Will Hunting*."

"That's a great movie."

"The best."

I grin. "That scene in the park? Where they fight."

She nods. "All in slow motion with that John Rafferty song playing in the background?"

"That song makes the scene. Or what about in the bar when he tells off that Harvard dickwad?"

"Or his whole 'Why shouldn't I work for the NSA' speech?"

We nod in unison. I stare at her too long, and her cheeks flush, which makes me think this party was the best idea I've had in a while.

My mind wanders to my plan to not screw around once the

season kicks in. But it's still preseason, which means maybe there's still a little time to have some fun. And my idea of fun is standing a foot away.

* * *

FORTY-FIVE MINUTES LATER, we're still talking. I'm trying to use this rare moment to find out everything I can about this girl. She's usually so closed off. Maybe it's the beer, but tonight everything about our conversation is easy.

When I ask about her family, she says her mom took off when she was younger, and her dad raised her. He was a firefighter but passed away. She's close to her uncle. A nerd to the core, she was on the high school newspaper for four years before attending Boston University.

We're discussing college when her eyes get that flinty edge again. "So, you weren't embarrassed to go to Boston College since, you know, it's inferior to BU?"

"No more than you were going to a school that basically accepts any kid off the street."

A smile plays on her lips. "Yeah, BU accepts more kids. Not every school can master that Stepford vibe you have going on at BC."

"It's tough, but someone has to do it." I click my tongue. "But it must be painful to not have a football team. That it sucked so bad, your school dismantled it."

"True." She clutches her chest like she's rubbing an ache. "But you know what took the edge off? Kicking BC's ass in hockey last year. And the year before that." She holds up her beer. "Cheers."

I let her have her moment, that smile on her face too cute to diminish.

She tilts her head, her hair falling over her shoulder. "Have you seen Clementine lately?" Clementine is my ex-girlfriend from high school and one of my best friends from childhood. We went years without talking because I hurt her when we were dating, but last year we finally made up.

"Fourth of July. She and her man came to my party." My eyes travel slowly over Maddie's face. "See, you should've come instead of blowing me off."

"I did not blow you off." But Maddie's words lack conviction. "Okay, maybe I did blow you off." Her nose crinkles adorably. "Sorry."

"Is there any possibility you might consider blowing me off less?"

She fights that gorgeous smile. "I'll take it under advisement."

"Good, because I don't know if my ego could stand another rejection."

She taps me on the chest with the neck of her beer. "Your ego is coming perilously close to jamming in the doorway when you walk through it. I'm pretty sure I'm in no danger of harming your precious ego."

"You'd be surprised. I'm a sensitive guy." I give her my sincerest look and then bat my eyelashes.

She stifles a laugh. "I'm sure. You have 'sensitive guy' written all over you."

"You shouldn't be so quick to judge. You might hurt my feelings." Her look of incredulity only encourages me. "I do have a soft side, McDermott. If we hung out more, you'd see it."

I bump her shoulder and she laughs, bumping me back. "All right. Maybe."

This girl is the one I met last fall. The one who laughs freely. The one whose eyes sparkle. And damn, speaking of eyes, I could stare into her baby blues all day. They remind me of calm ocean waters. Except when I look into hers, I'm not calm. If anything, my heart kicks up a notch when she's around.

I should be a good host and circulate among my guests, but

I'm not sure if I'll get another chance to see Maddie any time soon. She might be saying we'll hang out, but I know we're both busier than hell.

Nicole runs up and yanks on Maddie's arm. "Spencer just called. I need to use your laptop. Production might have messed up one of my segments, and I have to double-check it from my account."

"Okay." Maddie looks at me with a hint of disappointment in her eyes. "I guess we're calling it a night."

"What?" Nicole looks offended. She holds out her hand. "Just give me your keys. I saw your laptop in your bedroom. You stay and I'll be right back. You live next door, for fuck's sake. This will take me ten, fifteen minutes tops, and then we can all hang out." She turns to me and gives me an exaggerated wink, one that has Maddie tensing up again.

"But you'll need my password to use my laptop. I... I should come."

Nicole sighs again. "Just give me the code." She waits for Maddie to give her the info, but Maddie purses her lips. "Jesus, Madeline. I'm not going to fuck up your shit. I just need your code for five minutes. Get your fanboy Brad to change your login on Monday if you're that worried."

Maddie blows out a big breath. "Fine. It's DunkinDonuts411."

Nicole nods and runs off. I chuckle, and Maddie's cheeks turn pink. "Don't mock my love of coffee. This is serious business."

"Oh, I agree, doll face." She smiles and ducks her head. Is she embarrassed? Too fucking cute. "C'mon. Let's go shoot some pool."

I grab her hand and pull her toward the game room. She tugs me to a stop, and I turn around.

"Don't be too quick to think you can get one up on me, Sloan." She pokes me in the chest and grins. "I'm gonna kick your prep-school ass," she says, punctuating it with her Southie bravado.

I lean down until I can feel her breath on my face, and she stills. "I love a good challenge." I tap her on the nose and her eyes narrow, like she doesn't know if she wants to shoot me dead or fuck me.

Oh, yeah. I like riling up this girl.

CHAPTER 11

MADDIE

DAREN STUDIES THE TABLE, a serious expression tightening his jaw that's covered in the slightest stubble.

"Take all the time you need, Daren. I'm still going to win." It's probably a toss-up as to who will emerge the victor, but I rather enjoy getting a rise out of him. He's so damn full of himself. It would be nice to bring him down to Earth.

He looks at me briefly before that smirk reemerges.

"Whatever, McDermott. Number four in the corner pocket." Daren leans over, and I take a long look at that muscular body. His polo stretches across those broad shoulders down to his trim waist. He shifts slightly, and my eyes drop to admire that ass. Wowzers.

I suck down my beer. I'm not a big drinker, but it's definitely helping me relax. And I need to relax. Fortunately, I can be completely tipsy and not look it. I have my great Irish genes to thank for that talent. And I'm totally buzzed at the moment. Which works since I live next door and can crawl home later if I have to.

Buzzed. That's a funny word, I giggle to myself.

I'm sure I'll regret the alcohol tomorrow morning, but I want to chill for five minutes. I don't remember the last time I went to a party, so I might as well enjoy tonight.

Truthfully, I'm relieved not to have to do any more sports segments. Okay, yes, I was pissed yesterday afternoon because I had spent so much time prepping for Daren's interview, but now I'm realizing it was a blessing in disguise.

And Daren... He's not so bad. My tummy squirms when I think about how bitchy I was to him before our first interview. But he hasn't made me feel bad about it. If anything, he's been super sweet. Adorable, even.

I never did get a chance to apologize to him for insulting him that day. But maybe I can tonight when there are fewer people around to overhear our conversation.

The game room is tucked off down the hallway from the living room, and guests filter in and out. This seems to be the one area he really put time into decorating. It's decked out with a flatscreen, several game consoles, a pool table and a couple of arcade machines. On the opposite side of the room hangs his collegiate BC jersey in a dark frame, and beneath that is his Heisman.

But I know his achievements, and those two reminders of his accolades barely scratch the surface. When I think about it, he's actually pretty humble about it all.

He's so different from Jacob, who never missed an opportunity to tell you how awesome he was. I used to think that reflected his confidence, but now I know he's just an arrogant prick. Daren is so much more comfortable in his own skin.

I keep expecting Daren to run off and circulate with his guests, but he doesn't. He has girls dropping at his feet like he's anesthetizing them with his charm, and yet tonight, he's hanging out with me.

Look, don't touch, Maddie. Good-looking guys like him come with a price tag, one you can't afford.

I finish my beer, wishing men could be a less painful experience.

When Daren sinks the ball, he turns to me with a serious expression. "Bite me, McDermott."

He crosses his arms in front of his broad chest, making his shirt stretch more, those beckoning hazel eyes full of mischief.

"Gladly. Where?" Holy shit. Did I just say that?

A devilish smile ghosts his lips. "Careful, sweetheart. Don't want you to break off more than you can chew." Heat pulses in my veins, the ground shifting beneath me. His grin widens as he turns back to the table and takes aim.

What am I doing? Why am I flirting with Daren? I should go, but I've been waiting around for Nicole to return. She's been gone forever, and I'm about to send out a search party when she texts. *I logged off your laptop. Going to see if I can get Quentin naked. Left your keys on Daren's kitchen counter in the bread basket.*

Jesus. If Nicole thinks it's a good idea to sleep with the guys she's covering for her job, she's an idiot. She would get fired if Roger found out she was sleeping with Quentin. Spencer might not care, but Roger is old school, and he'd never let that slide.

I shake my head.

"What?"

I look up to find Daren studying me. "Nothing." Holding up my phone, I shrug. "Nicole left." I debate what else to say. But it's not like Nicole is some source I have to protect or even a good friend. "She's taking off with Quentin." Giving him a "birthday blow," according to her message. Then again, she might be lying. I can't tell with her anymore.

His eyebrows lift. "Okay then." He chuckles.

"I should get going too."

Daren's laughter fades, and he looks like he wants to say something when a few people join us and yank the darts from the board hanging across from the pool table. "Come on, Sloan," one guy says. "Let's do teams." He motions between me and a petite redhead. "If the girls win"—his eyes lewdly roam his date, who giggles—"they get… rubdowns."

"Rubdowns?" My eyebrows quirk up. Clearly, we're talking about more than…

"Back massages," Daren says, giving his teammate a pointed look.

"Fine. Back massages," he says with air quotes. "And if we win…" The guy hugs his date, letting his hands drop to her ass.

"Drinks on them next weekend," Daren says, cutting off his friend before he takes a drink of his beer.

The guy rolls his eyes and pats Daren hard on the chest, mumbling, "Cock block."

* * *

"Are you sure you don't want any help?" Daren's little chuckle irks me. A lot.

His teammate and that girl ran off a few minutes ago, leaving Daren and me alone in the game room. So we started over, and Daren said the only thing we were playing for was bragging rights because he'd enjoy beating my Southie ass. As if.

My eyes narrow. "Why do you think I *need* help?"

I might be halfway to drunk—okay, more than halfway—but I'm certainly cognizant enough to know that if I win, I want to do it on my own. And would I even be using the word "cognizant" if I were drunk? I think not. I am *so* not drunk. I am in fine playing shape.

I tighten my lips to mask my hiccup.

He's right behind me, but I won't face him. No way. He's trying to get under my skin. Trying to distract me so he can win. And he's *so* distracting. He's been staring at me every time it's my turn, and I can't focus.

He clears his throat. "And don't worry about those holes in my wall. Thanks for christening it, by the way."

My eyes narrow into little slits. I find it hard to believe I suck this badly when the board is only eight feet away. I mean, how damn hard can this game be? But between Daren's piercing hazel eyes and his cologne, wafting over when he's standing in my shadow, it's like my brain has been dumped in a deep fryer.

I stare at his otherwise immaculately painted wall. How is it that no one has missed the board before? I can't really be the first person to put a hole in it.

"It's just a game of darts, Maddie. It's okay if you lose. I won't hold it against you." He sidles closer, standing at my side. Staring. A small growl forms on my lips. And then he adds, "No need to get all huffy puffy."

"I am *not* huffy puffy." If he's not careful, he's going to get a dart aimed at him.

Despite my obvious irritation, he doesn't move. He just stands there, watching my profile like I'm the most interesting thing he's ever seen.

And then I can actually hear that little smirk break out on his face.

At that, I whirl to face him, to let him know these childish mind games won't work on me. Only spinning requires equilibrium, which apparently I lack at this moment, and I go stumbling into his hard body.

"Whoa, Maddie."

You know that moment when you realize there's no way to save face? Especially when it's planted into the hard chest of a ridiculously good looking man? Yeah, I'm in touch with that right now.

Whoa, Maddie?

I mumble into his shirt, "I'm not a horse."

His chest vibrates with laughter, irking me more. But before I can come up with the words to put him in his place, I realize how tangled up we are. His large hand grips my hip while his other arm is wrapped around my back. I'm clinging to his huge biceps, my boobs pressing into him as I gasp a breath.

I tilt my head back, way back, until my chin rests on his chest and I can see him peering down at me.

"Stop. Staring."

His eyebrows raise. But then his eyes travel over my face. "Stop being so insanely beautiful."

I stutter out a breath. I'm not sure if that's the best line I've ever heard or the worst. But based on how much I'm enjoying being this close to him—except for the cramp in my neck—I'm going to go with best.

"Stop batting your eyelashes at me and trying to distract me." I try to keep a straight face, to say that with conviction, but Daren shrugs with a smirk ghosting his lips.

Slowly, he lifts me until I'm fully upright, but he tightens his hold, his arms enveloping me in a hug as he leans down to rub his nose down my neck.

Oh my ever-loving God.

His gruff voice in my ear sends another shock through me. "What makes you think I'm trying to distract you?"

He places an open-mouthed kiss on my neck, and my jaw unhinges.

I swallow, hoping he can't feel my heart trying to gallop out of my chest. Because this man's body, all big and hard, is about the most magnificent thing I've ever felt.

My breath comes out in short puffs. "I, uh, I think this kind of behavior can get you disqualified. I'll get Southie bragging rights for life."

"Mm. But what a way to go." He pushes me back and lifts me onto the edge of the pool table. I blink to find him standing between my legs. "Maddie." He says my name in a whisper.

His hand wraps around the back of my neck, and when we're nose to nose, he pauses to look into my eyes. "You should know I've thought about doing this all summer." And then his mouth closes in on mine.

CHAPTER 12

MADDIE

Somewhere between his minty breath on my skin and those calloused hands riding up my thighs, I think I've lost all sense.

I have a two-hundred-and-twenty-five-pound quarterback parked like a Hummer between my legs, touching me like I'm the most magnificent thing he's ever felt.

He's been thinking about kissing me. Girls have been throwing themselves at him all summer, and he's been thinking about me.

I ignore the little voice that desperately wants to compare him to Jacob because for once in my life, I'm not going to overthink this. I don't care about the rumors swirling around Daren's personal life because I don't plan to be in it long enough to find out whether or not they're true.

This is about having a good time, plain and simple. And the man plastered to my body is all the encouragement I need to shut off my brain.

Besides, if my ex can bang cage girls two at a time, I can cut loose too. Just once.

Daren growls against my mouth, and my heart races.

See, Jacob. I can make someone come undone.

Thoughts of my ex fade as Daren fills my vision. His six-three frame is dizzying this close. I'm overwhelmed by his size, by the power in all of these taut muscles beneath my fingers. Daren is a damn diesel engine.

His lips make a slow sweep of mine. I let him take his time even though I want to crawl up his enormous body.

Is he trying to drive me crazy with these relatively chaste kisses? *How can this be chaste, Maddie? You're basically straddling the man in an upright position.*

Taking a deep breath does nothing to clear my head. Daren smells crisp and clean, his woodsy cologne making me want to lick him all over. *Hmm. Food for thought.*

His hands grip my waist, his fingers tightening, and as he nibbles on my lower lip, something in me snaps.

I tangle my fingers into his dark hair and yank him closer. He groans when my tongue slides into his mouth, and he scoots me right to the edge of the pool table so that our hips align. *God, yes.*

I grip his shirt, and a little whimper escapes my lips when his fingers squeeze my ass. This, this kiss detonated whatever's been building between us, and the only signal going off in my head right now is the one screaming to get under his hard body.

His kisses grow hungrier as his hand rubs up and down my side. Just close enough for his thumb to graze the swell of my breast.

Grab me. Squeeze me.

These wanton wishes go unheard while my need grows. Holy crap. I'm making out with Daren in the middle of his party.

I squeeze my eyes tighter, hoping to God people stay in the living room. Because I do not want to stop.

The hem of my dress is bunched against the top of my thighs, and when his fingers traverse the hooks on my garter, he pulls back and looks down.

"Fuck me, that's hot, Maddie."

It's my turn to laugh, even though I'm out of breath. "What did you think I wore underneath all of those suits?"

When Jacob and I broke up, I stocked up on slinky lingerie as a treat to myself. I figured if I wanted to get over him, I had to feel good, and garters and lacy underwear have a way of lifting a girl's spirits.

Daren's eyes lift to mine, the hunger in his look making me shiver. "I'll never be able to watch you on TV again without thinking about what you have underneath those snug skirts. C'mere, you little wildcat."

I laugh at the nickname. That's a first. No one in the history of my life has ever considered me wild. Focused, yes. Determined, definitely. But never wild.

We're about to lip-lock again when laughter in the other room breaks the spell. For both of us, apparently, because Daren frowns.

"Let's take this party somewhere else," he grumbles, scooping me up into his arms. I muffle my squeal. Next thing I know, he's whisking me into a dark room across the hall.

He kicks the door shut behind him before I find myself pressed up against it. I'm teetering on my heels, but Daren's keeping me upright.

His mouth descends for one panty-flooding kiss before he stops. Why... why is he stopping?

There's that frown again. "Babe, how much have you had to drink tonight?"

My back straightens. "I'm not drunk, if that's what you're asking." *Of course that's what he's asking, dummy. Maybe if you weren't drunk, you could answer the question.*

Daren swallows. "I just want to be sure..."

"That you're not forcing me to do something I don't want to do? Trust me, I'm willing and able." *Wow, Maddie. Eager much?*

He chuckles. "Mm. How willing, gorgeous?" he asks, placing small kisses against my neck.

I don't know what comes over me. Maybe I'm a little insulted he's not so carried away with lust that he has the time to talk, or maybe *I'm* so carried away with lust I can't control myself. But I grab his hand that's snaked into my hair and lift one finger to my mouth where I kiss the tip. I tilt my head down so I can peer up at him in what I hope is a sexy come-hither look.

"Willing enough." My tongue slides out in a slow swipe of his skin, and his eyes widen as my lips close around him.

His other finger joins the first in my mouth, and he watches like a man possessed.

"Fuck."

I let his fingers linger on my mouth. "That's what I'm aiming for." I laugh and tug him closer so I can do my best to make him come apart.

Because right now, I need to know I can.

CHAPTER 13

DAREN

My cock aches to have her mouth on me the way she just teased my fingers, but I want to take my time with this girl.

Tonight is unexpected. Sure, I'd seen some of the appreciative glances Maddie threw my way these last few weeks, but the minute we'd make eye contact, she'd close off, making me wonder if I was making this shit up. Making me wonder if that flirtatious banter in our interview was all for show.

Apparently not.

Maddie arches her back against the door, her hair a disheveled, black cascade around her shoulders. In the dark room, I can make out her parted pink lips and smoky blue eyes that stare up at me through our mutual haze of lust.

On the exterior, this girl looks as straight-laced as they come, but right now, she has her skirt hiked so those garters peek out just enough to make me want to snap them with my teeth. And don't even get me started about those fuck-me heels.

Wildcat is right.

"I'd be lying if I said I hadn't thought about doing this to you," I murmur as I duck down to graze her neck with my lips.

She groans and tilts her head back. "Yeah?"

Deciding it's better if I don't say exactly how long I've thought about getting her bare-ass naked, I suck gently, not hard enough to leave a mark, though I want to. But she's on TV. She doesn't need some asshole marking this beautiful skin, at least not anywhere visible.

She swallows, and I palm her breast and give it a hard squeeze as I press her up against the door. Part of me wonders if I'm being too rough, but her loud moan tells me otherwise.

Yeah, I'm gonna enjoy making this girl fall apart.

"Hang on, babe."

I scoop her ass in my hands and lift her up before slipping between her parted legs. Once I have her wedged against the door with my hips, I reach for her silky smooth thighs.

Even through my jeans, I can feel her heat, and I surge forward to get closer, tightening my grip on her. She cries out and wraps her legs around my waist. Her nails bite into my shoulders, her head falls back against the wall, and the vision of this girl is so magnificent, I want to sear it into my brain for future reference. Because, Jesus Christ, Maddie is fucking gorgeous.

My mouth teases her lips, but she's not having any of that. Her fingers thread through my hair, and she yanks me closer.

"Impatient?" I chuckle.

"Fuck you," she mumbles, never leaving my lips.

"Trust me, I'm trying."

She laughs, her body shaking against mine, and the sound is magical. I don't know why, but something about that sound makes me feel lighter. This girl is always so serious these days, but tonight she's been different. Tonight, she's let me in.

I can't think too long because her tongue licks against my lips, and when I dip into her mouth, she sucks my tongue in a rhythm that makes my cock strain harder against my jeans.

And then she's pushing out of my arms, demanding that I put her down.

Shit. Did she change her mind?

When her feet hit the floor, she grips my shirt, her serious expression putting me on edge. But then she slowly spins us around, and once my back is up against the door, she lowers her hand and palms me, leaning up to whisper, "I want you in my mouth."

My jaw tenses as I watch her drop to the floor and unzip my jeans. She licks her lips as she lifts me out.

"Hello, there," she whispers.

Did I suffer a concussion at practice today and I'm really bedridden at Mass General? Because Maddie's on her knees talking to my dick, which stands at attention.

And then she stares up at me as she places an open-mouthed kiss on my tip.

I can't fight the groan that leaves my lips as she rubs her soft cheek against me in a slow tease that has me swelling in appreciation. And then she takes a long lick up my shaft, keeping her eyes trained on me, and I fist her hair in my hand, careful to not yank her closer. But fuck, it's hard when her lips part to take me in and she envelops me in her hot little mouth.

"Fuck, Maddie."

Her eyes light up, and she takes me all the way, swallowing me down the back of her throat.

"Goddamn, woman. Don't you have a gag reflex?"

Her hand works me as her mouth slides up and down, and I clench my eyes closed, unable to watch the show or it will be over before it starts. She moans while I'm in her mouth, and the vibration nearly pushes me over the edge.

"Stop." I slip out of her grasp, and she gives me a pout of disappointment that can only be described as half sex kitten, half innocent school girl.

Reaching down, I lift her into my arms before I stalk over to my desk, shoving shit out of the way to make room for Maddie's delectable ass, which I place on one end.

Wrapping my hand around the back of her neck, I angle her for a kiss because that mouth is too damn hot to not explore again. She whimpers, clawing at my chest, and I reach down under her dress, snaking my fingers around her panties.

"Babe, you're drenched."

She laughs softly. "You think?"

I watch her face as I stroke the delicate skin between her thighs. Her head falls back, her hips tilt forward, and her choppy breaths make me want to take her hard and fast. But then she reaches forward and tugs back the hem of her dress so we can both watch my hand disappear into the black silk of her underwear.

Some day when I'm on my deathbed, I hope I can remember Maddie McDermott hot and wet on my desk, because I'm pretty sure I've found heaven.

"Harder, Daren," she groans.

But I can't go any farther without seeing the rest of her and feeling her on my skin. I pull away to strip off my shirt, pleased with the appreciation in her eyes as they travel over my chest. I stand there and let her look. My jeans are barely clinging to my hips, and I'm pretty sure my hair looks like I've been electrocuted, because I have been. By her.

When her eyes make it back up to mine, she takes a deep breath and reaches for the tie at the front of her dress. In the slowest tease known to mankind, she unwraps herself like an early Christmas gift.

A black, lace bra cups her generous breasts, and boy shorts finish off this brilliant ensemble. Even better, though, is the tantalizing strip of skin between those garters and her underwear that calls out to me. But I need her naked before I have a taste.

"Take off your bra, Maddie. Now."

My voice is gruff, mostly because it's hard to speak. I'm pretty sure I sound like a dick, only instead of being put off, Maddie's lips tilt up in a smirk.

"Make me."

Fuck.

My hands are on her, and the material is off before I can process that I might have ripped it. Maddie reaches up and pulls my hair, yanking me into a kiss as I grip her breasts with both hands. She moans into me, her thighs widening so I can wedge myself closer.

I break away. "You're going to pay for being so mouthy."

She smirks, gripping the base of my cock and jerking me off.

"I'm counting on it."

Her throaty voice makes the blood pound in my ears until the only thought I can process involves Maddie's pussy in my face.

"Oh, yeah, babe." I pull away, slipping out of her hands. Gripping her ankles, I yank until she slides back onto the desk. She lands with a squeal and a laugh, but in two seconds flat, I have her panties off and her legs wrapped around my neck, and that laugh turns into a breathy, "God, yes."

Chuckling, I lean in, appreciating how her skin is bare except for a small landing strip. Mm. Time to land.

I whisper against her damp skin, "Quid pro quo, Wildcat," before I take a long lick that has her arching off the desk. I set a slow, tortuous pace, her scent intoxicating me, tempting me to go faster.

"More, Daren."

Her legs drop open, her fingers parting herself. Goddamn, this woman makes me want to combust.

Kissing Madeline is heavenly. Feeling her body against mine? Divine. Going down on her? The fucking Super Bowl of sex.

Finally, I rub against that little bundle of nerves, and her legs clamp against my head.

"Hold still." I hold one leg open with my arm and brace my shoulder against the other. She writhes beneath me, her breasts heaving, her hair a wild tangle on my desk. Keeping my eyes pinned on her, I slide my tongue back and forth. She gasps, fighting to watch me. "Feel good, babe?"

"Yeah," she pants. "Soooooo good." Her thighs tremble when I press a finger into her tight entrance while teasing her with my tongue. It only takes two or three more strokes before she comes apart in a litany of screams and curses. For a girl who never curses, those dirty words feel like a badge of honor.

She pulses against my mouth, and I stroke her skin until she begs me to stop.

Maddie's panting and sprawled out naked on my desk, the moonlight illuminating her pale skin. Tossing an arm over her face, she laughs this hoarse, delighted laugh. After a moment, she brushes the hair out of her face and stares back, flushed and out of breath, and so fucking sexy my chest aches. Her lips slowly tilt up, and she hooks her finger into my jeans that are still somehow hanging down my ass.

"Come here, Heisman. Show me how you throw for a touchdown."

I grin, licking her off my lips. Tonight just got even better.

Thankful for the condom in my wallet, I suit up and press close to this beautiful woman, who seems to spark with light as I touch her. A few minutes later when I push into her and she claws the shit out of my back, the only thought registering in my brain is I can't get enough of this girl.

CHAPTER 14

DAREN

A BREATHY SIGH wakes me up. When I open my eyes, it's still dark outside. I want to check the time, but a gorgeous woman is draped around me.

Maddie's head rests on my chest, her arm wrapped across my waist, her leg thrown over mine. The sheet rests just above her hips, and I take a moment to appreciate how her perfect curves fit against me.

Reaching down, I drag the comforter up over her shoulders and she snuggles closer.

I'd be lying if I said having her here didn't feel incredible. Maddie is every guy's dream girl. Beautiful. Intelligent. Feisty as hell.

Guilt washes over me.

I'm not ready for anything serious, not when I have my first preseason game this weekend. And Maddie is definitely not a fuck-and-forget kind of girl.

I never should have done this, brought her to my bed. Last night happened too quickly. One minute we were flirting, and the next I was ripping clothes off her body.

Shit. I think I actually ripped clothes off this woman. The caveman in me is pretty pleased, but the sane part wonders how pissed she'll be when she tries to get dressed in the morning.

I should've slowed down, but there's something about Maddie that makes me want to push her to the edge. All those cold shoulders she threw my way this summer only increased my curiosity and attraction.

But fuck. I never hook up without talking about expectations. Because this can only be about having a good time. Nothing more. Not after Veronica nearly imploded both of our lives on her way out the door.

And now I feel like a dick for thinking that Maddie might want anything more. Had I brought it up, she probably would have laughed in my face and told me to make sure I didn't choke on my ego.

Closing my eyes, I let myself enjoy what went down before I have to deal with the fallout.

Christ. I lost count of how many different ways we went at it. The best part? She looked just as unwound as I felt, digging her nails into my ass and moaning my name. I harden against her warm thigh as images of her lying across my desk flash in my head.

Fuck, no, Sloan. Don't go there. Let the woman sleep.

Tilting my head, I catch a glimpse of the clock. I still have a couple of hours before I need to get up for practice.

Maddie sighs again, her pouty lips inches away, and I'm more than tempted to sweep my mouth against them even though I've been listing all the reasons tonight was a stupid idea.

But we should talk. Make sure we're on the same page.

To be honest, I'd be surprised if she wants something serious. Not with how closed off she's been.

Absentmindedly, I stroke her back, her soft skin soothing against my calloused palms. She smells sweet and floral, the faint scent of her perfume lingering. I bury my nose in her hair, unable to resist this connection, even though I'm worried it's one I never should have made in the first place.

CHAPTER 15

MADDIE

I'VE BEEN HIT by a car. Or beaten up by a mugger. Or mauled by a bear.

I jerk to sit up, but my sore body protests, and all I do is flail.

Why is my head pounding like it's been backed over by a semi? Did I drink last night?

Every muscle cries out as I attempt to roll over. But I'm pinned down somehow. Probably by that bear.

Squeezing my eyes shut, I realign my expectations about how fast I can move. But I'm so hot. I'm usually freezing first thing in the morning. I want to kick off the covers, but that would require motion, which I'm not sure I'm up to right now.

Huffing out a breath, I finally peek through my crusty eyelashes to find one very muscular arm wrapped around my waist. That arm leads to one exquisitely defined torso. My eyes finally make it up a little higher until his sleeping face comes into view.

Daren. Oh my God. I slept with Daren. And I'm still in his bed. Holy shit.

My heart thuds in my chest, which I will to still because I'm almost sure the blood roaring in my ears is loud enough to wake him.

Gingerly, I lift the sheet off my chest. Yup, still naked. Well, awesome. This isn't awkward.

Through the narrow slit in my eyes, I can make out dark curtains in his room and the faint light of morning.

Shit. Shit! What time is it? I need to get to the studio.

I gently grab his hand and lift the tree log off my body before I roll out from under him. Nausea swirls in my stomach, a reminder of how much I drank last night.

Please don't throw up all over this man's bed.

Despite the pain pulsing throughout my sore body, I eventually end up in a wobbly crouch on the floor like a ninja. I glance down. Okay, a naked, half-drunk, wobbly ninja.

Where the ever-loving eff are my clothes? I lift the sheet, hoping to find my dress, but all I see is... Wow, Daren. Full frontal. Nice.

Get a grip, Maddie! Stop ogling the man while he's sleeping, you creeper.

I tiptoe around the bed in a half crouch, trying to be quiet, which works until I step on a wrapper that crunches beneath my bare foot. Squinting, I try to make out the package. Trojan. Make that two packages.

I swallow.

Sex. We had lots and lots of sex last night.

Blurry images come rushing back to me. Of us making out on his pool table. Kissing against the door. Going down on him.

I smack my forehead. Oh, God. I basically begged to give him a blow job! *Well, I'm sure I'm not the first.* The thought makes me wince.

But I don't have time to drown in my mortification. I need to get dressed and get the hell out of here before we have some painfully awkward morning-after conversation where he tells me this was a one-time thing, and I try not to sock him in the eyeball.

Why do men always assume girls are so needy? I am a modern woman. I am fully employed with health insurance and a retirement plan. I don't need this man to feel good about myself. I will show myself the door, thank you very much.

Embracing my inner Beyoncé, I stand up straight. Except my stomach protests the motion, and I have to wrap my hand over my mouth to keep in the evil contents from last night. After a moment of being absolutely still, the nausea subsides.

I spot a stocking hanging over a lamp. And then my garters on the floor by the armoire.

My temple throbs, and I press a clammy palm to my forehead before I gather my trail of clothing.

Ducking into his office, I spot my dress and another stocking. Great. Almost there.

I'm halfway convinced I might walk out of here fully dressed when I spot my bra in two pieces on the floor.

Did the man actually rip that off my body? Holy hell. I'd be impressed if I didn't have to walk out of here bra-less. I know I live next door, but seriously. A girl needs her bra. And that one wasn't cheap.

The tattered fabric dangles off the tip of my finger, and I scowl. This is not how I wanted to start the day.

CHAPTER 16

MADDIE

ROGER STANDS at the head of the table, and bodies fill every chair from one end of the room to the other. I sit straight, my legs crossed at the ankle, dutifully jotting notes.

"The Assemblymen hope this initiative will appeal to taxpayers..."

The meeting drones on, and I try my best to pay attention, but when I shift in my seat, my thighs and everything in between ache, a constant reminder of what I did two nights ago. Grateful when the meeting disperses, I drag myself back to my cubicle.

After twenty minutes, I finally give in. I have stories to work on and deadlines to meet, but it's like an itch I have to scratch.

Checking to make sure no one is watching, I pull up ESPN's webcam coverage of today's preseason game. It's the first half, so Brentwood, the veteran quarterback, is still playing. Daren probably won't get any time until maybe the third quarter, or at least that's what the sports guys have been saying. I may have eavesdropped on their conversation this morning when I was refilling my coffee.

Rearranging everything on my desk so things sit at a right angle to my laptop, I stick in an earbud to listen while I attempt to finish an assignment. As the guys predicted, Daren looks like he's going to play five minutes into the third quarter. The Rebels are up by seven points, which doesn't seem like a big lead, but I'm guessing the coaching staff wants to see if Daren can hold his own.

I tiptoe across the hallway and stare up at the flatscreen TV where two sports guys watch the game. Fortunately, Nicole is covering the event, so she's not here to comment on my sudden interest.

Why I'm sneaking around to watch this is beyond me. I shouldn't care what happens today. I mean, I guess Daren and I are friends, so I should have a friendly interest. Not a holy-crap-we-screwed-like-sex-crazed-bunnies interest, which is definitely what's going on in my head right now.

Nerves flutter in my tummy, and I fight the urge to bite my nails, which I haven't done in years. Yes, I'm nervous for his game. We talked about his practice schedule the other night. How his practices go from sunup to sundown every day. When I knew I had to cover him for these segments, I did a little research. He had a reputation for being one of the few guys who didn't party in college, throwing himself into football, but now it's not a stretch to say he eats, breathes and sleeps the game.

My lips twitch up. It's hard to not admire his drive. His determination.

So maybe I'll watch for a few minutes and get him out of my system.

Sure, Maddie. Like you did this weekend?

I release a frustrated breath. Yeah, so maybe I rode him like a bareback rider at the rodeo, but in no way did I sign on for more than one night of fun.

So then why am I so eager to catch a glimpse of him right now? And why was sex never that hot with Jacob?

Because you never let go.

Honestly, I thought dating Jacob was letting go. Dating

someone so different had been difficult on many levels. Even though he pushed himself in the arena and in training, he somehow never grasped *my* work schedule, often complaining that I didn't make enough time for him.

Is that why he cheated?

I glance down at the phone in my hand, a constant reminder of his blow job cameo a few clicks away.

Before Friday night, I would've said Jacob and I had a healthy sex life. I tried to make sure he was satisfied. He always came. What man doesn't? And I got there too most of the time.

Not like Friday night, though.

Nothing with Jacob was ever that desperate, that needy, that perilously close to pushing me to some kind of precipice.

No, Jacob was a nice exploration of the missionary position. Every time. Never anything dirty. Never hard. Never, ever out of control. I couldn't remember him trying to rip off my clothes or me being so hungry to have him in me, I thought I'd die trying to press him into my body.

Not like with Daren.

Cheering draws my attention back to the game. My heart starts to race when the camera zooms in on him. I step a little closer to the screen.

There's that jaunty little strut. Daren crosses the field in those tight football pants, and my mouth waters. I can't quite make out his face, but that confident swagger reminds me how it feels to be under him. To have him drive into me. To have him bite me.

My toes curl in my heels thinking about that man's body. Jacob had a great body. But nothing short of coming face to face with a naked Channing Tatum could've prepared me for the magnificence that is Daren Sloan.

The broadcast cuts to his headshot and stats from his senior year at BC. Jesus, he's beautiful. Did I really sleep with this magnificent specimen?

No, you didn't just sleep with him. You pressed his face between your thighs until your eyes rolled back in your head.

An image flashes behind my eyes. Of Daren hovering over me. Of cut muscles and sweaty skin. Of glorious ridges and pulsing heat.

And holy mother, there was a *lot* of pulsing heat.

Now that my hangover has fully retreated, my mind has been filling in the blanks from Friday night. How his rough hands gripped my now tender skin in heated exchanges as I tried to claw my way closer. How wide I had to stretch my legs so he could press his way in. How good he felt when he finally pushed—

"Madeline."

I nearly jump out of my shoes. Twisting around, I come face to face with Roger.

"You okay?" he asks, waving his hand at me. "You look a little flushed."

"Do I?" I press a sweaty palm to my forehead. "It's warm in here. Are you warm? I'm warm." Oh, God. I'm standing here in the middle of the office about to spontaneously combust over Daren. *What's wrong with you?*

Roger eyes me curiously. "Did you eat lunch?"

"No," I say, pointing to him. Bingo. Lunch! "I have not eaten yet. And I do get a bit lightheaded."

"So go grab a bite. You know, I never say things like this, Madeline, but don't push yourself too hard. You're often here when I come in, and you're still here when I leave. I love your drive, but I don't want you to burn out."

Nodding, I agree. "Yes, sir. No burning out. I get it."

He points to the screen. "Good game?"

"Uh, I'm not really sure. I just popped in here a moment ago."

"I'm guessing you've heard then." He scratches the back of his head, a wrinkle forming between his brows.

"Heard what?"

"You're back on the football segment." He presses his palms

into his tired eyes. "I'm not sure why Spencer switched you out for Nicole after his big to-do last week, but viewer emails came flooding in wanting you back after Nicole's segment ran yesterday." Dropping his hands to his waist, he raises his eyebrows. "So you're back on. Be ready to go on Thursday."

No, no, no! Dread fills my stomach. How can I cover Daren? I slept with him this weekend. No, we fucked, dirty and hard and more than once.

Roger frowns again. "You're too young to get an ulcer, kiddo. Just aim for the same vibe you did the first time, and everything will be okay."

I nod, forcing a weak smile, and he shuffles out of the office.

Same vibe? How the hell do you convey the same vibe after you've placed your mouth on someone's... Oh, God. I went down on Daren. I scratched the hell out of his back. I said things to him you couldn't get me to say at gunpoint.

I'm going to throw up. I bolt for my cubicle only to run into Brad.

"Hey, Madeline. Just wanted to see if you wanted a coffee. I'm headed out now."

I shake my head. "No, that's nice of you, though. Thanks."

"No problemo." He looks me over. "You okay? You look like you've seen a ghost."

A strained laughter leaves my lips. "Just, uh, trying to get a grip on everything I have to do today."

"Been pretty busy lately, huh?"

"Yeah. Busy. Really, really busy."

He scratches his head, messing up his sandy blond hair. "Well, let me know if things change. I'd love to take you to lunch some time to catch up."

Nodding, I try to smile. "Yes. I will. Thanks so much. Some time we'll have to do that."

When I'm finally alone in my cubicle, I know only one thing will ease my distress. Work. Lots and lots of work.

CHAPTER 17

DAREN

THE WOMAN IS NEVER HOME. I assume she sleeps tucked under her desk at work. I've caught a few of her interviews on TV, so at least I know she's alive.

I figured seeing Maddie on TV would take the edge off, remind me why I should be over the moon that she skipped out on me early Saturday morning. But it didn't. In fact, it pissed me off. Especially on the field when she invaded my thoughts. Because when I'm playing ball, I've never had a problem blocking out distractions. Even during the ugliest times with my ex, I could always channel what I needed and clear my head.

The fact that I can't now is troubling. Keeping my interest in Maddie on lockdown this summer only made our hook up that much more explosive. And like a junkie, I need another taste.

After being bombarded by thoughts of her for the last four days, I've had enough. So when I catch a glimpse of her striding up to our building through my window, it doesn't take me long to make a decision.

When Maddie reaches her door, she balances her groceries on her hip while she reaches into her purse.

Tonight, her hair is pulled back in a sleek ponytail. A tailored white blouse hangs wide at her collarbone with the weight of her purse tugging on her sleeve. I stare at her slender neck that leads down a path I hope to travel again. My fingers twitch to trail across her soft skin, to feel her pulse pound in her chest because I'm pushing her to the edge.

I lick my lips, which does nothing for my thirst.

And then it becomes clear. What I need to do.

A plan formulates in my head, and like a play on the field, I wonder if going out on a limb will get me to the end zone or sacked. I haven't had to extend myself for a girl in a while. Usually, they're just available. Which sounds like a douchebag thing to say, but it's true. And it's boring. What's the fun in pursing what's readily available?

More than that, though, I'm tired of the safe plays. Because even when you play it safe, shit still falls through.

"Need some help?" I call out to Maddie from my doorway.

She spins, dropping her groceries with a small scream.

"Sorry. Didn't mean to scare you." I'd laugh except she looks genuinely freaked out. Bending over, I help her pick up the fruit that's rolled across our shared hallway.

One of the bags has torn open, and she obviously can't hang on to her groceries while she balances her briefcase, purse, and keys.

"Here." I hand her a stray apple and take the keys from her.

She still hasn't spoken or made more than fleeting eye contact. Guess we're back to her being closed off, which does not bode well for my plan.

However, the fact that I feel fucking electrified seeing her again is the only answer I need at the moment. Girls don't play hard to get with me. Girls hang on my arm in public or crash whatever event I'm at wanting to screw. But this one sneaks out of my bed in the middle of the damn night, and I feel like I might suffocate if I don't see her again. None of this makes sense. I suppose playing hard to get makes a difference. Except I don't think she's playing anything. Because she doesn't look pleased to see me.

Maddie's teflon armor sets off every alarm in my head. Christ, does she regret what happened?

Bracing myself for a rejection, which is likely given her what-the-fuck-do-you-want expression, I return my attention to her keys. Three hang on a hoop, which is attached to a small charm. One key is obviously for her car, the other for our mailbox, so I grab the third and slip it into the door.

Once it's open, I turn the chain over in my palm. "Paris?" The miniature Eiffel Tower gleams in my hand.

She stills, and her eyes drop. "Just somewhere I've been hoping to visit." Her eyes sweep up, a hint of sadness behind them. "My parents honeymooned there."

I want to ask more, but she scoots past me and heads for the kitchen. It's dark except for a small lamp on the counter.

Clearing my throat, I ask, "Is Sheri around?"

She shakes her head. "Out of town."

"I came by earlier this week. But you weren't home."

She turns to face me, her eyebrows raised like that was the last thing she thought I'd say, but then she schools her features. "I've been working overtime."

"Why do you look surprised I came by? You left my bed in the middle of the night, Maddie. I wanted to make sure you're okay."

She unfreezes and places the groceries on the counter before reaching over to flip on the recessed lights above. Her white blouse is paired with a gray pencil skirt and black heels. Simple yet stunning on her.

She keeps her back to me when she speaks. "That was a mistake, Daren. We never should have slept together."

I chuckle. "Sweetheart, you make it sound so mundane. I believe we 'fucked each other's brains out.'"

The sharp inhale of her breath gives me some satisfaction that she's been affected by this. I know I have been. Were it not for my brutal training schedule and Sunday's game, I would have camped out in front of her door sooner.

Because when I woke up alone that morning, I should've been relieved. Instead, I was disappointed. And now, days later, she's hijacked my brain, my dick and everything in between. Before I'm tempted to wonder if this is one-sided, her chest rises and falls like she just came in from a workout, and I smile.

For all of her aloofness, I think she wants this too. Because a person doesn't forget sex that sublime.

Finally, she turns around.

"Can we talk about what's going on here?" I ask, motioning between us.

"What do you mean? We are talking." Her face is impassive, which only gets under my skin.

"I mean, can we cut the bullshit and get real for a minute?"

Her eyes narrow. Good. I can work with anger. "Real? Okay. I can get real. We hung out. We hooked up. It was fun. Now it's over. Is that what you want me to say?"

She rolls her eyes at me before she returns to her groceries. I step up behind her and still her hands, caging her in.

"Stop." Leaning down to whisper in her ear, I fight the urge to toss her over my shoulder, carry her back to my cave, and spank her ass. "What's with the fuck-off vibe? I thought we worked past that."

Her shoulders still. "This can't happen," she whispers.

"What can't happen?"

"This. Us. I thought you just wanted a good time on Friday night. I don't understand what you're doing here."

"Ouch, Wildcat. That hurts. Where's your neighborly affection? I thought we got along well. So I want to hang out again. What's the big deal?"

"So you just want to fuck me?"

I laugh. "I wouldn't put it as bluntly as that, but yeah," I say, leaning closer, "I'd love to fuck you again. But truthfully, I like your company. That feisty mouth and all. Nudity is optional, but I'd be lying if I said I didn't want it on the menu."

Goosebumps break out on her arms.

"We can't."

"Why?" She's quiet for so long, I grab her shoulders and spin her around. "Why, Maddie? You can't tell me you didn't enjoy what we did. Because if I recall, you enjoyed it at least three or four times on Friday night."

Her cheeks flush with embarrassment, her eyes looking anywhere but at me. I tilt her chin up. "Look at me and tell me you don't want to hang out again. Say those words, and I'll leave you alone."

She braces her shoulders back. "Hang out? As what? As friends?"

"Yeah, as friends."

"Friends with benefits?"

"I don't know. Something like that." I let go of her and run my hands through my hair, my frustration growing. "Let me put my cards on the table. I don't screw around. Not during the season. If I'm in a relationship, fine. But I don't fuck around with girls. I don't drink. I don't party. One, because I'm not wired that way, and two, because football sucks up every ounce of energy I have. I don't have the time to date a girl right now. And relationships come with baggage I'd rather not deal with. God knows I come with more than a carry-on, and judging by the mistrust in your eyes, you do too.

"So me coming here breaks my own rules. Because I'm not looking for anything serious. I just got out of a long-term relationship, and I'm not interested in diving into another. At the same time, I think you and I definitely connected. We had fun even before I got you naked. And the naked part? It's given me spank bank material for the next several years." Her eyes widen, a smile ghosting her lips. "But you do live right next door, which is pretty convenient. So if I'm faced with the choice of rubbing one out at night or having your hot little body wrapped around me, then I'm gonna choose door number two. But I'm a modern man, so this arrangement would go both ways. I seem to recall you having a pretty insatiable sex drive yourself. If we do this, I'd be at your booty call command."

I expect her to laugh or tell me I'm wrong and say we didn't connect on some kind of cosmic level when we were naked. Instead, she braces her hands on the counter behind her. "We can't."

"So you've said. I need more than that."

Shaking her head, she sighs. "I'm back on the sports segment, Daren. I'm interviewing you on Thursday. I'm not sure if you realize this, but sleeping with a source is generally frowned upon in journalism."

Okay, that kind of sucks. I get her reluctance. But I still think there's a way we could go about this without jeopardizing her career. "This is sports. It's not as though you're covering Watergate. I'm a quarterback, for fuck's sake."

"And I need to maintain a professional relationship with you. It's bad enough I've basically licked my way up your body."

Goddamn. What a memory. "Thanks for the visual, babe." I wink and she blushes again. "Let me ask you this. How are you supposed to cover me? What angle are you supposed to take?" I don't mention the obvious, like horizontal, diagonal, or upside down.

"The same way we did the first interview. You teach me the basics of football." She shrugs. "People really liked our rapport. They liked the quasi-flirting, so I need to keep things light."

"Give me more credit. I was fully flirting with you." She cracks a real smile, and I'm wondering if we're getting any closer to the goal. "Think of it this way. We need to have a good relationship so you're more relaxed in front of the camera? Right now you look like you'd rather get your appendix removed with a rusty blade than hang out with me."

Her smile grows. "Not true."

I edge closer and lean down to whisper in her ear. "Think of this as my way of helping you to relax around me." I stroke her soft hair, and after a moment she leans into my palm. "Our own kind of aversion therapy."

Her head tilts back. "How do you know about aversion therapy?"

"I was a psych major, or at least I was for two years before I switched to business, but I paid attention."

She studies me, her teeth nibbling on her bottom lip. "So this would just be something casual?"

I nod.

"And you're not going to screw around with other girls?"

"Nope. I would just screw you. Frequently."

She fights a laugh and then her smile disappears. "But we wouldn't be in a relationship?"

"Just friends." Even as the words leave my lips, I recognize how that doesn't feel right, but I'd be an idiot to think we could start some kind of relationship right now. One where I'm always off at football practice or recovering from a game, or trying to find the energy to wine and dine her when I need to be thinking about the hundred new plays I still have to memorize.

She holds her breath in the world's longest pregnant pause before she speaks again. "On three conditions."

To be honest, I've been waiting for her to knee me in the nuts for making this proposal. But Maddie always surprises me. And I like surprises.

"Shoot."

"One, you really are monogamous. You're faced with girls who throw themselves at you on a daily basis, and I understand that temptation, but if you want to mess around with other people, we can't sleep together. However, since we're *just friends*, it shouldn't be a big deal for you to give me a heads up. Can you do that? Can you be that honest?"

I answer without hesitation. "Not a problem." I push closer until she's up against the counter again. Her chest rises and falls in a quickening breath. "What's the second condition?"

Her tongue swipes against her lower lip, and I fight the urge to taste it myself. "That we keep this a secret. We can't tell anyone, which means we can't go out. My job is on the line, and I don't want to jeopardize it with a casual fling."

Bracing myself on either side of her, I run my nose against the slender column of her neck, inhaling her sweet scent. "Deal." She shudders against me, her breasts pressing into my chest, but she's quiet. Too quiet. "And the last condition?"

"That we always use condoms."

I nod. "Goes without saying."

She takes a deep breath and nods. "I'm on birth control. It's just... "

"No explanation needed. I understand."

Maddie takes a deep breath and whispers, "Okay."

And just like that, we are happening. Fuck yeah.

I kiss her forehead and the tension in her body melts. "Will it be a stretch to pretend you like me during our interview?" I ask, resting my hands on her hips, leaning back to see her beautiful face.

She shakes her head, trying to fight that smile again.

"Can you admit you missed me?" I kiss her cheek and that smile widens.

Taking a deep breath, she nods, her hands coming up to rest on my chest. "Yes, I missed you."

"Madeline," I whisper, enjoying the way her full name sounds on my lips. "Have you thought about what we did that night? Do you replay it in your mind?"

Her hands tremble against me. "Yes."

With those words, the clarity I've been desperate for since she fled my bed settles over me. I don't know why, but I need this. I need her in my life. It's like her presence settles something inside me.

Wrapping her in a hug, I lift her off her feet until she laughs, and I swear I feel lighter than I have all week.

When I place her on the floor, I let her body drag against mine slowly before I thread my hands into her hair and pull her into a kiss. Her lips are soft when I brush against them, but she pulls back as I seek her mouth. She's keeping in a laugh, her eyes playful. I lean in again, and she backs away, her lips tilting up. God damn it.

"C'mere," I growl and pull her against me for a searing kiss. She gives up her coy game and moans into my mouth, her tongue eagerly stroking mine. When I think my dick is about to break through the zipper in my jeans, I come up for a breath and press my lips against her forehead.

"Why, Maddie McDermott, does this mean I can get you naked now?"

Her arms tighten around my waist. "Yes, you can get me naked."

"Thank fuck."

She laughs against me, but before I can sling her over my shoulder and carry her back to my place man-style, her phone rings, and Eminem's *Lose Yourself* blasts through her quiet kitchen. Her smile drops, immediately replaced with that no-nonsense demeanor.

"I'm sorry, but I have to get this."

CHAPTER 18

MADDIE

SETTING DOWN THE PHONE, I look up, expecting Daren to give me that judgmental sneer I got so accustomed to seeing from my ex. Jacob hated that I'd drop everything for work, which is a total double standard. Men do it all the time without a second thought, but if a woman does it, she's cold, heartless, or worse.

Daren frowns for a moment and then sighs. "I get it. Work calls." He motions toward my cell with a smirk. "Eminem, huh?"

I smile back, distracted by his sexy charm as he runs his hands through his already disheveled hair.

The relief in me is palpable. I didn't realize how much that bothered me about Jacob. How his judgment weighed on me.

But it's still early. Wait until you're half naked in Daren's bed and the phone rings.

I shake my head, wanting to clear my thoughts of the negativity. "I swear they call at the worst times."

The words just come out, like I'm testing him. Maybe I am. Why, I'm not sure. He said it himself. We're just fuck buddies, which is a new frontier for me. It should bother me, taking something as serious as a sexual relationship so casually. But it doesn't. A part of me feels liberated, like I'm taking charge of my life and getting what I want. Because I want to have sex with him again. He made me come so hard I half wondered if I had blacked out. I've never come more than once with a man, and I'd probably light on fire and go straight to hell if I tried denying I've thought about little else this week.

He's marking new territory for me left and right. Can I still consider him my first one night stand if we plan to sleep together again?

What a stupid thing to be mulling over right now when I have to get back to the office.

After listening to the message on my cell, I mutter, "I… I need to go," as I try my best to ignore the throb between my legs. He felt huge against my belly a few minutes ago. I take a deep breath, trying to find a sense of balance. Being around Daren is disorienting, like I'm on a non-stop carnival ride.

He nods, a resigned smile on his lips, like he understands the demands of my job.

I should be racing out of here, but I can't help but study Daren, who showed up on my door wearing a worn, long-sleeved Henley and jeans. He's rich. Loaded. But nothing about him screams obnoxious wealth aside from his address. Even his condo, although decked out with lots of big boy toys, isn't flashy.

He glances down at his watch, a beautiful Patek Philippe, a luxury watch without the flash of a Rolex. That frown returns. "It's late. Can I drive you?"

I can't help the shock in my voice when I ask, "Didn't you just have a ten hour practice?"

He tilts his head, unsure of where this is headed. "We watched film and had meetings in between the scrimmages and workouts, but yeah, it lasted about ten hours. Why?"

Who knew Daren Sloan was such a sweetheart? My heart melts a little, and I resist the urge to stroke his handsome face.

That's when this sinks in. How this is a bad idea. The worst. I may want to experience some casual fun, and sure, "hanging out" with Daren might help me be more relaxed when I interview him, but this man is all kinds of sexy *and* he's thoughtful.

When my phone buzzes again, I know I don't have time to think about this any longer. I decline Daren's offer because I'll need my car to get home later. He makes me promise not to walk out in the middle of the night alone, and my heart thuds a little faster.

"I'll get security to escort me."

He grabs his phone and looks up at me as though he's waiting. "Well, are you gonna give me your number or do I have to wait on your doorstep like a lost puppy whenever I want to see you?"

"I don't know." I look him over, unable to resist messing with him. "Are you housebroken?"

"Hmm. I'm not gonna pee on your leg if that's what you're worried about, but I can't guarantee I won't bite."

And then he gives me that look, the one that makes me want to incinerate. Would it be strange to hand him my panties right now and beg him to find hidden places on me to leave his mark?

I give him a weak smile because it's all I can do to focus. Reaching for a pad of paper, I scribble down my number, jamming it in his outstretched hand a little too hard. But then those bear paws grab my elbow as I head for the door, and he leans down to whisper, "Let me walk you to your car."

Of course he wants to walk me to my car. He isn't the cad that Jacob was. Why did I even date Jacob? The reasons, which I could rattle off a few weeks ago, seem fuzzy all of a sudden.

Daren soothes back a stray hair behind my ear and says, "By the way, I'll be thinking of you later." I glance up at him and he gives me a devilish grin. "In the shower." And then he nips my earlobe.

What was I doing? It takes me a long moment of shuddering breaths to remember I have somewhere to go. Something to do. Even though I can barely stand upright.

I close my eyes, struggling to focus.

Work.

Right. Because I put work first.

* * *

I RUN my thumbnail back and forth across my bottom lip as the sports producer edits the footage. Admittedly, my life is easier when I don't have to shoot, edit and write my own segment, but it's also nerve-racking to have other people obsess over my video. I've always been pretty thick-skinned when it comes to criticism, but covering something so high profile has been harder than I thought.

Hearing my voice in the otherwise silent room makes me cringe. "Today, Daren is going to show me how to throw the perfect pass. He says it starts with lining up your fingers in just the right spot."

Even as those words left my mouth, I could see the look in Daren's eyes, and I knew he was fighting the urge to turn that into a dirty joke. What I didn't expect was for him to wrap his arms around me to show me how to reach back and throw it.

"Nice job, McDermott," Spencer says behind me, making me flinch.

"Uh, thanks." I feel tempted to look outside to see if hell has frozen over.

Spencer stands by me, and I get one step closer to biting my nail. Please tell me I only *imagined* blushing when Daren got up in my space.

"He obviously likes you more than Nicole."

"Maybe he was just enthralled with those ridiculous shorts you had me wear."

At least you can't see the shorts from this angle. Wait. *Now* you can see my short shorts with the team's name emblazoned on my ass. Thank you, Douchebag Spencer, for making me wear them.

He clicks his tongue at me, and I fight the urge to knee him in the groin. "Those shorts were genius. I'm glad I have a pair in three other colors."

"Good thing." Asshole.

Deciding I'd better get away from him before I commit a homicide, I try to duck out of the editing suite, but Spencer calls my name.

When I turn around, he doesn't bother looking up from his tablet. "Don't get too busy with news. I'm going to need you to do a few sports promos."

At this rate, I'm never going to cover real news. I fight to keep a scowl off my face.

"What about the bachelor contest? Doesn't she need to do that voice over too?" the other producer asks.

"What bachelor contest?" And while we're at it, why don't we do a cute puppy contest? Or a most adorable baby contest? When the hell am I ever going to do real news? Since starting this job, I've barely done anything of substance. Although my golden-winged warbler story finally aired, producers made me trim it down so much that if you blinked, you would have missed it. The Rebels are already breaking ground on the new parking facility, and no one seems to care about the endangered birds but me. Typical.

On the inside, I'm stomping my feet, but outwardly, I haven't budged a muscle.

Spencer waves me off. "Something we're reviving. I'm still working out the details. I'll call you if I need you. I might use Nicole."

A bachelor contest? *Please, God, let Nicole cover that.*

Once I'm safely back in my cubicle, the sweet solitude doesn't last long. Nicole strides in looking as snarky as ever. The thin thread of friendship we developed Friday night died the moment she found out I was back on the football segment.

After forty-five minutes of total silence from my cubicle mate,

I brave the waters.

"Do you know anything about a bachelor contest?"

She laughs, but the look in her eyes when she turns around is anything but humorous. "Don't you know anything?" She blows her hair out of her face. "It's Boston's Number One Bachelor Contest, featuring four of the top local athletes. The money raised at the November gala goes to charity, and everyone pats themselves on the back at Thanksgiving when a few more turkeys get handed out."

I don't have time to be insulted. I'm too worried about what this contest means.

"And those bachelors would be…"

Rolling her eyes, she counts on her fingers. "Daren, of course. That hottie on the Bruins, the new Red Sox Pitcher, and some boxer."

Letting out a breath, I thank God she didn't name my ex. Not that he's as widely known as the athletes she just named, but it would be my dumb luck he'd get picked.

She spins back to her desk, and I can't take this unspoken standoff we've been having any longer. "Listen, Nicole, I'm sorry about all of this. Please know I didn't mean to steal your segment or step on your toes. It has to suck that I got reassigned to something that should have been yours. I'm sure I'd be livid if the roles were reversed."

Her shoulders relax a bit, and she nods. She's silent for so long I think she's tuned me out, but then she sighs. "I would have done the same thing, put you back on. My vibe with Daren just didn't happen."

"If it makes you feel any better, I feel like an ass every time I have to do it. Especially in those stupid outfits Spencer is always forcing me to wear."

When she faces me this time, her smile is genuine. "Okay, that actually does make me feel better." She nods, and it seems like we've called some kind of truce. For now, at least.

CHAPTER 19

MADDIE

MAYBE IT'S the stress of this morning's interview or the fact I just worked fourteen hours, but by the time I trudge up the stairs to Sheri's condo, I'm so tired I can barely put one foot in front of the other. So when Daren texts, asking if I want to come over for a late-night snack, I can barely manage the strength to operate my thumbs.

Too tired. Sorry. Raincheck?

My cell rings a minute later. "Hey, Wildcat."

As exhausted as I am, his voice—raspy and low—sends a wave of adrenaline through me.

"Is this a booty call? Because if so, unless you want to have sex with a dead person, I'm pretty useless right now." Nice, Maddie. Way to talk sexy.

He laughs, and the sound makes me melt a little. "No, not a booty call. Just wanted to ask what you were doing tomorrow night."

Part of me wants to be insulted that he's asking me to do something at the last minute, but then I have to remind myself that we're not dating, that we're just an arrangement of convenience, and a pang of disappointment hits me.

"McDermott, did you hang up on me for making you blush during our interview?"

"Oh, God." How embarrassing. I drop my head onto my pile of pillows. When I regain my composure, I sigh. "I can't even deny it because I saw it on film. What's worse is that my producers loved it. Ate it up. Did Spencer put you up to the whole 'let me wrap my arms around Maddie to show her how to pass' nonsense?"

Daren chuckles, and his amusement irritates me more. "No, that was my own stroke of genius. What? You didn't like when I touched you?"

"No, not at all." Lie. Lie. Lie.

"Hmm. I call bullshit, but that's okay. I'm fine with needing to convince you that you like when I touch you. Love it, even."

"Don't you think that's a bit conceited?"

"Not at all. I'm very in tune with my talents, and making you come, hard, is one of them."

My mouth drops open, and the only thing I hear through the phone is the sound of my own breath, which comes out in short puffs.

He laughs. "And Maddie? I plan to make you come again, all over my face, the next time I see you."

A small squeak leaves my lips, and even though he renders me speechless, I can't deny the throb between my legs. No one has ever talked dirty to me before, and I like it. No, *like* is too weak a word. Part of me wants to claw through our common wall to get an up-close-and-personal demonstration, but the other part of me, the sensible part, says I need to get to bed so I can prepare for an early start in the morning.

And this? Messing around with Daren, someone who suddenly seems like the focal point of my career, can't be smart, and I've always done the smart thing.

Taking a deep breath to clear my head of dirty delusions, I

know what I have to do. "As much as I'm sure I'd enjoy taking you up on the offer, I'm really busy right now, and—"

"You didn't answer my question. What are you doing tomorrow?"

My shoulders sag. "I have plans with Sheri, and we haven't hung out in a while. She's coming in from New York, so I'm not going to blow her off just to—"

"Just to blow me."

A laugh escapes me even though I'm trying to be serious. "Right." I want to dredge up the willpower I had thirty seconds ago to be sensible, to get some distance, but there's something so disarming about this guy that makes me a little insane and out of control.

"Isn't Friday night her book thing?"

How in the world does he know this? "Yes. Should I be concerned that you know when her dirty book club meets?"

"Maybe I've been invited. Is that so difficult for you to believe?"

I snort at his assertion. "Yeah, right. So anyway, I have plans with Sheri, and I'm working the rest of the weekend."

"So I'm shit out of luck is what you're saying."

"I'm saying maybe some other time." *Is that what I'm saying?* Ugh, I don't know anymore. But if I can get some time away from Daren invading my thoughts, maybe I can make some better decisions before I get myself fired.

"Damn. I was thinking you'd give great blow jobs in the shower."

Um. Yeah. Clearing my head? Not so easy with that visual in mind. Because honestly? I'd love to give that a try.

CHAPTER 20

MADDIE

THE BOTTOM of the Ninth is loud and packed with people. The baseball-inspired bar has a few Red Sox banners and memorabilia hanging from its dark, wood-paneled walls, but it isn't over-the-top. Like most places in Boston, an eclectic mix of people fill the restaurant, spilling out from around the shiny metallic tables.

I'm not sure how the girls expect to hear themselves talk about the book they're reading, but I'm just glad to not be working tonight. Tension radiates from my shoulder blades, and I arch my back and drop my head, trying to work out the knot that's been intensifying all week.

We're sitting at a large, rounded corner booth with several of Sheri's friends. I snagged the end seat because I get claustrophobic when I'm blocked in.

"Diet Coke?" Sheri asks with a judgmental eyebrow as she taps on my glass.

"I have to work tomorrow. I can't function with a hangover." As last weekend clearly illustrated.

"I've been meaning to ask, how did Daren's party go?"

Sheri and I have been playing phone tag all week, which worked for me since I really didn't want to talk about what happened with Daren. Our friends-with-benefits arrangement feels like a big dirty secret, one I don't want to discuss with anyone. Even though I consider Sheri a good friend, it only takes one slip-up for a rumor to start that can get me fired.

"Fine. It was fine. Nicole wasn't a total B for once, which was a surprise. Well, until I got reassigned to the sports segment. She gave me the silent treatment all week, but I guess that's to be expected. I feel bad about it, but there's nothing I can do."

Sheri drops an arm around my shoulder. "That sucks, but this is your career, and it's not as though you can turn down this opportunity."

Guilt twinges in my stomach for not telling her what happened with Daren last weekend. I know she'd be supportive. She's the one who planted the idea of getting together with Daren in the first place. But I can't tell her at a packed restaurant.

One of Sheri's friends sitting across from me starts freaking out across the table. I follow her line of sight.

Speak of the devil.

Daren and two of his friends stroll in, and my heart kicks into overdrive.

At first I wonder if Sheri somehow tipped him off, but she looks just as surprised as everyone else.

Of course, this is one of the closest restaurants to our condo, so it's not a shock that he'd come here. A waitress scrambles to seat them, and a sea of people part for the guys to pass.

Clearing my throat, I return my attention to the girls at my table, and with the exception of Sheri, they all look lovestruck. But Sheri hobnobs with the rich and famous on a daily basis, and I know she has her heart set on a musician she met on the set of her dad's last movie.

Two seconds later, the girls all turn to me and start talking at once.

"Maddie! Oh my God, he's gorgeous!"

"What's it like to interview him?"

"Do you think he'll take a photo with me?"

Laughter spills from my lips, and I tell them a little bit about shooting our segment. As I listen to myself talk, I realize this is the most attention I've ever gotten for a story. I've been so frantic trying to get a good news assignment that I haven't enjoyed the one that's fallen into my lap. Even if Nicole is still slightly miffed or Spencer wants me there because I have long legs. My job is to get girls interested in football, and right now, I'd bet money every girl in front of me plans to watch this weekend's game.

Confidence wells up inside me, and I surprise myself when I say, "Do you want me to get Daren to come over and say hi?" Their squeals give me the answer.

Standing up, I smooth my skirt. I wasn't planning to see him tonight. I lean over to Sheri and whisper in her ear, "Do I look okay?"

She gives me an enthusiastic nod. "You look hot, Mads," she says, low enough so no one else hears her.

I know she'd tell me to run to the bathroom to touch up if she thought I needed it. I'm glad I wore my hair down and kept on my high-heeled Mary Janes. Hopefully, that sophisticates my simple knee-length pleated black skirt and white collared shirt, which has a schoolgirl vibe.

I'm almost to his table when a guy comes over and taps on Daren's shoulder.

"I'm so sorry to bother you, but my son would die if I could get him your autograph."

I stop mid-stride, hoping to hell Daren isn't a jerk.

Daren puts down his drink and wipes his palm on his jeans. "Hey, man. No problem." He shakes the guy's hand before reaching into his back pocket. "I can sign the team's schedule. Sound good?"

"Oh, yeah. That would be awesome. Thank you so much!"

When the man gets his personalized autograph, he looks like he wants to hug Daren. As he starts to walk away, he adds, "I'm sure my wife wants me to tell you she loves you." He rolls his eyes, and Daren laughs.

"Well, tell her I said hi, and I appreciate her watching my games with her awesome husband."

The guy nods, a huge grin on his face.

Too sweet.

"Maddie?"

I turn back to the table to find Daren and his friends staring at me.

"Hey, stalker. I knew you wanted to crash the book club."

He beams a smile, and I swear my knees want to give out from under me. *Wow, that's powerful.* Someone should harness the strength of those dimples.

I smile at his two friends. "Sorry to interrupt your evening, fellas. Daren, can I call in a favor? The book club girls really want to meet you."

"Ah, his adoring crowd awaits," Quentin jokes before Daren socks him playfully in the arm.

Daren gets up, and I start to back up, but then he reaches out and pulls me into a hug. "Good to see you, Madeline."

I swallow, hoping I still have the strength to stay upright when he releases me. God, even the way he says my name is sexy. A shiver runs through me.

"Nice to see you," I whisper into his neck. Before he releases me, I take a quick sniff because I honestly can't help myself, and I'm treated to the scent of soap and crisp cologne, and my heart flutters at the reminder of last weekend.

As we part, he laughs and leans closer. "Did you just sniff me?"

"What? No. Weirdo." I roll my eyes like he's ridiculous.

He motions toward our table and places his palm on my lower back as we weave through the restaurant.

Expectant faces greet us when we reach our table. A flurry of chatter erupts, and I sink back into my seat, amusement bubbling up inside of me.

The girls fire questions at him and pass him cocktail napkins to sign, and it's a little comical to see this six-foot-three man hunched over trying to autograph scraps of paper. Just when I'm realizing I should offer to get him a chair, Camille, an investment banker who happens to be a blonde bombshell, scoots over, squishing in the other girls across from me, and pats the now vacant seat next to her.

He glances at me, and I smile, letting him know he should join us. As he sits, he calls over his friends, who pull up two chairs to squeeze in at the end. I'm pretty sure this is a fire hazard, but the wait staff seems too enthralled by the present company to mind.

Quentin and I chat for a while, but I keep finding my gaze on Camille and the way she's leaning into Daren when she talks. How she flips her long hair over her shoulder and leans over, flashing him her cleavage.

In case he doesn't get the hint, she bats her eyelashes at him. Who actually bats their eyelashes? Camille, the investment banker, that's who. But my moderate irritation is quickly surpassed by a hot sting that starts in my chest and sweeps through me when she wraps her hand around his forearm.

He doesn't flinch or look annoyed. No, Daren just keeps talking and signing whatever the girls hand him.

This. I need to remember this. Because girls throwing themselves at Daren is the norm, not the exception.

I feel like a fool for forgetting my vow to never date pro-athletes.

Wait. We're not dating. We're friends who have sex. I only asked him to be monogamous because I don't want to expose myself to some nasty disease.

Which means he can flirt all he wants, right? He's not my property. I'm not his. That's the point of this arrangement. I'm not allowed to be jealous.

Oh my God. I'm jealous.

I'm not even dating the man, and I'm jealous.

Brilliant, Maddie. I want to facepalm myself for getting into this situation. For agreeing to this arrangement. For inviting him over to our table. For allowing myself to care what Camille does and doesn't do to this guy I'm... fucking.

I swallow, needing something stronger than a Diet Coke.

When the waitress delivers my vodka martini, Sheri gives me a strange look, her eyes shifting to Camille and Daren across the table and back to me again.

Ignoring the question in her eyes, I grab my phone and check my emails. Anything to get my act together. In my head I realize there is no reason I should be pissed. Daren has fans. Lots of them, many of whom are women. Hell, even our sports segment hones in on that interest. So why I'm sitting here like some wounded girlfriend is something I can't quite comprehend.

One of the girls giggles across the table, and my mouth opens of its own volition. "So Daren, are you taking a sudden interest in romance novels?"

He laughs and rubs the stubble on his chin. "Is that what we're calling it? I thought Sheri said you guys read smut."

My roommate nods enthusiastically. "Maddie is trying to pretend she isn't reading erotica."

"I'm not reading erotica, freak. I came to hang out with you." I honestly don't have a clue what they're reading this week.

"She's missing out. Little Miss Manners doesn't want to dirty up her Kindle."

I don't have to look up to feel Daren smirking. Rolling my eyes, I frown. "I can handle whatever you throw my way. I'm not some priss."

I grab my drink and I'm mid-sip when Sheri adds, "Besides, I don't think Maddie's ready for cocks and clits."

My drink spurts across the table as I choke. I cover my mouth, horrified to look like such a dork in public.

Determined to grab back some control, I turn to Sheri once I've caught my breath. "Just make sure my mouth isn't full the next time we talk about cocks, and I won't have any trouble swallowing." I dab the corners of my mouth with my napkin.

How is that for manners? I am *so* not a priss.

Everyone laughs, cheering me on, but when my eyes reach Daren, his are smoldering hot.

But a minute later, his attention gets diverted when Camille pulls out her business card and leans into him as she explains how she'd like to "handle his portfolio."

I bet.

And while I'm tempted to play with fire, I've had enough of this game for tonight. I finish my drink and tell Sheri I'm running to the restroom and then I'm taking off.

Her eyebrows pull tight. She whispers back, "I'm sorry. I was just joking. You know I didn't mean anything by that, right?"

Giving her a small smile, I nod. "Of course. I have an early call time tomorrow, so I should get going."

I wave bye to everyone at the table as I leave money on the table to cover my share, but people seem to be deep in conversation. Camille has lassoed Daren's attention again, so I don't bother trying to flag him down. Because that looks desperate. And I'm done with feeling desperate.

As I skirt around Quentin, I pat him on the back and wish him luck on his game Sunday.

He grabs my wrist and pulls me closer so he can whisper, "You know this is part of the gig, right? Daren has to talk to fans. He has to talk to girls. That's his job."

Ugh. Am I that transparent? My defenses rise. "Absolutely. And no offense, but what should it matter to me what he does one way or another? We're just friends."

He nods slowly, looking like he doesn't quite believe me, and releases my arm.

Just friends. Friends with benefits.

But maybe we shouldn't be.

* * *

GRATEFUL TO GET AWAY from that trainwreck, I head toward the back of the restaurant and down the long, dark hall that leads to the restroom where I can finally drop my defenses.

Staring at myself in the mirror, I try to get my act together. I feel like an ass. For caring what Daren does. For being so obviously bothered by Camille that Quentin said something.

See, this is why I, Maddie McDermott, do not embark on a sex-only relationship. How do I call this thing off?

I wash my hands and press my cool palms against my neck.

"This is supposed to be simple," I tell myself in the mirror.

So I'll keep things simple. Next time I see him, I'll tell him I'm too busy to follow through on our arrangement. I'm sure he can appreciate that. And judging by the girls at our table ready to strip naked and gyrate on his lap, I'm pretty sure he can get casual sex anywhere.

With a sigh, I grab my purse and reach in to check my phone. I have one text message. From Daren. *Where'd you go?*

My mind races with a dozen different things I should write back, but I settle on something simple. *It's late. I have to get up early.*

I toy with the idea of saying something snarkier, but like I said, I shouldn't care.

I'm tucking my phone back in my purse as I walk out of the bathroom when I turn right into Daren.

"Jesus Christ, you scared me." I laugh as I press my hand to my chest.

He has his phone out, and he's reading my text. He doesn't look amused. Straightening my shoulders, I move over as a woman edges around us to walk into the restroom.

Daren takes my arm and walks deeper down the hallway and around the corner where an exit door stands open. It's dark, the only light coming from the moonlight outside. A cool breeze blows in, smelling of ocean air and rain.

"What's this about? What happened back there?" he asks, releasing my arm.

"It's nothing. I needed to go. I told everyone goodbye, but you were busy talking, and I didn't want to interrupt."

His eyes travel over my face in a slow sweep, a small smile pulling at his lips. "Are you jealous?"

"No, not at all." The lie comes out easily enough.

"You shouldn't be. You invited me over to your table. I was talking to your friends."

"That was very kind of you. I appreciate it. But they're not my friends, I mean, aside from Sheri." *Do it, Maddie. Say what needs to be said.* "Honestly, I'm glad we have a chance to chat because I really can't do"—I wave a finger back and forth between us—"this."

He tilts his head. "What do you mean, *this*? You don't want me to take you back to my place, strip off all your clothes, and fuck you until you're hoarse from screaming my name?"

My mouth drops open, and a pulse starts between my thighs.

He chuckles and steps closer, forcing me back against the wall. He tugs at the hem of my skirt. "Whatcha got down there, Maddie? I may have been talking to other girls at your table, but I can promise the only thing I was thinking about was what you have hiding beneath this skirt."

I brace my hands on his chest—to push him away or hold myself up, I can't decide. "We're... we're a bad idea, Daren." I hate that my voice is shaky.

"Hmm. Or maybe we're the best idea." He brushes my hair away from my neck where he places a hot, open-mouthed kiss.

God. Damn.

My hands clutch at his shirt, and he nips at my delicate skin. I can't stand it any longer and wrap my hands around his neck and pull him closer.

"You feel so good," I whisper, shocked by my honesty. But Daren does that to me, gets me to say things I'd never dare utter.

He grabs my knee and pulls it up over his thigh and presses his hard body against mine. "I've had a hard-on all week thinking about you, and my hand isn't doing it any justice."

When he talks like this, I could melt on the spot. Hell, I *am* melting, my panties soaked, and we haven't even done anything.

I burrow my face into his chest, his scent enveloping me. My heart is galloping in my chest, and I know I have a dozen reasons why I shouldn't be hooking up with Daren, but I can't think of a single one when he's standing between my legs.

He tilts my face back until we're nose to nose, his huge frame filling my vision. "Tell me later why we're a bad idea. But tonight let me show you all the reasons we work." And then his mouth descends to mine.

CHAPTER 21

DAREN

GODDAMN. She's sexy. Even with the doubt behind her eyes.

I could tell she wanted to call things off. But the way her eyes widened as I got closer—how her breathing shallowed, how her cheeks flushed without me even touching her—are signs I'm not crazy. Signs that she wants this as much as I do.

Her tongue strokes mine in a teasing dance, but her fingers tighten in my hair as I press harder against her.

I nibble her lip and tighten my hold on her hips. "Come home with me tonight."

When our eyes meet, hers are wild and luminescent in the dim light.

Maddie's a glowing ember, and doesn't even know it. And I want to stoke the fire. So fucking bad.

The sound of voices down the hall makes her push away. Reluctantly, I let go of her.

She holds her fingers to her lips. "We shouldn't be doing this here."

I grab that hand and place a soft kiss on her wrist. "C'mon, sweet thing. Let's take a walk on the wild side."

And then I turn for the exit behind us, pulling her behind me.

The parking lot is packed, but it's dark in the back where my SUV is parked under the branches of a large tree.

Cold rain pelts us, and before I have a chance to worry she'll be pissed she's getting drenched, her laughter rings.

Spotting a large puddle, I pick her up with one arm around her waist and one under her knees. Her gasping breath energizes me, and I turn back toward my SUV and resume our run.

I've never heard her so relaxed, so at ease that she giggles. Yet, here she is, gripping my shoulders, delight and shock on her face.

When we reach my car, I release her legs, letting them dangle as I hold her to my chest. Her shirt is damp and sticking to her skin.

"You're soaked."

She nods, and something in her eyes tells me she's admitting to more than just her clothes being wet. I set her down on the ground, pleased to see her as out of breath as I feel.

Reaching into my pocket, I hit the key fob and the locks to my SUV snap open, but instead of reaching for the front door, I reach for the back.

Confusion tenses her brows until she gets what I'm suggesting. Her eyes dart around the parking lot, assessing the risk.

"Let's be young and stupid. For once." I run my thumb along her lower lip.

In what seems like a split-second decision, she nods and lets me lift her into the back seat. Following behind, I slam the door shut and reach for her.

I may have broken out the dirty talk a few minutes ago in the restaurant, but I don't know what I expect from her tonight. Maybe nothing. Maybe everything. I'll do whatever she wants or nothing at all. I just know I need to be in her space and breathe the same air. I've been daydreaming about this girl all damn week.

No sooner do I think to say we don't have to be physical than she's hiking her skirt up so she can straddle me. Let me just say that a pleated skirt never looks so fine as when Maddie McDermott wears one. She has this naughty schoolgirl vibe going on that has me instantly rock hard.

My hands dip under her skirt and grip her gartered thighs. The fact that Maddie wears garters is seriously hot as fuck.

"I've been thinking about you," I murmur as she grinds against my lap. She stares down at me, her hair damp and tangled. Her fingers slowly unbutton the top two buttons of her blouse, the sight of which has me wanting to rip off every button in a race to see her creamy skin.

Her hips keep a silent rhythm in what's turning out to be the world's best lap dance. Thank you, Jesus.

I kiss her neck as the fabric falls away to reveal a white lace bra that pushes her perfectly rounded breasts into my face. So I do what any red-blooded man would do. I bite one. Not too hard. Just enough that she grinds down harder and moans. I grip her other breast in my hand and squeeze before I push the lace down around both lush mounds. Goddamn. What a sight.

Latching on to one nipple, I suck and tug and pull. Her hands pull me closer, like she's cradling me, while a breathy little pant escapes her lips.

When I break away to inspect my handiwork, a droplet falls from her damp skin. "You're wet." I glance up at the raindrops still glistening on her cheeks as I snake a hand between us to push aside her soaked panties. "Everywhere."

But I can't give her what she wants. Not yet. So I tease around her soft, pouty skin until her eyes screw shut and her head falls back. "Harder, Daren."

"Not until you tell me you want this."

Her head snaps up, and as she begins to shake her head no, I reach for the one place on her body I know will make her say yes.

"Say it, Maddie. Tell me you've thought about this all week like I have."

Choppy breaths escape her mouth as I rub faster, slicking the moisture along her swollen folds. Her eyes shut for a moment and she nods her head. "I did. I do. I don't know why I want to lie about it. Why I can't just admit this." Her hips tilt, grinding harder into my erection. "Yes, Daren. I want you. It's making me a little crazy, in fact. But I—"

"Shh. Now let me make it better." I grip her hair and pull her down, and our mouths collide in a frenzy of tongues and lips and groans.

Before I get her to ride me—because, please, God, let her ride me—I have to see this. I have to watch her fall apart.

When I flip her onto her back, she gasps. Her legs fall open, and seeing this gorgeous girl with her breasts surged up over her lace bra, garters dressing the sexiest pair of legs ever to grace this good Earth, and a face that makes angels weep, I know that whatever happens between us, I am one lucky bastard.

CHAPTER 22

MADDIE

RIGHT NOW, with Daren pinning me down, looking at me like I'm the only meal he's had all week, I feel like one lucky girl.

Maybe it's crazy. Maybe this is the dumbest thing I've ever done, but when he asked me to do something young and stupid, every part of me screamed to let go. To be with him. To take a chance.

And right now, with him tossing my leg over the back seat and pushing my other leg farther apart with his shoulder, I'm both embarrassed to be this exposed to him and so turned on, I could come if he blew on my wet skin.

I've never been with a man like this, someone who just told me what he wanted and pushed me to go there. Someone who saw my desire and urged me to seek what felt good.

Why haven't I? I've had lovers. But nothing has ever come close to the way my body feels when it's being tugged apart by Daren Sloan.

Yes, we had all kinds of sex last weekend, but I'd drunk too much. The memory of what we did came to me in waves all week. But I couldn't appreciate it in the moment like I am now.

He kisses his way down my body, and I feel dizzy. From the

sound of rain beating down on the roof of the car. From Daren pressing me into the damp leather. From his cologne and the scent of his skin. Dizzy and falling. Fast.

When he reaches my now bare skin, a wicked smile lights his eyes. "Your hot little pussy is going to feel so good like this." And then his mouth reaches me in the most erotic kiss I've ever seen.

My hands tangle in his soft hair, and he angles lower. His eyes find mine as he takes a long lick. That's all it takes for me to shatter apart, but then he sticks two large fingers in me, and I'm coming harder, so hard that white spots dot my vision.

His name leaves my lips in a sharp cry as I arch my back off the seat. "Fuck. Fuck!" My head thrashes as I writhe beneath him. "Come here. Get in me. Right. Now."

When he gets up, I can barely stand the loss, but I hear a zipper, and a wrapper tears, and then he's back, pressing my legs wider.

He angles at my entrance, and I hook a leg around his hips and pull him in.

He's so thick and hard, I almost can't take it. But I want it. The pressure. The way he stretches me to the brink. He sinks deeper and my breath catches.

"This. God, this," I gasp. My hands claw at his back. I'm lost, so lost in how he feels. In how I feel when I'm with him.

The groan that rumbles in his chest makes me more frantic, but he sinks even deeper and then stills.

In a pained voice, he asks if I'm okay. I nod and nudge him with my hips. He chuckles and then pulls up on his arms so he can look down where we're joined, and I'm mesmerized by the sight of him pulling out of me. Back and forth. So slowly. Wow. That's… hot.

He's almost all the way out when he faces me again and presses a soft kiss to my lips. "How do you want it, babe?"

"Hard. Please, hard."

And then he moves, pushing into me so swiftly that my body

slides up the seat. His hands grip my hips, holding me down as he sinks in and out, but what sets me off again is when he leans down to bite my neck. I can't help the cry from my lips or the way I clutch him to me. Because nothing has ever felt so good as when he brings me to this breaking point.

He must agree because he's swelling inside of me, and a minute later, I can feel the pulse of his release as he collapses on my body.

Holy mother of orgasms.

After a few minutes, he pulls me on top of him, where I listen to the strong beat of his heart. The rain comes down, a soothing pattern on the roof of the car that lulls me into an even drowsier state.

"We should get going," he says as he draws lazy circles on my back. "Come back with me. Stay the night."

"Mm. I have an early morning." My head is still blissed out.

"I'll set an alarm. Stay with me. We can just sleep, but I want you in my bed tonight."

I close my eyes, unprepared for the fluttering in my chest. I should tell him no. I should go home, sleep between my own sheets. But there's something vulnerable in his voice that makes me want to tell him yes.

Clearing my throat, I ask, "So you want me to choose young and stupid again, huh?"

He chuckles, the rumble beneath me satisfying. "Yeah. That's probably what this is, but I don't care. You feel too good to care."

I have to agree.

* * *

IT'S STILL DARK when the alarm goes off. When I open my eyes, I recognize the dark gray comforter and the arm wrapped around my chest. A small bolt of fear races through me, but as I think about the night before, about how sweet and caring Daren's been, my apprehension melts away.

He loaned me a BC t-shirt last night, swearing that's all he had, but I know he was just making me pay for all of those "friends don't let friends go to BC" jokes I've told him. I thought coming back here would be awkward, especially since I let him violate my body six different ways in a public parking lot, but he was so easy-going and fun, I forgot to be uptight. Thank God for tinted windows.

When we got to his place, he made me hot chocolate and snuggled me up on his giant bed and then tickled me until I was laughing so hard, I snorted. Yes, so ladylike. But that only made him laugh harder and then he kissed me until I was practically begging him to have sex with me again. What kind of girl does that? Me, apparently. And the jerk made me say, "Pretty please, Daren, stick your big dick in me."

Of course, I said it.

Rolling my eyes at myself, I try to scoot out from under his arm, but it just tightens.

"Where you going, Wildcat?" he asks gruffly in my ear.

"To work out, remember? And then I have to get to the studio. Sorry to wake you up." My whole body aches, and my girlie garden is still having aftershocks from last night, but I need to stay on schedule. I roll into him and brush his bangs off his forehead and lean down to kiss him between his eyebrows before I can second-guess the gesture. "Go back to sleep."

"Wait. I'll come with you."

"What?"

"I'll go running with you. That's what you do in the mornings, right?" He rubs his eyes and then gives me the sweetest smile.

"Don't you have practice later? And a game Sunday night?"

"Yeah. So? Today is a light practice, and I'm probably only gonna play one quarter."

He starts to get up, but I put two hands on him to hold him

back. "No. Nope. You can't do this." I'm suddenly wide awake. "You're on a very specific workout plan. I don't care what you think you're playing on Sunday. You don't know for sure. What if you end up playing half of the game or more and you're tired from running with me today? I can't have that on my conscience."

The grin on his face is so adorable, I make a mental picture of it.

"That's really considerate of you. But I assure you I can handle it."

Then he pulls me down on top of him, and I laugh. He kisses my neck, and I groan. "No. No, you aren't coming with me."

He nips my skin, and I feel him harden between us.

"Let me give you a workout. I promise you'll use your leg muscles. On all fours."

Then he slaps my ass before he rubs the offended skin. A throb grows between my legs as he moves my thighs down to straddle him.

"Did… Did you just spank me?"

He grunts in my ear. "Yeah, and I'm fully planning on doing it again if you try to get out of my bed right now."

I sit up on him and his grip on my thighs tightens. Bracing my hands on his chest, I laugh. "So you think you're the only one who gets to punish around here?" I rotate my hips in a slow circle, the thin fabric of his boxers separating us.

His eyes darken and his fingers sink deeper into my skin.

Pulling my shirt up so he can see my bare skin grinding on him, I say, "What if this is as close as I let you get this morning?"

He watches as my thighs pull his boxers taut over his impressive length. If I had any shame, I'd be embarrassed that he can probably feel how wet I am, but I'm pretty sure I left my modesty on the floor of his car with my underwear.

He laughs. "I'd say it's still one hell of a way to wake up."

And then he pulls me down to him and gives me my morning workout.

CHAPTER 23

MADDIE

I CAN'T STOP SMILING. It's downright idiotic. It's eight at night, I'm still at work, and this grin won't stop.

It's been three days, and I'm still riding a high. We've texted a few times, but I wouldn't go over Saturday night because I didn't want to keep him up late before a game. He banged on my wall and yelled that could be us breaking his headboard. I laughed but stuck to my guns.

Oh, and our interview last week? The segment ran Saturday and got such a huge reaction that ESPN replayed it on Sunday before his game.

He looked phenomenal on the field. So in control. So confident. Every time the camera zoomed in on him, I wanted to lick the screen.

My laptop blurs in front of me, and my fingers rest on my lips like they can still feel Daren's rough fingertips grazing my skin. This—whatever I'm doing with him—is by far the most reckless thing I've ever done. I am sleeping with the source of my sports segment. I could go down in flames in so many ways. And I'm exhilarated and terrified in equal measure.

Is this what it feels like to be a thrill-seeker? Why people jump off mountains with a tiny little parachute? All I know is I want another hit.

And then his text comes in, and that smile somehow grows wider.

Hey, Wildcat. Thinking of you.

Thank God he doesn't write "u" instead of "you." What? A girl has to have standards.

I force myself to finish up my web report before I reach for my phone. *I might be thinking about you. Possibly.*

His response: *Naked, I hope.*

Every time I watch baseball, I'm going to blush. Guess you hit a home run in the bottom of the ninth. I'm being a cheese ball, but I can't help it. I mean, we freaking hooked up in the parking lot of a restaurant.

Babe, I hit a goddamn grand slam. I fucking won the World Series.

I snort into my hand, nearly dropping my phone.

"You're getting laid, aren't you?"

And then I do drop my phone. Spinning in my chair, I see Nicole, who is standing in the doorway with her arms crossed. "My guess? Daren 'I'm so hot every girl wants my cock' Sloan.'"

"Jesus, Nicole. You startled me." My heart is racing in my chest. God, does she know? "I have no clue what you're talking about."

Her eyes narrow. "I mean, good for you. At least it takes that permanent scowl off your face." I scowl? What? She thrusts her hand on her hip. "Just know you're not the only one. He's probably banging every girl from here to Hollywood."

My stomach twists as she stomps off. Another text message buzzes in on my phone, but I can't bring myself to look at it.

She's probably right.

No. Daren promised he'd tell me, break things off, if he ever wanted to sample other options.

It's this moment that finds me cursing my ex because I trusted him so wholeheartedly that I ignored all the signs he was unfaithful. And now, whether or not Daren is hooking up with other girls, he bears my knee jerk mistrust.

An hour later, I'm about to drag myself home when Spencer pops his head in my cubicle. "We're doing promos all week for Boston's Number One Bachelor Contest, so I need you to lay off the news assignments."

"I thought Nicole was covering that story."

He gives me a bored shrug. "People seem to like you on the sports segment, so I'm going with a hunch."

I love how he says "people" like me, as in, he doesn't. *I don't like you either, buddy.*

Well, that would explain why Nicole looked like she wanted to tear me a new one. This should be her story. She's been campaigning for it all week. Lord knows I don't want it.

Glancing down at my color-coded notes for the other assignments I'm working on, I can't quite believe what he's asking me to do.

"But I'm doing research for two news stories already, and I'm hoping to do a feature on this homeless shelter that—"

"Yeah, I don't give a shit. Give the work to someone else, and bring that darling smile that everyone seems to love and be ready tomorrow morning at eight." He starts to walk out and pauses. "And would it kill you to wear something sexy for once? If you wear a business suit tomorrow like you're covering City Hall, I'm firing you, so go home and find something that boosts ratings."

And then he's gone with every ounce of pride I used to have in my job clutched in his money-grubbing hands.

I spend the next several minutes moping around as I try to get a grip. But by the time I head home, I have an idea that I hope gets me a small reprieve. God knows I need one.

CHAPTER 24

DAREN

Any semblance of contentment goes down the drain the moment I see that text from Veronica.

Can we talk?

That would be a resounding fuck, no. I'm actually surprised it's taken her this long to reach out to me. But we are over. And no amount of crying on her part will repair the damage done in our relationship. I'm sick of her lies. Of her drama. Of her bullshit.

Besides, any feelings I had for her withered and died the night of the draft when she leveled that bomb at me. The moment she left, I packed up the shit she had at my place and shipped it to her mother's the next day.

Jeanine pops her head into the locker room, jarring me from the foxhole I retreat to whenever I think of Veronica. "Daren, I need you out here in five. The other guys are here, and the station is ready to tape."

When the door closes, Quentin struts over naked and mimics her voice. "Daren, I need you out here because all of your adoring fans are ready!" And then he pretends to make out with himself.

The guys laugh, and I toss a jockstrap at his face. He ducks with a laugh and shakes his bare ass at me.

I tilt my head back and laugh. "I see how it is, Q. Jealousy is an evil thing. Not everyone can be Boston's number one bachelor."

Dumbest contest ever, and if it didn't raise millions for a few great causes, I'd never do it. Besides, the guy who wins gets the donation to his charity matched by the sponsoring corporations, and I plan to get the St. Martin's Homeless Shelter expanded threefold.

My parents might be rich now, but my mother's family was homeless at one point when she was a child, and that always resonated with me. Bad things happen to good people every day, and my family found help in this charity back when it was a one-room food pantry behind a grocery store. So yeah, I'll stomach a silly bachelor contest if it means I can help St. Martin's.

Brentwood rolls his eyes at me, not caring that I'm obviously joking. He's been bitchy all week, and I've been tempted to ask if he needs tampons. But then, I don't know any woman with PMS this bad, so it's an unfair slight to females.

By the time I get to the conference room, the guys are each standing by their respective female fans, who have been rounded up to coo over us. Five Rebel cheerleaders hover in the corner, and when one spots me, she beelines over and hugs me.

"Hey, Daren."

I give her an awkward side hug while my eyes search for the girl who has been front and center in my dirty dreams all week.

A fire-engine-red dress in the corner catches my attention.

Sweet mother.

Maddie glances over her shoulder, and I catch my breath. Her black hair is down, tousled like my hands have been in them. Doe eyes stare back at me in a moment that drowns out the thirty other people in the room.

I've never seen her so dressed up. Although she looked awesome the night of my party, the color red amps up her sexiness, which I didn't think was possible. Today, she looks like a flame, from the silky smooth fabric wrapped around her like a second skin to her sky-blue eyes. Damn, she's mouthwatering.

Her pouty lips give me a flirty smile before she returns her attention to the camera guy, and I take a gasping breath when our connection is broken.

Voodoo woman.

I haven't had time to connect with her this week. And when I say connect, I mean fuck her senseless. I intend to rectify the situation as soon as possible. She's supposed to come over tonight, thank Christ.

That Spencer asshole grabs the mic that's been set up in front of a black backdrop and welcomes everyone, promising that the only reason we're doing this on my home turf is because the team has the available space. Jeanine winks at me from his side, and I know that's all bullshit. I'd bet money she talked Spencer into doing all of our group promo shots here. Why it makes a difference where it's shot is beyond me.

Spencer motions toward us. "We're adding two more athletes and breaking you into two teams. The group that gets the most money will get your cause featured in prime time segments, which can raise additional revenue for your charities. We'll still do an individual winner, but this is another way to generate interest. One team of three guys will go with Maddie for interviews and promos, and the other will go with Nicole." He motions to the two girls who wave behind him.

After a few more introductions, I get ushered toward Maddie, and as we're gearing up to shoot our first promo, the back door opens and some tatted-up fighter walks in with what appear to be cage girls. He looks vaguely familiar.

Maddie tenses next to me and curses under her breath.

The guy heads straight for Maddie, and the way his eyes crawl up her body make me want to launch my fist into his face.

"Hey, babe," he says to Maddie, which doesn't seem to bother the two girls draped over him. "You're looking as hot as ever."

Maddie shakes her head, closes her eyes for a moment and then points across the room. "Jacob, you're with Nicole. And do me a favor." She waits for him to lean forward. "Don't talk to me. In fact, you can pretend we've never met."

The arctic air blowing off her is enough to give me chills. He starts to open his mouth, but Nicole trots over to usher him to the other side of the room.

"You know that guy?" I whisper to her when he's out of earshot.

Maddie taps the mic that's clipped to her dress and asks, "Now what gave you that impression?"

Even though she's clearly brimming with tension, as soon as we're taping, she's all charm and smiles as she beams confidence into the camera. I love her focus. She can block out that drama and get her shit done like a pro.

Pride fills me for my girl.

Whoa.

No, Daren. My friend. My fuck buddy. But definitely not *my girl.* Don't forget that.

Surprisingly, though, our interview is strangely awkward. I can't totally pinpoint why. Was it the conversation with that fighter guy or is she pissed the cheerleaders are grabbing onto me? But damn. That's all at the direction of her boss. Spencer tells the girls to sit on my lap and wrap their arms around me.

I guess I can't be surprised Maddie's all business, getting the segment done before she's off interviewing the other guys.

But that's not what bothers me. That's not what has me second-guessing our arrangement.

I can't lie. Slipping like that, thinking of Maddie as mine, scares me a little. Okay, it scares me a whole helluva lot.

I've done monogamous sex before without getting attached. In retrospect, that basically describes my entire relationship with

Veronica. Because now that I've had some space, I realize I didn't love her. And she sure as hell didn't love me.

I tell myself I won't fly into asshole mode and ignore Maddie when she calls, but that's a moot point because she doesn't call like she said she would. Our Tuesday night plans come and go with radio silence.

By the time Thursday morning rolls around and I head out to the field for our weekly *Football 101* interview, I'm feeling like a dick for not at least texting her yesterday to ask if she was okay after the run-in with that MMA fighter.

Turns out he's her ex. Guess I'm not the first jock she's dated.

But we're not dating, so scratch that.

She's cordial during my interview, and I can't decide if her nonchalance is a relief or irritating as hell. Getting distance from her should be a good thing. If we're just fucking around, then none of this should bother me.

But it does.

I'm hoping to get a moment to talk to her afterward—to say what, I'm not sure—but Jeanine is hovering like a starved vulture and ushers me over to a group of sorority girls on the sidelines to shoot more hype footage for the bachelor contest. I don't know why I've turned into her pet project, but it's taxing.

On my drive home, I'm in a foul mood, so when my cell rings, I press the Bluetooth button on the steering wheel and grunt hello.

"Son, now what kind of greeting is that? You sound like a constipated bear."

I chuckle. "Hi, Mom."

"How's my favorite son?"

"I'm your only son, Mom. If I'm not at the top of your list, I'm doing something wrong."

"Guess who I saw the other day?"

This can't be good. "No idea."

"Clementine." *Here we go.* Mom's never gotten over my

breakup from my high school sweetheart. But this is not the shit I want to talk about today. Or ever. "Have you talked to her lately?"

My mom is digging around for something. "We talked a couple of days ago. Why?"

"I was wondering if you've read her new book. My friend says it's fantastic!" She lowers her voice to a whisper. "But I heard it has sex, so I'm reading it on my Kindle where I keep my *Fifty Shades*."

That is... something I don't need to know. "You really called to tell me this?"

Mental note, avoid Clem's new book and my mother's e-reader.

"No, I called to find out if you've ever considered asking her out again. The two of you grew up together. You were inseparable. That girl always had her heart set on you."

"Mom, that ship has sailed. She's got a boyfriend. They're practically married. Honestly, I don't have those kind of feelings for her anymore. Never mind that if I messed up her new relationship, Jax would choke me with his bare hands."

My best friend Jax, Clem's twin brother, almost broke my face when he found out what I'd done in high school. And I let him. Because I fully deserved it.

"But you two were so good together."

I shake my head. "No, we weren't. I was a dick." And if I'm being totally honest with myself, she never looked at me the way she looks at Gavin. The asshole.

"But have you apologized for what happened with Veronica?"

My hands grip the steering wheel. "Of course I apologized. I'm tempted to ask what you know, but that might be awkward."

"Son, I've known all along what happened in high school, how you broke Clementine's heart"—she lowers her voice again—"by sleeping with Veronica." She clears her throat. "But I knew you were going through so much then, and I didn't want to add to your situation."

Fuck. This never gets easier.

Yes, I was the cocksucker who cheated on the girl I'd been crazy about since I was in diapers with a woman who would make me miserable. That's some karmic shit right there. Reason number one why I should never be in a serious relationship again.

"Did you call me to crack open my chest and dig around with a pitchfork?"

Her little laugh rings through the phone. "Good heavens, no. I just want you to find a good woman, someone to anchor you. Someone to tell you the truth when you don't want to hear it. A nice girl who will take care of you, maybe even when you don't deserve it."

An angelic face with stark blue eyes comes to mind, but I shake my head. Because dating Maddie in any kind of serious way is epically stupid. I can't go out on a ledge again.

The lie slips off my lips easily. "I'm not interested in dating anyone right now."

"You know who is so beautiful and really seems to have her act together? That sports reporter."

Please don't say Nicole. I need to date another blonde cheer-leader type like I need a hole in my head.

"That dark-haired beauty, Maddie. Is that her name? I love your interviews with her. She's adorable, and I've seen her news stories too. Oh, that girl has her head on straight. I bet if you'd ask her out—"

"I'm pretty sure she's not interested, Mom." Something tells me that after this week, Maddie really isn't, and that just puts me in a pissier mood. "Okay, this was fun, but I gotta go."

"Son, I'm sorry. Don't listen to me. I only want you to be happy."

"I'm fine, Mom."

"You know, your father misses you."

Christ. This conversation won't stop. Discussing Mason definitely will not alleviate my stress. "That's… I don't know what to do with that. Mom, I'll talk to you later, okay?"

Her sigh of disappointment is cut off when I curse at a driver for nearly sideswiping me.

"Oh, you're driving. Why didn't you tell me? Did you know that most accidents happen because people are on their phones?"

"Okay, Miss CNN, thanks for the tip. You'll be happy to know I'm on a hands-free set, but I'll call you soon."

By the time I get home, any thoughts of calling Maddie have disappeared. I might miss her like hell, but maybe space is what I need to clear my head.

CHAPTER 25

MADDIE

When I suggested that we cover the bachelor event like a contest between two teams, Spencer couldn't have been more pleased. Although this meant finding two more athletes, this is Boston. Handsome jocks abound in this city.

What I didn't count on was Spencer's newfound interest in mixed martial arts, and before I could blink, Jacob had been added to our roster of athletes in the bachelor contest. His fight in Vegas had catapulted him into superstardom, and Spencer was frothing to get him on board.

The upshot to all of this is that I'm now splitting responsibilities with Nicole, who was so grateful to be back on board, she actually brought me coffee the next morning to say thanks.

I wouldn't say we're friends now. I'm not delusional. But hopefully, this arrangement means I still have some time to cover news.

I rub my eyes, not caring if it smudges my mascara. Jacob left me three messages since I saw him on Tuesday. I've never been the kind of person to delete messages before I listen to them, but I'd rather fall into a paper shredder and be doused in lemon juice than waste one more minute on that man.

down, but he lifts my chin until I'm staring into his hazel eyes. "Just don't hurt me." It comes out a whisper.

He shakes his head with a small laugh. "I was about to tell you the same thing."

I chew on my bottom lip. "Why don't we try this honesty thing? No pressure to be more. Just enjoy each other's company like we said we would. With the option to reassess."

Those dimples creep out again for a sneak attack on my heart. "I like this idea."

He tugs me down to him until we're nose to nose. I'm about to lean down that last inch for a kiss when he winces.

I realize I'm leaning on his shoulder, and I jolt back. "I'm so sorry. Are you okay?"

He's in pain, but he gives me a huge grin. "I'll be fine. Get your ass back here."

Laughing, I lean down, and I'm expecting that kiss. Instead, he wraps me in his arms and gives me a hug, and a little piece of me melts.

"I've been thinking, " he whispers in my ear, "that I might be able to kick your ass at *Plants and Zombies*. "

I laugh. *Goofball.* I have no idea what the hell he's talking about, but I decide to take him up on the challenge.

"A chance to win some Southie bragging rights? Bring it, Sloan. "

* * *

A FEW HOURS later I realize I'm about to die an inglorious death and get splattered all over the pavement. But at the last second, I duck, and the shot goes wide and blows up the shed behind me.

I glare at Daren. "Nice try."

He chuckles and shakes his head, his eyes never leaving the television screen.

If you think this man ever gives less than a hundred percent, you'd be mistaken. PlayStation, for example, is serious business.

Honestly, I suck at video games. I've never understood the appeal, but I can't deny how much fun we're having. But I play to win too, so I made him put on a t-shirt so he wouldn't distract me with those abs.

"Death!" I scream as my pea shooter takes down his zombie all-star football player.

Daren shakes his head and releases the death grip on his game controller. "Beginner's luck."

A little snort leaves me. "Aww. Are you a sore loser? Big, bad Daren Sloan got his ass kicked by a little girl. Someone call CNN."

He shrugs. "Didn't want to break your spirit."

Laughter bubbles out me. "That was big of you." I crawl into his lap, toss my arm around his neck and kiss his cheek. "But you still lost. I think you need to be my slave."

He snorts. "Slave, huh?"

I nod, and he squeezes me to his chest. "The job is simple. Feed me peeled grapes. Maybe fan me with a few large feathers."

"So you're looking for an old school slave. Like, Egyptian times."

"Cleopatra had it good."

He laughs. "I don't think she ate grapes. Dates maybe."

"Fine. Feed me dates."

"All right, princess. Dates it is. But only if you can handle the tickle test."

I stiffen in his arms. *Tickle test?* "No, Daren."

The words are barely out of my mouth when his hands dart to my waist. I'm screaming and laughing and trying to fight back, except when we land on the floor, he pins me down. "Aww, you didn't pass," he chides as he reaches down to squeeze my thigh, which makes me convulse with laughter.

"I hate you!" I scream and try to wiggle out of his clutches as I giggle hysterically. Finally, I manage to push against his chest. He pauses long enough to shake his head.

"Nah, babe. I'm adorable. What's not to love?"

He places a warm kiss on my forehead and rolls over, pulling me with him.

He's right. The thought sends warmth through my chest. What's not to love?

CHAPTER 26

MADDIE

FOR THE LAST WEEK, we've been trying to do more of the friend thing. It's become this unspoken effort on both our parts.

We've been busy, but I've stopped by to drop off a batch of brownies because I thought it was overdue, and he brought by an iced coffee when I had to stay up late. He texts me silly memes, and I pretend they're not funny. I complain about the world's problems, and he surprises me with references to Howard Zinn and Noam Chomsky.

Yes, Daren is a smartie. You see this hot athlete, and it's tempting to write him off as nothing but a charming jock, but he's so much more than a pretty face.

Knowing Daren's kind of brainy definitely fuels my attraction to him. And not spending time with him all week is only sending that lust into overdrive.

One thing is for sure. It's pretty damn hard to concentrate when Daren is sitting next to me shirtless. His elbows rest on his knees and the intensity on his face is captivating. It's the look he gets when he struts out onto the field.

For the last hour, he's been studying today's game while I

research a potential story on my laptop. Every so often, I look up and watch him unobserved.

His hair is longer than when I first met him, and right now, it's a sexy, disheveled mess. A few strands hang down by his cheek, and I want to brush it off so I can see his face. He arches his back, and all of the muscles in his shoulders pull taut.

Wow, did I mention there were flexing muscles? Because there are. A lot of them.

"See something you like, McDermott?"

Busted.

I shake my head and look down at my laptop, hoping I'm not blushing. He laughs, and when I finally look up, those big hazel eyes do me in. But I won't give in to his charm. Yet.

"Whatever, Sloan. Stop thinking the whole world wants to hump your leg."

"You're cute when you blush."

"Go to hell."

He laughs again, and I go back to reading, trying my hardest not to smile because I know he's watching me.

We work in companionable silence until I hear him groan, a flash of pain registering on his face.

"Do you need to lie down again? I'm sorry. I'm hogging this side of the couch. I should move."

Today's game was better than last week's, but he's still sore and has to ice down. I start to get up, but he tells me to stop as he scoots closer and deposits his head in my lap.

I blink down at him once. Twice. Three times.

"I'm not crushing you, am I?" he asks as he takes the remote and rewinds a play.

"No." I have to clear my throat and say it again because nothing comes out of my mouth the first time except air.

It takes me a full five minutes to focus on my article, especially since the last time Daren was resting his head on my thighs, he was facing the other way.

With my laptop propped on the arm of the couch and Daren using me as a pillow, I attempt to study before tomorrow's meeting where I hope I can propose this issue for an in-depth news assignment.

The city council wants to ban the filming of porn unless condoms are used, but critics say that will only push filmmakers underground where participants will be more exposed to hazardous conditions.

I skim the words until I find what I'm looking for and read until my eyes are bleary. I'm just about to call it a night when I accidentally click on the wrong link and a porn site with full-frontal nudity pops up.

Oh, God. Penises are… everywhere. Big ones. Fat ones. Squatty ones. Who knew they had that vein? Which is kind of hot. But those thick ones with all that skin scare me. You'd think I knew what a dick looked like after putting it in my mouth, but it's not like I've ever taken a really good look.

My head tilts to the right. *That one is kind of pretty.*

I catch my breath. *Wait, why am I surfing porn right now? And why won't this page close?*

"That feels good."

I look down to find that I'm running my fingers through Daren's hair. And he's looking at me. With… that look. The one that makes my skin hot. Or was that the porn? I guess it doesn't matter because I'm… hot.

"I'm sorry. I didn't realize I was molesting you."

Ugh. Nice choice of words, Maddie.

He laughs and flips onto his back and stares straight up at me. "You weren't. But that could be arranged."

My hand is already in his hair, so I brush it out of his face and stroke back, massaging as I go. His eyes drift shut, and he licks his lips. He has gorgeous, full lips, emphasized by a five o'clock shadow that makes him look downright sultry.

A sexy groan rumbles in his chest, and my cheeks burn

because all I can think about is porn and how I want the man in my lap naked.

He grimaces as he shifts again.

"I hate when you get tackled," I say as I trace his cheek with my finger.

"I didn't realize you watched my games. But I guess you have to for your interviews."

"That, and I want to watch you play, Daren."

A smile tilts his lips, and he opens his eyes. "Yeah? I thought you didn't like football."

Looking away, I sigh. "It's not what you think." I shake my head. "I'm sorry I made you feel like I'm not into what you do. You're really spellbinding out on the field."

"So you've watched more than today's game?"

"Yes." I bite my lip, unsure of how much more I should say. But I don't like secrets, and this definitely feels like a whopper. If we're friends, I need to tell him. I take a deep breath, and try to quell my racing heart. "You probably don't remember this, but I interviewed you in high school."

"What?" He sits up quickly and winces. He's still frowning when he faces me with a what-the-hell-are-you-talking-about look.

Now my heart is really thundering in my chest. I don't know why I'm nervous. *Maybe because you want him to remember you.* "It was a long time ago. I'm sure you won't remember."

His eyebrows lift as his eyes widen more. "And?"

"And, like I said, it was a long time ago. Sophomore year."

"Where were we? Was it before a game?" The crinkle on his forehead deepens.

I lick my lips, buying me a moment. "It was after your game against Blackwell."

He stares at me. "The championship game?"

"Yes, Clutch, the championship game."

His eyes light when I call him by his high school nickname.

He wasn't supposed to play that day. He was a JV quarterback playing the bench on a varsity game, but after the starting QB got injured and the second-stringer choked, the coach took a chance and played Daren. And the golden boy came through. Scored twice and won the game.

"Why didn't you tell me? What happened to not liking football?"

Nodding, I swallow. This whole conversation makes me feel sick, but I want him to know the truth.

"I was a sports reporter in high school, Daren." Now he really looks confused. "Look, I didn't lie that day when I told Spencer I didn't like football. I haven't liked the game in a long time. But I used to love it." I run a hand through my hair, pushing back wisps that have flown loose from my ponytail. Memories I haven't wanted to think about in years come rushing back, and my stomach turns. "I realize none of this makes sense, but it's a long story, and I know you need to watch your film."

He shakes his head. "I'm done studying for tonight. Fill me in. Why did you stop covering sports?"

God, why did I say anything? Pressing my lips together, I will my emotions to calm down. But when I start talking again, it comes out a whisper. "Covering sports was something my dad and I did together." I shrug, feeling overexposed, and struggle to describe what happened.

"I was hoping to get this internship with a neighborhood newspaper, covering kids' leagues. I had to submit a few samples of work, and my dad thought it would be fun to write about the state championship, so I could do a mock assignment. So he took me to your game, and afterward, I asked you a few questions."

His brows are pulled tight, the look of shock still lingering in his eyes. "Where were we? Still on the field?"

Nervous laughter spills from my lips. "No, I ambushed you on the way to the parking lot."

He's quiet for a moment, and when I look up, his honey-colored eyes are wide with recognition. "You asked if I was scared when I walked onto the field to play."

I still, shocked he remembers that detail. "Yes."

He motions toward me. "You had glasses and a purple streak through your hair."

I smile. "That would be me."

"Don't take this the wrong way, Maddie, but you were like this hot, athletic nerd." I laugh, and when I glance up again, he's rubbing his jaw. "I asked you out."

"Maybe," I whisper.

"But you didn't call me back."

I lick my lips, my mouth dry. "So you called?"

He looks incredulous. "Yeah, I called. Twice."

My lips tilt up in a smile. "I didn't mean to blow you off. Trust me, I was pretty excited you asked for my number even though it was a total conflict of interest." *Much like this is now.*

I force myself to stop thinking about work. Yes, I could get fired for whatever I have going on with Daren, but I'm in too deep now to walk away.

A smile lifts his lips. "I made myself wait a few days before I called." He chuckles, and those dimples do me in.

Taking a deep breath, I brace myself for what I need to say. I haven't talked about what happened that week to anyone in years.

I never even told my ex what happened.

My stomach hurts, but I force myself to go on. "I didn't realize you called because I lost my phone that weekend. And when I found it, I had about forty messages, none of which I listened to." Daren looks confused, and I shake my head, needing to start at the beginning. "We had a record-setting cold front blow in the night of your game. Pipes froze all over the city, flooding whole blocks. My dad was a fireman. We had just gotten back from your game when he got called to work, and I was on this crazy high. Your game was exhilarating, and then I interviewed you, and you asked me out."

I motion to my face. "You were so cute with that black grease on your cheeks and your hair hanging in your eyes. My dad was watching me talk to you from the car. When we drove home, he joked there was no way you and I were going on a date unless he chaperoned."

My eyes water, threatening to overflow.

Daren's fingers thread through mine. "What happened, babe?" he asks softly.

Breathe. Inhale. This is the past. Don't let it control you. "Dad walked into a two-story on Grove Street that night and never walked out. He helped rescue a family of four and their yappy dog. The official report says it was an electrical fire. It started as a two-alarm but quickly escalated. The temperatures dropped so fast that night. One of the hydrants failed."

A wave of emotion that I've worked years to dam up cracks fissures in my heart. I shake my head, trying to keep the tears at bay. "A crew was scheduled to check the hydrants in that neighborhood, but budget cuts scaled back the frequency. Maybe if they had done the safety check... If the city council hadn't been so concerned with elections that year... If they thought about the men who risked their lives every day to do their jobs instead of the bottom line..."

Daren's thumbs brush back the tears tumbling down my cheeks. "C'mere." Wrapping me in his arms, he scoops me into his lap where I nuzzle into his neck and cry.

* * *

When I open my eyes, I realize Daren is carrying me into his bedroom. He places me on his bed and then pulls out a BU t-shirt and yoga pants from his dresser and hands them to me.

"Do you really have Boston University paraphernalia in your house?" My throat is hoarse from crying like a crazy person.

"Gotcha some jammies." He smiles, making my heart flip in my chest, and I momentarily forget my embarrassment.

But then reality sets in, and I drop my face into my hands. "Daren, I shouldn't have unloaded all of that on you. I got carried away. I just haven't talked about that night in years."

He wraps his hand around the back of my neck tenderly, and I stare up at him. He's still shirtless, only wearing sweatpants and a few bruises, but he's still somehow larger than life. "Thank you for sharing that with me. I'm so sorry you lost your dad." His eyebrows pull tight. "And I'm so sorry I made you cover football this summer."

God, that is not what I want him to take away from this.

"I'm not."

Because right now, something in me feels lighter. I haven't spoken about my father in so long. Too long. If Dad knew what I've accomplished, I'm sure he'd be proud of me. Tears well in my eyes again, and I blink them back.

Daren looks like he wants to say something, but he shakes his head. "I'll be back in a minute. After icing my shoulder all night, I need to warm up." He kisses my forehead and heads into the bathroom where I hear the shower turn on.

It takes me a minute to find my bearings, and when I do, I realize I don't want to be alone.

CHAPTER 27

DAREN

TILTING MY HEAD BACK, I let the water pelt my skin. Before I moved in, I had the shower redone with four ceiling shower heads, so it's like a rainforest in here. But I need it. After practice when I can barely move, I crawl in here and my muscles can find a little reprieve.

But tonight my body isn't what needs help.

Breathing in the steam, I close my eyes and try to figure out what just happened. I know I've been telling myself this is casual, that we're just friends—really good friends—but my relationship with Maddie feels anything but casual right now.

Christ, the way she looked at me with tears trailing down her pale cheeks, I thought my heart was going to rip out of my chest. Usually, Maddie is fierce, tough. It's one of the things I love about her.

Not that I love her.

Well, I obviously care about her. A lot. Probably more than I should at this point, but I admire the hell out of her. The way she gave herself over to covering stories that make a difference instead of inconsequential football games. She's more than just a beautiful girl with an awesome laugh. More than a sexy woman with a great personality. She's just... more.

It's a little bittersweet to think about how things could have been different.

She was one of the only girls to ever turn me down in high school. At least that was how I thought about it then. I figured she had blown me off, and now I feel like a giant douchebag.

Fuck, I was full of myself. The girl lost her dad that weekend. Of course she wouldn't have thought twice about some idiot jock.

And having so much unresolved shit with my own father makes me feel like a bigger dickwad. I know I need to call Mason and sort through our shit, but the very thought sends a wave of exhaustion through my bones.

I rest my palm on the tile and breathe in the steam and try to clear my head. The click of the door handle startles me, and I turn to see Maddie standing in front of my open shower.

"I'm cold too." Her wide blue eyes are red, and her cheeks are flushed, but she's still a fucking vision. She bites her lower lip, something I've come to understand is a sign of her nerves. Which is funny because she never does it when she's on air. She tilts her head, an uncertain look in her eye. "Can I join you?"

The expression on her face does me in, and even though the smart part of me says we should get some space from each other, that this has gotten too intense too fast, a bigger part of me wants that closeness, and I want it with her.

We haven't slept together all week, and my fist is getting old fast. But when she came over last weekend and made me dinner, I knew our rules had changed. Because I wanted to get to know her better, and now that I do, I don't think I could stop our trajectory even if I wanted to.

I nod, and a beat passes before she shakes out her dark mane and loose waves fall around her face. It's like she's moving in slow motion, my anticipation growing as she reaches down for the hem of her t-shirt and pulls it over her head. A minute later, she's bare before me, shivering in the cold.

Her vulnerable expression tugs at something in my chest, and it's almost overwhelming.

"C'mere here, babe."

She steps in, and water sluices over her pale skin, down her shoulders and across those lush breasts. She closes her eyes and tilts her head back, and I catch my breath as her lips part, everything losing focus but that beautiful face.

When I am old and gray, I want to remember this moment and the girl before me. I'm not a religious man, but if I believed in angels and signs, I'd be tempted to think the vision before me is beatific.

Her sky-blue eyes open and search my face, and it's this moment that makes me fear she'll find me wanting. But she smiles, and it's unguarded, and it digs into the part of me that I swore I'd never open to another woman again.

She seeks my embrace, and my arms wrap around her and fit her soft body to mine. My lips rest on her hair, her cheek pressed to my chest.

I'm fighting this hard-on, but I can't help it. She's curvy in all the right places and wet. Her plump breasts are pushing against me, and she's pressing her lips to my neck, which only sends the blood rushing to my dick. And before I know it, everything aches, and my fingers itch to yank on her hair while I sink into her.

I expect her to push me away for being an insensitive asshole, so when she presses her hips harder into me, I'm unreasonably elated. So I let my hands roam her back, drifting against her wet skin, and when I tug her closer, my thumbs drag against the sides of her breasts and her nipples pebble against me.

Maddie's head tilts back, her lips seeking mine, and my hand grips her hair. She moans into my kiss, opening herself, stroking her tongue against mine.

Her taste is so sweet, it makes the ache worse. And then she tilts my dick between her legs and squeezes her thighs as she slides across me, back and forth, slick and hot, her bare skin like satin.

"Fuck, Maddie. You feel good." I grab her ass to control her movements and revel in the little panting sounds she makes. "I've missed you this week."

She looks up, blue eyes dark, her pupils wide, and with a shy smile says, "You've seen me."

I shake my head before I nibble on her plump bottom lip. "That's not what I mean."

She swallows as I kiss down her neck and palm her full breasts that are slick with water. Her back arches into me while she continues her dirty slide on my cock, the one that makes me want to throw her down on the tile and fuck her hard.

But then she grabs my face to kiss me, and she stares into my eyes while she sucks my tongue in a way that makes me a little insane with lust. I'm about to hoist her into my arms when she falls to her knees and takes me into her mouth.

Fuck. Fuck. Fuck.

I want to say it's her hot, wet tongue that unravels something inside me, but it's the expression in her eyes as she watches me that has my chest expanding in new and uncertain ways.

Her lips drag over the length of me before her tongue takes long, slow licks at my head. I tangle my fingers through her long hair, and she leans sideways into my palm. Closing her eyes, she takes me deep, and I could come right here, but this isn't what I want. What I need. What I think she needs.

"Maddie." Her name rushes from my lips. "Need to fuck you, babe. Hard."

She nods, and I haul her up and spin her around, placing her hands against the tile.

Condoms. I need condoms. The asshole in me wants her bare, something I've never considered before, but the bigger head in me prevails, and I step away before I do something stupid. I remind myself that wearing condoms was one of her conditions when we first started hooking up, and right now when she's vulnerable is not the time I want to ask her to reconsider.

I kiss her neck and delight when she shivers. "Be right back. Don't move."

My feet trail water across the bathroom floor, but thankfully I find what I need quickly. When I turn back, I find Maddie peering at me over her shoulder, a sultry smile tugging on her lips as she watches me grip myself to roll on the condom. The appraisal in her eyes makes me harder, so I let her watch as I stroke myself. But I'm selfish, standing here, jerking off so I can see her reaction.

Her mouth parts and her eyes widen as my hand moves down my cock, and she's standing there with her hands up, ass out, like she's about to get frisked. Fuck, yes.

Steam rises all around her while her breasts heave, and wet tendrils trail down her porcelain skin. Breathtaking. She's just breathtaking.

Some Neanderthal urge to toss her over my shoulder and lock her in my room forever takes residence in my chest. This girl. God, she just does it for me in a way no one has before.

Suddenly, the idea of this being casual is painful. Because there's no way in hell I'm letting go of Maddie.

I make quick work of the condom and stalk back toward her. Gripping her hips, I tug her ass toward me, and she arches. Christ. I want her.

My hands grip her breasts while she drags herself against my dick. She's tall for a girl, but she's the perfect size for me.

"Don't drop your hands, Wildcat," I whisper in her ear. A shuddering breath leaves her, and I pinch her taut nipple between my fingers. She arches more, and I thrust along the cleft of her ass, which only makes her pant. Damn, I love that sound.

I reach down, dragging my fingers between her legs. A groan

rumbles in my chest when I feel how wet she is, how swollen and ready, and I push two fingers into her.

"Daren. Yes."

Fuck, I love when she says my name.

"What do you need, baby?"

"Y… You. I need you. Inside me. Now."

She's panting and pushing against my hand, and my dick is angry from not having a turn, but that's too bad because I need my mouth on her first.

I kneel behind her and take a long lick up her swollen slit.

She gasps and bucks backward. "Fuck, Daren. Fuck."

That's all the encouragement I need, and I rub her clit with my thumb as I caress her slick folds. But it's when I lick farther up against her tight rim that she screams and falls apart, her swollen nub throbbing against my hand. *Interesting.* I file that away for future reference as I stand.

Keeping the pressure with my hand, I stand and nudge my cock into her snug pussy, and I'm rewarded by her frantic thrashing as she presses back into me and bucks.

Goddamn, she's so tight. I thrust harder, pushing to the hilt, and she's screaming, "Yes!"

Within minutes, she's coming on me again, pulsing hard, and I'm swelling into her.

Then my mouth finds that silky expanse between her neck and shoulder, and I bite and suck because I need more of her. All of her.

She stills, and I pause to feel the race of her pulse against my tongue, appreciating how my heart is beating in the same rapid-fire rhythm.

"Baby," I whisper against her ear, and she turns to kiss me. I tilt my hips and drag against her, and she moans.

Not to be outdone, my little wildcat reaches down and wraps her hand around the base of my cock as I continue to push into her, and I am done.

Tugging her hips up, I damn near lift her feet off the ground when I come with a shout because she's the best thing I have ever felt.

She's gripping the shower rail with one hand and laughing at how carried away I've gotten. We're both gasping and out of breath and somehow sweaty in a shower.

Eventually, I set her on her feet and gently ease out of her before I turn her around in my arms. "That was... wow."

The smile on her face makes my heart beat just a little faster. She nods slowly, a shy expression on her face as she glances down. "I could get used to that wow."

When she looks up, I stare into those bright blue eyes, feeling a little lost and a little found, confused as fuck and like I'm staring at my answer. And then I tell her in all honesty, "I could too." Because no matter what, I'm not letting go.

CHAPTER 28

MADDIE

THIS HAS TO BE A MISTAKE. A tall bouquet of lavender roses takes up half the reception desk.

"Are you sure?" I ask Susan, the secretary, who will be retiring next month. I lean over and smell a bloom. Wowzers, they smell great. So sweet, almost fruity.

Susan raises an eyebrow. "Someone is getting a little Hammer time." She giggles, and I wrinkle my nose. *Hammer time?*

No way will I even hint at my sex life while at work, so I school my features.

She waggles her eyebrows at me. "The courier said it was for Madeline McDermott. That would be you. And this wasn't cheap. It's Sunday. No one delivers on Sunday."

I feign indifference and thank her for paging me before heading back to my cubicle.

The arrangement is heavy, and I have to wrap both arms around the glass vase. I'm a little afraid I'm going to trip in these heels and land in a swan dive.

When I'm back at my desk, all I can do is stare at the bouquet.

Daren did not just send two dozen roses to my job. He'd never. Would he? For something that's casual?

A pang in my chest aches as I think about what that means.

I've been freaking out all morning over what I told him last night. It just poured out of me. The poor man probably didn't know what to do with crazy Maddie and her big mouth. Because "casual" does not mean detailing how your dad died before you went into a tailspin. How it led you to change the whole direction of your life.

Of course Daren was sweet. He's always sweet. He was freaking Prince Charming, consoling me while I sobbed all over him. Well, before I pounced on him in the shower. And then he became one of those guys in Sheri's dirty books, which I'm thinking I need to start reading.

I bury my head in my hand, still not quite believing I threw myself at him like that. But my jaw still aches, a reminder of exactly how far I went. Jeez.

After unloading that story, I wanted to be close to him. It was like I was addicted to him, to how safe he made me feel.

And I am not the kind of girl who throws herself at men, but that's what I did last night.

When I snuck out of his bed at four thirty this morning, he reached for me and told me he'd miss me, and I felt like a lightning bug, buzzing and alive with hunger for him.

But by the time I got to work, though, the excitement had worn off. Because men say all kinds of things in the middle of the night when a girl is naked.

My palm presses into my stomach to quell my nerves.

"Open the card, Maddie. Stop being a freak," I whisper to myself.

The card, like the bouquet, is exquisite and written on a thick cream card stock. *For the girl with the purple streak in her hair. I owe her a date. xo*

"Damn, that's kind of awesome," Nicole says over my shoulder, making me jump.

"Jesus Christ, you scared me." My heart bangs away under my palm where I clutch my chest.

Thank God Daren didn't sign that card. Because, holy crap, he sent me flowers! That giddy feeling I've been fighting all day comes flooding back, and I can't help the smile that lifts my lips.

Turning my back to Nicole so she can't see my stupid grin, I take a deep breath and try to calm down. I'm not sure how much Nicole saw, and I don't bother to ask when I tuck the card away and try to focus on my mile-long to-do list. But it's hard.

Daren sent me flowers. A whole freaking field of flowers!

The teenage Maddie who secretly swooned over him during our first interview is doing a cartwheel and spirit fingers.

I shouldn't be this excited. I need to have realistic expectations. He's an NFL player for Christ's sake. *Calm down, Maddie.*

And shit. I'm. At. Work. Part of me wants to die from happiness while the other half is considering hiding the bouquet behind the recycling bin.

"You're really not going to tell me who they're from?" Nicole huffs.

"Nope."

My heart thunders in my chest. *Please go away, Nicole.* I really don't want her blabbing to the office.

Leaning forward to smell the bouquet again, she whisper-yells, "Is that a hickey?" as she points at me.

My hand rushes to cover my neck, and she busts out laughing.

"Nah, just kidding. But clearly you're sexing up someone who *could* give you a hickey. And really, instead of that scowl on your face, you should be thanking me, because if I had gotten that gig interviewing him, maybe he'd be sending *me* roses right now." Her eyebrows tilt up before she starts whistling the NFL theme.

She never says his name. She doesn't need to. But the look in her eyes says it all.

My heart is beating fast and sweat builds on my neck. Damn it. I hope no one heard her comment. I'm so pissed that I fell for her dumb "look at that hickey" tactic, I'm not sure where to begin, but we're interrupted when Brad clears his throat.

"Hey, Maddie." His jaw is tight as he hovers in the doorway.

I return the greeting as I try to cool off, unsure why he's shooting daggers at me with his eyes. Realizing I'm still clutching my throat, I lower my hand. "Hey, Brad. Did I forget to email you? I thought I submitted the paperwork you requested for the system upgrade."

He scratches the back of his head and shakes his head. "No, I thought you might need... That you might want... Actually, never mind. You're right. You turned everything in."

Turning on his heel, he disappears around the partition.

Weird.

"Looks like your fanboy is jealous," Nicole says, motioning toward my flowers.

I can't help frowning. "What? No way. We don't have that kind of relationship. We're friends." While he might have asked me out when I first started this job, from all of our interactions since then, I thought he's been okay just being friends.

She shrugs. "Whatever. All I'm saying is he could give a shit about how many times my laptop freezes. He only ever asks you."

Huh. "Well, we've chatted a few times, and we've had coffee once or twice on our lunch breaks. Maybe he's just having a bad day."

"Or maybe he's lamenting the day little Maddie got herself a boyfriend."

She swivels back to her desk, and butterflies take flight in my stomach. *Boyfriend.* Is that what Daren is?

I try all day to keep that smile to a minimum, but it's parked on my face like a Broadway billboard.

CHAPTER 29

DAREN

"Earth to Daren. Hello, douchebag."

My best friend Jax stares at me across my kitchen table.

"What?" I ask, confused why he looks so pissed. I just fed the man.

"If you check your phone one more time, I'm gonna shove it up your ass."

I roll my eyes with a laugh.

When a text comes in a minute later—the fifth one like this today—I start to get pissed. Glaring at Jax, I point my phone at him. "Did you sign me up to get porn pics sent to my phone? Or to get offers for sex"—I hold up my phone to read—"'in your area. Discreet and convenient.'"

He barks out a laugh. "No, but I wish I had. That's hysterical."

"I've been getting them all day. I wonder if Quentin did this." But really, this isn't his style. Quentin would roll up on the corner with three girls and offer me one. "Fuck. I need to change my number."

Jax asks for my phone, and I hand it to him.

"Won't Dani mind that you're looking at porn?" I ask, deciding I need to give him shit.

He laughs and shakes his head. "Dude, she watches it with me. She rocks my world. And anyway, her bod is way hotter. And the bonus? She won't melt if she stands too close to the radiator."

Okay then.

He tosses my phone back at me, and after I delete the text and block the number, I stare down at it, waiting for the one text I *do* want. I know the florist should have delivered the arrangement by now, but Maddie hasn't called or texted, and I'm starting to get worried I went overboard.

Jax is talking, and I nod back at him. Then he murmurs, "I'm a hoe and I want to give you a blow."

I nod again.

"Put your man nipples away. They're turning me on."

I stare at him. "What?"

"Exactly, dickhead. You're not listening." He glares at me a long minute before tossing a napkin at my head.

"Sorry. I guess I'm a little distracted."

"Ya think?" He chuckles. "This has to be about a girl."

"Why do you assume that? Maybe I'm waiting on a call from my agent."

"This can't be football because you're usually serious as fuck about it, and it can't be about that cunt Veronica because she just pisses you off."

"Hey, don't call her that." I might still be pissed at her, but that's no excuse to call a woman that word.

He places his hand over his heart. "So sorry. Let me rephrase. It can't be about that *bitchface* Veronica."

Like that's better. I shake my head, not interested in talking about her anymore. Or ever again for that matter.

"This has nothing to do with her. She's off, hopefully getting her life together. I wish her well." Even as I say those words, I realize I don't mean them. Not yet. I'm still too angry. But I know myself, and someday, I think I will mean it. At least, I hope I will.

He gives me a look and then rolls his eyes. "I'm not gonna

recount all the ways that chick made you miserable. She even made you stop calling my sister by the nickname you gave her when you guys were in diapers."

Emmie. I couldn't say Clem or Clementine when I was little, so she was my Emmie. After she and I worked through our baggage last fall, Veronica pitched a fit, making me swear I'd never call my ex-girlfriend by that nickname. I'm not sure why it was so important to her. Maybe it suggested too much familiarity. I don't know. But the one time I slipped, Veronica threw a plate across my kitchen, shattering it against the wall.

Jax makes a face. "I'm just glad you got both of your heads straight."

He would think I was with Veronica for some weird sex reason. But in the last year we were together, she and I barely slept together. We were too busy arguing.

"Was it over my sister? Because you guys started talking again?" Jax asks, lowering his voice, sounding almost regretful. But that's crazy, because Jax would never feel bad over me breaking up with Veronica.

I rub the back of my neck. "That was part of it, I guess. But you and Clementine are two of my best friends. My oldest friends. And if Veronica didn't understand my need to work through things with Clem, then she never understood the kind of person I want to be." Sighing only partially eases the ache that still lingers. "You and your twin sister are a package deal. It sucked only having you around. No offense."

"Ouch, bro." He gives me a pained grimace, and I toss a crouton at his head, which he dodges with a laugh.

"How's your girl doing?" I ask, hoping his favorite subject turns this conversation into something less depressing before I put my head in the oven. "And please don't tell me any more shit about the two of you and porn," I mumble under my breath.

His eyes light and he smiles a big, goofy grin. "Dani's fucking awesome. What can I say? I love her."

I laugh and grab my Gatorade bottle for a drink. "Have you guys set a date?" Shockingly enough, my former manslut best friend fell in love last year with his sister's roommate. Taking the saying "Go Hard or Go Home" seriously, he asked Dani to marry him during half time at a Celtics game while on the kissing cam.

"No, we're gonna wait until she's done with school, and I can finish out my first season."

Nodding, I can't help but be proud of him. He got recruited to play pro soccer, and for the first time ever, he's focused on all of the right things.

"Remind me to thank Dani for setting you straight."

He laughs. "I do it every day."

Aww, shit. There he goes, getting that little lovesick look in his eyes again.

I clear my throat, deciding to come clean after Jax's little display of affection for Dani. "So... I've *maybe* met someone."

His hand freezes midway between his plate and his open mouth. "I knew it!" He slams his fist down with a laugh. "And she's not some she-devil lunatic parading as a normal human being?"

"She's pretty awesome, actually." I'm tempted to tell him more, but it's still early, and I promised Maddie to keep us under wraps. Although we made that agreement when we were just sleeping together, I'm hoping last night changed something for her. It did for me.

"And?" He drops his fork and waits.

"And nothing. She's a friend, and I like her. She's really talented and funny and driven. She has her shit together, and I enjoy spending time with her."

Silence settles between us until his lip turns up into something that resembles a snarl. "Dude, that's all you're gonna give me? For real?"

"Sorry, man."

He holds his hands up. "Fine. I won't pry because you're obviously serious about this girl." Then his eyebrow lifts. "But she's hot, right?"

"Fuck, yes, she's hot. Now stop digging."

We eat in silence, and then he chuckles. "I bet she's psyched about your bachelor contest, huh?"

Oh, hell.

That stupid thing. I wish I could just donate money to the St. Martin's Homeless Shelter like I have in the past, but my financial situation isn't the same anymore, and I have to budget more carefully.

But hopefully the contest doesn't upset Maddie. Besides, she has a front row seat. She's one of the hosts of the event, so I know she understands why I'm doing this.

Even so, I wish we could date like normal people and not have everything we do scrutinized.

I nod at Jax. "It'll be cool. I'm sure we can handle it." I hope.

CHAPTER 30

MADDIE

THE DOOR to Daren's condo whips open as I lift my hand to knock, and I jerk back, surprised to see Jax on the other side.

"Maddie!" Jax says, a smirk on his face once he realizes who I am. His eyes shift to Daren, and he says something under his breath.

"Hey, Jax. Long time no see. How's it going?"

"It's going well. I love those segments you've been doing with dickhead here. You do a good job of making him look like a stud." Then he elbows Daren with a laugh.

Glancing back and forth between the two of them, I'm almost certain they're having a full-on dude conversation without saying a word.

I take in Daren's faded jeans and snug gray t-shirt. Gah! Just the way it clings to his chest makes my mouth water. "Clutch does a pretty good job of looking like a stud without my help."

A huge, dimpled smile spreads on Daren's lips, and I'm pretty sure that look alone is enough to dissolve the panties from a girl's body.

Jax starts to punch Daren again, but Daren gets one in first, and then in a split second, he has Jax in a headlock.

"What were you saying, asshole?" Daren asks Jax in a sweet voice.

"Your momma."

They both crack up, and Jax shoves off his buddy.

Daren dusts off his hands and says, "Don't talk about my momma. She changed your diaper when you were little." He smacks the back of Jax's head. "She's seen your wee willy winky, so shut the fuck up."

"Thanks for that reminder." Jax shivers and makes a face as he grabs his crotch.

"Okay, boys. This is a fascinating study in male bonding, but I need to go in a minute, so…" I look to Daren, and he nods.

He turns to Jax, yanks him in for a quick hug with a slap on his back, and then tells him to get the fuck out. A second later, he's pulling me into his condo, shoving his buddy out and slamming the door.

"You're a dick, but I love you," Jax shouts from the other side.

"Love you too, sweetheart. See you next week," Daren yells back before he turns to me, a coy expression playing on his lips.

"Hey."

"Hey."

We stare at each other, the room quiet in a way that emphasizes how loudly my heart is beating. *Jesus, calm down.*

Then we both start talking at the same time.

"Thank you so much for the flowers."

"I'm sorry if the flowers were too much."

We stare at one another again and laugh.

Why am I playing it safe? Stop being so damn rigid, Maddie.

I clear my throat. "This is stupid, Daren."

His head tilts to one side, his expression suddenly serious.

Stepping closer, I wrap my arms around his neck. His hands automatically fall to my waist.

It's hard to miss the relief in his eyes. "What's stupid, baby?"

Even though I should probably tell him not to send me

anything at work, the bouquet was such a thoughtful gesture that I can't bring myself to do it. No, what I want to do is kiss him senseless.

I stand on my tiptoes and press my lips to his, and his fingers tighten on my hips. "Why would you apologize? I loved the flowers." I kiss him again and lean into his big, hard body. "No one has ever sent me lavender roses before. They're beautiful. Breathtaking."

He whips me around until I'm pressed against the door, and his hand goes to my hair, tugging until my lips fall open, so he can kiss me deeply. So deeply I feel it like a tidal wave in my girlie parts.

"Mmm." I lean back and smile, loving how he fills my vision. "I wish I could get naked with you, but I have some research to do tonight, and I'm afraid if I indulge in your brand of orgasms, I won't be able to function."

He chuckles as I kiss him again, and then I nuzzle into his neck, taking a moment to breathe in his crisp cologne that's faded but still smells so yummy I can almost taste it. Plus, I'm squirmy, that pulse between my legs going a million miles an hour.

"It's okay. I need to study some film. Wanna work here? I promise not to violate you before ten p.m."

"That sounds perfect." I kiss his neck and then break away from him before I give into my overwhelming urge to strip naked and do it against his door. "Let me run home and change into something more comfortable, and I'll grab us some snacks." I really don't want to hang out in a suit and heels.

His eyebrow lifts. "How comfortable are we talking? Like, pasties and a thong comfortable?"

I laugh and smack him playfully on the arm. "No, goofball. Yoga pants and a t-shirt." I lean in for one more quick kiss before I head for the door. "We'll save the pasties and thong for the weekend." Then I give him a wink before I run back to my place.

CHAPTER 31

MADDIE

WE NEVER SAY we're more, but our early agreement seems too rigid for what we are. I mean, we're definitely friends, and I'm wholeheartedly enjoying the benefits, but somehow Daren seems more like a boyfriend than anyone else I've ever dated.

Maybe it's the way he smiles at me when he thinks I'm not looking. Or the way he puts my feet in his lap while he's studying film. Or even how he likes to wrap his arm around me when we're watching TV. Whatever this is, I like it.

Sometimes I stay over. Most of the time, though, I go home. I don't want to make assumptions, so I try to take it day by day despite my typical need to plan out my life in five-year increments. But I love that he always tells me to stay.

And while I want to define what we have, I'm afraid to burst our bubble, to mess with our equilibrium. So we don't talk about what we are, and we don't share how we feel.

I shake my head, determined to keep this simple. What we have works, and it's two parts thrilling and one part terrifying, but I've decided to be a big girl and trust him. Because even though we're sleeping together, I've come to think of him as my friend first and not just my lover.

The weight of his stare catches my attention.

"I don't know what you think you're doing, Clutch, but it's not working."

His laughter tells me I'm right.

Even though I don't look up, I know Daren is watching me. I ignore him, but I can't hide my smile. We're hanging out at his place another evening. I told him if we worked for another hour, I'd play *Plants and Zombies*. After that one win, I've been on a huge losing streak, but I like to talk smack, and he's too much fun to rile up. I love how serious he gets. How his jaw tightens and his lips thin out. Even how he yells at the screen. Boys and their video games.

At least it's something fun we can do while we're camped out at his place. It's one of the self-imposed restrictions we've made. We can't go anywhere public. If we're seen together in any kind of social setting, that could suggest we're involved romantically. Spencer made a lewd comment about us after taping our weekly segment, which I don't totally understand. The jerk told me to flirt, to make Daren seem appealing.

Maybe I'm doing it too well.

My stomach twists. I hate sneaking around. I've finally given in to biting my nails again, which means I have to hold the mic a certain way on camera so you can't see how neurotic I've become.

One thing is for certain. I can't blow this. I might be moonlighting as a sports reporter, but if I'm to be taken seriously in news, I can't be seen having an affair with the guy I'm covering each week.

Despite how guilty I feel for breaking nearly every rule in my profession by having this relationship, I know Daren is different. I know this means something. What, I'm not sure, but I want to find out. Because maybe down the road, when I'm not covering his team and he's not my weekly feature, we could happen for real.

Football season only lasts five months. I just have to get through this one season. And then… maybe.

So here we sit at Daren's another evening.

I actually love it. I'm so used to toiling by myself—working on articles or researching stories—it's nice to have someone to keep me company.

Besides, Daren is usually wiped after practice anyway, so we veg out in sweats and try to prepare for the following day.

Except right now, Daren isn't studying his playbook. He's staring. At me.

When I look up, he glances away and returns to his McDonald's sundae.

The man has the appetite of a T-Rex. I've learned to get *dozens* of eggs and *loaves* of bread when I go shopping. While he eats pretty healthy generally, tonight he splurged and made a quick snack run, which he claimed would help him study his playbook. I called bull, but he kissed me on the nose and promised to get me a Dunkin' Donuts iced coffee, so I gave him a free pass.

But now he's not studying. He's staring. Again.

I don't look up from my laptop. "What?" I mumble on the pen I'm chewing. Ick. I'm chewing a pen, but the jerk's making me nervous.

"You look cute all serious over there." I can hear the smile in his voice, but it's only nine, which means we should work another hour before any nighttime activities begin. But his cologne is wafting over, and I'm dying to run my nose over his neck.

I squirm in my seat. God, just the thought has me on edge.

"I can't focus when you're staring at me, Clutch."

"Wanna bite?" He dips his spoon into his chocolate sundae. It has nuts sprinkled on top.

Mmm, I would commit an assortment of crimes for a bite of ice cream, but I've missed a couple of workouts this week, and Spencer will freak if I gain any weight.

When I decline, he frowns. "Stop thinking about calories, Maddie. You're fucking perfect. Your body is a testament that God exists."

I can't help smiling. "Okay, Sloan, that was a good one." I take a break from my screen that's starting to get blurry from staring at it so long and face him. Daren's just wearing sweats and a plain white t-shirt that stretches taut over his muscular chest, but heaven help me, he makes cotton look good. What is it about this guy in t-shirts?

Even decked out in something this casual, he's sinfully sexy. His hair is damp from a shower, and it hangs into those flirty hazel eyes. His skin is tan from long afternoons in the sun, and I want to run my lips over those strong cheekbones and down his stubbled jaw.

With a mischievous grin on his face, he scoots over until we're thigh to thigh, and then he scoops up a big bite and raises it to me. But just as I'm leaning forward and opening my mouth, he pulls away and eats it.

"What the eff?"

He laughs. "What the eff? Babe, I've hard you say all kinds of dirty things when we're together, so I know you can do better than that."

"Fine," I huff. "What the fuck, Daren? Give me a bite right now."

He holds up his sundae, a devilish glint in his eyes. "So you want it in your mouth?"

My face burns and my jaw drops open. No one has ever talked to me like Daren. He can turn my most innocent statements into something sexual. And I won't lie. I like it.

I take a breath. "Yes… I want it in my mouth."

He sets the spoon on the coffee table before he dips his finger in the ice cream, but as he brings it near me, I eye him skeptically, wondering if he's going to whip it away again. Instead, he dabs it across my lips.

"That's a good look for you."

My thighs clench. I know full well he's trying to turn me on. It's working. Well, two can play this game.

"Mmm," I groan, slowly licking my lips. "It's sweet. And kind of salty. Just the way I like it."

He's not smiling anymore.

But I am.

Daren dips his finger back in the sundae and brings it to my mouth. I lick the tip and smile before I open wider and suck him deeper. A little moan escapes me as I reach up and guide his finger in and out, making sure to keep my eyes trained on him as I swirl my tongue around him.

His nostrils flare, his breath hot on my cheek as he leans closer. When I release him from my mouth, I smack my lips and raise my eyebrow. "I'm sorry. You were saying?"

Next thing I know, my laptop is gone and I'm horizontal on the floor with one very large Daren Sloan hovering over me.

Now I'm the one gasping as he knees my legs wider to nestle between my legs where I feel him hard against my thigh. My legs wrap around his waist, pulling him down so I can thread my fingers through his hair.

"Maddie," he whispers just before our lips meet.

He rolls against me, and the feeling is so exquisite my back strains to arch against his huge body.

He kisses down my neck, stopping to bite me just hard enough that I know it'll be red when we're done but gone by morning. Every light suck sends a pulse between my legs, and in about two seconds, I'm dying for more.

"What are you doing to me?" His words come out strained, like it's been torture to admit.

Suddenly, it's a race to see how fast we can get our clothes off. I'm ripping off his shirt, and he's tugging down my pants. I'm pulling at him to feel his weight on me again, and he's squeezing my ass in that way that tells me he's unraveling.

185

When his mouth connects with my nipple, he grips my wrists and yanks them above my head, holding me down with one massive hand while the other finds its way into my panties.

"I'm really wet." I don't know why I feel the need to state the obvious.

He grunts his approval before plunging two thick fingers into me.

My eyes are about to roll back into my head when he taps that spot. He always knows just where to touch. Just how to stroke.

But when I lean back, something out of the corner of my eye makes me flinch.

"Babe, what's wrong?" he asks, stilling his movement. His eyes follow mine to stare at my laptop.

"Nothing... Nothing." I laugh. "God, I'm being paranoid." I tug my arm down and throw it over my face. I'm out of breath and pissed at myself for ruining this moment. "I could have sworn the camera light on my laptop was on. I'm just... being paranoid."

He pulls my arm down and places a quick kiss on my forehead before he gently disengages from between my legs. Then he lunges over and slams down my laptop with the back of his hand.

"There." He turns back to me and licks his fingers. "Where were we?"

"Oh my God. Did you just lick me off your hand?"

"Yup." He grins. "Wanna taste?" But instead of using his fingers, he kisses me long and deep, my tangy flavor mixing with his usual minty taste.

"You're dirty," I pant, wrapping my legs around his waist. "I like it."

He thrusts against me as we kiss, and when he nudges at my entrance, every part of me is screaming to take him bare, but before I get the chance to tell him, he's reaching for a condom.

Sitting back on his haunches, he rolls it on before flipping me over on my stomach. The thick area rug beneath me feels coarse against my sensitive skin.

"Here." He tucks a soft chenille throw under my face. I turn back to look at him, wondering why he thinks I need this. He grins. "Don't want you to get rug burn."

I laugh, a little touched by his thoughtfulness and a whole lot turned on by the prospect of whatever we're about to do that would include rug burn.

Daren lifts my hips and then scoots a pillow underneath me to raise my ass up. His hands ghost over my back before his lips kiss a trail down my spine.

My blood is thrumming in my veins, my skin on fire from his touch when he parts my cheeks and drifts a finger down between my legs.

The sound of me panting seems so loud, and I'm burning, desperate for more. I scoot my ass up higher, and his teeth bite into my skin.

Argh. Yes!

Everything about this seems so wrong, so filthy. And I'm desperate for more.

He widens my legs and settles between my thighs, skating his length back and forth across my wet skin. He pushes against my entrance only to back off again.

Damn, he's such a tease.

I moan his name and dig my fingers into the carpet. Then he utters those words.

"What do you want, baby?"

I don't think about it. I don't have to. "Your cock. Fill me, Daren. Fuck me."

He makes a sound in the back of his throat as his fingers spread me wider, and he pushes his thick hard length in all at once.

A gasp escapes my mouth, the feeling too intense, riding that border between pleasure and pain. He eases out of me while he grips my hips to hold me still and then thrusts back in.

"You're so deep." I stretch my arms above my head, relishing the fullness. "Fuck, I can't take it."

He groans when he enters me again. "You should see how good you look like this." His hand comes down in a hard smack on my ass, and I flinch, not expecting the contact. But oh my God, it feels so good, the sting a direct pulse to my clit. He must agree because he does it again.

His big body stills. I close my eyes, so turned on, I could light on fire right now. When I realize he's massaging my inner thighs, squeezing my skin around him, pressing me around him and then somehow opening me wider, I start to mewl into the carpet.

Holy shit. Yes.

His fingers press into me and him at the same time, and I know he's watching the whole show. Knowing he's seeing our bodies connect this way has me thrusting back.

What's he doing to me? I've never felt so good before.

But then he trails his wet thumb up higher to my back entrance, and presses down lightly, and I swear I see constellations behind my eyes.

"Oh, God." I've never entertained getting any action there before Daren, but his teasing touch has me clenching down on his cock.

His thrusts resume, but his thumb never leaves my backside. He presses harder and harder as his rhythm speeds up, and when he bridges that tight ring of muscles, I come undone, screaming into the carpet. He follows a moment later, pulsing hot and thick inside me as I quake from this epic orgasm.

A few minutes later, we're still sprawled on the floor, a tangle of arms and legs.

"Don't go home. Stay with me tonight, Maddie." His voice is hoarse and rough, just barely above a whisper.

His head rests between my breasts, and I thread my fingers through his hair. "Are you sure? I don't want to be one of those girls."

When he looks up at me, he's frowning. "What are you talking about?"

"You know, one of those girls who takes over your closet and bathroom, leaving tampons where you expect to find your aftershave."

He laughs. "Sweet thing, I can barely get you to leave your toothbrush here. Trust me, you're in no danger of outstaying your welcome. Leave all the tampons you want."

His eyes grow pensive, and I brush the hair out of his face. "What's on your mind?"

He pauses, and I wonder if he's going to answer me, but then he says, "I'll be on the road soon."

I nod, knowing that his season is about to get crazy. My chest squeezes, and I blink back unexpected heat in my eyes. "I know. I'll miss you."

The tension in his face relaxes. "I'll miss you too." He kisses me, and it's soft and sweet, and makes my heart ache with his tenderness. When he pulls away, I miss those lips even though they've been pressed to my body all night.

He slumps on me again, and I wrap all my limbs around him, loving how he keeps me warm, loving how sated I feel. We stay, tangled together until his breathing is slow and steady. Finally, I slap his naked but very firm ass.

"Okay, Sloan. You're putting my extremities to sleep."

He grunts and starts to lift off me. When he raises his arms above his head in a catlike stretch, I'm treated to six feet three inches of a very naked man of steel. Ripped shoulders lead to strong pecs. He's built but not overly so. Not abnormally bulky like some athletes.

But he's a big boy. With big boy parts. One part in particular gets my attention as my eyes drift down his washboard stomach. Wowzers.

He lets me look, a sly grin lighting his eyes. "I'm thinking we might need to put your laptop camera to good use when I'm gone."

"Mm. So you want to have Skype sex? Is that what you're saying?" I tear my eyes off his nakedness and look up.

"I think that's a damn good idea. I bet you have some good moves for me. Especially since you've been watching all that porn lately."

I gasp. "I have not been watching lots of porn." Okay, maybe I've watched a little, but I've rationalized it as research for my assignment.

He laughs, loving that he can get a rise out of me. I enjoy the show as he turns and heads toward his room.

"Get in my bed, McDermott," he calls out, not giving me an option to go home.

I grin, and yell back. "Are you going to behave tomorrow? You can't grab my ass like you did last week." Even though no one was around, we can't take any chances. We can't be so touchy-feely when I interview him.

His voice echoes down the hall. "But I like grabbing your ass. I consider it the highlight of my day."

Me too, Clutch. Me too.

CHAPTER 32

MADDIE

WE WERE SUPPOSED to go straight to bed, but forty-five minutes later, I feel like I just ran a marathon. "I think I'm going to skip my workout tomorrow." My throat is hoarse. From screaming. My head rests on his shoulder, and we're both sweaty and still panting.

"You just burned like two thousand calories. I think you're good to go." He rubs my back, and I let out a sigh, feeling deeply sated.

"You should teach a class on how to give a girl an orgasm. Or three."

He laughs. "C'mon. I'm sure it's not that difficult to do, though I'll take the praise."

Perhaps it's the sex-induced coma talking, but I just come out and say it. "No, it's actually quite an accomplishment. I've never come three times in a row before I met you. Jacob was lucky if he got me there once."

Daren's quiet. God, why did I say that? We never talk about our exes.

He clears his throat. "What happened between you two? Why didn't it work out?"

I roll my lips, grateful it's dark in here. "He had a penchant for sex with other girls, and I walked in on him getting a blow job from a cage girl."

"Fuck."

"What about you? What happened with Veronica?"

Daren blows out a breath, releasing me to run his hands through his hair. "It's late. You sure you want that story now?"

He's either trying to dodge or he's exhausted. But the thought that he doesn't want to answer makes me think he's hiding something. Feeling suddenly vulnerable, I pluck myself off his chest. "No. It's fine. You don't have to tell me."

Straining to look around the room, I spot my clothes on the floor and start to get up when his hand comes around my arm. "C'mere."

I sit on the bed, debating what to do.

"Maddie, get your ass back here."

I shake my head. "It's cool. I'll see you later."

"Fuck, woman." Two seconds later, I'm on my back again. "Stay. The. Night." He tucks me to his chest and threads his fingers through my hair. "We didn't love each other. That's what happened." When he sighs, his grip on me loosens, and his head dips back into his pillow. "It's a long story, and when I tell you the whole thing, I'm pretty sure you're going to think I'm an ass."

"That's possible."

He laughs humorlessly. "Veronica and I got together in high school. But it's not some childhood sweetheart story."

His body is taut, and he's radiating tension. I should let him out of his misery. "Look, I know it had something to do with Clementine. I read her book."

Another tight laugh escapes him. "Awesome. Well, then. You know I'm a dick." With that, he releases me and tucks his arms behind his head, like he's resigned to whatever judgment I deem appropriate.

I roll my eyes and scoot over, dropping onto the pillow next to him before I turn to face him. "Tell me the story." I run my palm over his cheek. "It was a long time ago. Whatever happened, I want to hear your side of things. It's worse if you just let me wonder about it."

Because if he doesn't tell me, I know where this relationship, or whatever this is, is headed—nowhere.

I only need one thing from him. Honesty. And if we can't do this now, I won't delude myself into thinking we'll figure it out later.

Steeling myself, I prepare to go home, prepare to let this thing between us go—anywhere but where I was secretly hoping it was headed.

Closing his eyes, he sighs. "Fine. But don't say I didn't warn you."

CHAPTER 33

DAREN

THIS CONVERSATION HAS every chance of ending with Maddie walking out the door and never coming back. Especially given how she caught her ex.

It figures I'd find myself in this position. And I can fully admit I deserve it. I find myself bracing for the worst because when karma fucks you up the ass, she's not gentle.

Clearing my throat, I start at the beginning. "I can't really tell you about Veronica without explaining my relationship with Clementine."

I wonder if this will be weird, for me to talk about someone who has become Maddie's friend too, but when I glance at Maddie, she nods.

Returning my attention to the ceiling, I stare at the long streak of light streaming in from the street. "Clem, Jax, and I grew up together. As I'm sure you gathered from reading Clem's book, their parents are epic assholes, so they spent a lot of time at my house. We lived next door."

Maddie's quiet, and the pressure of what I need to say weighs on me like a concrete slab. "Clementine and I didn't get together until our senior year in high school. We'd joke about dating, but I

194

think we were both afraid it would change our dynamic. So, for the first three years of high school, we dated other people. But at the end of the night, we always ended up together, hanging out, goofing off. She and her brother would sneak into my room, and we'd stay up watching horror movies or playing video games."

"Sounds like fun," Maddie says softly.

"Yeah, we had a blast." I blow out a breath, not wanting to continue, but knowing I need to. "So Clem's best friend was this chick Veronica, and she and I did *not* get along. She seriously annoyed the shit out of me. Freshman year, we argued all the time, and it sucked because Clem and Veronica were often a package deal. As we got older, I'd end up having to drive Veronica home because she didn't have a car. I didn't want Clem to have to do it in the middle of the night, and Jax would never do it because he never fucking liked her. Anyway, after a few years of playing chauffeur, I guess Veronica and I got to know each other better. We stopped arguing as much. She stopped trying to get a rise out of me. By senior year, I suppose we had become friends."

"Hmm."

I don't bother to look at Maddie because I'm positive she's silently calling me an idiot. And she'd be right.

"I'm not sure if you know this about Clem because she's pretty private now, but in high school, she was the 'it' girl. The party followed her. She was homecoming queen. Prom queen. Student Council president. I forget what else. Oh, she was like a state champion runner. The girl had more talents than she knew what to do with. All of this meant she was pretty fucking busy. Busier than me, which is saying something because football was all-consuming. On more than one night, Veronica would go to her house, find she wasn't home yet, and come hang out with me. When you're seventeen and stupid, this makes sense. In retrospect, I'm guessing she came early on purpose."

Scrubbing my face, I take a deep breath. "This all meant

Veronica and I ended up spending way more time together than we should have. Because I adored Clementine. Worshiped the ground she walked on. And I suppose I was just being an insecure jackass because one night while she was over waiting for Clem, Veronica told me it was all one-sided. That Clem didn't feel the same about me that I did about her, but that she didn't know how to break it to me. Veronica pointed to the fact that Clem committed to BU early action and never considered attending BC with me even though it has a great writing program, which is what she wanted to do. Now, you might say that our schools are only forty minutes away on the D-line, but Veronica seemed to think this meant something. That this was Clem's way of letting me down easy because she didn't know how to break up with me."

I venture a glance at Maddie, half wondering if she's asleep because she's so quiet. But she's wrapped around a pillow. Her large blue eyes, which look black, widen. "Sounds like Veronica was manipulating you."

Shrugging, I sigh and roll onto my side to face Maddie. "Yeah. But it doesn't matter. I was stupid. A smart person would have realized Clem had a lot on her plate and would have expressed what I was feeling to her, but I guess I just started shutting down too. Whatever the case, I suppose the bigger issue was the fact that Clem was not into public displays of affection. I mean, the girl would barely let me hold her hand. Knowing her family, none of this should have surprised me. Her mother is an ice queen, so I couldn't blame Clem for not being affectionate. From reading her book, you know she was a virgin, too, and I didn't want to be an ass and pressure her. She said she felt weird because she obviously knew a lot of the girls I had slept with before we dated, and she felt inexperienced. It kind of bugged her out. But I gotta say that after a while, after months of her growing more and more distant, it got me thinking about what Veronica told me."

Memories flood back to me, stinging with a bittersweet ache. "Anyway, that spring everything went to shit." Thinking about it makes me mildly nauseous. Clem and I may have worked through the past, but if I could visit my high school self and kick my own ass, I would.

Maddie brushes my hair out of my face. "What happened?" she whispers.

What happened? I nearly ruined one of the best friendships I've ever had.

I blow out a breath. "It was a strange week. Every time I saw Clem, she was busy. She wasn't calling me back. She seemed preoccupied when I did see her. Of course, Veronica *was* around, and she suggested that Clem liked some other guy because we saw them talking in the hall. It was all probably innocuous stuff, but our distance had been growing, and it was starting to get under my skin. I missed Clem, my best friend. I missed hanging out with her. Being around her. Not worrying about hugging her. That's what's so strange. Before we were dating, I hugged her all the time. We goofed around. I'd carry her on my back. We'd laugh at everything. But that all stopped senior year. It was like she was a different person when we were dating. I guess I was too. I was training really hard and talking to coaches at different colleges, but it sucked that our dynamic changed so dramatically."

I'm quiet, letting the memories wash over me. Maddie threads her fingers through mine. "You don't have to tell me any more if you don't want to."

"Nah, babe. You should probably hear this. You know Clem, and I don't want shit to be weird between us. It's just... I've never talked about it before."

She stills. "Really? Not even with Jax?"

"Especially not with Jax." He had a front row seat for most of it. I'm sure he doesn't want a blow-by-blow.

I rub my chin, the scruff scraping my palm. Closing my eyes, I can see the whole thing in slow motion. "It was late spring. After school, I had to see a doctor to get the results of a physical so I could participate in a summer training camp. As I was going over the results with him, I noticed my blood type, which is B. And for some reason that caught my attention. Because I knew my parents were both type A."

It was a moment that rocked my world off its axis, and I'm sure the man had no idea. "I mentioned that to the doctor, and he laughed and told me that was impossible. That I must be mistaken because there's no way two type-A parents could have a type-B kid."

"Oh, shit." Maddie's hand tightens in mine.

A weak laugh escapes me. "See, the reason I remember Clementine not being around at the time is because I was going out of my mind trying to figure out what that all meant. I mean, who the fuck were my parents? Did my mother cheat on my father? Was she even my mother? I tore through damn near every photo album in the house looking for similarities. Looking for some sign that I was who they claimed I was."

I haven't thought about this shit in so long, it feels foreign. Like I've come home to a closet full of clothes I haven't worn in years that don't quite fit anymore.

Maddie whispers, "Why didn't you talk to Jax about what was going on with your parents?"

"Dating Clementine had changed the dynamic for all three of us. So Jax and I weren't tight that spring. And Jax had some girl drama of his own at the time."

"He never told you what that was?"

I shake my head. "Which made me think it was pretty bad because he went from dating one girl senior year to sleeping with everything in a fifty-mile radius. But he was pretty pissed at me for what went down with his sister that spring. We didn't talk again for almost a year. If he and I hadn't ended up at the same college, I'm pretty sure we wouldn't be friends now."

I'm quiet, feeling sucked into the past, something I try not to think about.

A few minutes later, Maddie rolls closer until her lips press into my shoulder. She doesn't say anything, and I'm pretty sure she doesn't expect me to continue, except now I need to. Now, I want to get it off my chest.

I clear my throat. "That week, I asked my mom what her blood type was. I lied and told her it was for a project at school, a genetics assignment where we had to analyze our traits to see which parent was dominant genetically. I was trying to gauge her reaction. Well, she looked like I had just set our house on fire. She mumbled something about being late for an appointment and almost sprinted out the door."

"Ugh. That's rough." Maddie scoots closer, and I lift my arm to tuck her against me.

"My dad runs a Fortune 500 company. This isn't shit you can just go around talking about. I was a mess, trying to figure out which of my parents was the liar. Which one let me think I was theirs. I was so fucking pissed. My dad was always talking about me inheriting the hotel that he inherited from my grandfather. Who, it turns out, is not really my grandfather."

"Jesus. Daren. I'm so sorry."

While every part of me loathes this story, it's strangely comforting to finally tell someone. I hold Maddie a little tighter, knowing what comes next.

"All I knew that day was that one of my parents had lied to me my whole life. I walked around in a daze. You know how you can space out when you're driving familiar roads? End up at a certain spot with no recollection of getting there? My whole day was like that. I didn't remember going to class, but I must have. I don't remember getting in the car, but obviously I had. All I remember is sitting at a traffic light. It was raining, pouring. And for some reason, I glanced to the side and saw Veronica waiting at the bus stop. She had an umbrella, but it didn't help much. She looked like a wet cat. So I rolled down my window and told her to get in."

I press my lips together, wondering if shit would've turned out differently if I hadn't given her that ride. "I should have just driven away, let the girl catch the bus. But I felt bad for her. And, really, deep down, I think I wanted to destroy shit. Burn everything down to the ground. You know Newton's Law of Motion? For every action, there is an equal and opposite reaction? I had always had a great life. Been on top of my shit. Been the star athlete, made my parents proud. This, this moment was the rubber band snapping back. Because it all felt like a fucking joke. So when I pulled up behind Veronica's house, and she gave me those big puppy-dog eyes and told me how much she missed me, how she wouldn't treat me the way Clementine did, I thought fuck it. Fuck it all. And I lit the match."

* * *

MAYBE IT'S BEEN EASIER to talk about this because we're lying in bed in the dark. But now, I want to see Maddie's face, to gauge how much I disgust her. So I loosen my grip on her shoulder and wait.

She sighs. So much can be said in a sigh.

I imagine the worst is going through her mind. But then she surprises me and tightens her arm on my chest.

"How long did this go on?" she asks quietly.

"Few weeks." I blow out a breath. "I felt like shit every day I didn't tell Clementine. And in those rare moments I forgot and then suddenly remembered what I was doing, it was like the air got sucked out of my lungs." Groaning, I shake my head. "Veronica and I only slept together that one time, and then there were a couple of partial hookups that always began with me intending to do the right thing and break things off. I needed to come clean to Clem. I planned to tell her everything. When I told

Veronica we had to stop, that I had to tell Clem, she freaked out. Threw a vase at my head and swore she'd tell her first. But it didn't matter because Clem found out anyway."

"I know. It's in her book."

"Yes, it is. So in case I want to think it wasn't as bad as I imagined, I can flip that fucker open and confirm how big of an asshole I was."

Maddie laughs softly, and I'm surprised she finds any humor in the situation. Because I feel nauseous walking down memory lane.

She rolls onto her stomach and leans up on my chest. "Yes, you were an asshole. But I can see you were going through a lot." Silence lingers between us, and I take a strand of her silky black hair between my fingers. "Maybe you didn't handle it well, but we all do dumb things in a crisis." She's quiet again, and I'm still reeling from the fact that she hasn't run out the door yet. "So what happened with Veronica? You guys obviously stayed together."

"Yeah. For all the wrong reasons."

"What do you mean?"

"When our friends found out what happened, people hated her. Even though I was just as responsible, no one gave me shit. Well, no one but Jax, but I welcomed that with open arms. Every bit of it." I tell her about the fight we had, how he almost broke my jaw. How he managed to avoid me our entire freshman year in college. "But it sucked anyway because he and Veronica never liked each other, so we couldn't all hang out once he and I worked through some of our issues." And not being able to hang out with your friends and your girlfriend blows.

Taking a big breath, I continue. Because I know I haven't answered Maddie's question. "We shouldn't have stayed together. But Veronica didn't have any friends at BC. And her home life was really bad. Alcoholic parents who bordered on abusive. At the very least, they were negligent. I felt like she needed someone, so I guess I was that someone. The only problem—well, there were a few—but the main one was she never trusted me. Since we had hooked up while I was dating Clementine, Veronica had me pegged as a cheater even though I never considered it. No matter how ugly our fights got, it never crossed my mind. I won't do that again to someone. But she just didn't trust me. And that shit gets exhausting. I got to the point where I needed someone who believed me, who believed in us."

Maddie rubs my chest, just over my heart, like she knows it hurts having to talk about the past. "It must have been a relief to finally talk to Clementine and tell her what happened with your parents."

I close my eyes, tilting my head back. "I never told her."

"What?" Maddie jerks against me, and I look up at her. Even in the darkness, I can see her frowning. "Why didn't you tell her what happened with the blood type?"

"I didn't want to give her excuses. I needed to own what happened and let her know it messed me up all these years not being friends with her. And I wanted to apologize for not being there for her in college when all that shit was going down with that professor." I sigh. "Truth? Before we talked last fall, I really had no idea Veronica was probably lying to me when she said my relationship with Clem was one-sided. All this time, I assumed it was true."

Maddie sits up more, pulling the sheet tighter over her chest. Is she leaving?

Her head slants to the side, and in the dim light, I can tell she's biting her lip. "You guys got engaged last fall, right?"

"Yeah." My gut burns at the thought.

She looks at me for a long moment. "So why get engaged if all you did was argue?"

I stare back, wishing I had a thousand different answers than the one that leave my lips. "I figured that's what you do when your girlfriend tells you she's pregnant."

Silence.

Long minutes stretch between us before she speaks. "What... What happened to the baby?"

The words feel bitter on my tongue. "There was no baby. She lied to keep me from breaking up with her and then later faked a miscarriage. She finally came clean about it the night of the draft."

"Jesus."

Maddie immediately wraps her arms around me. We lie there in silence, and then she swallows. "So you wanted a family?"

"Of course. You know, not right out of college, but at some point. But I never would have let her carry my child on her own, especially not with the shit that I went though with my parents."

Maddie nods, and I thread my fingers in her hair, loving how having her here dulls the pain of the past and makes me believe that I can have so much more in the future than what I had with Veronica.

"You're a good man. Maybe people don't tell you because they focus on your moves on the field, but you're a good person, Daren."

She presses a kiss to my chest, and I realize I've never had anyone like this, a woman in my life I could be so open with.

"I proposed to her before I realized how so much of our relationship was built on lies. So many fucking lies. It wasn't until talking to Clem, after we were already engaged, that I started really piecing it together." I laugh, humorlessly. "We probably never would've lasted, but I was willing to try for the sake of the baby. But between the deceit and Veronica hating football, it was too much. In college, maybe she initially liked the attention she got from dating me. But it wasn't all positive. Girls gave her a hard time. Told her all kinds of lies to get close to me. I know that wore her down. But at the end of the day, while I thought I loved her, the truth was I loved one thing more, and we never got past that."

"The game."

Nodding, I let out a breath, relieved that Maddie gets what I'm saying. "Yeah, she hated that I always put football first. It's not as though I ever promised her anything different. She knew my priorities."

"Hmm." Maddie runs her finger over the edge of the sheet. "Jacob hated how much I worked. He didn't understand that about me, which is crazy because he spent most of his days in the gym. But for some reason, it wasn't okay that I was as committed to my career as he was to his."

"How did you guys meet? What's the story?"

She groans and flops onto her back next to me, and I roll to face her. "My coworker got food poisoning. He sounded like he was on death's door, so I helped him cover his segment. I didn't know much about mixed martial arts, aside from the fact that they beat the hell out of each other in the ring. Anyway, I filmed Jacob's match and interviewed him afterward. And as soon as the camera stopped rolling, he asked me out."

"Didn't waste any time, did he?"

"No, he didn't. I guess I liked that. In college, guys never really asked me on dates. I was always working and not at the bars with my friends, so my social life was non-existent. Anyway, I liked that he was confident. We both grew up in Southie, so we had similar backgrounds. He's a few years older than I am. I didn't know him growing up, but once we started dating, I realized how our friends all kind of knew each other in one way or another." Blowing out a breath, she curls up on her side, and I brush the hair out of her face. "We had fun going out. But I was always taking on last-minute assignments, which would ruin our dates. He hated that. I can't say that I blame him, but it would've been nice if he had just broken up with me instead of banging girls behind my back."

I run my finger over her cheek. "I'm sorry he hurt you."

Pulling her closer, I kiss her forehead. "But I have to say I'm glad you guys broke up. Because now you're here."

A smile tilts her lips. "With you?"

"Yes, with me." I stroke her hair. "And you haven't run out of here screaming after hearing all my baggage, so I figure that's a good thing."

Her soft laugh strums my heart a little faster. "Everyone has baggage, Daren." Looking into her eyes, I don't see judgment. I don't see disdain. I see a friend. "It's learning not to make the same mistakes that matters."

"Maddie?"

Her eyes widen. "Yeah?"

"I'll try not to be one of your mistakes."

She arches up and gives me the sweetest smile before placing a kiss on my lips. "I have a feeling you won't be."

Reaching for a blanket, I pull it over us before I grab her and fit her to me. This girl has no idea, but I think I just fell for her a little harder.

CHAPTER 34

MADDIE

WHEN THE ALARM GOES OFF, I swear to God, I want to stab it. Repeatedly.

The obnoxious ring continues, but I can't move to turn the damn thing off. Exhausted, I peel open my eyes and realize I'm still at Daren's. He's half-draped on top of me, which is usually how we wake up when I stay over.

His face is pressed to my bare chest, his thigh draped over mine. I brush the hair out of his face—his beautiful, scruffy face. The face I would kiss right now if it weren't glued to my breasts.

I chuckle. "Hey, Clutch. I need to go to work." He doesn't budge, his deep breaths coming in a consistent rhythm. "Honey, come on." I finally shake him a little. "I need to go to work, but you're on top of me."

He groans. "But I like being on top of you."

Laughing, I attempt to roll him off again, but he squeezes me tighter and says in a sleepy voice, "Have a good day, babe. I'll miss you." He leans up and pecks me on my cheek before he flops onto his back and passes out again.

I love how easily he says those words. Little flutters of happiness bubble inside me.

He told me so much more than I expected last night. The man poured his heart out. I can't say it was easy to hear about his relationships with Clem and Veronica, but knowing I'm the first person he's ever opened up to about what happened in high school makes me think maybe we could really do this.

After a quick shower, I wrap a towel around me and dig around the living room, looking for my phone. I never walk off without it, but Daren and I got carried away. When I unlock it, I find four messages. *Shit.*

My leg jiggles as I listen. The first one has me in a panic. Roger wanted me to come in early, but by the last message, he had the problem under control. Another reporter is already covering my shift and I can work from home if I want. *Okay.*

I call Roger, just to be sure.

"Sorry for that first message, Maddie." He sounds distracted. Papers shuffle in the background.

"No problem. Sorry I couldn't make it. I accidentally left my phone in the living room and didn't hear it ring."

He yells at someone in the background and then coughs into the phone. "I'm serious about you working from home. I'm afraid I'm going to walk in one morning and find you keeled over your desk, dead from exhaustion, and I don't want to be held responsible for it."

A little laugh escapes me. "Are you sure? I can get a little done on that—"

"Keep your butt home. Or else. I'll see you tomorrow."

Before I can respond, he hangs up.

All righty.

After tossing on one of Daren's t-shirts, I grab a cup of coffee and settle down at his kitchen table. It's strange to have an unexpected free morning. I dare say it's delightful.

All of my stuff is here already, and rather than dragging everything home before I'm caffeinated, I opt to wake up and read through the headlines first. Powering up my laptop, I scroll through a few stories and jot down notes on some follow-up ideas.

My stomach gets the best of me after a while, and I wander to the refrigerator. When I glance at the clock, I realize it's much later than I expected. Almost eight-thirty. I figure Daren will be up soon and I decide to make us breakfast.

Daren.

God, I don't know why last night made such a difference, but the stupid butterflies in my stomach are rioting at the thought of him.

If someone had told me I'd be grateful I found my ex cheating on me, I would have laughed in their face. But right now, I am grateful because it brought me to this point. It brought me Daren.

Which reminds me.

Pulling out my phone again, I slide my finger over the images until I find the one I want. The one of Jacob and that girl.

And then I hit the delete button. Because that part of my life is over.

Feeling lighter than I have in months, I head back to the kitchen.

A stupid grin pulls at my lips as I pull out what I need from the fridge. Eggs, cheese, mushrooms, tomatoes. I crack several eggs in a bowl and am about to start whipping them when two large hands come around my waist.

"Jesus Christ, you scared me!" I just barely get the bowl down on the counter in one piece.

Daren burrows against my neck and kisses me. "I thought you had to work."

"My schedule changed at the last minute, so I'm working from home. Well, here for now, but I was about to get out of your hair."

He growls against my ear, sending goosebumps down my arm. "Stay. If you don't have to go, don't. I have practice, but I shouldn't be too late." His hands wander under my t-shirt. "Mmm. No underwear. Easy access."

I laugh and attempt to keep myself upright. "I'm trying to make you breakfast."

He nibbles on my neck for a moment before he stops with a growl. "I need to get going. I wish I could just hang out with you today."

He nuzzles against me, and my heart floods with emotion.

I open my mouth to say something, but nothing comes out.

Daren slowly spins me around. I wrap my arms around his neck.

He grins. "Gotta say I like seeing you in my kitchen first thing in the morning."

Jesus. Could he be any sweeter? How on God's green earth did I ever resist him in the first place? "Go shower. I'll make you a quick omelet before you go."

His face burrows into my neck, and he just holds me for a few minutes. When he steps back, for the first time in my life, I totally understand what it means to be captivated by someone's stare. The emotion behind Daren's eyes makes me hold my breath.

He clears his throat. "What are you doing tonight?"

Thinking about my to-do list, I shrug. "Just paying bills. Doing some laundry and a little research. Why?"

"Think you could do that another night? I'd like to take you out."

I still. "Like as in a—"

"As in a date."

He wants to take me out. A real one. Teenage Maddie nearly passes out.

We've been on lockdown at his place since we started getting together. Him asking me out definitely makes this feel more like a relationship. My stomach flutters at the thought, but before I can get carried away, I remember the reason we've been hiding out in the first place.

I start to open my mouth, and he shakes his head. "We'll be

careful. You won't get busted, babe. I promise. I'd never do anything to jeopardize your career."

Staring back at him, seeing the sweet expression on his beautiful face, the last thing I want to do is say no. Because, holy shit, Daren Sloan wants to take me on a date. We've been sleeping together for weeks, so I'm not sure why this makes me practically giddy, but the thought of us spending time together like a real couple does funny things to my heart.

Taking a deep breath and a leap of faith, I nod. "Okay. Let's do it."

CHAPTER 35

MADDIE

SMOOTHING my hands down over my silky midnight blue shift dress, I look down at my phone to check the time. Seven fifty-eight PM. I'm two minutes early.

It feels odd to be standing on the corner of Boylston Street in the middle of Copley Square, but this is where Daren told me to wait. I balked when he said he'd meet me here because nothing about this location feels like the "we'll be careful" promise he made me this morning. And even though everything inside me wants to duck behind that carefully manicured bush a few feet away, I can't stop thinking about what he asked me this after-noon when he sensed my reservation on the phone. It was four simple words: "Do you trust me?"

I didn't have to think. I just answered. "Of course." Because I do trust him. Wholeheartedly.

But that doesn't mean I'm not nervous.

Those words, though, they're enough to get me to this point. To take that leap.

So here I stand. On the corner of one of the busiest streets in the city, hoping like hell this doesn't blow up in my face. Taking a deep breath, I try to focus on that word. Trust. *Yes, I trust you, Daren.*

The clop clop of horse hooves draws my attention, and I look up to see a black carriage roll down the street. One minute later, it stops in front of me. The driver side door pops open, and an elderly gentleman gets out, walks around and opens the passenger side.

His gravelly voice calls out, "Miss McDermott, your ride awaits."

What? I look at the old guy, who seems harmless enough, but I'm from Southie, and I do not just randomly get in vehicles, horse-drawn or not, with total strangers.

"Maddie." From the shadows in the back seat, Daren leans down and shoots me one of those killer smiles.

My stomach flips at the sight of this man who's now decked out in a suit and tie, looking altogether like he stepped off the cover of *GQ Magazine*. Boston's sexiest bachelor is right.

I glance around, and pedestrians stroll by, totally not giving a second glance to the carriage. Or me. Or the hot man waiting for me.

Jesus, Maddie. Relax. You'll be hidden back there.

Laughing, I clasp his outstretched hand and plunk down next to him. "This is crazy."

"Maybe, but I owe you that date, Wildcat. It's about six years overdue."

I bite my lip, realizing that he's counting back to when he first asked me out in high school.

"This is so damn sweet of you."

He leans closer, wrapping his arm around me and pressing his lips to my neck. "*You* are so damn sweet."

My fingers immediately thread through his hair as I tilt my head to give him access. "Where are we headed?"

"Toward the harbor. A friend of mine owns a great French restaurant, and he's giving us run of the back terrace that overlooks the water." He pulls back and studies my face. "It's secluded. Don't worry." He leans back, and I know he's sensing my nervousness.

"Daren. This is great. I don't mean to be weird about work. I'm sorry I'm being so paranoid. Thank you. I love that we're taking a horse-drawn carriage. I've never been in one."

I lean up and kiss him. His hand cradles the back of my neck, and I close my eyes, relishing how much I love being with him and how hard he's trying to make tonight perfect.

Snuggling into him, we watch the city pass by as we meander through the cobblestoned streets. When we reach *Mon Ami*, we duck into a back entrance and walk out onto the most majestic view of the ocean. Because the terrace is elevated, there's no way anyone on the street can see us.

Daren's friend, a chef named Christophe, serves us himself. Once he takes our order and pours two glasses of wine, we're alone on this beautiful deck. Twinkle lights decorate the alcove and a cool breeze blows off the water.

"You always come through in a clutch?" I ask, appreciating how my words get those dimples to pop out. "When did you have time to plan this?"

His eyebrows lift. "I'm not sharing trade secrets."

I laugh, totally enthralled by having all of that charm leveled at me. "Well, I'm impressed. But that's nothing new. You always seem to impress me."

Those dimples deepen. He watches me until I start to squirm, and then he raises his glass of wine and waits for me to lift mine before he whispers, "To taking chances."

"To taking chances."

CHAPTER 36

DAREN

I'M NOT sure why it's taken me so long to do this, but taking Maddie out was the best damn idea I've had in a while. I hadn't realized how much I needed to get her out of my condo. Not that I don't love spending time with her there. I do. But this girl deserves to be treated special.

"So you and Jax actually buried Clementine in mud all the way to her neck? And she didn't kill you?" she asks, laughing, before taking a sip of her wine.

"Oh, she definitely tried to kill us. But we were seven. I'm sure if we tried that today, you'd never find our bodies. But that wasn't half as bad as when we dyed all of her white socks pink. Her mom was pissed and thought Clem had screwed up her own laundry by accident, so she refused to buy her new clothes. All through sixth grade, she walked around with pink socks."

Maddie's eyes widen. "You and Jax sound like little terrors."

"We were. I'm surprised Clem never poisoned our food or put a hit on us."

"I'm pretty sure if you had filled my training bras with pudding and frozen them, I might have considered those possibilities."

I snicker. "I guess we were little bastards. That poor girl never ate a Pudding Pop again."

She covers her mouth to chuckle. "So what's the worst prank you and Jax played on each other?"

Pausing, I shake my head. "We did a lot of crazy shit, but the most embarrassing was probably when Jax de-pantsed me in seventh grade in front of all of the eighth grade girls."

A snort of laughter leaves her, and she covers her mouth. "Well," she says, raising an eyebrow when she's done laughing, "I'm sure you gave those girls plenty to talk about."

I can't help but grin. "Probably the highlight of their year."

"Oh, lord." She looks toward the exit and then points toward the back. "We should call back Christophe. You might need help getting that ego out of the restaurant when we're done eating."

I chuckle, and she winks back at me. Damn, this girl is cute.

"What about you, Maddie? Please tell me I'm not the only one who got in trouble growing up. You strike me as the kind of girl who always followed the rules."

She frowns, and her shoulders sag. "I was kind of a boring kid."

I set my fork down and reach over to grab her hand. "That's not possible. A girl who covers sports? Nothing boring about that."

A smile tugs her lips. "My dad loved that I covered sports. That was our thing. Football, basketball, baseball, hockey–he loved it all. Took me to games when he could afford it. It was tough for him as a single dad, but you'd never know it. He was just the kind of guy who always looked on the bright side, always thought I could do anything I put my mind to. He made me believe I could be a broadcaster even though I was really shy growing up."

"Really? I'd never take you for being the shy girl."

"It was hard to overcome–don't get me wrong. Taking journalism classes in high school helped because I could prepare questions ahead of time and know what I wanted to ask. It took some of the pressure off."

I run my thumb along her wrist and watch as goosebumps spread up her arm. "You couldn't have gotten me to admit this in high school, but when you interviewed me back then after the championship game, I was nervous as hell. I was so sure I sounded like an idiot when you sounded so polished and self-assured."

"I did not sound self-assured! My hands were shaking, and I was almost positive you could hear my heart hammering in my chest. I thought I was going to pass out from holding my breath. You made me forget to breathe, Daren."

Her face flushes, and she glances down, looking mildly horrified at her confession.

I laugh and reach down to scoot her chair closer before I plant a kiss on her cheek. "I know the feeling."

* * *

WHEN WE'RE DONE with dinner, I grab her hand and lead her across the street for a quick stroll. It's ten o'clock on a Tuesday night, so I know we don't have to worry about the tourists who typically frequent the wharf-side park.

Once we're under an ivy-covered archway and covered in shadows, I press her up against a pillar and kiss her until her hands tangle in my hair and her chest is heaving.

I brush my nose with hers and love the desire in her eyes when they flutter open. "I could kiss you all night, but I know you need to get up early. Let's get you home."

Her eyebrows furrow. "You, uh... don't want me to stay with you tonight?"

I kiss that spot on her forehead and leave my lips there until she stops frowning. "Of course I want you to stay with me. I always want you to stay with me. But if you come back to my place, we're not sleeping." Her chest vibrates against mine as she laughs. "So, let me get you home. You need some rest."

Dipping my head, I kiss her neck, and she moans. "I can't believe you're taking me home."

"My dick can't either. He's livid." She laughs, and I bite down on that soft spot underneath her ear, and that laughter turns into a breathy sigh. "But tonight's not about sex." Her fingers thread through my hair again, and it's taking every ounce of willpower to not give in. "Tonight is about showing you how special you are to me. I know we've done things backwards, but had we met under normal circumstances, I would've wanted to take things slowly and show you that you're worth the wait."

She lays her head against my chest, and I kiss her hair. "Daren, if you're not careful, you're going to make me clingy."

I squeeze her just a little tighter. "I'd like to see what clingy looks like. Are we talking with clothes or without?"

She laughs again, and the sound does stupid things to my heart. Yeah, I'm in deep with this girl.

When I drop her off at her door, I kiss her nose. "Want to come over Thursday night and play *Plants and Zombies*? "

She pushes up on her toes and places a soft kiss on my lips. "Can I be the Fire Pea? I like the Gatling gun."

"Sure thing, Wildcat. "

She winks at me. "It's a date."

CHAPTER 37

MADDIE

THE WAITRESS SETS down my coffee, and I realize I'm smiling like an idiot. I've never been one to daydream, but Daren does that to me. Puts me in this strange place where all I want to do is fantasize about the next time I'll see him.

I shake my head, trying to focus.

As I sit in the coffee shop waiting for my lunch date, nerves perk up in my stomach. Daren and I might be undefined, but there's one person I want to talk to if I hope to move forward with him.

I spot her gorgeous blonde hair across the room and wave to her. When she reaches the table, I get up to hug her. "Clementine, it's great to see you."

"It's been too long! I don't think we've hung out since that sex toy party Jenna had at the beginning of the summer." She shakes her head with an embarrassed grin and tosses her stuff into the booth before scooting in. Her roommate Jenna throws these crazy parties where all the girls go home with vibrators. It's way over the top and tons of fun.

I was a little apprehensive about what Daren would think about me hanging out with Clem, but when I told him, a huge smile broke out on his face, and he told me to give her a noogie for him.

Grinning at Clem, I tell her, "Jenna would probably love the book club my roommate Sheri belongs to. They read tons of smut."

She nods and leans closer conspiratorially and whispers, "My new novel is a little smutty."

"It's the first thing on my TBR list. I've just been slammed with work. Sheri's out of town right now, but when they have their next get-together, I'll give you guys a heads up, and you can check it out."

"Sounds like fun. You know, I've been reading more erotica lately because Jenna bet me I wouldn't, and I have to admit some of it is pretty good. But that girl is pushing me to write dirtier books, and that shit isn't happening. No way am I writing sex scenes about a cock stroking her folds like a free-range chicken."

I nearly choke on my iced tea.

We talk more about books, and she fills me in on her new novel and what she's been up to since graduation. We've been gabbing for a while when I finally get the nerve to say what's on my mind.

"Clem, you know how grateful I am to you for getting me that interview, right? So many big things happened for me after that segment."

"No thanks are necessary. Besides, you took it easier on me than Matt Lauer would have." Clementine got thrown into the limelight last fall when her identity as a well-known young adult author got blown by a former professor. For the average person, this wouldn't have been a big deal, but she's the heiress of two business tycoons, so she had media trucks parked on her street for days when her pen name was leaked.

"I don't know about that. You answered some pretty uncomfortable questions." Like whether the cheating boyfriend in her book was based on Daren, which she denied. I can understand

219

why. I would've lied too. At the time, Daren was up for the Heisman, so their names made headlines for weeks.

I'm so glad Daren and I had that talk last week. I'd never be ready to hang out with Clem like this if we hadn't. But now comes the hard part.

I take a steadying breath and decide to rip off the Band-Aid. "I actually wanted to talk to you about something, and I'm not sure how you're going to take it."

Her eyes widen dramatically. "You can't just drop that on my lap. Spit it out." She laughs, and I continue.

"Okay, you know how I met Daren the day I interviewed you?"

She nods.

"And you know how I've been interviewing him every week for that sports segment?"

"Yeah, I love those segments. They're great. You and Daren have great rapport. Your chemistry is off the charts."

I wait for her to connect the dots. A minute later, her eyebrows tilt up and her mouth falls open. "Holy fuckballs. You guys are dating!" She's grinning, so I'm guessing she's not pissed.

"Shhh!" I look around, making sure no one is listening. "We're not official or anything, but yes, we have been spending a lot of time together. I moved into a condo next door to him this summer, and then he had this party, and we… we…"

She shakes her hand at me. "Say no more. It's none of my business. I'm just so glad he's met someone awesome!" And then she jumps out of the booth and comes around to hug me again. *Whoa.*

I laugh into her embrace, relieved she's okay with this.

She shoves my shoulder. "I have to tell you I knew he was into you that day. When I introduced you guys, he was totally gawking at you."

"He was not." Oh my God. Was he? I don't think I believed

him when he told me he's been interested in me since then. Nerdy teenage Maddie does a high kick and spirit fingers.

"He was too. Seriously, he's an amazing guy." She looks down. "Honestly, he and I never should have dated. We were never right. I want you to know that in case you feel any weirdness about he and I being friends."

I start to shake my head, but she puts a hand up. "Veronica hated that he and I worked through things, but Daren is a really loyal person. Which must sound weird given how he and I broke up." She groans. "I'm not explaining this right." She blows her bangs out of her face. "He has always been there for me and Jax. When all that shit went down with my professor last year, Daren rode in on a white horse and got me a place to lie low, a killer attorney, helped me figure out a plan. Given that my book was about our relationship, I'd say he went above and beyond what anyone would expect of him."

My eyes fall to my lap. I'm not sure what to say.

"Hey." Clem waits until I look at her to give me a rueful smile. "He and I both made mistakes. I played a role in what happened too. I'm not excusing his behavior, but we were young, and we did stupid things. And in the big scheme of things, that part of our relationship was a drop in the bucket. I've known him my whole life, and aside from our breakup, he's saved my ass so many times I've lost count. My brother's too. I just... I want you to know you can trust him. You won't find a better man."

I take a deep breath, trying to process everything. My stomach flutters, and I can't help the smile that plays on my lips. "He is a good man, and I really lo—" The word on the tip of my tongue makes me catch my breath. "I really like him."

A knowing smile tips Clem's mouth upward. "I'm glad you really *like* him. Now don't fuck him over or I'll have to kick your ass." Then she gives me one more squeeze and tells me I need to read some smut because it's great for my sex life.

All righty then.

CHAPTER 38

DAREN

I'VE NEVER BROKEN my training routine for a woman. Yet here I am in the middle of the night, contemplating how I can talk Maddie into having sex one more time before I leave for my game.

My eyes trail down her bare back as I listen to her soft breaths.

I've always gotten eight hours of sleep, always trained with the sole focus of the game, always pushed myself to live between the goal posts. But something's changed. As much as I love the game, I love her more. So I sleep less, I daydream about her when I should be studying, and I plot out ways we can spend more time together. Yeah, I love Maddie.

Christ. That's scary. You think you love someone—I thought I loved Clementine and I certainly cared for Veronica—but this, Maddie, she fucking makes my world go round.

Maybe I'm being a pussy. But I've lived in the spotlight for the last four years. Most women want that spotlight. But Maddie? She could give two shits about that kind of stuff. Her mind whirls with passion for the underdog, for injustice, for righting wrongs.

She shot a feature last week at the St. Martin's Homeless Shelter, and it damn near brought tears to my eyes. Her boss wanted quick shit for promos, and she managed to shoot enough footage for a whole segment and got the go-ahead to do in-depth features for all of the charities.

Her soft sigh next to me makes my heart quicken.

It's the third night in a row she's slept over. For the last few weeks, I've only gotten her to stay two nights a week, so this feels momentous. I'm tempted to give her a key and tell her it's so she doesn't have to lug dinner over from her place. I can't say it's because I want her here all the time. That might freak her out.

She calls my name in the dark, and I pull her back to my chest and plant my thigh between her legs.

"What time is it?" she asks, her voice a sexy rasp.

"Too early. Go back to sleep, sweet thing." Even though my cock wants to get up close and personal with her, the girl needs to sleep. She's always running at high speed. I don't want her to wear herself out.

Maddie lets out a sleepy moan. "Did you remember to pack your gray suit?"

"Yes, sweet thing. I packed it. And that awesome t-shirt someone just got me."

She giggles. She got me a t-shirt that says, *Not just a pretty face.* I told her I'd take it to every away game as my good luck charm.

I kiss her neck. "Babe, I left my new number on the coffee table."

"I can't believe you had to change it again," she grumbles into her pillow.

It's the second time in two weeks. If I find the asshole who's been signing me up for every porn and sexting site on the East Coast, I'm going to break his nut sack.

Maddie's breathing evens out, and I'm starting to think she fell asleep when she says, "I'm sorry I can't drop you off at the airport. Will you text me when you land?"

My chest tightens, and I inhale deeply, trying to memorize the scent of her hair. "Of course."

Her arm reaches up and snakes around my neck. "How are you feeling about the game? Do you think you're going to play?"

"Hmm. Not sure. Probably not, but I have to be ready in case."

She massages my scalp, and I groan. "Wish I could be there," she whispers. "Look out for Wilkinson. You know he's a sneaky bastard. He sacked the Bears' QB twice last weekend. I realize that was preseason, but still."

I smile, knowing she's been paying attention to the film I've been studying this week. This is what sets her apart from every other girl I've gone out with. She knows the game and is taking the time to learn it even better.

"Yes, ma'am." My arm tightens around her waist. "Are you still planning to watch with Jax and Clem?"

"Yeah." She's quiet for a moment. "Is that okay? That I'm hanging out with your friends?"

"Fuck, yes, it's okay. Why wouldn't it be okay?"

She lets out a sleepy laugh, and it lightens the pressure I'm feeling about Sunday's game. "I don't know. I… I just didn't know if it was too much."

"Too much?"

"Yes, too much. As in too big a step for what we're doing."

My eyebrows raise, and I turn her onto her back and slide over her, fitting myself between her thighs. "And that would be? What are we doing?" I kiss along her jaw before I lean back and make her answer.

"Seeing each other? Sleeping together?" She threads her fingers through my hair. "I don't know what you want to call *this*."

"You mean dating?"

She blinks, staring back with those big blue eyes before a smile forms on her lips. "Is that what we're doing, Daren?" Her arms tighten around my neck before she leans up to kiss me.

"I should hope so," I mumble against her mouth. "Because if not, I sure as hell want to be dating the beautiful naked girl in my bed." I kiss her again until her fingers tangle in my hair. "I'm sorry I woke you up."

"I'm not. I'll miss you."

My heart beats faster. "Get some rest. You have a long day ahead of you."

She sighs and nods reluctantly. I kiss her forehead before I get out of bed, relishing how much I love seeing her first thing in the morning. Which makes me realize how much I'd love to wake up to her every day.

CHAPTER 39

MADDIE

"Maddie, calm down. It'll be okay," Clementine whispers as she places her hand on my knee to stop me from jiggling my whole leg.

"Sorry. You're right." I just want Daren to do well. He's been studying plays and working out like a fiend, and I hope he shines today if he gets the chance.

We're at Clem's house, sprawled out on a giant sectional. Actually, it's her boyfriend's house. Clem moved in with Gavin this summer, and they look blissfully happy together. They're sharing the house with her old roommate Jenna and Jenna's boyfriend Ryan.

Laughter booms from the front hall, and a minute later Jax strolls in with his arm wrapped around his fiancée Dani.

"You guys are late," Clementine says with her hands on her hips. "And you both look like your hair just got run through an electrical socket."

Dani's eyes widen as she flattens down her hair, and Jax laughs and hugs his sister. "Don't give me shit. I just got in last night from Los Angeles. Can you blame me if I miss my Dandelion?"

Clem rolls her eyes and then gives him a reluctant smile. "Fine, loser, but I need you to go make the cheese dip. I love that recipe. I still can't believe you came up with that all by yourself."

Dani gasps and turns to Jax, who chuckles and says, "What? You made it for me, so now it's my recipe."

"Good thing you're so cute, because you're insufferable most of the time," Dani says with a straight face, but Jax leans down to rub her nose with his, and she gets a hazy look in her eyes and sighs.

Gosh, they're cute together.

It's strange to be around all of Daren's friends without him here, but they're a fun group.

Gavin sits on the other side of Clem before he pulls her into his chest and kisses her on the forehead.

"Hey, cuteness," she whispers to him.

"Hey, love bug," he mumbles back.

They look so content together it makes my chest ache. I wonder if there will ever be a time when Daren and I can be out together in public. I hate that we have to sneak around. I hate that I was constantly looking over my shoulder during our date.

It's a sick disease, this thing with Daren. He infiltrates my every thought, dances through my dreams at night, and fills my head with flights of fancy. Because when I allow myself to think about my future, I want one with him so badly my heart hurts with longing.

It's been just over two months since he knocked me on my ass while I was out jogging, and honestly, I don't think I've recovered.

After I swore up and down that I'd never date another pro athlete, here I am, wishing Daren could be here right now, missing him so much it's hard to breathe.

And that's when I finally admit it to myself. I'm in love with him.

A smile lifts my lips.

Falling for Daren has only made me realize that I didn't know what love was before I met him. Because nothing in my life has prepared me to be consumed. To be devoured whole by this emotion. To feel disassembled and somehow reconnected in a bigger, fuller way.

"Whatcha smiling about over there, Maddie?" Jax asks as he strolls up. Before I can answer, he scoops Dani up off the couch and sits back down with her on his lap even though there's plenty of space. So here I sit between two of the world's cutest couples.

Jax kisses Dani before he returns his attention to me and waits for my answer.

"Just excited for Daren's game. You're going to think I'm ridiculous," I say, "but I'm a little afraid for him to play and a little terrified for him not to."

Jax grins. "Don't worry about Daren. He's got this covered. Trust me." He motions toward me. "I see what Daren likes about you. You're a big step up from his last girlfriend." He curses under his breath. "Veronica was like that Fenway hot dog stand that looks like it might give you a good case of *E. coli*, and you're like the fucking Chrysler Building at Christmas, all lit up with twinkly lights."

My mouth drops open for a second, not sure how to respond to that statement. Did he just compare me to a building?

"Jax, lay off Maddie," Clem says. "You got Daren's text." She shoots him a glare.

I look back and forth between the twins as they have a silent conversation.

"What... what did Daren say in this mysterious text?" I ask.

Jax tilts his head, but when I look back to Clem, she has a smile plastered on her face.

"What?" I sigh. "What, guys? Just tell me."

Jax laughs with a wink to his sister. "Daren said to take it easy on his girlfriend or he'd have our asses."

"Jesus, Jackson," Clem huffs beside me. "Don't you know how to be discreet?"

"What? You know they're dating. Get over it."

"Seriously, shut the fuck up. Are you trying to advertise this information to the whole neighborhood? Because if so, there are a few people in Allston who didn't hear."

I start to laugh, resigned that the cat is out of the bag with his friends, and reach for my beer. "You guys are all close, so I trust you won't rat me out to my boss, but yeah, we're trying to keep it on the down low."

Jenna flounces in and jumps on Clem's lap, making Clem groan underneath her weight. After slinging an arm around her friend and nudging Gavin over a bit, Jenna turns to me with a raised brow. "Do people still say 'down low'?" Her Southern drawl is so charming, I'm pretty sure she could talk the devil into doing her favors.

"Probably not." I chuckle to myself that I'm being this lame right now. "By the way, I'm supposed to give you all Daren's new number."

"I have his new number," Jax mumbles as he takes a pull of his beer.

"The one he got two nights ago?"

"What the fuck? He changed it again?"

Nodding, I text it to Clem, and she forwards it to the rest of their friends. "He keeps getting tons of"—how do I say this?—"unsolicited material sent to his phone."

"In other words, porn." Jax shrugs. "Not sure why he needs to change his number for that."

"If you received thirty sexts and fifty-two photos from random women in less than two days, it might get annoying."

"Holy shit. Fifty-two?" He blows out a breath and stops to think a minute. "Were they hot?" Dani elbows him in the gut, and he laughs. "Just kidding, babe. You know you're the only porn I need."

Everyone lets out a collective groan before Clem reaches around me and smacks her brother on the back of his head. "Please do not say shit like that again."

Dani and Jax laugh, and she drops her head on his shoulder as he nuzzles her hair.

"Speaking of sexts," Jenna says, "I brought last week's prize for our Out-Skank winner!"

"Jenna, you're putting my legs to sleep. Get off." Clem nudges her off her lap.

"I'm sorry, Out-Skank?" I make a face. "That sounds like an STD I need to avoid."

Jenna gasps. "Oh, girl. We need to include you in our thread. Give me your number."

Next thing I know, I'm getting dirty messages from the three girls for their weekly sexting game.

Jenna: *Care to douse my taco in your special sauce?*

Dani: *I need to squeeze that beefy brat between my buns.*

Clem: *Drizzle your icing on my pouty muffin.*

Covering my mouth, I snort-laugh into my hand. "Okay, wow." I look between the three girls. "I'll play this with you, but you have to swear you'll never show my messages to anyone." Because I can already see the headline: *News Reporter Madeline McDermott Involved in a Sexting Scandal.*

"Cross our hearts," Jenna says, motioning across her body. Clem and Dani nod. The three of them are grinning from ear to ear like getting me to participate is some big feat.

Jenna holds her hands out. "This week, we're doing a Disney theme. And the prize is something that's eight inches of fun from my box of sin."

Before I can ask any questions, their thumbs are in motion. Clementine mumbles, "Bring your A-game, Maddie. We play to win."

Gavin pulls her back to his chest and says, "My girl can get a little competitive, Maddie. Just warning you."

"Pshaw." Clem gives him a quick peck and keeps texting. My phone buzzes with three pings a moment later.

Jenna: *Some day my prince will come, preferably on my tits.*

Dani: *Beauty, have you met my Beast?*

Clem: *Jump on my magic carpet. I'd like to give you a ride.*

I tilt my head, chuckling, while I stare at my screen. "Have you guys ever thought about making an Out-Skank app? I bet it would be all the rage. Like some kind of drinking game."

Dani snaps. "That's an awesome idea!"

The announcer gets our attention when they wrap up the preview with a quick mention of the new QB for the Rebels, and they debate whether or not we can expect to see him play. Daren's college stats flash on the screen next to his gorgeous face.

How does he get better-looking every time I see him?

Which reminds me of our interview three days ago. Because holy hotness, that man strutted out in full gear—those skin-tight white pants, football pads, and jersey, with his helmet tucked under his arm—and my ovaries damn near exploded.

"Aww, look at Maddie," Jax says. "She's in love."

I turn to him, forcing myself to glare, because holy crap, am I that obvious?

His fiancée chides him, and he chuckles.

The front door opens again, and Jenna's boyfriend Ryan strolls in, holds up a giant case of beer in one hand and a stack of pizza in the other, and yells, "Let the festivities begin!"

As he puts down the food, his eyes land on me, and he waves. We've never really met before, but I know he's the lead singer of a popular local band. Sandy blond hair waves in his eyes, and he has that whole rocker vibe going on with black jeans and a faded Aerosmith t-shirt.

Ryan points to me and says, "You must be Daren's girlfriend."

My shoulders sag. Seriously, at this point, I'm pretty sure the postman in the next county over knows we're dating, because Daren's friends suck at keeping secrets.

Jenna runs up to Ryan and plants a wet kiss on his mouth. "Hi, cutie pie," he mumbles against her lips.

She turns back to me and shakes her head. "I swear he's the last person. No one else knows. Just us." She motions around the room to the three couples.

I laugh in defeat. "Okay, that's fine, but you really can't tell people about us. I could lose my job. It's a major conflict of interest. That's why we can't do anything together in public."

Gavin clears his throat and smooths back a long strand of hair from Clementine's face. "Maddie's serious, guys. She'd get fired for this. You can't tell anyone."

He's a journalist, so I'm sure that's why he's backing me up right now. But my stomach falls hearing someone else confirm my worst nightmare.

Clem must sense I want to hurl my breakfast because she nudges my shoulder. "You can trust us. I promise."

"You really can't go out together?" Dani asks, a concerned look on her face.

"No. We really can't. I mean, he took me out last week, but it was all undercover and sneaky."

"That's so weird considering you interview him on TV every week. Those segments are great, by the way. I've learned so much about football. Like how to call a play and how you need to hold the ball." She freezes in that iconic Heisman position, a serious expression in her eyes.

Jax chuckles. "You don't need any help holding balls, babe."

A wad of paper goes flying and hits him in the face. "Jackson, stop. I just threw up a little in my mouth." Clementine makes a gagging sound, and everyone laughs.

The camera cuts to the crowd, and even though they're playing in Atlanta, there are a number of Rebel fans dotting the stadium. Mostly women. Wearing Daren's jersey. And here's a random fact. His jersey set a record for sales, selling more this summer than any other professional athlete's.

A shot of several women decked out in Rebel gear flashes on the TV. Their jerseys have been modified for maximum cleavage, and they're bouncing up and down in unison, their boobs waving at the camera. They're screaming for Daren, and one holds up a sign that says, "Marry me. We'd make cute babies."

Hysterical. If it didn't make my stomach turn in on itself, I'd be tempted to laugh.

But I try to focus on what's important. Daren. The game. Wanting him to do well. Because those women don't mean anything for our relationship, right?

Before I can head down that path of doubt, I close my eyes and take a deep breath. I told Daren I trusted him, and I have to believe he won't hurt me.

CHAPTER 40

DAREN

WHEN COACH TELLS me to warm up after the third quarter, we're up by six points.

A few weeks ago, he mentioned he wanted to move to a two-quarterback system, switching off between Brentwood and me the way we did in preseason, but I kind of thought he was full of shit. It's not unheard of at the pro level, but it's definitely unusual, especially if the starting QB is effective, and Brentwood is, the bastard.

I've sensed some unspoken urgency to get me ready, but with Brentwood in his prime, I still don't understand why. It's tricky maneuvering into the second QB spot, bumping the guy who had the job last year into a third rotation permanently.

Coach motions for me with eight minutes left in the fourth. "You've got this, Sloan. Keep that head of yours calm. And don't forget to check all your options before you commit."

I nod and snap on my helmet.

Quentin and I stand on the sideline and wait to take the field at the same time. As Brentwood struts by, he grabs my shoulder and leans in. I'm thinking he's going to say something encouraging. Instead he grunts, "Don't fuck up."

I laugh. Because this guy is known as a legendary inspirational speaker. And he is in a huddle. I've heard him pump up the guys. But I guess I don't qualify as someone worthy of that positivity.

When the ref blows the whistle, I jog on. And I'm unprepared for the applause that greets me. It's so overwhelming, it damn near brings tears to my eyes. I know I had a good track record during preseason, but I'm pretty sure my national appeal grew tenfold when Maddie's segments got picked up by ESPN.

And damn, I want to make that girl proud.

"Don't fall for your own PR, man," Quentin jokes, whacking me on the back.

"How else will I know how awesome I am?" I tease.

"You *are* awesome, motherfucker. Now let's kick some ass." He fist-bumps me, and after the huddle, it takes a couple of plays to calm down. Adrenaline is an interesting chemical. I feel like I could hoist an SUV off the ground right now, but it's also messing with my accuracy. Finally, after two shaky first downs, I spot my chance when I drop into the pocket. I feel it in my gut as I watch my opponents spread on the field like chess pieces. When Quentin jukes the defense and breaks free like his ass is on fire, I step back and release the long pass, knowing that Q will hit his mark.

When he catches the ball in the end zone with a minute and fifteen seconds left on the clock, firmly putting the game out of reach for our opponents, there's only one person on my mind. And I love that she's watching.

Actually, I just fucking love her.

* * *

I send her a quick text as I head for the showers. *We won.*

She texts back almost immediately. *You kicked ass, Clutch! Muah!*

I may have just played my first regular-season NFL game, but all I can think of is getting home to celebrate with my girl.

By the time we're done with the after-game interviews, I'm wiped out. Quentin is still grinning from ear to ear as we reach our hotel rooms.

"I think we make a good team, Sloan." He pats my back as I reach for my keycard.

"Back atcha, Q." I'm about to open my door when giggling on the other side makes me pause. I double-check the number on my key, which matches up to my door.

I stare at my door again, straining to hear, but there's only silence.

Did I take a hit to the head this afternoon? I swear I'm hearing things.

Turning to Quentin, I call out to him, "Dude, have you been pranking me by signing me up for porn sites?"

"Nah, man." He chuckles. "But that's funny shit."

"Yeah, it was fucking hysterical until I had to change my number."

When I get my door open, the giggling starts again. I hit the lights, and two very blonde, very buxom, very naked women are sitting on my bed.

Shit.

Running my hand over the back of my neck, I groan. "Okay, ladies. I'm both flattered to find you here and a bit perplexed by how you got through security." It's not as though I have a room under my own name. Only a handful of people know this is my suite. But the girls have my number painted on their faces, so they clearly knew I was staying here.

One starts to talk, and I wave her off. "I need you to get dressed. As lovely as I'm sure you both are, I'm not interested." I look down at my watch. "You have three minutes to leave before I call security." Grabbing my suitcase, I check to make sure the nudists aren't also kleptos.

Just then, my phone buzzes. My stomach turns over when I see Maddie's name. Because this is not the shit I want to explain her. Especially after what her ex-douchewad did to her.

By the time the girls leave, my head is pounding. I call Maddie and we talk for a few minutes. She asks if I wore the t-shirt she got me.

I reach into my carryon and pull it out. I tell her it's my good luck charm, and she sighs into the phone. It's wistful and sweet, and I wish I could see her face. But I hear the fatigue in her voice. I know it's late there, and she has to get up in a few hours, so I tell her to get to sleep.

I wish I could do the same, but I toss and turn half the night. Because I really do think honesty is the best policy. I've fucked up before, and I don't want to do it again.

If I hope to stand a chance of something real with Maddie, I need to be up front about the stupid shit that happens, even finding fangirls in my bed. But I hear the guys in the locker room complain about this all the time. That their long-term girlfriends can't handle the shit that goes down in the NFL, and before too long, they break up.

My worst fear is Maddie will be overwhelmed by it all and call things off. Between the pressure she faces at work and the insanity I just found curled up in my sheets, I don't want her to give up before we've given this a chance. And honestly, I know I'm crazy about her, but I have no fucking clue if I'm more invested in this than her.

I laugh humorlessly, the sound echoing in my silent room. I got into this not wanting strings. Just some good company. Some hot sex. In other words, something easy. Yeah, basically I was delusional.

The worst fucking part is I'm scared we're going to tank before we ever get started. This should be the honeymoon period with candlelight dinners and long nights by the fire. Except I can't take her anywhere because of her job.

Two nights ago I asked if we could sneak out again for another date, and she said we couldn't. That she was too scared we'd get busted.

Apparently, our vibe is *too* good during our interviews, because her boss, that dick Spencer, told her the other day she'd better be keeping the flirting with me on camera.

My jaw clenches at how fucked up things feel all of a sudden.

In the morning, as I board the team's bus to the airport, Quentin gives me a what-the-fuck face when he sees me. "Dude, you look like shit. Aren't you supposed to be reveling in your win yesterday?"

Rubbing my palms against the stubble on my face, I groan. God, I just want to unload. And Quentin is one of the happiest-go-lucky assholes I know next to Jax. Well, Jax post-meeting Dani.

Quentin drops into the seat next to me, and his eyebrows arch. "Wanna talk about it? Wait, let me guess. Chick problems?"

"Actually, yeah, I could use a little advice."

"Dude, did you fuck those girls in your room last night? Because that shit won't go down well with your girlfriend. Maddie does not look like someone who lets that go."

"What?" My heart slams in my chest, and I lower my voice. "How the fuck do you know I'm dating Maddie? And of course I didn't fuck those girls. Christ." My temple throbs, and this conversation just started.

He chuckles, the smug bastard, and he grips his chin like he's deep in thought. "Well, one, I see how you guys look at each other when you think no one is looking. It's kinda cute to be honest. Two, I see how you *don't* look at all the girls who fling their boobs in your face on a daily basis. Three, you look panicked this morning, so I'm guessing it had something to do with those girls in your bed."

"Fuck." I scrub my face harder. "I kicked them out. Of course I kicked them out. How did you know about them? Did you have something to do with that?"

"Nah, man. Not my style." He holds his hands up in defense. "So get that scary look out of your eyes. I wouldn't do that shit to someone. The only way I knew was because I walked down the hall to get some ice as the girls were leaving."

I blow out a breath, wishing for a do-over, starting from the time I got to my hotel last night. What I would do differently, I'm not sure. But I can't fuck this up with Maddie. That much I do know.

"Okay, Q. Lay it on me. How do I handle this? I think I should just tell Maddie what happened, but I want to do it in person." This isn't shit I can talk about on the phone.

"Fuck, no." He looks at me like I might be insane. "Nothing happened, right?"

"Swear to God. I didn't even look at them once I noticed them on my bed. Just told them to get dressed and get out."

"Dude, no need to be a fucking Boy Scout." He pats my shoulder like I'm some pathetic loser. "This is why you can't tell her."

I lean forward, hoping I can figure this out before our plane lands this afternoon.

"It's elementary, Daren. If you tell her this shit, you plant the seeds of doubt. Then, every time you have a road game, which is pretty fucking often, she's going to wonder if there are naked girls in your bed. So even though you had nothing to do with this situation, if you tell her, you're still gonna pay the price."

Yeah, I can't deal with that again. Because Veronica constantly accused me of cheating on her. Although I never even considered it, if a woman came within a ten-foot radius of me, Veronica immediately assumed I wanted to fuck her. It was exhausting trying to reassure her.

Groaning, I sink deeper into my seat and turn toward the

window where rain starts to pelt the bus. "Fuck. How did everything get so fucked?"

He chuckles. "Welcome to the NFL, the land of endless pussy and irrational expectations."

CHAPTER 41

MADDIE

I can't put my finger on it, but Daren's different. When he came home from his first away game, I expected to see unbridled enthusiasm. I thought he'd be bursting with details about the game, the way he was during preseason. Like a kid in a candy store.

Instead, he seemed so buttoned down. Measured. Careful.

When I asked if something was wrong, he hugged me and said he was just stressed. That he hadn't realized how much pressure he'd be facing.

So I try not to make any demands. Because I hate those girls who want their guys to live and breathe the air they exhale. There's nothing I want more than for Daren to succeed, so if that means we have to spend less time together this fall, so be it.

I know how much this means to him, and I'm okay making sacrifices. As soon as this first season is up and I stop covering sports, he and I can be normal people and go out for real. I'm sure he's tired of hanging out with me at his condo all the time. I feel bad about turning him down for another date, but I can't take that risk. Not after Spencer made that comment. I swear he scrutinizes our footage in a way he hadn't in the past. Maybe I'm just being paranoid, but my instincts tell me I need to tread very carefully.

To help Daren focus, I'm trying to text him less during the day so he can direct all of his attention on practice. And I've stopped staying over as much so he can get more sleep. But I miss him. So much.

With his schedule, he's gone a lot. For practice, games, travel, promotion, and charity events. We still do our weekly interviews and the station is promoting the hell out of the bachelor contest, which is around the corner, but I miss our quiet times together. A month and a half of the regular season has felt like the blink of an eye and a lifetime in equal measure. Work keeps me so crazy I can barely breathe, but not spending time with Daren makes me watch the clock and wish for an end to this misery.

But I'm doing my best to suck it up. So tonight, I'm hanging out with a few friends from college to get my mind off Daren. But when I realize where we're meeting, my heart sinks. The Bottom of the Ninth. Because the last time I was here, I was with Daren.

Midway through the evening, when I head back to the bathroom, I can't help but think of how he pressed me to the wall and kissed me senseless. The memory is so strong, it makes my heart ache more.

As I head back toward my table, I hear laughter and turn to see Daren on the opposite side of the restaurant with a small crowd of people. He's sitting with several teammates and a few girls are squished in with them, hanging on his every word.

Right at that moment, I'm so insanely jealous of not being able to do this, of not being able to have something so simple as a dinner out with Daren and his friends, tears sting my eyes.

Blinking quickly, I dart back to my table and scoot into the booth. I'm in my own world, nodding when my friends speak even though I can't process a word. So when the waitress brings a giant cake lit with candles and places it down in front of me, I'm altogether speechless.

And then everyone sings Happy Birthday. To me.

Holy shit. It's my birthday.

Tears stream down my face, and my friends hug me and hand me presents, all the while thinking I'm crying because I'm happy. But everything inside me feels numb.

Because there's only one person I want to spend my birthday with. And he hasn't a clue it's today.

* * *

I DON'T PICK up the phone when he calls later that night. I know I'm being immature, but I'm too emotional to have a conversation. What's crazy is I know those girls were probably with the other guys. But why do they get to enjoy his company when I can't, and I'm his girlfriend?

I'm dying a slow death of a million small cuts.

During my mid-morning break the next day, I put on a happy face and call him. We chat for a while, and he tells me about his evening out with the guys and mentions everyone who was there. It matches what I saw, and I feel like shit that my feelings could still be so fucked up despite his willingness to tell me everything.

I don't mention my birthday. It seems a little pathetic, so I decide it's not important.

Really, it isn't his fault he didn't know. I hadn't thought about it until my friends broke out the cake. But for some reason, this doesn't make me feel any better. Between the distance created by our schedules and my stupid birthday fiasco, my heart feels like it's in tatters.

Deep down, I know the answer, why I'm such a train wreck right now. My birthday has always been rough since I lost my dad. My uncle Patrick always tried to make it special, but it never took the emptiness away. He left me a message last night, too, telling me we needed to hang out soon so he could give me my presents.

I wipe away a few stray tears. I need to get a grip. Be strong. Or get out of this relationship because this can't be healthy. I feel like a crazy person.

But the idea of calling it quits when Daren has done nothing wrong makes me want to slap myself. He's a good man. A great friend. A fantastic lover. I would be certifiable to end this.

By the following Friday, I'm starting to finally feel a little less insane. I'm curled up on the couch with a cozy sweater, a glass of wine, and Clementine's new book, hoping to finally get a little time to unwind when the doorbell rings.

I open it to find Daren with two dozen long-stemmed roses in one hand and a rectangular box wrapped in silver paper in the other.

"Hey. What's the occasion?"

"Maddie, I'm so sorry I missed your birthday. Why didn't you tell me? I feel like such a jackass. Sheri texted me this morning, asking me to check on you since she's been gone so long, and she mentioned feeling bad about missing your birthday."

He sets the flowers and gift down and hugs me, and I throw my arms around his neck and close my eyes. His large hands run up and down my back, and before I realize what's happening, tears are streaming down my cheeks.

I try to sniffle quietly, and he stills. "Aww, babe. I'm fucking this up, aren't I?"

I shake my head. "No." God, why can't I stop crying?

"I am. I know I am. Fuck." He squeezes me tighter. "Can you stay over tonight? I feel like I haven't seen you in months, and it's tripping me out."

Nodding, I start to wipe the tears when he moves my hands. He holds my face gently and wipes my cheeks with his thumbs. "Maddie, I'm good at football, but let me tell you right now that I suck at relationships. I never say the right thing. I can't even get your birthday right."

"It's okay. I just feel so much distance from you. It has me wondering if I did something wrong."

"God, no. You're perfect. I'm the fuckup."

He leans down to brush his lips against mine, and all the anxiousness I've been feeling for the last several weeks starts to melt away as he presses my body into his.

What starts as a gentle kiss turns frenzied a minute later. I'm gripping his shoulders, and he's pulling on my hair to kiss me deeper. I reach for his belt buckle, and he tugs at my shirt, and we're a tangle of clothes and limbs, desperate to get closer.

By the time we're in my bed, I'm so exhausted, I can barely form a sentence. But literally the second we're done, Daren falls asleep, still nestled inside me.

And wow, the boy is a deep sleeper. I somehow manage to roll him off so I can clean up in the bathroom. When I curl up next to him a few minutes later, he murmurs my name and says he's sorry.

The next day, he's out the door by eight a.m. I have to go into the studio later, so I try to enjoy the rare morning to sleep in. But something keeps nagging at me.

As much as I loved sleeping with Daren, a part of me is still unnerved. He never told me what's bothering him. Because something obviously is.

CHAPTER 42

MADDIE

THE DIAMOND TENNIS bracelet glimmers in the mid-morning sun. It's beautiful. Delicate and sophisticated.

I can't believe he bought this for me and didn't even ask me to open it last night. We got so carried away, I hadn't thought about it until I got up to get some coffee this morning.

Grabbing my cell to call him, I wait for his line to ring, only to hear that the line has been disconnected.

Ugh. Did he have to change his number again? I thought the prank porn had stopped, but maybe I'm wrong. How the hell is someone getting his number time and time again?

Maybe I can duck out of work early today and pop in to see him.

All day, I sit in the editing booth and finish up a follow-up to the porn segment I've been working on. My stories have been running for the last two months, but with the vote coming up next week, this is my last shot to make a difference. It's been a challenge to track down people who are willing to talk, but I think what I have is compelling.

I'm fine-tuning some last-minute video of a porn star named

Ella. She can't be older than eighteen, and she already has several chart-topping videos.

Her small voice wavers when she talks. "This isn't the life I wanted for myself, but at least I make enough to pay my way through college. I'm not doing drugs. I don't drink." She toys with a frayed edge of her faded tank top. "I don't plan to do this forever, but I didn't have many options when I was kicked out of my house last year."

Ella's gotten a GED, and she attends community college classes part-time.

"If this law gets passed, I'm afraid it'll give the filmmakers a reason to not require everyone to get tested for STDs. It'll push everything underground where it goes unregulated." She shifts in her seat and her brown hair tumbles over her shoulder.

I ask her if she'll stop participating in these films if the law is passed and the shoots get riskier.

"I don't think I have a choice. I have bills to pay." She blows out a frustrated breath. "This is all so ironic. Men hate wearing condoms, except the men on the city council want the guys in these films to wear condoms, which in turn means people won't watch because they're not turned on when they see the plastic."

People can say what they want to about her, but I think she's brave to be standing up for this cause. I hope when viewers watch the segment, they hear her story and don't simply objectify her. Because this girl is so much more than a pretty face and a young body.

What you won't hear in my piece is the fact she's raising her little sister, a detail she doesn't want made public in case social services take her away. But since their mother is a drug addict, Ella doesn't know what else to do to keep her safe.

"She's hot," someone whispers in my ear.

I nearly fall out of my chair to find Brad behind me.

"Jesus." My heart is racing. "You scared the crap out of me."

He snickers. "Sorry, Maddie. I brought you something." He hands me my favorite iced coffee from Dunkin' Donuts.

"Tha... Thanks." I give him a weak smile, too freaked out to put any effort into it.

He launches into his plans for the weekend even though I didn't ask. He's grinning and talking away.

"I'm glad to see you in such a good mood. You've looked kind of bummed out lately."

He shrugs and leans against the cubicle wall, ignoring my need for personal space. I push back in my chair to create some room between us.

"Listen, I'd love to talk some more, Brad, but I'm on a really big deadline. If this goes well, I might have a shot at doing more primetime coverage, which is where all the serious news gets done. It sure as hell would beat doing bachelor contests."

He shakes his head. "That has to be insulting to a woman like you. Between that and the football bullshit, it's a wonder you have any time on your hands to do this." He motions toward my screen. "But it's probably also why your laptop has been crashing so hard lately." He tsks, a strangely snide expression on his face. "Gotta lay off the hardcore porn sites, Maddie. They're full of viruses. It took me an hour to fix your operating system this morning."

"What?" My head rears back. "What are you talking about? What do you mean hardcore porn sites?"

"Sweetheart, your search history doesn't lie."

I feel my cheeks burn. But I will myself to stay calm. I'm a grown woman, and I'm just doing my job. "Then maybe you should check my history a little more carefully because everything I searched is relevant to my assignment. Ask Roger."

"Maddie, hey, I'm sorry. Listen, I was just kidding."

Ignoring him, I turn back to the editing booth and wait for him to leave. When the sound of his footsteps fade away, I take the drink he just brought me and toss it in the trash. Asshole.

My day gets worse when I walk into my tiny office to find my ex-boyfriend talking to Nicole.

"Hey, hot stuff. How are you?" Jacob asks, looking delighted to see me.

What the hell is going on this afternoon?

Nicole looks back and forth between the two of us. "*That's who you've been boning the last few months?*"

"What?" Am I trapped in the Twilight Zone right now? "No, I am not *boning* Jacob."

I take a closer look at my ex. He seems bigger, brawnier, but he's starting to look like a caricature of himself with a big body and a little head. Well, two little heads.

"You're seeing someone?" he asks, appearing hurt.

"Like you care. Seriously, who I see is none of your business." I start to pack my bag. "What are you doing here?"

"Nicole had a few questions for me, so I thought I'd drop by and answer them in person."

I turn back to them and roll my eyes. "Okay, Nicole, I know we've never been the best of friends, but off the record, I dated Jacob for about a year. We broke up in May when I found him in bed with another woman. Feel free to sleep with him. I am being a hundred percent honest when I say I really don't give a shit if you do or not. However, you should know that if the asshole says you're exclusive, he's lying."

He gets a pained look in his eyes, like he might actually be hurt by what I said, which pisses me off more. He has no right to be hurt.

Nicole starts laughing, and I grab my bag and stalk out of my office.

I'm so looking forward to seeing Daren, to washing off this horrible day, but when I get to his place, he's not alone.

He's sitting at the kitchen table with financial documents spread across from one side to the other. And Camille, Sheri's friend, is sitting next to him, laughing. As I walk in, she grabs his arm and smiles up at him but addresses me.

"Hey, Maddie." Her forehead wrinkles. "That's your name, right?"

Ahh. The girl gloves come off early. *Bring it, bitch.*

She leans toward Daren to grab a piece of paper, which is really just an excuse to press her boobs into his arm. He doesn't even notice. Typical. Men can be so clueless sometimes.

"Hey, Maddie." His eyes finally swing up to mine. "Camille is offering to do the investments for the homeless shelter pro bono. She's also helping me out with some financial issues I need to clear up."

I bet she is.

Camille looks between us like she's confused why he's explaining that to me. Inside, I'm screaming, *Because I'm his girlfriend!*

Just then, Sheri walks down the hall from the bathroom. "Holy shit, Maddie! I haven't seen you in ten years!" She rushes toward me and leaps up for a hug, nearly knocking me over.

She's been in New York for the last several weeks to work on a new film with her dad.

"You'll be happy to know your condo is still in one piece," I joke. "What are you guys up to?" I look toward Camille, who has returned to basking in Daren's attention.

Sheri shakes my arm like we're twelve. "We're about to head out for our book club, but she needed to pop by to see Daren first. You should join us out tonight."

Not happening.

"I'd love to, but I have so much work to do. I just wanted to swing by and thank Daren for something, but I can see he's busy. I'll catch you guys later."

I know Camille doesn't mean anything to Daren. Just because I don't trust her doesn't mean I don't trust him. But I'm so fucking tired of having to hide my relationship with Daren. I'm so fucking tired of denying that there's anything between us. Of women like Camille thinking it's okay to make the moves on Daren when I can't even enjoy an evening out with him.

Before anyone can respond, I'm gone, eager to take a hot bath, blast Nirvana, and drown my sorrows in something alcoholic.

When I get to my room, I turn off my ringer, strip out of my clothes and head for the tub where I ignore the world. Because right now, the world can kiss my ass.

CHAPTER 43

DAREN

I swear to God, I can't do one thing right this week.

Get it together, asshole. This is football. This is the one thing you can do. Put up or shut up.

Gritting my teeth, I reach back to release the pass, but my throw goes wide, and Quentin shoots me the finger.

Coach has had enough and stalks toward me. "Son, I don't know what crawled up your ass and died, but I need you to dislodge it and play like this means something." He shakes his head. "Where's the guy who played for me in preseason? I want him back. You're playing hard, and you're playing tough—and at the end of the day we're winning—but something ain't quite right here." He turns his back to the rest of the guys and lowers his voice. "Is there anything you need to tell me? Did you get arrested last weekend or get a girl knocked up or something?"

I choke on my own spit. "No, sir."

He gives me a curt nod. "Okay, then. That's a relief." His head tilts. "Girl problems?"

My shoulders slump, and like a fucking Buddhist Zen master, he says, "Ask not what she can do for you, but what you need to do for her." With a stiff pat on the arm, he adds, "And then, once you've got that shit straight, have a little fun out here, okay? You're depressing me."

Once practice is over and I'm stuck in gridlock traffic, I give in and decide I need some advice. Glancing at the date on my dash, I realize I can't call Jax because he's traveling to a game. I know I could call Clementine, but I don't want to be the douchebag who calls his ex-girlfriend when he needs help with another woman.

So that only leaves one other person, and I haven't spoken to him in months.

"Daren, my God, it's good to hear your voice."

The guilt from not calling him in so long forms a knot in my throat.

"Hi, Dad."

He sighs. It's the sound of relief, and I know it's because I've been calling him Mason for the last several years. But I was too hurt to call him my father.

"To what do I owe this wonderful call?"

Fuck, and he has to be nice about it. "I need your advice."

The last time I called him for help, Clementine was all over the news. Yeah, it takes a major crisis to go there these days. I saw him more in college because my mother nagged me until I gave in, but I've had a hard time letting go of the anger. I know he didn't mean to crush me, but he did, and no apology or amount of money can ease that pain. My guess is that huge Heisman banquet he threw for me was part of his apology, but he should know by now I don't care about those kind of gifts. But lately, even Maddie has been encouraging me to see him.

My father laughs. "Is this about a woman?"

I roll my eyes. I swear he can read my mind. "Of course."

He chuckles again. "Well, lay it on me. Your mom and I were about to have dinner, but I'm sure she won't mind if I take it in the study so we can talk."

If I weren't starting to feel like I was losing Maddie, I'd never do this. But one thing is for sure. I can't lose her. And Mason has stayed married to my mom all these years, even when she was raising someone else's kid. I figure he must have really loved my mother to marry her after her fiancée took off. She never even heard from the asshole again.

I know. That's who I should be angry with. My real father. But he died when I was in high school—my senior year, in fact— so I never had a chance to tell him to go to hell. That's one of the things that made this whole thing worse. Finding out that I had a real father—right after he passed away.

Maddie's right, though. I need to get over this shit with Mason. He's always treated me well. I'm not sure why I'm still angry about this. I guess part of it ties into how finding out he wasn't my real father had a chain reaction in my life that I'm only now recovering from. But I gotta own that shit too.

Shaking my head, I man up and tell him the short version of what's happening with Maddie, minus the coma-inducing marathon sex.

He hums over the phone. "You gave her a diamond bracelet, and she's barely spoken to you for the last week? Son, something about that equation doesn't work for me." He's silent for a moment. "What happened the last time you saw her?"

Shit. That feels like a lifetime ago. "Okay, part of that problem was I had just changed my number, and I thought I had given her the new one. And we had our weekly interview yesterday, but she was all business."

"Well, tell me what happened a week ago. It seems the drama started there, right?"

I nod even though he can't see me. "I was working with this woman, a financial advisor, on some investments, and Maddie came over. She said hi and that she was heading home to work. And since then, she's barely returned my calls or texts, which is unusual for her."

There's that chuckle again. "Son, what does this financial advisor look like?"

What? "I don't know. Medium height. Blonde. Wears too much lipstick and her perfume makes me gag. Why?"

"Is she attractive?"

I pause to think about Camille. "I guess. I haven't really thought about it. I'm not into blondes."

"What does Maddie think of this woman?"

"She barely knows her. I think she met her one other time. Hell, I barely know Camille."

"Ahh, you're still so young. I remember being this clueless."

"Seriously, you're not helping here."

He laughs. "Sorry, son. Okay, tell me what happened the first time she met Camille."

I roll my shoulders, trying to ease the tightness in those muscles. "We were all at a restaurant. Maddie was there with her roommate Sheri and several of Sheri's friends for this book club they have. Maddie invited me over." I scratch my head, wondering how the hell this means anything. "I sat opposite Maddie and next to Camille because that was the only seat available, and I signed autographs for the girls."

"And?"

And what?

I blow out a breath. "I looked up, and suddenly Maddie was gone. My buddy Quentin told me she left. So I tracked her down, and I guess you could say we've been together ever since."

I'm still waiting for the punchline, waiting for all of this to make sense.

And then I remember the conversation Maddie had in the back hallway by the bathroom. I had asked her if she was jealous, and even though she denied it, I knew she was lying.

"Oh, God. She hates Camille, doesn't she?"

"My guess is yes, she's not her biggest fan."

"And Camille was at my house when she came over the day

after I gave her the bracelet. Maddie said she wanted to thank me for something, but she couldn't say anything specific because no one is supposed to know we're dating."

"Sounds like you know what to do."

I rub my forehead and try to finish driving home without getting in an accident. "What would that be, Dad? What would you do?"

"Grovel. It's the only way to go. As long as you're being honest with her, I'm sure everything will work out."

My lips twist at the irony here. He's telling me to be honest.

Long after we get off the phone, I'm still mulling over his words. It takes me a good hour to stop being pissed at him all over again. And then his advice to be honest sinks in.

I know I haven't told Maddie everything, but the crazy shit is just getting crazier, and I don't want to freak her out. But maybe she senses I'm not telling her the whole story.

I have nothing to hide. I haven't done anything wrong, but I want to protect her, protect us. And I hope I haven't done just the opposite.

But with the bachelor contest this weekend, I know I don't have a lot of time to make this right. The last thing I want is to do this event with all of this awkwardness between us, so I head for her place resolved to tell her everything.

Except when I get to her door, no one is home.

And she doesn't call me back.

CHAPTER 44

DAREN

WHEN I LOOK around the hotel's grand ballroom, a sea of tuxedos and shimmery dresses greets me. The bachelor contest might sound like a silly affair, but there are some big fundraisers in attendance. Having grown up coming to these kinds of galas trained me to spot the heavy hitters. If I weren't on a mission, I'd be slapping their backs, trying to get their donation dollars to go to St. Martin's.

It takes me a few minutes, but I finally spot Maddie. Stunning in a floor-length red ball gown, she damn near floats across the floor. Holy shit. This girl makes me lose my mind, and she doesn't even know it.

Her hair is shorter, drifting just below her shoulders, and my stomach sinks. She's making changes. Don't girls always talk about cutting their hair? And I'm the asshole she didn't tell, the idiot who didn't know her birthday, the douchewad who protects a piece of his heart because he doesn't want to get hurt.

That realization stops me in my tracks. I've never told her I love her. I didn't want to move too fast and freak her out or go out on a limb and get pummeled.

Christ, I *am* an idiot.

As I'm walking up to her, one of the other contestants, a guy who plays for the Red Sox, places his hand on her lower back and whispers in her ear. She smiles shyly and pulls back, shaking her head.

What the fuck is that about?

He's looking at her like he wants her for breakfast. No fucking way, asshole. Not happening.

I stalk up to them. When her eyes meet mine, they cool. "Daren." That's it. She says my name, and the lack of emotion behind it kills me just a little bit.

The idiot next to her returns his hand to her back, and fury coils in my stomach and makes its way through my chest.

"Maddie," I say. "Can I talk to you a second?"

Her lips twitch. After a moment, she starts to nod yes, but an announcer tells everyone to grab their seats.

"I have to go, Daren. Maybe we can talk afterward." Then she turns on her heel and heads for the front of the room.

Idiot boy leans toward me. "Holy shit, she's hot. I call dibs on fucking her."

My jaw tightens so much it aches. "You ever talk about her like that, and I will launch that sorry-ass throwing arm through that wall over there."

He rears back and holds up his hands. "Kidding, man. Kidding."

Blowing out a long breath, I look for my table.

I need a break. I need the stars to align in my favor tonight, and I have to make this right. There is no way in hell I'm letting my pride fuck this up. I'm going to lock her in at my place and tell her all the crazy shit that's been going on, and she might be pissed that I haven't told her, but it's better than this. Because I know for a fact that I'll lose her if we don't talk this through.

When I spot my table, I curse under my breath. *Fuck you, stars.* Because who am I sitting next to? Camille.

Goddamn it.

"Daren!" she squeals too loudly. Gone is the financial planner. Someone has replaced her with a fangirl, because she jumps up and all of her parts jiggle in her overly snug dress. A second later she hugs me and presses herself all over me. *No, no, no.*

I give her a quick pat on the back, nearly gagging on her perfume, and step back. When I look up, Maddie is staring daggers at us from the podium.

Running my hand through my hair, I drag my seat farther away while I glance around, hoping to find a way to move somewhere else without offending Camille. Her firm is donating so much money that my whole table is filled with her coworkers.

I sit and wave down a waiter for a Scotch. I've never drunk hard liquor during the season, but these are special circumstances. And tonight I need a fucking drink.

After welcoming everyone, Maddie says, "I have to give a special shout out to my co-worker Nicole Stanton, who can't be with us this evening. She came down with the flu and sounds terrible." She holds up her phone. "But I've been receiving hate mail from her for the last hour for stealing her gig, so at least we know she's alive."

Everyone chuckles, and she smiles sweetly at the crowd. "I guess I have my hands full tonight. I mean, I just get the worst jobs. Interviewing Boston's sexiest bachelors all night. Jeez. I need a raise."

People laugh, and my heart is seizing up from an overdose of her charm.

She's so effortless up there. Sweet and charismatic. Funny and flirtatious. I've seen her on the news, and I've gotten to know her easy-going style during our interviews, but to watch her up there, without a single notecard or teleprompter, she's so fucking impressive. My chest swells with pride.

Maddie introduces every bachelor, and they banter back and forth up there. I know she has to hype the guys, but each time she smiles adoringly at them, my heart aches a little.

After each introduction, a special segment featuring the bachelor's charity is shown on the screen behind them. At several points in the evening, people have tears in their eyes from her stories.

Finally, she introduces her ex, and he strolls up there and drapes his arm around her. She stiffens and pushes his arm off her. "Hey, stud, haven't you ever heard you're not supposed to touch the merchandise?"

She plays it off like a joke, and the audience laughs. She keeps his intro short, just long enough to not diss him, and then she plays the video about his charity.

It's for an after-school program in South Boston. When it's over, she leans toward the mic and says, "I actually grew up going here. It's where I learned about journalism. They brought in a local broadcaster, and right then and there, I knew it's what I wanted to do."

From the expression on her face, I'm wondering if that program had anything to do with the internship her dad tried to help her get when he brought her to cover my high school game.

She clears her throat. "Jacob, I'm really proud of all that you're doing for our neighborhood. Great job." She sounds sincere, and Jacob's shoulders slouch.

He reaches over to hug her and whispers something in her ear, and she nods. Before he walks backstage, he leans closer and kisses her cheek.

Everyone "awws" and she wipes her eyes. "Enough of this mushy stuff. Let's get to our final bachelor." I realize she's calling me up, and I make my way to the podium as I smooth my tux.

I give her an awkward hug, and she smiles toward the crowd, careful to avoid eye contact with me.

"With some of the best stats in football for a rookie, Daren Sloan has dominated the field this fall. He's known around these parts for being the go-to guy in a clutch. A Heisman winner, a two-time All-American, and a three-time All-Conference player,

Daren's reputation precedes him. So it comes as no surprise that the Rebels are in contention for the playoffs. Nor does it come as a surprise that his charity, St. Martin's Homeless Shelter, raised the most money tonight. Because if you know Daren, you know he plays to win. He eats, breathes, and sleeps football. It's hard to be around him and not be impressed with his professional commitment."

I'm touched by her words, but I'm even more moved by her story about the shelter. After an overview of some of the resources St. Martin's provides, she introduces a man named Sam, and the moment I see his face, tears fill my eyes.

I turn to look at Maddie, but she stares up at the screen. Sam wasn't in the original segment that already aired on the news.

Sam's weathered voice comes through the speakers. "Daren comes here several times a month. He helped me fill out a job application once. I know he cares about the people of this city. How many football stars do you see eating lunch with the homeless? And yet he sat with me for an hour, listened to my story about how I lost my home. Before he left, he gave me a hug and said he'd find a way to help me. And he has. He put his name down as my personal reference and got me a job at a local hotel."

Sam's voice cracks, and I have to turn my back to wipe my eyes. "The only thing Daren asked in return was that I come back here when I had a chance and try to pay it forward by helping others. I hope his charity wins because I know for a fact that this place changes lives. It changed mine."

The lights come on, and there's a hushed silence. When I turn to face the audience, the applause is deafening.

When they're done clapping, Maddie says, "Congratulations, Daren. You raised six million dollars, which will be matched not by one corporation, but two. Last night, we got word your father's corporation, Sloan Industries, will also be contributing, which brings your total to eighteen million dollars. The shelter will be able to afford all of the renovations they need to stay open and expand to help twice as many homeless in the Boston area." She turns to me finally, and says, "I'm so proud of you. Congratulations."

But before I can thank her, she takes a deep breath and places her hand against her stomach. "Which brings us to the dating portion of the evening," she announces into the microphone.

The women in the audience start cheering, and Maddie laughs that slightly artificial chuckle she does when she's on film. She calls up all of the athletes, who stand behind her.

Maddie motions toward us. "Six very lucky women will go on exclusive dates with these bachelors next week, so I hope your calendars are clear. But before you accept this date, you should be fully aware of what you're getting yourself into. Because with so much popularity come the fans. And let me tell you, these boys have quite the admirers."

She turns back, and when our eyes meet, her glare is glacial.

Shit. This can't be good. When she returns her attention to the audience, a smile is plastered to her face.

"Without further ado, I call this segment Buyer Beware."

Everyone laughs, and if my stomach could sink any further, it would. When we signed on for this contest, the guys agreed to be roasted. And something in Maddie's eyes tells me I'm about to go down in flames.

The segment starts with girls screaming over the Red Sox douchebag I nearly pummeled earlier. Athlete by athlete, the fans talk about what lengths they'd go to get close to us. A girl jokes about how she was arrested after following one of the guys onto a plane. Guess TSA didn't find it amusing. Finally, the segment cuts to a shot of me with the guys on the team before cutting to footage of screaming girls who are sitting on top of my SUV.

As images of the women project onto the screen, the voice of one of my teammates says, "Daren has the most insane fans I've ever seen. They've locked themselves in his car. Naked. Snuck into his hotel room at away games. Naked. And they've flooded his phone with all kinds of pics. Naked pics. We even have a locker full of underwear girls leave for him. He's a lucky bastard."

The kicker comes at the end. It's a photo of a buxom blonde. And she's only wearing a red t-shirt. The image instantly stops my heart. Because the t-shirt says, "Not just a pretty face." It's the one Maddie gave me at the beginning of the season. The fabric comes down to the girl's thighs, and then you see her bare legs. Worse, though? She's standing in front of a rumpled bed.

Except I have no fucking clue who that girl is. *What the everloving fuck?*

Of course, everyone thinks it's some random pic, but the girl who gave me the custom-made t-shirt sure as hell won't.

The segment ends with a big "buyer beware" warning sign and hazard lights. The audience laughs, roars because they think it's hysterical, but when the lights turn up, Maddie is wiping her eyes. Fuck.

After clearing her throat, she introduces tonight's biggest corporate donor, who will announce the winners of the dates with the bachelors. Maddie steps back to let the donor take the mic and turns to walk off stage. I grab her wrist.

"Let me explain, Maddie," I say low enough so she's the only one who can hear.

Her head drops, and all of her beautiful hair cascades forward. "I'm pretty sure you had that chance." She sniffles and pushes back her shoulders as a tear escapes. "All I asked for was honesty." Her chin quivers, and she adds, "I'll drop off the bracelet next week."

"Don't do this. I know that looked bad, but nothing happened. I swear to God I never touched any of those girls. And I have no goddamn clue who that girl was in my t-shirt."

She gives me a sad smile. "Daren, I've heard that excuse before. Maybe it didn't come from you, but it might as well have." She wipes away another tear. "I'm sorry, I can't do this."

As she walks away, I start to go after her, but her boss Spencer stops me and motions toward the podium. "Don't even think about leaving, Daren. You need to go accept an eighteen million dollar check. I'm pretty sure that trumps a piece of tail."

What the fuck?

A corporate suit is calling my name from the stage as I watch the love of my life walk out the back of the ballroom.

My head is pounding as I wander back to the podium. *What the hell just happened?*

CHAPTER 45

DAREN

"Dude, you look like shit." Jax kicks the pizza box at my feet and pushes off the mountain of laundry at one end of my couch before he drops down next to me.

I barely grunt a response as I stare at ESPN. They're replaying last week's interview Maddie and I did, and I've been rewinding it for the last half hour, torturing myself. The only reprieve I've had is the fact that my date for the bachelor contest is a seventy-five-year-old widow named Lucille.

Pointing the neck of my beer toward the TV, I say, "Right here. She knew. Look at her eyes. She fucking knew all those girls were sneaking into my room. All I had to do was tell her. That's it. Maybe it would have hurt her, maybe she would have been pissed, hell, maybe she wouldn't have believed me, but it's better than her thinking I'm an outright liar. All I had to do was open my fucking mouth and tell her."

"Have you groveled? Begged her to listen? Sometimes ya gotta beg, man. I myself have done that once or twice with Dani."

"Dude, if I could fucking find her, I would. She isn't taking my calls, and Sheri swears she has no clue where Maddie went. Maddie just told her she was staying with a friend, that she didn't want to be next door to me. That she couldn't handle the head-board once that got going. Whatever that means. The girl packed a bag the night of the contest and left."

"What about her job? You could track her down there."

I glare at him. "Idiot, she'll lose her job if her boss thinks we're sleeping together."

Jax looks confused. "I thought he already knew about it."

"He could have been talking out of his ass to get me to stay at the gala. I have no idea, and I'm not willing to risk Maddie's job to find out."

"How about you just wait for her to leave her job? Like, camp out by her car until she comes outside."

I make a face. "You creeper. I'm not going to fucking stalk her."

My buddy punches my arm, and I sink deeper into the couch. "How did your game go last weekend?"

I close my eyes. "Like you need to ask. I played like shit. We won, thank fuck, but I had very little to do with it."

"And you're drinking during the season. Gotta say this is a first. Even when Veronica was acting like a crazy bitch, you'd just put all that shit aside and play football like it was your lifeline."

"It was. I don't know how I got away from that." I rub the spot on my chest that's been aching for days. "I just can't get my head straight. It's like I can't fucking breathe."

We're quiet for a while, and I listen to Maddie's voice come through the speakers. God, I feel like a pathetic asshole, sitting here watching our interview over and over again.

Finally, Jax turns off the TV. "Some of the guys and I are headed out to get tattoos tonight. Wanna come? Sometimes you gotta brand that shit on you so you don't forget. Life lessons and all that. It's better than sitting here, being a sad sack."

Laughing, I close my eyes. "I'm pouring my heart out to you, and you want to get a tattoo?"

"Yup."

My shoulders slump. "Fine. Fuck it. Let's go."

* * *

JAX'S FRIENDS meet up with us on Boylston Street, and Jax grumbles, "I can't believe this is the place the guys picked."

"Why? Are we going to get tetanus from their needles or something?"

He shakes his head and groans. "I wish."

We walk in, and I'm relieved to see such a spotless parlor. It's a beautiful setup, actually. Exposed brick walls, two rows of black leather chairs, framed artwork everywhere.

A tatted-up guy walks up to us and motions to Jax. "You gonna let me ink you up, man?" Then he laughs.

"Fuck, no. I'm not an idiot." Jax turns to me. "Here, you can do Sloan."

I look back and forth between them, a little more than certain that they hate each other. "Bro, you're freaking me out," I tell Jax.

"Brady might be an asshole, but he's a great artist. I promise you'll be happy with his work." Then Jax smacks me on the back and walks off to talk to his friends.

Brady shrugs. "I'm old friends with his girlfriend Dani."

"You mean fiancée."

"Whatever." He sighs and runs his hands through his black hair. "We doing this or what? You have some idea of what you want?"

I check out the lines that snake up both of his arms. The guy has some really nice pieces, which assuages my anxiety.

Nodding, I describe what I'm looking for, and he motions for me to grab a seat while he sketches the design.

Two hours and three beers later, I'm still not sure how to get Maddie back. This might be the dumbest thing I've done yet, but I'm hoping the effort counts for something.

267

* * *

THE NEXT MORNING, I'm so grateful I don't have to haul my ass to an early practice I could cry. My mouth is pasty, and my eyes are glued together. I groan and try to sit up.

"Want some coffee?" a female voice calls out.

What the fuck? My heart starts to thud in my chest. In a panic, I look around and realize I've been passed out on Jax's couch. And that voice must be Dani's.

Thank you, Lord. Because I really can't deal with another girl trying to break into my place. I take a deep breath to calm down. "Yeah, thanks, Dani."

Dropping onto one of the bar chairs, I gratefully take the coffee. I smile at Dani, but her mouth twists into a frown.

"What's wrong?"

Her frown deepens. "I might not be the best person to tell you this."

I lean forward. "Tell me what?"

"You're going to be upset. Jax said he'd be right back. He went to grab some bagels. He really should be the one to tell you."

"Dude, you're seriously freaking the fuck out of me."

She chuckles and then frowns again. "Okay, but don't shoot the messenger. Promise?"

I nod, about to pass out from holding my breath.

She motions back toward the living room, and I follow her. "You should sit down first."

I comply, hoping to hell she gets to the point soon. Then she turns on the TV.

"What are we looking for?"

"It's everywhere. I won't have to look too far."

Click. Click. Click.

And then she stops on some celebrity gossip show. The word "scandal" is emblazoned in red letters.

Dani looks at me warily. "Maybe we should start with the

video first. This will all make more sense if we start there. But the video isn't on television." After switching to the internet, she glances at me a second before her eyes dart away. "You know. Because of legal reasons."

No, I don't know.

My skin is crawling as I wait for her to play the damn thing already.

She clicks around and finally ends up on some file sharing website.

The video is grainy. Like something off a phone. It shows a couple on a bed. Some naked guy is straddling a girl's chest. He sounds like he's enjoying a blow job. The dude is ripped and tatted up. Suddenly, I recognize the ink.

"Holy shit. That's Jacob. Maddie's ex."

Dani nods slowly, a sad expression in her eyes like I'm not understanding the images in front of me.

A sinking feeling settles in my stomach. His ass is blurred, and so are parts of the woman's body. But then, for a split second, you see her profile when he leans back.

"What the fuck?" I'm going to be sick. "That's not... That can't be."

When the video ends, Dani clicks back to the celebrity gossip TV show.

A sleazeball reporter says, "In case you missed it, let me catch you up. Files leaked off of WNEN in Boston late last night that has the whole city talking. During a network restructuring, a pornographic video popped up in their dropbox for advertising clients, who occasionally use the studios to film. We can't show you the video for a number of legal reasons, but the scandal has rocked the news station. Many speculate the video features MMA fighter Jacob 'The Killer' Callahan due to his recognizable tattoos. Just last weekend, he was featured in WNEN's bachelor contest."

The camera cuts to footage of Jacob leaning in to kiss Maddie when she introduced him at the gala. "After this sweet moment between the notoriously tough Callahan and WNEN reporter Maddie McDermott on Saturday night, his fans are all wondering if this is the mystery woman in the video. McDermott told the audience she grew up in South Boston, which is where Callahan grew up. Sources tell us the two dated for almost a year and have recently grown cozy again, pointing to the footage as evidence they're back together."

My vision blurs, and I lean forward to press my palms into my eyes.

"I'm so sorry, Daren." Dani sits next to me and gingerly rubs my back. "Take a deep breath."

"I don't believe it. She hates him. That can't be recent video. And who the hell took it? Maddie would never agree to be taped."

But then I think about the jokes we made about having Skype sex while I was on the road. Would she agree to be filmed for this asshole? I feel like my world just got kicked off its axis.

The douchebag on TV starts talking again. "We were just admiring her new haircut, which might mean the footage is as recent as a few days ago." They show the video again, commenting on the woman's length of hair and how similar it looks to Maddie's.

I stalk off to the bathroom where last night's beer comes rushing out.

Fuck. Fuck. Fuck.

After the tattoo I just got, this serves me right.

CHAPTER 46

MADDIE

How do you know your life is about to fall apart?

For me, it started at Dunkin' Donuts. The girl across the counter had just handed me the large coffee when a guy tapped me on the shoulder and asked if I was really the chick in the video. When I asked what he was talking about, the ten people in line behind us all whipped out their phones in a race to show me.

There I stood, mouth agape, coffee dripping down my arm as I realized I was looking at the video I took of Jacob getting deepthroated last summer. The same video I deleted months ago.

But it wasn't until some jerk leaned toward me and asked if I do that for all of my boyfriends that I realized he thought *I* was the girl in the video.

At which point the coffee slipped out of my hand and crashed on the floor, splattering everyone.

I flinch as Roger taps his desk, shaking me from my thoughts. "How did this happen?" he asks, looking pissed to be having this conversation.

I open my mouth—to say what, I'm not sure—when Spencer answers. "We're not sure, Roger. I'm on it, though." I didn't even realize he was in the room.

"You sure as hell had better be on it. Because the last time I checked, hacking into someone's phone was a federal offense."

Spencer scoffs. "Assuming what Maddie said was true."

Roger glares at him. "I think Maddie has been perfectly upfront here. She disclosed her past relationship with Jacob in detail. I think we can trust her side of the story. Because I seriously doubt she would upload a self-condemning video to our servers." With a pained expression, Roger turns to me. "Is there anything else I need to know? Anything at all?"

After a moment, I shake my head. Because now is probably not the time to tell him I've been having an affair with Daren for the last four months.

My stomach turns over, and I cover my mouth, willing myself to not vomit.

A knock on the door has the three of us looking up at two men in expensive suits. "Risk management. We're here from the legal department."

Susan the secretary pokes in her head a second later. "Boss, the phone lines are flooded. Everyone from CNN to MSNBC wants to know when we'll have a statement."

He waves her off. "The vultures aren't going anywhere. They can wait." Roger rubs his five o'clock shadow. "Maddie, do you have an attorney you can call?"

Oh, God. "I... I don't know."

"Really, Roger?" the risk management guy asks.

Roger points back at him. "Don't act like you're not ready to ruin this girl's career over some stupid viral footage. People are starving in the streets every day, politicians take payoffs like I pop my vitamins, and the only thing you care about is this fucking video." He slams his desk drawer shut. "The truth here is we shouldn't give a shit who is in this video. We shouldn't be spending the resources of our *newsroom* on this story because it's not a goddamn news story!"

Whoa. My eyes tear up as I realize he's on my side.

"Maddie," Roger says like a sigh, "find an attorney. Call someone. You shouldn't go in with those guys without one. I know your side of things. That's enough for today. Think you can get someone lined up for tomorrow?"

I nod even though I have no clue where to start.

On my way out to my car, I'm swarmed by reporters who scream in my face.

"Maddie, when did you do that video?"

"How long have you and Jacob been dating?"

"Were you together the night of the bachelor contest?"

Finally, I can't stand it, and I stop to address the cameras. "I am unequivocally *not* the girl in the video. Jacob and I broke up in May, and aside from the bachelor contest promo shoots and the event itself, I haven't spoken to him since."

I begin to push my way through the crowd, and they keep barraging me with questions.

It isn't until I'm parked in South Boston that I break down and cry.

* * *

I'M LYING prone on the twin bed in the spare bedroom at my uncle's house. The tears stopped a little while ago, but only because numbness set in.

I stare at my crap from high school, wishing my uncle Patrick hadn't gone to such lengths to help me settle in here after my dad died. I never had the heart to tell Patrick how my posters and photos and yearbooks all just reminded me of my father and made the pain worse.

Jesus. What would my dad say about this? How horrified would he be right now?

Burrowing into the cotton pillowcase, I close my eyes and try to block out thinking about my father. But being surrounded by all of my shit from high school makes it tough.

"Maddie, honey, are you okay?" My uncle pokes his head through my door. Nodding, I wipe away the wetness on my face. He shuffles uncomfortably, his hands in his pockets. "Can I bring you something to eat? Maybe some soup?"

I give him a weak smile and agree even though I'm not sure I can hold anything down. But if I don't accept it, Patrick will worry. The door closes, and I close my eyes.

Patrick is only eight years older than I am, so he's more like a distant older brother than uncle, but he's always been here for me. My swan dive of public humiliation has to be hard for him. But he hasn't said much. Just that he loves me and knows I'll get through this.

Crashing at his house was my only option. I haven't stayed here in years, not for any extended period of time. I never wanted to be a burden—not that my uncle ever made me feel that way, but he did so much for me growing up, and I never wanted to take advantage of his kindness.

The low murmur of the TV in the other room is a constant reminder of what I face if I try to head back to Sheri's.

My eyes are swollen, and I feel so helpless. Tears burn in my eyes. I need to tell Daren the truth. He needs to hear it directly from me that I'm not the girl in that video. I know we're not together anymore, but I want to tell him I would never do that to him.

But that video looks so bad. That girl looks like me. I can't imagine what he's thinking. I hope he knows that looks can be deceiving.

All at once, I can barely breathe.

Oh my God.

Is this what he was trying to tell me? I never gave him a chance to explain because I was hell-bent on protecting myself. But what if I was wrong? What if there was an explanation for how that girl got his t-shirt? He's never given me any reason to doubt his sincerity or honesty before.

Do I really think he cheated on me? Could he treat me the way Jacob treated me?

Nausea roils in my stomach, and bitterness crawls up the back of my throat.

No. I don't.

Cursing from the other room makes me lift my head. My uncle's voice echoes down the hall. "Maddie! You need to see something! Get out here! Oh, shit."

Ugh, I can't take much more of this.

Lifting myself off the bed is difficult, my body feeling like it weighs a thousand pounds. Sluggishly, I walk toward the living room of my uncle's humble two-bedroom house.

When I round the corner, I see my uncle on the couch, his hand over his face. I'm about to ask what's wrong when I look up at his flatscreen and my worst nightmare comes true. Bile pushes up the back of my throat, and I cover my mouth.

Because the girl in these images having sex with Daren? That one *is* me.

CHAPTER 47

DAREN

AFTER I UNLACE MY CLEATS, I slump back and watch everyone move through the locker room. Several of the guys are watching something on a cell phone in the corner, and I'm hoping like hell they're not leering at Maddie.

Every news station is reporting the video with her ex was recent, but I can't bring myself to buy that story. She hates Jacob. I mean, doesn't she?

For once in my life, I feel paralyzed. Fuck, is she going to lose her job over that footage?

I scrub my face, three days' worth of stubble scratching my palms. Someone sits next to me, and I turn to find Brentwood leaning back against the locker.

I'm pretty sure the guy hates me, but for once, he looks sympathetic. "How is your girl taking this?"

"My girl?"

"Yeah. Maddie."

I start to shake my head, and Brentwood laughs. "Dude, don't even fucking deny you're together. I've watched you turn down chick after chick on the road for the last several months. Girls with sky-high tits and asses that wouldn't quit. So I figured you were with someone. And the way Maddie looks at you, any idiot with a pair of eyes can see she's in love with you."

A flicker of something in my chest lights. Hope, maybe? Why his words make me feel better, I'm not sure. Because I'm almost certain Maddie hates me right now.

He lifts his chin. "You've got a good head on your shoulders. In fact, you're exactly the kind of guy I want to take over my team at the end of the season when I retire."

It takes me a full minute to process what he just said. "What? When did you decide to retire?"

"When I got my fourth concussion last fall."

"I thought you were fully recovered."

"Man, it only takes one good hit, and I'm done. Dead in the ground. No, thanks. I'd rather spend the next fifty years with my wife and kids, getting fat on beer and brats and talking about the good old days. I've had a great career, and this season looks like it might end on a high note, thanks to you. I know I haven't praised you, but it's been harder than I thought to give up my team. So just get through this media bullshit. That's all it is. I see it every season. But I also know you're above it. You're always keeping your nose clean. Use those instincts now. They haven't let you down so far." He gives me a hard slap on my back that nearly knocks the wind out of me and takes off.

Fucking hell. I don't know what to do with the bombshell he just dropped in my lap.

The team is mine if I can keep my shit together. But does football mean jack without Maddie in my life?

Not really.

My instincts. What do my instincts tell me?

That there is no way Maddie cheated on me. That even after our argument, she'd never run off to fuck Jacob. She hates him.

A roar of commotion kicks up from the corner, and I look up to find half of my team staring at me.

"What?"

Nothing. No response.

"Seriously, tell me why the fuck you're staring at me. I've had a godawful week."

"Dude, don't kill the messenger," Quentin says.

Fuck me. I've heard that before. "Just spit it out."

"Well, I think we're all really interested in your sex moves, man. That thing you do with her on her back…"

"You're speaking a fucking foreign language right now."

Quentin ambles over and hands me his phone and then reaches over to scroll through a dozen images. Of Maddie and me. On my couch. Fucking.

"What the hell is this?" My fingers grip the device.

He clears his throat. "Gifs. You know, compressed graphics. They're like mini movies a couple of seconds long."

"I know what gifs are, asshole. That's not what I mean."

He clears his throat. "I don't know how to tell you, but there are like five different series of you guys. The story just broke. Apparently that one of her and her ex wasn't the only thing that landed on the station's server. These just got posted on some file-sharing website."

"Show me the rest." I need to know how far this goes.

They're shot in her bedroom, on my couch, one in the recliner, and one on the floor.

Fuck. Fuck!

I look up at the guys. Some are grinning. One dick tries to give me a high five.

Quentin leans in. "I'm sorry, man."

"I don't know how these were taken. She was paranoid about us getting found out."

"You sure *she* didn't take them? A lot of chicks out there would kill to do sex tapes with a guy like you."

"Go to hell, asshole. Maddie isn't like that."

"I'm sorry. You're probably right, but I thought it needed to be said."

One of the guys is scrolling on his phone a few feet away. "These gifs are clearer than the video of her and that Jacob guy. Like it was taken with a laptop."

My stomach clenches. Maddie thought she saw the camera light go off that one time we were going at it on the floor, after I teased her with the ice cream.

Christ. I scrub my face again. Maddie must be freaking out. I head for the showers where I try to get my head together. By the time I get dressed, I know what I need to do.

On my way out, Jeanine stops me. She looks ready to kill someone for my PR nightmare.

"Don't you dare think about going anywhere. You get your ass in the conference room. Here's how I want you to roll with this. You've been so squeaky clean that people are devouring this story. So just admit you and Maddie had a fling. End of story."

She ushers me into the conference room where the media immediately flash cameras. Really? How did they assemble here in the last hour? I'm the cause of this hysteria? What bullshit.

I sit next to my coach and Jeanine puts a statement in front of me and whispers, "I wrote this out for you. All you have to do is read it."

Coach says a few words about making a mountain out of a molehill and turns the mic over to me. I glance at the press statement and crumple it up.

I pull the mic closer. If football has taught me anything, it's that you have to man up. I can never blame losses on someone else. It's on me.

People are screaming out questions.

"Were you sleeping with Maddie when she was having sex with Jacob Callahan?"

"Did you know they dated in the past?"

"What did you think of the video with her and Jacob?"

"When did you guys start going out?"

I hold my hands up. "Okay, everyone, we're doing this my

way. So let's start by quieting down. I have something to say, and I'm guessing you want to hear it."

My eyes tear from one side of the room to the other to impress the fact that I want them to shut the fuck up.

"First, I really can't believe that you guys don't have more important stories to cover." Sighing, I decide to put it all out there. People can judge this shit for themselves. "Maddie McDermott and I met through mutual friends last year and got to know each other after she was assigned to cover the weekly *Football 101* segment. That video you've been alleging is her in a compromising position with her ex-boyfriend Jacob is total bullshit. She and I have been dating since the summer, and I know for a fact that she loathes her ex-boyfriend. So there is no way that footage is recent. I know she told you guys it wasn't her, and I believe her. Furthermore, anyone who knows Maddie can tell you she'd never do anything to jeopardize her career by allowing herself to be videotaped in that kind of situation."

"You mean nothing to jeopardize her career other than sleeping with the source of her weekly segments?" someone in the back shouts.

I laugh, but it lacks any humor. "Ladies and gentlemen, Maddie is a news reporter who was moonlighting to cover our fun little football games every week. Now if you think for a moment that her journalistic integrity was compromised because she was spending time with me, you're overestimating the value of football. Because when she wasn't here at the stadium or being forced to cover bachelor contests, she was covering real news, like homeless shelters and fire codes and—"

"Porn!" someone yells. "Don't forget that porn story she's covering, Daren."

"Yes, that's true. And while I think she raised some valuable issues for the city councilmen to consider, I don't appreciate the way you make her story seem so lecherous. Shame on you. I'm proud to call Maddie my friend, one of my best friends in fact, and I'm an even luckier bastard to call her my girlfriend. What you really should be trying to dig up is the asshole who hacked her laptop."

I get up, too disgusted with these people to continue. "Now if you'll excuse me, I need to find my girlfriend."

CHAPTER 48

MADDIE

Late afternoon light drifts through the blinds. The house is quiet. So quiet. My uncle said he had to run a few errands, but I think he needed some space. I'm guessing he went to his girlfriend's house to freak out over his niece, the deviant.

My lips twist. I don't really think he sees me this way, but God, do the websites have to show every damn gif, each one with its own little x-rated tag, like "Maddie McDermott sucking Daren Sloan off" or "getting nailed hard."

The news outlets are no better, flashing the word "scandal" over my headshot like I'm a criminal. So even though the "reputable" news sources won't show any images, they're giving this story more credibility because they're covering it.

My friends have seen this story. My coworkers. My boss.

I feel so numb. How the hell did I arrive in this spot?

My life feels like a wasteland, and I am ground zero for the wreckage. All of those years of slaving away. Trying to do my dad's memory proud. Trying to make a difference. All for naught.

In this silence I realize that, more than the job I'm sure I just lost, my heart really hurts over losing Daren. Because right now, as I'm grasping for a life vest, he's the one I want. He's the one I trust. He's the one whose arms I wish could wrap around me right now and drown out the world.

But what really kills me? That I turned my back on him over a rumor, over innuendo and speculation. Over shit like that video of Jacob that started the downward spiral of my career.

I'm a hypocrite. Here I am, dying to talk to Daren, to hear his voice, to have a chance to explain, when I wouldn't listen to his explanation. I wouldn't even take his calls.

One asshole reporter wondered if Daren had taken the gifs, and I laughed out loud. Daren would never do that to me. Never.

I sniffle, and a hand rubs up and down my side. Ugh, Daren always rubbed my side like this. At night, while I was trying to go to sleep, he'd rub my back until I'd drift off.

Daren.

That hand moves to my stomach and pulls me back until I'm up against a big, hard chest.

Oh my God. Daren.

My head whips around until I'm met with those honey-colored eyes.

I gasp, both elated and horrified to see him. What must he think of me right now? But I don't have time to ask because he pulls me closer and tucks me under his chin.

"Daren." A sob breaks through me, and my whole body quakes. *Oh, God. Oh, God. He came.*

"Shh, baby. It's okay. Everything will be okay."

He holds me tightly with one arm while the other hand rubs my back.

I breathe him in, the scent that's only Daren. Fresh laundry. Crisp aftershave. My fingers dig into his sides, like I'm afraid someone will storm in here and try to take him away from me.

His fingers tangle in my hair, and he kisses my forehead. "I'm here. We'll figure this out." I nuzzle closer, at a loss for words. "I'm going to find the asshole who did this to you, and I'm going to rip his balls off his goddamn body."

Laughter spills from my lips. It sounds manic, like it's coming from someone else. I'm crying. I might be hysterical. Do hysterical people know when they're hysterical?

His big palm runs up over my back and massages my neck, and I sniffle and try to get a hold of myself before I lift up so I can look into his eyes.

He reaches up and cradles my face. I lean into his hand, and we just stare at each other. His calloused thumb slowly wipes away a tear.

A deep sigh leaves him. "Maddie, I am so fucking sorry I didn't tell you everything. If I could go back and redo it all, I would, baby. But you have to know nothing happened with any of those girls. They were breaking into my hotel room, so that must be how one wore the t-shirt you gave me, but nothing happened. I don't even see other women since you came into my life. And that shit just kept getting weirder. With my past... I didn't want you to assume the worst." His eyes close briefly, and when they open, he shakes his head. "I just can't lose you."

"You didn't lose me." A shuddering breath shakes my body. "I... I should have let you explain."

"If... if you need to confirm any of this, ask Quentin. I was afraid the girls would make bullshit accusations, so after the first time it happened, I started bringing him with me back to the hotel to clear out the room. If you want to talk to him—"

"No." I shake my head. "I believe you. I don't need to ask."

I'm not sure if it's my own runaway scandal that's helping me see things differently or the fact that he's here now, but I know he didn't cheat on me.

He brings me closer and kisses my lips. Just once. Slowly. So tenderly.

Another tear escapes.

"Sweet thing, everything is going to be okay. Please stop crying."

I nod, believing in him, in us, to figure this out.

"And nothing is going on with Camille. I honestly hadn't thought twice about her offering to do work for the homeless shelter, and—"

"It's fine. I shouldn't have gotten so jealous. It's just that things were weird between us, and I let my emotions get the best of me."

"Baby, I would do things differently if I could."

"It's okay. We're okay."

He tucks me back to him, and we snuggle in silence. He doesn't ask me any questions, doesn't accuse me of any wrongdoing. Doesn't tell me I screwed up. Doesn't ask me about that video of Jacob. He just holds me.

All at once, the words rush from my lips. "That girl in the video. It's not me. It's the girl Jacob was cheating on me with." He lets out an audible sigh. "I would never do that to you. I would never jump from your bed into another man's arms. I just wouldn't."

Those arms squeeze me tighter, and he kisses the top of my head. "I know, babe." He's quiet for a few minutes. Then he asks, "Do you have any idea who would want to do this to you?"

I shake my head. "You mean who would want to destroy my career?" I blow out a breath, still not quite able to wrap my head around everything.

"Would your ex do this? Maybe make this video to make it look like you? To somehow get back at you?"

Sitting up, I turn to face Daren. Because he needs to hear the ugly details. "Jacob didn't do it."

"But you said he wanted to get back together with you. Maybe this was some kind of revenge sex thing."

"Jacob didn't do this. I mean, he didn't make the video." God, this is kind of humiliating. Daren looks a little surprised by my insistence. "I took it. With my phone."

Daren's eyes widen, and I continue. "That's the day I caught him cheating. I took a video so I could remind myself that I never wanted to trust him again. So when he called, apologizing or trying to rationalize this or confuse me, I could remember." My shoulders slump. "It was a stupid thing to do, but I was so crushed, so pissed off. But I never showed anyone the video. In fact, I've never spoken to anyone about it before you. And what's weirder is I deleted it a while ago. It shouldn't exist."

Daren's eyes soften. "C'mere." He pulls me to him. "I'm sorry you had to see that."

"I'm okay. I made peace with it. That's why I was able to delete it, but who the hell got their hands on my phone? I've never given anyone the password, and I don't remember letting anyone use it."

"Hmm. That's a good question."

"I need to call Jacob and apologize."

Daren's hand on my back stills. "Are you sure you want to admit responsibility?"

"I have no problem owning up to what I did. Do I think he'll take any legal action against me for taking the video? No, I don't. But regardless, it's the right thing to apologize, isn't it?"

Daren kisses the top of my head. "Yeah. It is."

"He has to know I took it. He's not an idiot. But I don't want him thinking I did it to get revenge. That I'd try to hurt him like that. No matter what he did to me, I'd never sink to that level."

Daren nods, and I'm relieved that he understands why I need to do this.

"So if it wasn't your ex, who else had access to your phone and laptop? Didn't you let Nicole use your laptop that one time?"

"What time?"

"At my party? Before I mauled you on the pool table." He chuckles.

"God, I forgot about that. Yeah, Nicole definitely had access, and I got so wrapped up in you and me hooking up that I never changed my password after she used it that night."

He's quiet. "You were wrapped up in us?"

"Uh, yeah. I couldn't think straight all week," I admit.

"Good. I was afraid I was the only one whose brain got scrambled by our night together."

Burrowing my head into his chest, I laugh. "God, no, I was a mess. I wanted you. I've always wanted you, but the reality that we had slept together totally threw me."

Calloused fingers draw my hair away from my face. "I've always wanted you too, sweet thing."

I smile like an idiot, glad he can't see me grinning. "Even when I was a geeky high school sports reporter?"

"Fuck, especially then." His fingers tighten in my hair. "You've always kind of kicked my world off its axis. Even in high school."

"We only talked for like fifteen minutes."

"That's all it took, babe." He kisses my forehead again, and I smile and close my eyes.

I feel such a huge relief knowing he's here. I have no clue how to deal with my crumbling career, but knowing Daren is in my corner makes me feel like I can weather whatever storm is ahead of me.

I feel his chest rise and fall in a steady rhythm. The sound of his heart is so calming that I drift in and out of sleep as I listen.

* * *

WHEN I WAKE a few hours later, I'm still wrapped around Daren. Or maybe he's wrapped around me. Whatever this is, it feels right. My world is falling apart, but having him here makes me stronger and makes me think I can face whatever lies ahead.

My lips are parched, and I start to pull away so I can get something to drink, but his arms tighten. "Where do you think you're going?" His groggy voice sends chills down my arms. His hard body angles toward me, and the bed squeaks underneath us.

I laugh, I can't help it, the ridiculousness of it all finally settling in. "We can't hide out here forever."

"We could try." His eyes crack open, and he grins. "I've rather enjoyed staring at your 30 Seconds to Mars poster."

"Ugh." I laugh and it feels good. "Stop. I haven't stayed in this room for years. My uncle just left up all of my embarrassing junk." I glance around, hoping nothing too horrifying is out. Like pictures of me in braces. I'm pretty sure I could go a lifetime without showing Daren those shots. "Speaking of my uncle, how did you know to come here?"

"I called Sheri. She wasn't sure where you had gone, but I asked if she knew where your uncle lived. I hoped he might know where you went in the event you weren't here."

"And how exactly did you get past him?"

A bigger smile tilts Daren's lips. "I knocked on the door. He was on his way out, but when he saw me, he slapped me on the back and pointed toward your room."

My jaw falls open. "That's it?"

"Yup." A beat of silence passes and Daren shrugs. "I don't know. Maybe he saw my press conference."

I still, unprepared for that answer. "You had a press conference?"

"*I* did not have a press conference. That bitch Jeanine pulled me into one."

I sit up. "And what did you say?"

His eyebrows lift marginally. "I'm sure if you pop on the TV, it's on somewhere."

He's so casual about the whole ordeal. I'd laugh if my whole life weren't hanging in the balance.

"What do I do?" I whisper. My fingers toy with a thread hanging from my blouse. I must look like a crumpled mess, still wearing my work clothes.

"Well, for starters, *we* need a bigger bed. My ass is about to roll off the side here."

I laugh and smack him on the thigh. "I'm being serious."

"Me too. I have a nice ass, and I really don't want it landing on something hard."

"Oh my God. Shut up."

He yanks me down to him, and I topple over in a mild fit of giggles. Once I'm all wrapped up in those arms again, he kisses my forehead. "Okay, I think you need to get your stuff. We'll stay at a hotel because I need a gym and, like I said, a bigger bed. Your uncle probably doesn't want to hear the coils on this one all night long because I fully plan on loving up on you at some point later this evening, 'cause, you know, makeup sex."

I blush and smile into his shirt, my heart fluttering at the prospect of reconnecting with him.

He squeezes my butt cheek, and I grin wider. "But before the sweaty sex, I need to call our attorney and get tomorrow situated."

I lean up. "What are you getting situated?"

"Your uncle said you needed to line up an attorney for tomorrow. I've already called one."

"I thought you said you didn't talk when you arrived. That he just pointed you in the direction of my bedroom."

It's dark in here, but it almost looks like Daren's cheeks are flushing. "Well, he might have said a little more than that."

"Like?"

"Like, 'Don't fucking have sex in my niece's bed.'"

"He did not." My eyes widen.

"He did." Daren barks out a laugh and strokes my hair as I collapse back on top of him.

"That's so fucked up, I can't even."

"Babe, I'm pretty sure everyone knows we have sex." He says it like a joke, but his laughter stops. I know he's pissed that there are images of us together like that.

"I'm so mortified." I shake my head back and forth on his chest.

Those hands grip me tighter. "Shh. It's okay. I already have a team of people trying to get to the bottom of this. We'll get some answers soon. Besides, sex is what happens in situations like these."

Sniffling, I look up at him. "Situations like what?"

His eyes run over my face, hovering on my lips before they meet my eyes. "Situations where the guy is so ridiculously in love with his woman he can barely function." Reaching toward me, he tucks a long a strand of hair behind my ear. "I love you, Maddie. So much."

Tilting my chin up, he kisses me. My heart is thundering so hard in my chest I'm sure he can feel it beneath me.

I blink back tears. "I love you too, Daren." Looking into those hazel eyes, I take a deep breath. "I always hated leaving your bed at night." My voice is barely above a whisper.

"Then why did you? You know I wanted you to stay."

Using the back of my hand, I wipe away the tears. "I just didn't want to be one of those girls who overstays her welcome, and you're too much of a gentleman to tell me."

Groaning, he pulls me tighter. "Sweet thing, c'mere."

Next thing I know, I'm on my back, and he's hovering over me. When his lips reach mine, he groans again, but instead of devouring me like I'm expecting him to, he gives me a peck and pops off me like he's doing a football drill. "Get your stuff. I need to get you to a hotel. Now."

I watch him cross the room and grab my bags. I've had a day from hell and I have no idea what's going to happen with my career, but knowing Daren is here somehow assuages my fear.

CHAPTER 49

MADDIE

As the door opens, Daren's hand returns to the small of my back and ushers me in. Wide-eyed, I take in the executive suite, complete with a living room, a small kitchen, and at least two rooms off the main area. "Wow, this is the VIP treatment."

"My father called ahead and reserved it for us."

My synapses must be fried from all the crying. Otherwise I'd remember that Daren's father *owns* this hotel.

Daren's father.

I pause, horror settling in my stomach for the millionth time today.

"What's wrong?" Daren pauses next to me.

My shoulders slump, and I shake my head. "Your father knows what happened. Has he seen our photos?"

"Yes, he knows, but I'm sure he'd rather have an extremity removed than check them out, so I think you can look him in the eye when we meet for dinner soon."

A gasp leaves my throat. "Dinner?"

"Yes, dinner. And before you go getting all weird about meeting my parents, you should know they're totally on your side. For the record, my mom has been your biggest fan since we started taping those segments this summer. She was damn near tickled pink to find out we were dating. Granted, I'm sure she'd prefer to forgo the sex gifs, but she'll recover."

Daren rubs my back, and I nod, still feeling shellshocked from the whole ordeal. "I'd like to meet your parents. If they aren't too horrified by the situation, that is."

Two big hands settle on my shoulders and turn me to face him. "My dad is an executive of a Fortune 500 company. I'm pretty sure he's been around the block. Nothing that you and I can cook up will shock him." Daren squeezes my arm. "I promise."

He heads into one of the bedrooms before he calls out to me. "I had Sheri pack some of your stuff and drop it off earlier. We're going to be staying here this week. I hope that's okay. I figured the security is a lot tighter at the hotel, and with a private elevator, we won't have the press breathing down our backs."

I wander in behind Daren and look around. Although this isn't the master, it's still a lovely room with a queen-sized bed, fluffy white bedding, and a mahogany dresser. My bags are already waiting for me.

"Daren, why do we have two bedrooms?"

He turns slowly to face me and tucks his hands into his pockets. "I wasn't sure where you and I were at. I didn't want to assume we were getting back together." He grins and looks embarrassed. "Okay, I hoped like hell we were getting back together, but if you needed some space, I wanted you to have it. So I got us a suite with two bedrooms."

Heat burns my eyes, and I roll my lips to keep them from quivering. "Of course I want us to be together. I don't want separate rooms."

We stand there staring at each other a beat, and Daren's eyes crinkle in the corners, a smile teasing his lips. And then his arms wrap around me.

I'm feeling like such a basket case, but he seems to understand.

Goosebumps break out on my arms as he rubs my shoulders. "Baby, you're freezing. Do you want to take a bath, and I'll call up some room service?"

Nodding, I smile. Just then, it hits me. "How were you with me today? Didn't you have practice?"

"Yeah. I went. To most of it at least. I'm taking the next two days off. I promised Coach I'd work out here, and he agreed that I needed the time to deal with this."

"You took time off? Can you do that?"

"I just did."

Closing my eyes, I take a deep breath because I know he's never taken a break like this before. He was known for being one of the most die-hard players at the collegiate level, and yet here he is taking time away from the game to help sort out this drama.

"Thank you, Daren. So much. You have no idea how much this means to me." I stare at him, trying to absorb how much he must care for me to make that kind of sacrifice. The feelings I have for him overwhelm me, and right now, there's only one way I can think of to show him the extent of my feelings.

I lean up and whisper, "Want to join me in the tub?"

Those mesmerizing eyes stare back, all the tension from us being apart this last week radiating off him. I step closer, just a fraction, hoping he'll give in, needing him to give in.

"Fuck, yes," he growls. His hands grip my hips as his mouth crashes to mine.

The stubble on his jaw nicks my lips, and all I can think about is pressing his face to my body, to feel that burn on my skin, on my breasts, between my thighs. The thought makes me weak, and I think I'd stumble if he weren't holding me up.

He pulls away, and I want to protest, except the next thing I know, he's tossing me over his shoulder.

I let out a squeal, and he slaps my ass, which is on display in this skirt.

"You've been a bad girl, Wildcat." That big hand comes down again, and I gasp, the sensation sending a deep throb to my core. "Fucking call me back when I leave you a dozen messages," he grumbles, stalking out into the living room and into the master suite.

In a whir, we move past an enormous bed with a mountain of lace linen and into the bathroom. Then he stops and lets me slide down his hard body. When my feet touch the floor, he flexes his hips, pressing his length into my belly, and I'm so overcome with need, everything aches.

Those fingers dip beneath my skirt and grip my ass, hard, almost painfully, but I'm so turned on that pain and pleasure meld together into the same thing. I glance up to find Daren staring behind me, into the mirror above the vanity.

"Goddamn, I love that you wear garters."

My breath leaves me, the idea of him watching us setting my skin on fire.

I lean forward, anchoring my hands on his chest and arching my back so he can get a better view. I look over my shoulder to see what he sees. Those big, calloused hands grip me and spread me apart, my black thong doing little to cover me.

"Baby." His gruff voice makes my body pulse, and it's all I can do to restrain myself. Because I want to let him control the pace. I want to please him. So much.

Our eyes meet in the mirror, and I say the words I know he loves to hear. "Fuck me, Daren." I lick my bottom lip. "Hurry." I reach between my legs, my fingers connecting with the damp, lacy material.

His hands tighten around me, and then in a flash, my butt hits the cold marble counter. He rucks up my black skirt and moves between my thighs as he grips my hips. Those hazel eyes blaze with hunger. "I've missed you, Maddie."

Before I can return those words, before I can tell him how much I love him, his mouth is on me, scalding me. His tongue slides across my lips, and I open to him, shuddering when those deep licks glide across my tongue. He grips my hair, tugging back until I open wider as he angles that massive body over me.

I pull up his t-shirt, and he reaches back with one hand to yank it off before he tugs my butt to the edge of the vanity and presses his hips into mine.

When his mouth connects with me again, I snake my hand down to stroke the erection that's straining against his jeans.

Daren brushes my hair off my shoulder, and his lips drift down my neck. As I stroke down on him, he sucks and licks.

"Harder," I pant. He's usually so careful to not leave a mark, but right now, I want to be branded. I want his lips and teeth and tongue to press into my skin and make me his.

He sucks that tender skin in a dangerous rhythm that matches the pulse between my legs, and as I'm about to yank open his jeans, he bites down, stilling me.

I moan, my hands gripping his body. The rest of me writhes, nearly convulses, and when he releases me, his tongue darts out to soothe his mark.

"Yes." It's all I can utter because words fail me.

My hands can't move fast enough to unbutton his jeans and reach into his boxer briefs. His hot erection juts into my hand, and I grip that velvety thickness.

He lets out a strangled moan as I stroke down, and I'm so desperate to feel him push into me, I can barely breathe.

And then his mouth is on me. Ravenous. Unrelenting. He grabs my wrists and pins them behind me as he thrusts his hips against mine.

My head drops back as my chest arches. I want this. Need this. Am desperate to feel his hard body against my delicate skin. But then he pulls away to kick off his jeans and boxers.

That's when I see it. The black marks along his rib.

"What is that?" I'm pretty sure my eyes are huge. Because the last time I was with this man, he did not have a tattoo.

His eyebrows lift, obviously not understanding.

"This?" I push him back so I can look at it more carefully.

Holy shit. Holy fucking shit.

He clears his throat. "Do you like it?"

"I love it. I mean, oh my God." My fingers skate across his skin. "But Jesus, Daren. What if we hadn't worked out? Your future girlfriend would be so pissed."

He chuckles, and all I can do is stare at the ink.

It's a gesture so sweet, heat burns my eyes.

I suck in a breath, mesmerized by this marvelously sculpted man in front of me. Sinewed muscle wraps down his arms and chest. Ripped abs draw me to that delectable V-shaped path I know well, that I've tasted and licked and long to do again.

And there, marking his skin, is the shape of his rib, outlined in ink, with the words *This one belongs to Maddie* written over it.

I suck in a breath. "You're not afraid you'll regret it? It's… it's forever." The weight of those words hang between us, and his lips pull up.

"That's kind of the point. I love you, Maddie."

I try to say something, but emotion overwhelms me. "I… I love you, too, Daren."

As his lips sweep across mine tenderly, my chest fills with new emotions I didn't even know existed. Those fingers thread through my hair, and I'm so lost in love with this man, he owns me, heart and soul.

Our touches grow feverish, the desire to have him fill me overwhelming as I claw my way closer to him. He breaks away for a moment and glances down.

"Babe, you look so fucking gorgeous like that."

I look down to realize I'm sitting with my legs splayed open and skirt scrunched at my waist. My blouse is hanging off my shoulder, and desperation toys with my self control.

When I look up, he's stroking his thick length. Eyes hooded, stomach clenched, he palms himself in slow, even strokes as my body throbs for more.

Slicking my lower lip with my tongue, I watch him, captivated. Slowly, I reach down to unbutton my shirt, loving the way his eyes widen as I strip off the material to reveal a pale pink lace bra that I unsnap.

"We have to make up for lost time," I say as the material falls away. "And I need to feel you bare."

We've never gone without condoms. And the thought of having him in me skin to skin is enough to make me combust.

His nostrils flare, and he works his jaw back and forth. "I got tested when you and I started getting together. I'm clean."

I nod. "I trust you'd tell me if you weren't." Scooting to the edge of the counter, I hike up my leg. "I'm good too. Got tested this summer, and you already know I'm on the pill."

He nods slowly, his eyes burning my skin as they trail over my breasts and down to my thighs. He's gripping himself harder, his cock huge in his hand, and all I want is to make him fall apart, so I reach between my legs and slide my fingers under the thin lace of my panties to rub myself.

"Fuck, Maddie."

I pull the material over farther so he can watch. Because I plan to take care of him better than any stranger, better than any of those girls with their cheap thrills. Because I know him. And I know his body. And I know what he likes.

Right now, that's watching me get off.

I spread my legs wider, and a moment later, he's on me, pushing my thighs as far open as they'll go and stroking me through the lace of my thong. "You're so wet, so fucking wet." He grips himself and pushes past the lace to nudge my bare skin with his cock.

Leaning back on my elbows, I push my hips out. His hand grips my shoulder to hold me in place. Then he whispers, "I've never gone bare before. You're my first. And if I'm being honest, I hope my last." He pulls me close for a kiss, my heart fluttering in a way that makes me wonder if I'll float away from euphoria because that's the second time tonight he's told me he wants something long-term.

He rests his forehead against mine, and our breaths mingle. As he pushes closer, I say the words I think I've always known. "I'm all yours."

His mouth ticks up in a sexy grin as I grip his hips and revel in the strength of the muscles flexing under my hands.

And then he's pushing into me. It's so good. He's so big and thick and hot. My head falls back, so that I'm half leaning on the mirror, and I glance down to see us connect. In this bright bathroom light, our every move is unmistakable.

He feels huge like this. I'm clenching down and his tip bumps into that spot as he pulls back, and I'm moaning and writhing for more.

Grabbing my knee, he pulls my leg over his shoulder and thrusts deeper.

I'm barely able to hang on, the fullness too much, too good. My head drifts back, and... Oh, God... "Daren." Every thrust has me gasping and clenching.

"Baby, fuck." His breath is hot in my ear, his fingers digging into my skin.

All of my muscles tighten, and I grip him closer. I'd inhale him right now if I could, his touch is so addictive.

His lips ghost against mine, and my hands fist in his hair and bring him to me. As we kiss, I suck on his tongue.

And then he's somehow surging bigger inside me. I gasp, "Holy shit. Holy shit. God. I... Ah... Please..."

He swivels us sideways so I can lie all the way back on the vanity, and he pushes hard, sending shockwaves through me. I start to quake, the sensation so fierce.

"Fuck, fuck, fuck!" I shout, arching into the cool marble

beneath me.

"Right there with you, babe," he grunts as he pulses inside me, and we unravel together.

When the sensations subside, his head drops to my chest, and my fingers tangle in his soft hair, and we lie in a sweaty heap, panting and spent.

"That was…"

"Yeah…"

Then we laugh, and he grunts again from the sensation because he's still inside me. He kisses my collarbone and helps me sit up.

I watch in a sleepy daze as he turns on the faucet and fills the enormous bath tub. He drizzles something pink into it, and the room starts to fill with steam and the scent of cherry blossoms.

"Baby, come here."

Sliding off the counter, I pad over to him. He crouches in front of me and unhooks my garters to slide them down my legs until I'm just standing in a pleated, short black skirt.

His eyes drift down my body in a slow, appreciative perusal. "That's a good look. You should prance around topless more often."

I grin and reach for him, helping him to stand, before I let the skirt slide down my hips. "Food for thought." I wink and head into the delightfully hot bath. I sink into the water and turn around to see my huge football player watching me.

"Get in. I'm not going to soak in a bubble bath all by myself."

His lips tip up on one side and he steps in, making the water swish around me. Once in, he hooks a finger. "You're crazy if you think I'm going to be soaking in this tub and have you way over there."

I laugh, the release feeling so good after such an agonizing day. But having Daren here makes my chest flutter and stretch, and I realize how much I want this and how close I got to losing the best thing that's ever happened to me.

CHAPTER 50

DAREN

Fᴜᴄᴋ.

She's crying.

"Babe. What's wrong?" Sliding through the water, she shifts between my legs. I pull her back to my chest, loving the way she feels against me. "Was I too rough?"

She laughs and shakes her head as more tears fall.

"No, that was perfect." She sniffles, and I stroke her hair.

Shit. This is about work. "Everything is going to be okay. I promise. We'll figure out who hacked you."

She sniffles and shakes her head. "This isn't about my job. I've basically accepted that I've lost it. There's no way a news station would hire me back right now. Rule of thumb in journalism: You cover the news. You don't become the news." Her hand comes up to her face to wipe a tear, and my heart breaks to hear the reality of her situation. But then she sighs. "I'm just overwhelmed about us. About how easy it is to screw everything up. I'm freaked out because I want us to work, and you have so many demands on you that are only going to intensify."

Silence fills the room. "And you're worried how those demands will affect our relationship if I'm constantly traveling."

She nods and sinks deeper into the water.

I squeeze her, lifting her higher, and push the hair off her shoulder so I can kiss that delicate skin. "I have a solution."

She stills, like she's stopped breathing.

"Move in with me. I know you live next door, but I fucking hate when you leave my bed, Maddie. I want you there all the time. The last thing I need to see before I go to bed is your beautiful face. And I want you there when I wake up. Our schedules are too busy to live separately. I'll never see you. Because, trust me, you're going to start getting amazing job offers, and soon you'll be going a hundred miles an hour because that's what you do."

The silence that greets me is deafening. Shit. And then it hits me. "You're scared because of what happened with your ex. Because you were just about to move in with him."

She takes a little shuddering breath and nods.

"Babe, look at me." I turn her around and wipe the tears that streak her face. "Is what you and I have at all like your relationship with him?"

She laughs and shakes her head. "No. Not even close. Honestly, now that I'm with you, I have no idea what I saw in him." She looks down. "Maybe it was just this idea of having someone be there for me. Like you said, I'm always on the go, always working. And it gets lonely. He was there, and I think he filled a void. This is going to sound crazy, but I'm actually glad I caught him when I did." She looks up, those luminescent eyes searing into me. "Because if he hadn't, I never would have met you."

"We'd already met."

"You know what I mean." She nibbles her lip. "Will it be weird? Sharing space with a woman again?"

My brow furrows. "Again?"

Maddie glances away. "Didn't Veronica live with you?"

"God, no. She had her own place on campus. We were planning to move in together after graduation, but we broke up in May." I study Maddie's reaction, enjoying the shy smile that peeks out on those full lips. "By the way, Sheri told me something about my headboard. That you left her place because you didn't want to hear it against your wall. Babe, you have to know that shit killed me."

Those big, blue eyes widen, and she glances down. "Oh, um. That." Maddie shakes her head. "I guess I didn't want to hear you move on. You know, eventually date other women."

Fucking hell. I scrub my face. "Babe, I can't help what happened before we got together, but I can tell you this. You're the only woman I've ever wanted to see first thing in the morning. The only one who made me want something other than football. Who made me think I could have more out of life."

Her lips twist as she fights a smile. "The only one?"

"Yup." I kiss her. "Now stop thinking I'm about to run off with some random chick. If you and I didn't work out, I'm pretty sure I'd barely be able to get up out of bed, much less mess around with other girls. So no more freakouts, okay?"

She nods, laughing.

When her laughter subsides, she raises her hand to my face. Smiling, I kiss her palm and lean closer to bite her wrist. She giggles, and I kiss up her arm until I reach her shoulder. "What do you say? Move in with me. Be mine." Pulling her so she straddles my lap, I tilt my head back and stare at this beautiful woman, who's soapy and slick and such a fucking vision my chest hurts.

She leans down to kiss me, and her hair falls forward, casting a curtain around us. "On one condition."

"Anything. Name it."

"I get to come to some of your games."

My heart? That muscle in my chest that's carried me through grueling practice after practice and workouts that made my whole body burn? It cracks open with the love I have for this girl.

"It would be my honor to have you there, sweet thing."

A wry smile lifts her lips. "Even if I'm rooting for the other team?"

I stare at her, straight-faced, and lock my jaw. Her smile drops, and then, when I know she's doubting whether she should be joking like that, I tickle the fuck out of her.

"Kidding! Kidding!" she screams, laughing.

Water splashes all over the floor, bubbles are in her hair, and I'm damn near positive I never want to get out of this tub.

CHAPTER 51

DAREN

MADDIE IS WEARING a charcoal-gray suit and a cream-colored blouse, looking like she's about to cover the White House. Realizing that this scandal has hurt her chances of doing something like that makes me sick to my stomach. Because this girl could do it. She has that kind of talent and drive.

I'm hoping today at least mitigated the damage.

It's been a long day of talking to attorneys, ours and WNEN's. We told her employer she forgot her laptop at home so my father's tech expert can take a look at it first. I'm afraid if we hand it over to the station, it'll mysteriously fall down a flight of stairs, destroying any evidence. Because for all I know, her smarmy producer Spencer did this so he could perv on her. Luckily, her battery died the morning the story broke, so she hasn't been online, which hopefully means no one has remotely hacked it this week.

When our team of lawyers finishes talking to her, Maddie heads for me with her arms crossed. She lowers her voice. "I'm relieved this is over for now, but I'm pretty sure I can't afford those guys. You should have talked to me first before you got the biggest law firm in Boston to represent me."

Of course I sent her in with the best lawyers money could buy. I want my girl to be protected. Because if her job tries to hold her in any way responsible for this, I will lose my shit. Our firm has already contacted the FBI in hopes of expediting the search for the fucker who hacked her.

Frowning, I shrug. "Money is no object. I'm paying for it, and before you give me any attitude, remember that we're a team. We're in this together, and if I want to pay to help my girlfriend deal with all of this bullshit, she's going to let me."

She rolls her eyes, but a smile is playing on her lips. "Why are you talking about me in third person?"

"I thought it would help you see how objective I'm being."

She laughs softly, resting her palm on my chest. "Okay, Clutch, but seriously. It'll take me like fifty years to pay you back."

I stroke my chin. "You can make me brownies."

At that, she really does laugh. "Brownies?"

"Yup. Every week. Think of it like you're working off the debt."

"So… basically a lifetime of brownies?"

"That sounds about right." I grin and kiss her on the cheek, whispering, "And if you want to serve those to me naked, I won't complain."

She swats at my arm, chuckling, and I pull her to me. "You're terrible."

"That's part of my charm." I bat my eyelashes, and her mouth opens as she inhales quickly. Did I just make her swoon? Good God, I love this girl. "Maddie, baby, how about we get out of here?"

By the time we make it back to the hotel, she looks exhausted. I tuck her into bed and head into the living room to make a few calls and update my parents. They've been Maddie's biggest supporters through all of this without any judgment.

My parents and I have talked more this week than the last

several years combined, and I'm relieved to be rebuilding our relationship. I still won't agree to accepting Mason's—um, my father's—inheritance, but for now we've tabled the discussion.

When I get off the phone, I'm about to order some room service when my phone lights up again. *Quentin.*

"Hey, man."

"Hey, stud. How ya doin'? Gotta say I don't envy you this week. We all miss you over here. When ya gonna be back?"

"Day after tomorrow. I'll get in a few practices before this weekend. Thank fuck it's a home game. Not sure if Coach will use me, so I hope you're playing nice with Brentwood."

"He'll play you. Trust me. But that's not why I called."

I shift the phone to my other ear. "Lay it on me."

"I've been thinking about Maddie and her situation. It got me wondering about something."

"Spill it. You're making me anxious."

He lets out a sigh. "Well, I started thinking about how those girls were always able to get into your room. They got around security, the room switches, everything."

That has my attention. "What are you thinking?"

"You only told a handful of people that you had moved rooms, right? But somehow those chicks always knew where to find you."

My heart is starting to thud hard. "Yeah."

"So I called up Shayna."

"Who's Shayna?"

"One of the girls in Dallas. The cute little blonde one who had those tattoos on her nipples."

"Christ." I run my hands through my hair. "I didn't get a good look at her, man. I saw that she was naked and asked her to leave. Obviously, when you offered to walk her out, you got a closer look."

He laughs. "Anyway, she tells me some guy told her how to get in your room. He texted her an update after you switched to that other suite down the hall."

"What the fuck?"

"Exactly. You got a pen?"

Blood is roaring in my ears. It takes me a full minute to realize Quentin asked me a question. "What? Yeah. Hang on." I head over to the desk. "Shoot."

He rattles off a number. When he's done, I'm still confused. "So this is Shayna's number?"

"Nah, man. It's the dude who told her how to find you."

* * *

WHEN I ENTER THE BEDROOM, I'm surprised to find Maddie awake. She's staring at the TV with tears streaming down her face.

"Babe, don't watch that shit. It's just going to upset you."

She sniffles. "I'm not upset." She lifts her head to me, a smile on her face.

I turn to face the flatscreen and realize she's watching my impromptu press conference the other day. It's being rerun on ESPN.

"I'm sorry about saying anything about you hating Jacob. That's no one's business."

She shakes her head. "It's fine. I called him a few minutes ago. He's not mad about the video leaking. He says he feels worse knowing what I saw that day. I told him I'm over it." A deep sigh leaves her. "He told me I could say whatever I wanted about that video—why I took it, what happened—and that he was cool with it."

My eyebrows lift. Guess the guy's not the dirtbag I thought he was. "He's been surprisingly quiet about it."

"He's up in Vermont training, so he wasn't super plugged in to the story." Her head tilts forward, and she wipes her cheek. Then she motions toward the TV. "I was just overwhelmed about what you said. The whole 'I need to go find my girlfriend' thing kinda got to me." Those big, blue eyes lift to mine.

"I'm a lucky bastard."

"Yeah, you said that."

I laugh and sit next to her. Hugging her to me, I get ready to share what Quentin just told me. "We need to talk."

"Mm?"

I unload all of the details, the ones I hadn't shared with her when I was on the road because I feared her reaction. But now's the time for her to understand how insane it has gotten. Because if we're in this for the long haul, and God knows I am, we need transparency. Being in public the way we are, it's too easy to twist the truth, and I need Maddie to trust me. Which means I have to tell her shit that won't always be pleasant, but she tells me she can handle it, and I have to trust she can.

She chews on her bottom lip. "So those girls always found their way into your bed on every road trip."

"Yup."

"And you'd walk in to find them naked. Every time."

"Yup."

"But you kicked them out."

"Yup."

She laughs. "Can you say something more than 'yup'?"

"Yup."

Blowing out a breath, she rolls her eyes, but she's fighting a smile. "Okay." She pushes her hair out of her face, and her expression grows serious. "Basically, you're saying that someone tipped off these girls so they knew how to find you."

"Possibly. But I'm not ruling out the idea that someone actually sent those girls to my room. It's too coincidental. I know NFL players can live crazy lives sometimes, but I've never been like that. I've never welcomed those kind of situations. And for it to happen in city after city? I don't think I'm *that* popular."

She laughs and reaches over to kiss me. "You probably are that popular, Clutch, but I'm not going to think about that now. What happens next?"

"I've already given the phone number Quentin snagged to our attorney and private investigator. Hopefully, they'll dig up something." I kiss her forehead, relieved to have all that shit out on the table. "Now, for the really important question." Her brows pull tight, and I kiss her nose. "Do you want a jersey with my number for Sunday's game?"

The grin on her face could light the night sky. "Hell, yes, I want a jersey." She rubs the scruff on my face, a rueful expression in her eyes. "Are you sure it's okay if I come on Sunday? I don't want to cause any problems or be a distraction."

"It's fine. I promise. Jax and Clem are coming, so you won't be alone." I trace a finger over her cheek. "I talked to Coach Reynolds this morning. Gave him an update. I'm planning to head in to practice day after tomorrow. Think you'll be okay without me?"

Her eyes widen. "Yes, of course. I hate that your schedule is being thrown off because of me."

I tug her closer. "You're the best part of my schedule."

CHAPTER 52

MADDIE

DAREN SOUNDED IRRITATED that I was heading to WNEN without him, but he can't miss any more practice, and I need to get a few personal items out of my desk. His dad sent a bodyguard to drive me from the hotel to the station. I've never given much credence to the necessity of having a bodyguard, but Hank is the size of a bulldozer, and having him around definitely makes me feel better.

When we step off the elevators, Susan nearly turns over her chair hopping up. I barely brace myself in time for her to tackle me in a hug.

"Oh, my dear. You poor thing."

I hug her awkwardly and try not to cough on a mouth full of her hair. "I'll be okay."

Hank clears his throat, and over Susan's shoulder, I see him silently asking if he should yank her off. I shake my head no and let the woman smother me. When she finally lets go, I straighten my blouse and ask if Roger is around.

"He's in a meeting, dear, but I can get a message to him if you'd like."

I shrug. "Tell him I'm clearing out my desk and that I'm leaving as soon as I'm done."

Officially, I'm on a paid vacation while the authorities investigate. But I know this job is over. Technically, I'm not supposed to come here, but Roger told me I could swing by to gather up my files.

My stomach twists at the thought of having to see my other coworkers, knowing they've probably perused my photos.

Daren says we're negotiating one hell of a settlement right now because our attorney assured us the station is at least partially responsible for the hack. My private files were found on their servers. There's no way around that.

When I reach my cubicle, I'm surprised to find a mountain of mail and gifts.

"The station has been flooded with things for you," a voice says behind me.

I whirl around to find Nicole. My eyes narrow, and I ask the question that's been tearing a hole in my stomach all week. "Did you have something to do with me being hacked?" I can't help the venom in my voice or the tears in my eyes.

Her face drops. "I must be a bigger bitch than I thought if you really suspect me of doing that." She closes her eyes a brief moment and shakes her head. "I had nothing to do with your scandal."

Ugh. She would use that word. *Scandal.*

Her lips purse. "I've had investigators up my ass all week, and I can assure you nothing is going to turn up."

I stare at her, unsure what to think. But in the end, it doesn't matter. Not really. My career is done. I blink back hot tears and turn to my desk, looking for the reason I dragged myself in here today.

Pushing over the mail, I breathe a sigh of relief when I see the familiar face smiling back at me from my bulletin board.

There he is.

Hi, Dad.

The tears come down faster, and there's no use wiping them away, so I don't bother. I tuck the photo into my purse and glance around. Color-coded file folders sit neatly on my desk, each one full of story ideas and leads and sources. Ignoring the urge to trash them all, I grab a box and toss them in along with a few other personal belongings.

I don't bother saying anything to Nicole. What is there to say?

As I start to head out of my cubicle, Hank takes the box out of my hands. I give him a grateful smile. Because we snuck in here when no one was expecting it, there weren't any cameras out front, but I'm not sure what to expect on my way out.

I'm bracing myself to brave any media outside that might have gotten wind of my presence when a small crowd by the elevators catches my eye.

Police. And guys in black suits.

My phone starts to ring in my pocket. I pull it out to see Daren's name. I answer it immediately. After our falling out, I promised him I'd always answer his call.

I don't get a chance to start talking because he asks me where I am.

"Um, I'm just about to leave the station. But it looks like something big is going down."

"He's going to be arrested, Maddie."

"What?" I'm having a hard time paying attention because the cops are headed toward me. Hank moves in front of me, and I have to arch up to see over his shoulder. I hold my breath as the cops stalk past us and into a room down the hall.

There's shouting and the sounds of a scuffle. I'm clutching the phone, and Daren is saying something, but all I can register is how I should be covering this story, whatever is happening right now. Except... that's not my job anymore.

A few minutes later, Brad emerges in handcuffs, and I stop breathing.

When he sees me, he shakes his head. "I'm sorry, Maddie. I didn't mean for this to get so out of hand."

"What, Brad? What got out of hand?" *What did you do?*

He fights the restraints and turns to yell, "It wasn't supposed to happen this way, Maddie. You have to believe me. " My stomach twists as I watch him struggle to look back at me. "I fucking love you, Maddie. I'd never try to hurt you!"

What the hell?

The authorities wrestle him into the elevator, and I stand there in shock as the doors close. I don't know how long I stand there, but I finally realize I'm still clutching my phone.

"Daren?"

"Yeah. I'm here. Maddie, are you okay? They're arresting Brad for hacking you."

I don't say anything at first. I can't. And when I finally do, I have to hold back a sob. Not because I'm crushed it was Brad—at least it wasn't someone I considered a close friend—but because this nightmare might be coming to an end. "Thank you for helping me. For being here for me."

"Aww, babe. Come back to the hotel. I can be there in an hour."

I shake my head. "No, finish with practice. I'll see you this evening."

"Maddie, listen to me. Have Hank drive you back. I'm on my way."

He hangs up before I can argue.

That night, I curl up in Daren's lap while we share a bottle of wine and order room service. He lets me cry and holds me and tells me everything will be okay.

For now, that's what I need to hear.

* * *

THE NEXT MORNING, I'm ready to get the whole story. I flip on the news. Brad's arrest is on every news station.

Daren's quiet as he prepares for practice. He told me what he heard from our private investigator last night, but I had a hard time processing the details.

Brad confessed everything. The stalking. His obsession with me. How he hacked my phone and laptop.

But that's not all. He sent the girls to Daren's rooms. He signed Daren up to get porn. He plotted to break us up, to turn me against Daren.

I watch the coverage, both relieved to have answers and horrified at what they are.

"Babe, you okay?" Daren has his workout bag packed, but the concern on his face makes me think he's reconsidering heading to the stadium, which is ludicrous.

I put on a brave face. "I'm fine. Or… I will be." Smiling, I haul my butt off the couch, run up to him, and throw my arms around his neck.

He chuckles and rubs my back. I breathe him in, wishing this day were over so we could hang out. But I know that's selfish of me.

"Go to practice." I peck him on the lips and let go of my death grip on him. "I was thinking about hanging out with Clementine today." She texted me last night and asked if I wanted to hang out and have a girlie afternoon with facials and manicures while we vegged and watched *Friends*. It sounded perfect. Especially since I'm nervous as hell about Daren's game tomorrow.

I watch for Daren's reaction because I know he's encouraged me to spend time with his friends, but I want to make sure he's really comfortable with it.

I'm relieved when he beams a smile. "Great. Make sure to take Hank with you."

"Yes, sir." I salute him.

His lips tilt up higher until those adorable dimples peek out. "See you for dinner?"

Nodding, I put my hands on his shoulders and push him toward the door so he won't be late.

He reaches down to grab his bag and stops to kiss me again. His lips are warm and soft, the perfect contrast to his scruffy jaw. This never gets old.

"Don't forget we need to leave by nine tomorrow morning," he mumbles against me.

"I won't." I'm so excited to finally see him play in person, but I'm concerned I'll be a distraction.

Like he can read my mind, his eyebrows pull tight. "Sweet thing, it'll be fine. Stop worrying."

I nod and let him kiss me once more before he heads out. I watch him step on to the elevator, and as the doors are closing, he yells, "My parents said you're coming for Thanksgiving next week, so don't make any plans. Your uncle is invited too."

My jaw drops open. That's one way to help me stop stressing about tomorrow's game. Tell me I'm meeting his parents.

* * *

WHEN DAREN RUNS off the field, I'm euphoric. Clem and I are jumping up and down, and Jax is screaming like a madman. But you can barely hear us over the roar of the crowd.

Daren threw a last-minute touchdown and won the game in overtime. I can barely catch my breath from the thrill of it all.

"Your boy did good, girl." Clem hugs me, and we continue hopping around like lunatics.

We finally calm down and head out to her car. Daren told us we shouldn't wait because he has field interviews and a post-game press conference.

He snuck us in the back way, through the player's entrance,

315

but now we have to brave the crowds on the way out. I grab my big, black sunglasses and fight the nausea in my stomach. Clem's lips twist when she sees me, and she hooks her arm through mine and pulls me close.

"If anyone says shit to you, I will shank them with a rusty object," she whispers.

I laugh, relieved that this afternoon has gone so smoothly. But we've been sitting in a box reserved for players' friends and family, so there's still time for the crazy to start.

We're headed for the exit when Jeanine, the Rebels' PR executive, stops us. "Maddie, I'm going to need you to join Daren for a quick press conference. The team thinks that if you do this together now, it'll help quell some of the hysteria surrounding you two."

I agree even though I'm not exactly Jeanine's biggest fan. I know Daren isn't thrilled with how cutthroat she can be.

Jax and Clem follow behind us. We wait in a long corridor. Finally, Jeanine ushers us into a huge conference room filled with media. Cameras immediately start flashing. It takes me a moment to spot Daren, who is seated next to his coach and a few teammates.

His coach waves me over, and Daren's mouth is tight. Shit. Did he not want me to come? He gets up and walks up to me, leaning down to whisper, "You don't have to do this. Jeanine wants this press conference, not me."

"It's fine." I look up at him and smile. "She says this is good for you and the team. That's all I need to hear."

His eyes wander over my face, and then he grabs my hips, pulls me close, and kisses me full on the mouth.

Holy wow.

Cameras start clicking like crazy, and all I can do is cling to this man as he kisses the hell out of me.

When we part, I giggle and cover my mouth.

The grin on his face is priceless. He turns to the cameras. "Any questions?"

Everyone stares back at us, speechless. Daren waves at them. "Great. See ya."

Then he turns on his heel and drags me out.

We're still laughing about it an hour later as we sit in traffic, trying to get back to the hotel. Clem and Jax drove to the game separately, so it's just the two of us in Daren's SUV.

"So I have a serious question for you." His voice is so somber all of a sudden, I turn in my seat to face him. "How fast can you pack so we can head home?"

Home. His home. *Our* home.

"I don't have much to pack at the hotel, but Daren, are you sure? I can stay with Sheri, and we can take things slowly. You have your hands full with the playoffs coming up, and—"

"Maddie, are you getting cold feet?"

"What? No, of course not. I just want you to be sure."

"I'm sure. I'm so sure I will swear on my Heisman."

I gasp. "No, that's sacrilege. Football gods, he's kidding." I shake my head. "There shall be no swearing on that trophy for any reason."

He laughs, and the sound fills the car. "Maddie McDermott, are you superstitious? I had no idea."

"I simply do not believe in messing with a good thing right before the playoffs." And yes, I'm a teeny bit superstitious.

He frowns. "Hmm. That throws a wrench in my plans."

"What do you mean?"

"If you aren't up for any change before the playoffs, then you'll have to wait for us to redo your office."

"What office?"

"The one we're making in the guest room, so you can work."

My heart warms at his offer. "You don't need to do that."

"I know, but I want you to have a space of your own. Oh, and one more thing. Keep next weekend open. After my game, we have plans."

"What do you mean we have plans?"

Tapping the steering wheel, he says, "We. Have. Plans." When I don't respond, he adds, "I plan to take my girlfriend on another date." And then he winks.

High school Maddie squees.

CHAPTER 53

MADDIE

THE LAST FEW months have been nothing short of insane, but moving in with Daren, having him with me, has helped.

After Brad was arrested, the media frenzy got worse, but soon another scandal replaced mine. The fallout, though, was significant. Roger resigned over how the station handled my story. Spencer used every outtake with Daren, every smile and interaction with him to milk the ratings. And there was nothing I could do about it. My old boss has since gotten another job. I apologized to Roger for lying to him about Daren, and he told me I'm a hard worker and will land on my feet once the dust settles. I know I disappointed him, but I also know I love Daren. So no matter how Daren and I got here, no matter how difficult our journey has been, I wouldn't take it back because he feels like my forever.

Nicole told investigators that Brad would ask her about me, and she merely thought he was nursing a crush and not being a full-on stalker. She maintains she didn't have anything to do with me being hacked, but I can't be positive she wasn't one of the anonymous sources that shared details only someone in my office would have known, like the flowers Daren sent me. I suppose it doesn't matter since I don't trust her anyway. Just last month, she was offered a job with a big celebrity news show in Los Angeles. She took it.

After Brad's arrest, I tried to block out the media frenzy as much as possible. I worked out in Daren's home gym. I took yoga classes and hung out with our close friends. For the first time ever, I stopped watching the news. Instead, I read Sheri's steamy books, practiced my new sex moves on Daren at night—which he loved—and learned to relax.

By February, I came to peace with everything. I even started getting offers from a few small stations in the Midwest to do news, and ESPN offered me a full-time job. I finally agreed to do a few sports segments a month for them because I could stay local. I told them in no uncertain terms that there was no way I was leaving Boston. Not with Daren here. ESPN agreed.

His team went all the way and made it to the Super Bowl. They lost in overtime, but Daren had a spectacular game. I couldn't have been prouder.

Now, flipping open my new laptop, one that Daren bought for me a few months ago, I take the Post-It off the camera and finish tweaking my weekly YouTube segment.

Daren was the one who suggested I try video blogging. I started with something simple. Me. People had so many questions about what happened, and I got tired of dodging the press, so I began by explaining how everything went down last fall and how I got hacked by Brad. He used a common spyware called a RAT—Remote Access Trojan—to lurk on my computer and spy on me. He gained full access to my email, docs, and camera. And after I noticed the camera light that one night, he made sure to turn it off the next time he filmed me. Then the creeper hacked my phone by emailing me a virus.

I guess I was lucky in a way. Because all of those gifs were taken from actual videos, but fortunately, those didn't leak.

Neither did my weekly Out-Skanking texts with Clementine, thank God!

My first video blog segment ended with tips on protecting yourself from RATting, which included getting the latest anti-spyware, covering your laptop camera when it's not in use, changing passwords frequently, and only using a secure server. Granted, there was nothing I could do to protect myself from Brad given that he was supposed to be the one to protect me from being hacked, but for the average person, those suggestions can help.

The morning after I uploaded the story, I woke up to find my little video trending on YouTube. Twenty-four hours later, I had almost a half-million views. Then the job offers really started to stream in.

But Daren's right. I've been running at a hundred miles an hour for too long, so I've been using this time to cover what I want, how I want. My segments are getting picked up by news stations, and I don't have to show any skin to make some asshole producer happy. Of course, I still cover football on occasion. But now it's because I want to.

"You ready?" Daren asks, slipping on a baseball cap.

"Yes."

He tosses the ball to me. "You need to watch Clementine closer this time. She got by you last weekend on a reverse."

Laughing, I nod. "All right, Clutch. But *you* need to remember that this is *touch* football and not actually tackle any of the guys. I was afraid you almost dislocated Jax's arm last time."

"He can take it. He's a big boy."

"No doubt. But still. Play nice."

"Babe, I always play nice." Daren bats his eyelashes innocently, and I shake my head, fighting a grin.

"And freaking pass the ball to Gavin. He's always open."

Daren grumbles, but I know he's just being a brat. I follow behind him, but he stops so quickly I stumble into him. He turns to me and asks, "If I pass to Gavin, can I have brownies when we get home?"

That's become our code. I chuckle, placing my hands on his waist. "Honey, you had 'brownies' this morning. Twice. Do you really need them again?"

His head rears back. "Sweet thing, I always need your brownies." And then he tosses me over his shoulder, smacks my ass, and carries me out the door squealing.

EPILOGUE

THREE YEARS LATER

DAREN

I CAN'T GET over how much fucking traffic there is for a Sunday night. My phone lights up where it's resting on the dashboard, and I check to make sure it's not Maddie before I toss it onto the passenger seat.

My head is all over the place. If I take a call, even with a hands-free setup, I'm likely to drive into the median. Christ, I need to calm down.

Deep breaths. Breathe the fuck in and exhale the fuck out.

Finally, I get to our neighborhood, which is decked out in Rebel flags. Partygoers from the corner bar rush out into the street and start cheering, and I laugh and try my best not to run anyone over.

I'm proud, but right now, there's only one person I want to celebrate with, and if I don't get home in exactly three minutes, I'm gonna lose my shit.

My wheels squeal to a stop, and I grab my phone and bag and race in. Maddie said she wouldn't freak out during the game, but I know how she gets. And she is in no condition to be stressed out.

When I open the front door, my eyes immediately land on

her. Her head tilts to the left and her left eyebrow raises as she picks up her phone.

"Daren Sloan, how the hell did you get home that fast? I told you I was fine. See?" She waves her arms at herself. "Fine." She starts to push off the couch.

"Don't, babe. Stay put. I'll be right there. Let me wash my hands first." Because you can't be too careful. You'd be surprised how many germs you'd find on doorknobs and handles. I really should get more disinfectant wipes.

In record time, I've kicked off my shoes and tossed off my coat. Maddie sighs back into the couch, and when I've washed up, I sit next to her and wrap my arms around her as gently as I can.

"Honey, I'm not going to break," she chides, tilting her head up to kiss me.

I nibble on her sweet bottom lip that tastes like cherry Chapstick before I scoop her in my arms. She squeals and grips my shoulders, and I kiss her long and deep.

"Mm. Why, Mr. Sloan, I dare say you missed me. Which is saying something since I saw you this morning."

"Why, Mrs. Sloan, of course I miss you. Every minute that we're apart."

She leans back and places her palm on my face, and I lean into her. Her black hair is tied back in a braid, and she's so damn beautiful, my chest hurts.

"You're a smooth talker, Clutch." She places a soft kiss on my lips. "I dare say you could have your way with me when you talk like that."

My dick hardens at the mere mention of having sex with my wife. If I thought she was beautiful when I met her, she's downright breathtaking now.

I cough, trying not to get ahead of myself. "Wildcat, I thought you needed to take it easy. Dr. Klein said—"

"Dr. Klein said I could do whatever I felt comfortable doing as long as I'm not on my stomach."

I work my jaw back and forth. "So last night—"

"Last night you needed rest. You had the conference championship today, and you kicked all kinds of ass. In fact, I just won a hundred bucks off your game in a pool the yoga girls put together."

My head tilts back as I bark out a laugh. "Babe, I don't know where to start with that." She smiles proudly and bats those long lashes at me. "So you held out last night because of *my* game?"

"Yes."

"And you *bet* on my game?"

"Yes."

"And you can get naked tonight?"

"Oh, yes."

That's all it takes for me to lift her up and stalk toward our bedroom. My little minx has been holding out. She giggles against my neck, and my heart starts to race. Because I am one lucky motherfucker.

I place her gently on our king-sized bed, and she looks up at me with such adoration in her eyes, I might melt on the spot. She unties her braid because she knows how much I love it loose when we're together.

Threading my fingers through her long tresses, I lean down to kiss her, and she opens her mouth to let me in. She sucks on my tongue in that way that makes me a little crazed with lust while her hands make quick work of my belt and jeans.

Reaching back behind my neck, I tear off my t-shirt. She grabs my neck and pulls me down to kiss her again while she handles me with long, confident strokes. After being together for three and a half years, this girl can still get me off in about two minutes flat if I let her.

"Nope. Not happening." I grab her wrist and place a kiss on her palm before I reach down for the hem of her shirt. She looks up at me shyly. I can see the hint of insecurity in her eyes. Which is crazy because she's just as hot now as she was before. "Babe, I love your body. You look amazing. Would I be this hard if you weren't?"

I stroke my cock and her eyes widen. She loves when I do this.

Her tongue darts out to lick her lips, and then she nods and pulls off her t-shirt.

A groan escapes me when I see her. My hands immediately fall to her full breasts, and I take care to not be too rough. Maddie likes it rough, but we're doing this my way. I'll get her there in the end, so my girl will just have to compromise.

"Scoot back."

She leans back on her elbows, and I kneel between her legs and hunch over her, taking my time to kiss a wet trail over her soft skin. When I reach her breasts, she falls back farther and threads her fingers into my hair.

I suck on her taut nipple, and she tightens her grip. And while there's nothing more I want to do than unravel my little wildcat, when I reach her swollen stomach, my breath catches in my throat.

"Hi, little slugger," I choke out before I rest my head on Maddie's tummy, being sure to not put too much weight on her.

She strokes my hair, and I close my eyes, overwhelmed by the many blessings in my life. She's eight months pregnant, and I want to spend every waking hour with my wife before he arrives.

I don't know how I'm going to handle leaving her for the Super Bowl in two weeks, but I've already chartered a private plane back. Maddie wants to come, but I'm worried the stress of traveling will be too much.

"Are you okay?" she whispers. "You haven't iced down tonight. I got carried away. We really should be icing your shoulder."

God, I love this woman. She always puts me first. Which only makes me raise her pedestal higher. "I'm fine, baby. I just love you so much I can't stand when we're apart. Especially when you're like this."

Soft hands push the hair off my forehead. "Come here."

When I reach our pillows, I pull her to me. My arm wraps around her tummy, and she places her hand over mine. "I'm sorry." Maybe this isn't a good idea.

Even in the darkness, I can see her scrunch her nose. "For what, honey?"

"I just don't want to hurt you. Hurt the baby."

She kisses my chest. "You won't. I asked the doctor."

"You did?" We've been pretty careful throughout the whole pregnancy—I mean, I've read about ten books on the topic—but in the last week, I swear our little guy grew like six inches.

"Yes, I did."

"Really?" Maddie might be a dirty girl between the sheets, but she's pretty modest in public. I can't imagine her asking her ob-gyn about our sex life.

"Really. I told her, 'Doc, my husband has a really big cock. Can he still fuck me hard?'"

I let out a choking cough. "Christ, Maddie." I laugh, and she giggles against me.

"Actually, my exact words were, 'My husband is well-endowed. How enthusiastically can we make love?'"

Now I really laugh. "You did not say 'make love.'"

She smacks me playfully. "I did too."

"When I said it, you threatened my balls."

"It doesn't sound right when you say it. It usually gives me the heebie-jeebies, but it sounds like the appropriate term to use when talking to your physician."

I nod, a smile still playing on my lips.

Yes, I told my wife I wanted to make love to her. Because yes, we have sex, and yes, we certainly fuck, but more often than not, what we do feels like some kind of metaphysical connection, and words fall short of describing it. What I have with my wife blows my mind. In fact, the word 'love' doesn't really do it justice.

Her hand strokes my chest, and a little breathy sigh leaves her lips as she kisses my shoulder, and just like that, I'm hard again.

She turns on her side, and I roll to face her.

Our lips meet in the middle, and I get on my elbow to kiss her deeper. I take my time even though my dick is screaming for more once she tucks my cock between her thighs and starts rotating her hips. I angle up higher to stroke her swollen, wet skin, and her breathing comes out in short pants. Reaching down, I spread her around me and still her hips.

"Let me do the work, baby."

I lift her leg over my thighs and grip my length to continue stroking her.

"Oh, God." Her head falls back, and I place open-mouthed kisses on her neck. She smells so good, like lavender and honey.

I'm about to sink into her when she stills me with her palm. She looks up at me with those big blue eyes. "Can I ride you? I've looked it up. It's totally safe," she pants.

"Get your ass up here then."

Except instead of facing me, she turns away for a reverse cowgirl.

When she sinks down, I swear white dots my vision. She's so tight and warm, I grip her hips to stop.

"You feel too good. Hang on a sec."

She glances over her shoulder with a sultry smile. Finally, after a few steadying breaths, I smack her ass. "Ride me, woman."

Her laugher rings in our dark bedroom, and she begins to move. I only let her go for a few minutes because I don't want her to overdo it.

"Lie back. I need to feel you."

I reach behind me for a few pillows and prop myself up higher so that she won't be uncomfortable. Because I know she's not supposed to lie flat on her back.

Pressing her palm to my chest, she starts to recline on me. I put my hands on her shoulders to ease her back to my body.

She turns slightly so she can kiss me, and I stroke her cheek. "You have no idea what you do to me."

Maddie opens her eyes, and I see my future reflected back at me in ways I never imagined. She whispers, "I know the feeling."

The kiss is endless, the kind that starts on your lips and travels down and grips your heart.

I'm moving in her, and she's arching her back. I palm her swollen breasts, and she moans.

Her body feels so warm against mine, all soft curves and slopes. Her breath comes out in short pants, and when I reach down between her legs, it only takes a few strokes for her to clench around me.

There's nothing like coming at the same time as your woman.

I pulse and swell inside her while she moans my name. Gripping her hips, I anchor her to me while I find my release.

We're both sweaty and spent, and I ease her off me, reluctant to lose our connection.

"Baby, you okay?" I lean over to kiss her.

Her eyes are closed, a smile lingering on her lips. "Mm. Definitely." She stretches up, and reaches over to grab me and pull me closer.

I kiss her forehead, and she sighs. "I love you, D." She reaches up to play with my hair. "You played a great game today. I was so proud of you."

"I love you too, sweet thing."

Then I close my eyes and rest my head on her chest, never more content with my life. And for the first time ever, it has nothing to do with football.

MADDIE

TEARS well in my eyes as I take in our friends who have gathered for our baby shower. I can't believe Daren did this.

He ushered me out of the house this morning with two errands, and by the time I got back, our place was clean and blue streamers covered every wall. Catered food lines the dining room table, and when my eyes reach Daren, who looks so handsome in a black sweater and jeans, I bite my lip to keep from turning into a big crybaby.

This man is full of surprises. When we got married two years ago, he whisked me off to honeymoon in France because he knew I'd always wanted to visit Paris. And just as I thought we were returning home, he took me to Italy... and then Spain.

I sniffle, overwhelmed by the love I see in my husband's expression as he watches me. He leans down to kiss me and whispers, "Surprise."

I shake my head at him and laugh, trying my best to blink back the heat in my eyes, but as our friends congratulate us, the tears start to fall. Across the room, Jax is hugging Dani, and next to them, Gavin has his arm around Clementine.

"You're early," Sheri says from the hallway. She barrels up to me, and Daren yells, "Be gentle, Sher-bear!"

She rolls her eyes but instead of giving me a normal hug, she kneels down and places her head and hands on my stomach. I look up at our friends, who laugh.

"Are you guys going to tell us the name already?" Jax asks while he shoves a finger sandwich in his mouth. I try to focus on the conversation, even though Sheri is whispering to my huge baby bump.

Daren smiles and motions to me. I shake my head and tell him to do it.

He rubs his stubbled jaw as he walks around to me, waiting until Sheri ends her convo with our child to drop his arm around my shoulders. "We're naming our son Daniel Mason Sloan. Daniel for Maddie's dad and Mason for mine."

I nod, feeling way too emotional for my own good. "But we'll probably call him Mason."

Everyone "awws" and Daren kisses my forehead.

We eat and open gifts, and I'm overwhelmed by the pint-sized onesies. I hold up the cutest outfit to my stomach and tears rush down my cheeks. "I love this." I read the words out loud. "Real men snuggle."

I look up, and Jax grins. "It's true."

"Thanks, guys."

Clem hands me a tissue, and once we've opened all the gifts, Sheri heads home, and Clem ushers the guys down to the baby room to help assemble the crib and baby swing.

As we stand in the doorway watching the guys open the boxes, Clem asks, "Are you going stir crazy now that you've stopped working?"

"Surprisingly, no. We have so much to do before Mason arrives, and I'm loving just having time for us. Besides, I know I'll be back in the full swing of things once I start co-hosting *Good Morning, Boston* in a few months. I was freaked out about leaving the baby, but the studio has a room all set up so I can nurse him."

"I think it's awesome that Daren's mom wants to babysit."

"She's the biggest sweetheart. I love that little Mason will be close to her."

"Is Daren really planning to take over his dad's hotel? When he told me, I wasn't sure if he was bullshitting me."

I laugh. "That's the plan. He wants to play for the Rebels for another two or three years and then retire. He knows he's been lucky because he's never been seriously injured. With the baby coming, he doesn't want to take any chances. So he's learning everything he can about the hotel and will help manage it in the off season. The board members are tickled pink because he's so well known and respected in this city."

Daren never told Clem what happened between him and his father. Well, his step-father. Daren thought it opened too many cans of worms when everyone had moved on. But he and Mason have worked through their baggage, and with the little one coming, it's been easy to move forward. Especially since Daren is proud to pass on the hotel to his children some day.

"I'm so happy for you guys." Clem reaches over and hugs me, and heat stings my eyes. I sniffle, and Clem shakes her head.

"Oh shit. I'm sorry. I don't mean to make you emotional." She laughs, but then I notice she's wiping her eyes too.

Jax tosses an empty box into the corner of the room, and he rubs his hands together in a dramatic display. "Let the assembling begin!"

"This should be good," Clem whispers to me.

Her brother holds up the directions and then, a moment later, flips them upside down and squints at them.

Gavin nudges Daren. "Dude, you might want to take those from Jax. I don't want the baby to roll out the bottom."

We snicker, and I'm about to burst from happiness.

There's something so wonderful about having all of my

335

friends in the same place. I love how close the guys have gotten. Jax and Daren have always been tight, but now Gavin is in with the boys too. He and Daren hang out all the time. Now that us three couples are married, I feel like I have two sisters in Clem and Dani. I'm a little sad Jenna and Ryan can't be here, but they're in New York for one of his concerts. They'll be back in town in a few days, though, so I know we'll catch up soon.

I look up to catch Gavin mouthing that he loves Clem, and when I turn to look at her, she's rubbing her tummy. She's wearing a loose fitting flannel, but from this angle, I could swear...

Holy shit. Is she...

My eyes bug out, and I gasp.

"Babe, what's wrong?" Daren is in front of me in two seconds.

"Nothing. Why?"

He frowns and tilts his head like he doesn't believe me. "You gasped. Are you having Braxton Hicks contractions?" He lowers his voice. "Because maybe we were too rough last night."

I laugh, and my friends watch with rapt attention as I pat my husband on the shoulder. "Honey, I'm fine." I raise my eyebrow and turn to Clem. "I was just thinking how fun it's going to be when we all have kids and they can play together." How did I not notice this when she hugged me?

Her face flushes, and I can't help but giggle. So I try to let her off the hook. "Dani, are you and Jax thinking of starting a family at all?"

Dani looks up thoughtfully. "We're going to wait a little longer. Our business is going really well, and we want to save up a good nest egg first."

Jax stands by his adorable wife and wraps his arms around her. "I don't know, babe. I think we could maybe do this." He looks around the baby room, and I see his wheels turning. "I'd love to have a little Dandelion as cute as you."

She leans forward with a sigh. "Really?" Her eyes are so hopeful, I can't help but squeal on the inside.

Jax leans over and kisses her. "Really." Then he lowers his voice. "And maybe we can start trying, like tonight."

Dani snuggles closer, a lovesick look on her face, and Clementine groans. "Brother, you need to learn what the word 'whisper' means." She shakes her head before walking up to Gavin. He hugs her, and their hands meet on her stomach.

Clem takes a deep breath. "We didn't want to announce this now because today should be about your baby, but since we're all talking about children, Gavin and I have some news."

"Dude, you knocked up my sister?" Jax asks, looking a little grossed out.

"Asshole, they're married," Daren says. "You were just talking about sexing up your wife when you got home."

Jax presses his palms into his eyes. "It's just a lot to take in." He inhales deeply. "Holy shit. My sister is gonna have a baby." A goofy grin spreads on his face before he hugs her, practically lifting her off her feet.

When the hug fest is over and we've all had a chance to congratulate Clem and Gavin, I ask how far along she is.

"Four months." She threads her fingers through her husband's. "It's a girl." She shrugs, grinning. "And a boy."

"Twins! Holy shit!" Jax looks like he's about to pass out.

Everyone erupts again, and after a round of hugs and congratulations, I shush them.

Turning to Clem and Gavin, I ask, "Do you have names yet? It's still early so there's still plenty of time if you don't."

Clementine grins. "We were thinking Paisley and Ryder."

If I could jump up and down, I would, but my boy might kick me in the kidneys and I'd hate to pee in front of my friends, so I opt for another hug.

When our friends have left, my mischievous husband wraps his arms around me. Giving him a stern look, I ask, "What happened to waiting until after Mason arrived to have the shower?" With Daren's season being so hectic, we thought we needed to minimize our stress.

He kisses my nose. "This one is just for our close friends. The one my parents are throwing is still on the calendar in a few weeks. I just thought you needed to see how special you are and how much you mean to me."

My eyes well with tears. "Stop. You're going to make you cry."

"I don't care. Let the tears fall. As long as you know that you're the best damn thing that's ever happened to me."

At that, big wet droplets slide down my cheeks. "Love you, Clutch. So much."

He leans down, and when his lips touch mine, he whispers, "Love you too, sweet thing. Thanks for being in my life."

I close my eyes as we kiss, knowing that this is just the beginning of our life together. And right now, I feel like one of the girls in Sheri's books, so lucky to have my very own happily ever after.

TO MY READERS

Thank you for reading *Kissing Madeline*. I would love to hear what you thought of my novel and hope you'll consider leaving a review on Goodreads and the vendor where you purchased it. If you haven't read the other two books in the series, keep flipping for the Dearest Clementine blurb.

If you've read the whole Dearest series and wondered what happened to Brady, he got his own book! Be sure to check out *Shameless*, which kicks off the Texas Nights series. You'll find the synopsis if you keep scrolling.

To receive an email alert when I release future books and get access to exclusive giveaways, head to my website (www.lexmartinwrites.com) to subscribe to my newsletter.

DEAREST CLEMENTINE

Twenty-year-old Clementine Avery doesn't mind being called bitchy and closed off. It's safe, and after being burned by her high school sweetheart and stalked by a professor her freshman year of college, safe sounds pretty damn good.

Her number one rule for survival? No dating. That is until she accidentally signs up for a romance writing class and needs material for her latest assignment. Sexy RA Gavin Murphy is more than happy to play the part of book boyfriend to help Clem find some inspiration, even if that means making out...in the name of research, of course.

As Gavin and Clem grow closer, they get entangled in the mystery surrounding a missing Boston University student, and Clem unwittingly becomes a possible target. Gavin tries to show Clem she can handle falling in love again, but she knows she has to be careful because her heart's at stake...and maybe even her life.

DEAREST CLEMENTINE, the first book in The Dearest Series, can be read as a standalone novel.

FINDING DANDELION

When soccer all-star Jax Avery collides with Dani Hart on his twenty-first birthday, their connection is instantaneous and explosive. For the first time in years, Jax isn't interested in his usual hit-it and quit-it approach.

But Dani knows better. Allowing herself a night to be carefree and feel the intensity of their attraction won't change anything when it comes to dealing with a player. So when Jax doesn't recognize Dani the next time he sees her, it shouldn't be a total shock. The fact that he's her new roommate's brother? That's a shock.

Dani doesn't regret that night with Jax, just the need to lie about it. Since her roommate has made it clear what she thinks about her brother's "type" of girl, the last thing Dani wants is to admit what happened.

Jax knows he's walking a fine line on the soccer team. One more misstep and he's off the roster, his plans to go pro be damned. Except he can't seem to care. About anything... except for the one girl who keeps invading his dreams.

Despite Jax's fuzzy memory of his hot hookup with his sister's friend, he can't stay away from her, even if that means breaking his own rules. But there are bigger forces at work–realities that can end Dani's college career and lies that can tear them apart.

Jax realizes what he's losing if Dani walks away, but will he sacrifice his future to be with her? And will she let him if he does?

FINDING DANDELION, the second book in The Dearest Series, can be read as a standalone novel. This new adult romance is recommended for readers 18+ due to mature content.

SHAMELESS

A USA TODAY BESTSELLER

Brady...

What the hell do I know about raising a baby? Nothing. Not a goddamn thing.

Yet here I am, the sole guardian of my niece. I'd be lost if it weren't for Katherine, the beautiful girl who seems to have all the answers. Katherine, who's slowly finding her way into my cynical heart.

I keep reminding myself that I can't fall for someone when we don't have a future. But telling myself this lie and believing it are two different things.

Katherine...

When Brady shows up on a Harley, looking like an avenging angel—six feet, three inches of chiseled muscle, eyes the color of wild sage, and sun-kissed skin emblazoned with tattoos—I'm not sure if I should fall at his feet or run like hell. Because if I tell him what happened the night his family died, he might hate me.

What I don't count on are the nights we spend together trying to forget the heartache that brought us here. I promise him it won't mean anything, that I won't fall in love.

I shouldn't make promises I can't keep.

ACKNOWLEDGMENTS

My first order of business is to thank my husband Matthew, who is the one who pushed me off the ledge and got me to take a chance and try my hand at writing fiction. If I had landed in a giant splat on the ground, I'd be blaming him too. haha. Seriously, though, thank you, Matt. You make me laugh every day, and you're the reason I have anything funny to say. Thanks for not killing me when I use our convos in my books. And to my girls, I may not want you to read my books, but you're the reason I write. Love you, little bears. A big hug to my awesome family in Texas and the best parents a girl could ever have. Love you!

I have the most kick-ass agent ever. Kimberly Brower, thanks for being tough on me and for being a great friend. My books are better because of your input.

RJ Locksley, you're a fantastic editor. I can't tell you how much I appreciate your feedback.

A huge thanks to Whitney Barbetti and KL Grayson, who helped me get my second wind. I seriously wouldn't have finished this book without you. Love you guys. #Trifecta4Ever

Jules Barnard, you deserve a medal for reading my crappy first draft. Still waiting for you to visit me in LA. *whistles*

Tackle hugs to Krista and Becca Ritchie, who showed me the ropes to self-publishing. You two inspire me.

M. Pierce, thanks for that wry sense of humor and encouragement. I appreciate you pushing me to redo my first cover. So many great things happened because of that advice. I owe you some pancakes.

To Sheri Thompson-Gustafson... Thanks for helping me pick out my covers and for holding my hand whenever I freak out, which is often. I wrote Maddie's roommate for you. Sorry I didn't give her big boobs. xoxo!

Cole McCade, I'm psyched I finally found someone who loves Harold Perrineau in *Romeo & Juliet* as much as I do. Thanks for helping me with my blurb. I owe you a few drinks. Let's line up that designated driver.

To my lovely former student Rachel... I'm so proud of your many accomplishments! Thanks for sharing what your life is like as a broadcast reporter. If I got any of the details wrong, it's all on me.

A big thank you to my betas, Alexis Durbin, Kristen Humphry Johnson, and Kristina Brooks. Your feedback was wonderful!

I also have to give a special shout out to Angie Owens and her eagle eye. Thanks for proofing this last minute!

Ass slaps and smooshy hugs to Doris Gray and Jullie Anne Caparas, who started the Dearest Series Fan Group. You two have done so much for me—scoured my books for excerpts, made me teasers, and helped me plan. You were the first to Out-Skank me... on Twitter no less. *tear* Thanks for the encouragement and endless laughs! I also have to thank the girls in my group for understanding my filthy mind and for being as twisted as I am. #ThatSkankLex loves you!

I really appreciate all of the friendships I've made with the #IndieChicksRock gang. Thanks for sharing so selflessly in the group. NAAU, I've learned so much from you.

Cristiane Karamanolis, thanks for all of your tweets and shares and endless love for authors. I feel lucky to know you.

Tarah Lockard, your teasers are gorgeous. I appreciate you taking the time to help me.

Kawehi Reviews, thanks for being one of my earliest readers!

Jacqueline Russell, you're a sweetheart for helping me with my promo!

Truly, I realize no one would read my books were it not for a few bloggers who picked up *Dearest Clementine* early on. Aestas, I can't thank you enough for taking a chance on a new author. Lanie and the Bookaholic Fairies, you rock my socks. Dirty Laundry Review, you girls are peas to my carrots. Three Girls and a Book Obsession, this is where I snuggle you.

Hugs and hair pulling (the sexy kind) to my friends at The Literary Gossip, Smokin' Hot Book Blog, Summer's Book Blog, Teacups & Book Love, Owl Always Be Reading, Schmexy Girl Book Blog, One Click Addicts, Give Me Books, ByoB, Kylie's Fiction Addiction, I Bookin' Love to Read, Hopeless Book Lovers, Smut Fanatics, Smut Muffins, Book Baristas, Four Chicks Flipping, Restless Book Obsession, INDIEpendent Book Babes, The Smut Slut, Desert Divas Book Addiction, FMR Book Grind, Second Bite Book Reviews, Smut Bags, Books & Tea, Once Upon A Book Blog, Red Cheeks Reads, Lauren's Book & Media Club, Bujoijoi22, Typical Distractions Book Blog, Literary Misfit, Painful Reads, Hopeless Book Lovers, BookCrushin.in, The Bookish Laurel, Little Read Riding Hood, The Never Ending Book, Reads, Calloway Books, Shelley & Courtney, Turning Pages at Midnight, Starbooks, Megpie's Book Blog, Read Review Repeat, and One More Chapter. I know so many more bloggers have posted my cover reveals and promos and sales and teasers. If I could smother you all in kisses, I would.

A huge thanks to Natalie at Love Between the Sheets for doing the promo for all three of my books. You're the best, Nat!

Lastly, to my readers... Thanks for reading my books and for all of your messages and tweets. It's bittersweet to come to the end of this series. This is the last full-length novel for Clem, Jax, and Daren as their stories have been told. However, since I've received so many messages about Jena and Ryan, I wanted to let you know that I'm hoping to write a companion novella for them. And Brady now has his own book, *Shameless*, because I definitely think he deserves a happily ever after! I hope you'll check it out.

Thanks for reading, y'all!

xoxo,

Lex

ALSO BY LEX MARTIN

The Dearest Series:

Dearest Clementine (Clementine & Gavin)

Finding Dandelion (Dani & Jax)

Kissing Madeline (Maddie & Daren)

Texas Nights Series:

Shameless (Kat & Brady)

Reckless (Tori & Ethan)

Breathless (Joey & Logan)

Varsity Dads:

The Varsity Dad Dilemma (Gabby & Rider)

Tight Ends & Tiaras (Sienna & Ben)

The Baby Blitz (Magnolia & Olly)

Cowritten with Leslie McAdam

All About the D (Evie & Josh)

Surprise, Baby! (Kendall & Drew)

ABOUT THE AUTHOR

Lex Martin is the USA Today bestselling author of Varsity Dads, Texas Nights, and the Dearest series. She writes contemporary romance novels, the steamy kind she hopes readers love but her parents avoid. A former high school English teacher and freelance journalist who's lived all over the country, she currently resides in her hometown of San Antonio with her husband, twin daughters, and a bunny named Dandelion.

To stay up-to-date with her releases, subscribe to her newsletter or join her Facebook group, Lex Martin's Wildcats.

www.lexmartinwrites.com

Made in United States
North Haven, CT
16 September 2022

24197275R00202